# ABSOLUTION

KAYLEA CROSS

**Absolution**



* * * * *

**Cover Art by**
**Sweet 'N Spicy Designs**

* * * * *

This book is a work of fiction. The names, characters, places, and incidents are products of the writer's imagination or have been used fictitiously and are not to be construed as real. Any resemblance to persons, living or dead, actual events, locales or organizations is entirely coincidental.



ISBN: 978-1494878498

# Dedication

To my boys and hubby—still love you to infinity (and beyond!). And for Katie, whose support and critical eye make me a better writer. Thanks, hon!

And to anyone who's ever faced their own battle with cancer, or watched a loved one during their fight.

Suck it, cancer.

# Author's Note

This is the fifth and final book of my **Suspense** series, and finally we get to see Luke and Emily's story! As you've probably guessed by now, Luke is my favorite character of the series, so I couldn't wait to write this story. It literally poured out of me and it's my all-time favorite book I've ever written. I hope it will be one of yours as well.

Happy reading!

Kaylea Cross

# Prologue

*Charleston, SC*
*Late November*

Emily Hutchinson lifted a hand and tucked the last few strands of her thick brown hair beneath the plastic cap the nurse had given her. The mirror above the sink of her private hospital room showed how pale her skin was. Her green eyes seemed too big for her face, and were full of shadows almost as dark as the ones beneath them. The thin gown she wore fell shapelessly around her thin frame. The two ties at the back let in a cold draft that went up her spine like the rake of icy fingertips.

Her day of reckoning had come.

"Emily?" the nurse called from outside the bathroom. "Are you nearly finished?

She took a deep breath, staring at her reflection and the fear in her eyes. She'd already lost her reproductive organs two years ago. After this, would she even still be a woman? "One second." When she was sure she had her composure, she stepped out of the bathroom.

The nurse, Patti, gave her a sympathetic smile. "They're ready for you."

Emily eyed the gurney that would take her down to the OR and fought back the wave of dread and grief swamping her. Stupid, to be this afraid now. She'd always known this day would come, as it had for her mother. And yet, with the moment of truth at hand, it felt like her veins were filled with ice water.

When Patti held out an encouraging hand, Emily took it and climbed up onto the gurney, maneuvering her IV pole around to the side. Shifting to lie on her back, her limbs were leaden. But her mind screamed.

"Your hands are freezing." Patti added an extra blanket and tucked them around her before coming around to offer another smile. "Everything's going to be fine. Jim's the best."

Yes, he was. Emily had known the surgeon for more than a dozen years, and there was no one on earth she trusted more for this operation. Knowing he would be with her in the OR brought her some measure of reassurance, but what was coming afterward scared the living hell out of her. The thought of what would happen after the surgery coated her skin in a cold sweat.

"Here we go," said Patti. "You just rest while I take you downstairs."

"Sure." At least her voice sounded normal. Calm, collected. As though she wasn't embarking on the fight of her life. No, that wasn't true. She'd begun that two years ago, only she hadn't realized it at the time.

The gurney's rubber wheels squeaked and squealed on the linoleum floor as it traveled out of the room and into the garishly lit hallway. Behind their station desk, the nurses looked up from their work when she passed to smile at her.

"See you when you get back," one of them said. Emily raised a hand in reply, her throat so thick with unshed tears she thought she might choke on them. The terrible void of the unknown yawned before her. She wouldn't know what Jim found until she woke up in recovery, and once she did, she wasn't sure how she could face the rest of it. As terrible as the surgery was, this was the easy part, and she knew that all too well. From here out, things got much tougher.

And sometimes, they became impossible.

Forcing the sickening thought away, she closed her eyes and concentrated on taking slow, deep breaths to calm her nerves. A soft ding told her they'd reached the elevator, and the metal rails of the gurney clanged against the door on the way through.

"Sorry about that," said Patti.

"It's okay."

The doors closed with a dim swoosh, then the motor hummed as they descended. When it dinged again, she opened her eyes as the doors pulled apart, revealing her friend Anne waiting in the hall. She came straight over.

"Hi, Em," she said, taking one of her chilled hands.

Emily squeezed back. "I thought you were away this week."

"Except for today. The rest of the week, I'm staying with a friend." She winked. "What, you thought I'd let you go home alone with no one to take care of you? As if."

The tears Emily had fought burned through her resistance. Pressing her lips together, she put her other hand over her eyes.

"It's going to be okay, Em." Anne's grip was warm and firm. "Nothing's going to happen to you on my watch."

A soggy laugh escaped. Anne was like that. Protective and fiercely loyal, even though they were only casual friends. “Thank you.” It seemed completely inadequate, but it was all she had.

“Don’t mention it.” Anne glanced up. “Ah, here comes Doc Hollywood now.”

Emily turned her head as Jim strolled up, tall and handsome in his pale blue scrubs, his clear, gray eyes full of warmth when he smiled at her. “How are you feeling, Emily?” He took Anne’s place and helped her push the gurney through the double doors of the OR.

“Fine. Just want this to be over.”

“Understood.” He guided the gurney next to the operating table so the nurses could transfer her. “We’ve got the A-team assembled for you here this morning,” he said, as the nurse tugged his mask into place and tied it behind his head. His wedding band flashed on the chain around his neck—he always wore it like that while in surgery—in the bright lights, and for a second her eyes stayed there.

Jim and his wife had been happily married for over thirty years. The same as she and Luke would have been if he’d stayed.

She cleared her throat. “I appreciate it.”

All too soon the anesthesiologist bent over her, his brown eyes looking into hers from behind rimless glasses. “Want me to give you a sedative?”

“No, thank you.”

“Okay, everyone,” Jim announced, all scrubbed in and gloved up as he stepped in next to her. “Emily’s one of our own. Let’s make sure she gets our best.”

The team assembled around her and her calm facade began to crumble. Tremors started in her fingers and spread to her hands, then down her arms and neck, until they wracked her whole body. Her teeth chattered. Jim took her free hand when the anesthesiologist pushed the cocktail of drugs into her veins. It burned all the way up her arm, each centimeter of progress a separate torture as it traveled toward her heart. She sucked in a deep breath and fought back a grimace, but failed.

"Almost done," Jim said, holding her fingers tight in his. Someone placed a mask over her face and she pulled in a couple of breaths. An awful pressure squeezed her head as the anesthetic took hold, making it feel like her head was being crushed in a vise.

A frisson of panic took root and she shook her head sharply, her body fighting all of it despite her attempt to stay calm.

"Easy, Emily." Jim maintained the steady pressure on her hand and kept talking to her in his low, calm voice. "Don't fight it, just let go. We're going to take real good care of you."

Her eyelids fluttered as the drugs finally did their work. She knew they would do everything they could for her. Anne would stay with her for a few days when she got sent home. But after that...she was on her own.

****

*Tribal region of Afghanistan*
*Next Day*

"Sir? Someone is on the satellite phone for you." Releasing his grip on the loaded pistol beneath his lumpy pillow, Farouk Ahmed Tehrazzi peeled his heavy lids apart and studied the man who had taken him in. Hazel eyes regarded him from the doorway of the crude bedroom the man and his wife had vacated for his use.

"Thank you. I'll take the call." He slid his hand out from beneath the pillow.

His heart pounded with anticipation. The rush of excitement helped to dull the exquisite agony in his belly as he sat up. The square of gauze taped over his new surgical incision was stained with blood. He'd popped two of the staples holding the wound together during his frantic escape over the Afghan border.

He took the phone from his host with a grateful nod and the man left. Tehrazzi brought the handset to his ear, conscious of the debilitating weakness in his muscles. His whole body hurt from the fever—his immune system's way of battling the peritonitis caused by his bodyguard's knife.

"Hello," he said in Pashto.

"It's me," a male voice replied in English.

His hand clenched tighter around the phone. Abdu. His eyes and ears until he got back on his feet. "What have you learned?"

"I have bad news, I'm afraid."

Tehrazzi's heart gave a sickening throb. "Tell me."

"The operation failed."

He closed his weary eyes. "He is still alive?"

"Yes. Ahmed died attempting to kill Doctor Adams. No one followed up on Hutchinson."

His jaw clenched so hard his teeth ached. Doctor Adams was the least of his concern now. His teacher was all that mattered. "What happened?"

"Security was too tight at the hospital. Communication broke down amid the confusion with Ahmed's death."

"Where is he?"

"The hospital released Hutchinson this morning, but I can't find out if he's left Vancouver yet."

Of course he'd left. His teacher would never stay in the same place, especially when he'd been targeted there. "What about his wife?"

"His wife? I thought they were divorced."

Tehrazzi suppressed a growl of irritation. That was irrelevant. She would be easier to find, vulnerable. And for all the years they'd spent apart, his teacher still cared deeply about her. That wouldn't have changed, and he still wore the precious medallion she'd given him.

Tehrazzi knew him too well to believe otherwise. Losing her would eviscerate him, even now. "Find out where they both are."

"I'll look into it and get back to you."

"Do that."

Tehrazzi hung up and laid back against his damp pillow. Perhaps he'd been thinking about this the wrong way. Maybe he should focus on the wife. He'd targeted other women in his teacher's circle because it guaranteed his teacher would respond personally. And every time it had worked.

He shifted on the thin straw mattress. Planning an operation like that stateside would be difficult. The Vancouver debacle proved how unreliable the men he'd hired were. For this to work, Tehrazzi had to be directly involved. And when the end came, he wanted to be the one facing off against his teacher. Allah willing, he would prevail.

The rough wool blanket scratched and hurt his fevered skin, but at least it was warm. Winter closed in on the mountains. In a few weeks the snows would make travel all but impossible. And his body…he wasn't ready to take this operation on yet. Much as it killed him, he had to wait until he was stronger. But what could he do in the meantime besides plan his next move?

His restless gaze fell on the pack he'd placed next to his bed. The book was in it. Stained and worn, its binding falling apart, he still carried it with him. For over twenty years he'd kept it as a reminder.

A frown creased his forehead. Christmas was only a few weeks away. Perhaps it was time to let go of his memento.

His hand shook when he reached for the pack and dragged it over, biting down on his lips to keep from crying out as his wound pulled. Reaching inside, he took the book out and studied the tattered cover in the dimness. He rubbed his thumb across the faded title. A barrage of conflicting emotions flooded him. Grief. Bitterness. Rage. And above it all, an aching, terrible loneliness.

Releasing a deep, slow breath, he laid it on his lap and called out for his host. The man appeared a moment later.

"I wondered if I might impose upon you to take a package into Kabul and mail it for me."

"Of course, I'd be honored to."

When he left, Tehrazzi stared down at the paperback cradled in his hands. This would be a Christmas gift his teacher would never forget.

*Yesterday is history. Tomorrow is a mystery. And today? Today is a gift.*

*That is why we call it the present.*

*—Babatunde Olatunji*

# Chapter One

*Baton Rouge, LA*
*Christmas Day*

The waiting made him edgy as hell.

Luke Hutchinson eyed his silent cell phone lying on the coffee table next to his whirring laptop and loaded SIG Sauer, and willed it to ring. He hated the waiting almost as much as the dread he couldn't shake. In the quiet of the room all his senses were on alert, anticipating…something.

All thanks to the tattered paperback novel he'd found on his front porch when he'd come back from his morning run. One look at the brown paper wrapping and his heart had gone into overdrive. Nobody sent him Christmas gifts anymore. But this was no ordinary gift.

It was a promise.

He stared down at the faded title and thought of the day he'd bought it for his young friend. It'd been a piss-poor substitute for his physical presence, but a gesture to show he cared, meant to help Farouk improve his English because Luke could no longer be there to teach him.

He swallowed a bitter laugh. Looking back, how had he not seen what was coming?

The title taunted him. *To Kill a Mockingbird.* The significance of the book worked on so many levels, and made his stomach clench tight as a fist. He knew exactly what it meant.

The student was finally coming after the teacher. Only Luke didn't know when that fateful meeting would happen. Or where.

A shadow moved outside the French doors that led onto the back deck. A quick flash of darkness.

Hackles rising, he shut the laptop to extinguish its lit screen, snatched up the gun and crept along the wall toward the doors, staying low and out of sight. In the kitchen, pale moonlight shone through the rectangular panes of glass, reflecting on the hardwood floor. The refrigerator hummed quietly. Nothing else stirred.

Pausing, he waited there in the darkness for a few minutes. The chances of someone sneaking up and catching him unawares were almost nil, but he was going to check things out regardless.

When nothing else disturbed the silence or caught his attention, Luke edged to the French doors. He threw one open and burst through it onto the deck, pistol aimed and ready. A cold breeze blew over his face and rustled the branches of the pecan trees edging the yard. The half moon threw its silver rays onto the grass and led his gaze to the dock that stretched out into the lake. Not a ripple disturbed the clear surface, and he didn't detect the sound of a motor. He relaxed his stance. Very few people had the ability to take him on, and fewer still worried him.

But Farouk Tehrazzi was more than capable of keeping Luke awake at night. The bastard had already come close to killing him several times.

Satisfied he was still alone on his property, Luke slipped back inside and rearmed his custom security system. He didn't sleep much so it wasn't unusual for him to be awake at this hour, but all night he'd had a gut deep certainty of impending doom. Something was wrong, he could feel it. After serving so many years in the shadowy realm of CIA counterterrorism operations, he knew enough to trust his instincts. And they screamed that the monster he'd created was on the move again. The "gift" he'd received merely confirmed it.

The call from his boss back at Langley that morning verified they'd lost their only helpful lead on Tehrazzi when he'd crossed over the Afghani border from Pakistan. Once across, he would settle amongst the Pashtun villages dotting the high mountain peaks of the Hindu Kush.

Luke ran a hand through his shaggy hair, his palm brushing over the newly healed craniotomy site at the base of his skull. That inconvenient surgery had kept him sidelined while Tehrazzi made his flight into the mountains of Afghanistan. Now, Luke was more than ready to get over there and finish what he'd started all those years ago during the Russian-Afghan war in the name of defending democracy for the CIA.

If only the Agency would let him get back to doing what he did best instead of gumming up the whole operation with enough red tape to gift wrap the Statue of Liberty. First it'd been because they wouldn't give him medical clearance to go into the field. Once he'd cleared that hurdle, it was because they hadn't signed off on the team he wanted. A former Green Beret named Davis was still over in A-stan working his magic, infiltrating the tiny villages and getting cozy with the warlords to garner new intelligence. Right now, that was the only part Luke felt good about. If anyone could find out what Tehrazzi was up to, it was Davis. He was the best at counter insurgency that Luke had ever seen during his career in Special Ops.

The grandfather clock in the hallway chimed midnight, officially making it Boxing Day. Luke glanced around his spartan living room with a sigh. Not that yesterday had resembled anything close to Christmas. On the few occasions he came home during the holidays, he never bothered with a tree or lights. What was the point? It only reminded him he was alone, and by choice.

This year, he didn't even have a Christmas card sitting on his mantel. For the first time in over two decades, his ex-wife hadn't sent him one. And she hadn't returned his calls, either. He'd phoned her twice to find out if she was okay after her sudden departure from Vancouver when he'd come out of recovery, and left a message the last time. Nada. It bothered him more than he wanted to admit.

Luke set the pistol on the coffee table and sank onto the couch to open the laptop screen. Yep, quite a life he'd carved out for himself. He'd spent most of his days tracking down terrorists in every war-torn and backward country on the planet, first as a SEAL officer, later in CIA paramilitary ops and contract work. He'd faced death more times than he could count, and taken more lives than he cared to remember. At this point, he didn't care if he bought it on the next mission so long as he got Tehrazzi in the process. With everything he'd gone through in his life, it would be a relief for the pain to stop.

If hell existed, he'd more than earned an eternity of torture and misery there. Though he doubted the devil could do much worse to him than he'd inflicted upon himself over his lifetime. If what he'd done in the name of duty didn't earn him a place in the underworld once he croaked, he always had the trump card of abandoning his wife and young son all those years ago. That knowledge never went away, no matter what he did. It stayed buried in his heart like a razor blade.

In fact, it was a miracle he'd been invited to his son's wedding a month ago, and wouldn't have been if he and Rayne hadn't tried patching the cracks and fissures in their relationship—if someone could call it that—six months ago. On his way to the airport Luke had almost turned around on the freeway and gone home. Would have been safer for everyone if he had. In the middle of a dance with Emily, the first time he'd touched her in over a decade, his head injury had finally taken its toll and landed him flat on his back in the middle of the dance floor. Out cold, and they'd dragged him off to the hospital. One brain surgery later, and voila, he was good as new.

Absently he toyed with the St. Christopher medallion hanging from a gold chain around his neck. Em had given it to him when he'd first made the SEAL Teams, and he'd never taken it off. Not once in over twenty years, until that surgery when one of the nurses had given it to Emily to hold. Maybe that's why she'd taken off so suddenly with the cryptic message of "having her own demons to face" and flown back to Charleston. Finding out he still wore the thing must have been a shock for her.

The laptop suddenly beeped with an incoming e-mail. When he opened the file from Bryn, he frowned. She was the cog in the wheel that joined him, his family, and most of his hand-picked team together. She'd just married a SEAL named Dec McCabe. Luke had enlisted him to track down Tehrazzi back in September when she'd been kidnapped.

Luke braced for bad news. If Bryn was back from the honeymoon already and e-mailing him at this hour on Christmas night her time, it had to mean Dec had been called out to join Dev Group. Which meant either something big was brewing in the Middle East that he didn't know about, or the top brass expected trouble in the immediate future.

*Hey, Luke. Just got off the phone with Rayne. Emily's not doing very well...*

His stomach dropped. Damn it, he'd *known* something wasn't right with her.

*Christa and Rayne are with her, but I'm heading to Charleston tomorrow, and thought maybe you should give her a call. Will keep you posted.*

*Bryn*

Staring at the screen, an awful hollow feeling settled in his gut. He'd known it had to be bad for Em to leave the hospital in Vancouver before he'd come out of recovery, but if it was bad enough for Bryn to fly down there...

He remembered the e-mail from his son on the last mission in Afghanistan in late September. *P.S. You might want to talk to mom ASAP.*

Jesus, he'd been too chicken shit to phone her after their last conversation had ended so disastrously, so he'd let it slide. Seeing her at Rayne's wedding was the first time he'd made contact since. She'd been pale, but he'd assumed it had to do with seeing him face-to-face and the fact their only child was getting married. But Christ, what if it was something way more serious?

*Shit.* Why the hell hadn't Rayne called him to tell him? Luke snatched up his cell phone and dialed his son, but it went through to voicemail. He tried Bryn, but the same thing happened. He jumped up from the couch and went to the kitchen. It took some digging, but he eventually found his daughter-in-law's cell number. He paced as he waited for the call to connect, then it rang once, twice, three times—

"Hello?"

"Christa, it's Luke." He didn't bother apologizing for the late hour, but she didn't seem groggy so maybe he hadn't woken her.

"Hey, Merry Christmas! How are you?"

He was too worried to make small talk. "I just got an e-mail from Bryn about Emily."

"Oh..."

When she didn't offer anything further, Luke suppressed an irritated growl. "What the hell's going on?"

"Just a second." He made out the sound of a door closing and then treads down wooden steps. She must be headed down the rear steps of Emily's house, toward the garden. Luke knew every square inch of that property, so he had a good mental image of where she was as he counted the seconds. After another few moments she came back on the line. "Sorry, just wanted a little privacy."

So Rayne and Emily wouldn't know who she was talking to. "What's wrong with her?"

"She's...sick."

Yeah, no shit.

"We only found out yesterday when we came in to visit for a few days."

Luke pictured Christa peering cautiously over the shrubbery to make sure no one in the house could see her. "Sick with what?"

"We're still prying details out of her, and she doesn't want anyone to know."

Luke clenched his jaw. If Christa's career as a national-level softball catcher didn't pan out, she could make a living working for the Agency with non-answers like that. "How bad is it?" Although he already knew it was pretty damn serious. It scared him to know Emily hadn't even told Rayne or Bryn about it.

"Uh...she's putting on a brave face, but— Hold on." A moment's pause. "Be right up," she called, her voice muffled as though she'd put a hand over the phone. So much for the covert op. "Sorry," she said to him, her voice a near whisper, "but I gotta go back in or she'll be suspicious."

"Is Rayne there?"

"He's uh...busy cleaning up the kitchen with her. Can I have him call you back in the morning?"

*It is morning*, he wanted to say, but held back the words. Luke was acutely conscious that his son had contacted Bryn instead of him, and that Christa hadn't offered to put Emily on the phone. Since Christa was the soul of politeness, he had to assume it was because she thought it would upset Emily to speak with him. Or that it might piss Rayne off. "They tell you not to talk to me?"

"What? No, it's just...I'm not sure if she..." Christa took a deep breath. "I'm not sure what to do," she admitted. "That's why I asked Bryn to contact you."

So Christa wouldn't be incriminated on her own. "Fine. Have Rayne call me when he gets a chance."

"Okay. I'm sorry I can't tell you more, Luke. I want to, but—"

"It's all right. I understand." He understood all too well.

"I don't want to interfere with your...relationship with her—"

*Relationship?* He almost laughed. What he and Emily had wasn't anything close to a relationship. He didn't even rank a spot on her Christmas card list anymore.

"—but Bryn and I talked about it and we both think she needs... I'm not sure if you're comfortable with it, but—"

*Jesus Christ*, he wanted to snap, *just say it already.*

"We think she might...need you."

*Ah, hell.* Luke closed his eyes as a wave of pain washed over him. Whatever was going on, Emily had faced it alone until today, and he was likely the last person she wanted to find out about it. He hated knowing that because it emphasized what a shitty husband he'd been and how badly he'd hurt her when he'd left all those years ago. "I hear you." But what could he do for her? They were barely on speaking terms.

Once he got off the phone, Luke debated the situation for all of three seconds, then went to his bedroom and took a duffel from his closet. Sitting around waiting got him nowhere, and he knew Tehrazzi was up to something. On the off chance Emily might be in danger, he would put an undercover security detail on her.

He packed enough clothes to last him a week, then got his gear together. Improvising was second nature to him, so he'd handle this situation the same way he would a military operation: his way.

To hell with waiting for his son to call him back. He was putting his ass on a plane ASAP and getting some answers from Emily face to face.

****

*Charleston, SC*
*Boxing Day*

Emily sat curled up on the porch swing overlooking her back garden, while her new daughter-in-law puttered around the yard pruning and cleaning up the beds for the winter. She loved Christa to pieces, and would be eternally grateful her son had married such a sweetheart, but if they didn't let her get up and help with something soon, she'd go nuts.

They'd made her lie on the couch all morning while they'd taken down the few Christmas ornaments she'd put up, along with the fresh cut Blue Spruce tree she bought each year. Tradition was important to her. The owner of the tree lot always put one aside for her and called her when it came in, but this year she almost hadn't bothered decorating at all. She wasn't exactly in a festive mood these days.

When Rayne and Christa had surprised her on Christmas Eve by showing up on her doorstep, they'd given her the best present in the world. Bryn's arrival this morning made it all the more special. Holidays were hard enough for Emily without spending them alone. She hadn't wanted them to find out what was happening and they'd been mad as hell she hadn't told them before, but now the secret was out and she was relieved.

"Aren't you getting cold?" she called out, glancing at her watch. Christa'd been at it for over an hour, and Charleston was chilly in late December.

"No, I'm good. Almost done here anyhow," Christa replied, kneeling as she deadheaded some of last year's perennials. Her face was hidden by her Team Canada ball cap that proudly proclaimed *You Only Wish You Could Play Like A Girl*.

Since she'd gotten ill, Emily had let the garden slide. It made her happy Christa was here to lend a hand because it was too beautiful to let it go by the wayside. Full of memories, too. Like the ones from her wedding reception.

*Quit thinking about him.* "How about some tea, then?"

Christa stopped what she was doing and looked up at her with narrowed eyes. "You move one toe off that swing and I'll come up there and duct tape you to it."

Emily laughed. "I might be more scared if I thought you really meant that."

Christa set down her spade and put her hands on her hips. “Don’t try me, and if we want tea, I’m sure Rayne will make it.”

Emily sighed. “I’m not an invalid, contrary to everyone’s opinion.”

“You’re supposed to be resting, and you should take advantage of that. Just for once let someone else do the work around here. We’ll be gone soon enough as it is.”

She wasn’t going to win this argument, so she might as well enjoy the break. “Have I told you you’re an angel?”

“About a hundred times.”

Smiling, Emily leaned back against the pillows and pulled the thick quilt around her more snugly. The air was cold, but not frigid. The tall palmetto that graced the center of the back garden waved its fronds gently with a soft rustling sound. Moving in swirling gusts, the slight wind coming off the harbor brought the briny tang of the water with it. The cool temperatures seemed to help the nausea that plagued her, and refreshed her sluggish brain. Both miraculous things, given how awful she’d felt lately, but she was much better today. The imposed rest was definitely helping. Good days were so rare for her now that she’d learned to cherish them.

The black, wrought iron side gate swung open and Bryn came through it, just returned from her jog. She pulled off her knit cap and grinned, long dark hair flowing down her back. “Hey, how are you guys doing?”

“Great,” she and Christa replied in unison.

Bryn rolled her eyes. “You two are like twins, I swear. It’s scary.” With her long legs encased in her tight yoga pants, she loped up the back steps and took a seat next to Emily. She ran a critical eye over her face. “You look better.”

“Feeling better, too. The air helps, along with the peppermint tea y’all keep shoving at me.”

"We do what we can." Bryn studied Christa's work for a moment with a shake of her head, her hair brushing across the middle of her black Nike jacket. "Did you guys inherit some kind of mutant female gene that I didn't? Is that why you can cook gourmet food, keep a spotless home, garden and do everything else in regards to running a show home and I can't?"

"You just need more practice," Christa told her without looking up. "As for me, I'd much rather be able to kick a terrorist's ass and walk away dusting my hands."

Bryn made a sour face. "It didn't happen *quite* like that." She tilted her head at Christa. "Where's your hubby?"

"Doing laundry." Her aquamarine eyes sparkled with humor. "Phase one of his domestic training is nearly complete."

Bryn shared a conspiratorial grin with her. "I like the way you think. I only had limited time to get Dec trained the way I want him before he got called out, so I'll live vicariously through you. You've got a better shot with perfecting Rayne anyhow. Mine won't be home enough to make the effort worthwhile."

Yeah, Emily knew how that went. As the wife of an active-duty SEAL, Bryn faced a tough transition, and while Emily didn't envy her, she was going to make sure she helped her friend through it. The same as Bryn and Christa were helping her now with their unexpected visit.

As much as she'd intended to fight this battle alone and not worry any of her loved ones, it was such a blessing to have them gathered around her, and more so to know they'd done it because they loved her so much. That in itself was better than any medicine a doctor could prescribe.

Beneath Bryn's nonchalance about her husband

getting called out to duty, however, Emily heard the terrible uncertainty she herself had once been forced to live with. She nudged Bryn's knee. "Heard from Dec?"

"Not since yesterday when he responded to my e-mail. He told me he's fine, and not to worry."

Their first Christmas together, and he was overseas someplace. Emily rolled her eyes. "Why do they say such ridiculous things to us? Do they think we're stupid?"

Bryn chuckled. "I guess it's all they can think of to put us at ease."

"Oh, please." As if anything could do that. She'd spent many a sleepless night glued to the TV watching cable news reports about developing situations and conflicts overseas. That's the only way she'd ever been able to guess where Luke was when he deployed during the years they'd been married. It had taken its toll over the course of their marriage, but she'd still been willing to stick it out until they were old and decrepit, sitting on this same porch swing together. Little good it had done her.

Pushing the thought away, Emily laid a hand over Bryn's and met her friend's dark eyes. "I know it's not much, but I understand what you're going through."

Bryn offered a smile. "I know, and I'm glad I've got you to talk with." She got up and stretched, reaching her arms over her head, five-feet-nine-inches of toned muscle. "How about something to snack on? It won't be homemade petit fours or anything, so I don't want you to be disappointed," she warned with a wry edge. "But I think I can handle some yogurt and granola parfaits with strawberries. Sound okay?"

Emily double checked with her stomach, imagining the flavors in her mouth. Luckily, her body didn't protest with all the signs that heralded a bout of vomiting. Things were looking up. "I think I will have some, thanks."

"Back in a flash." She passed Rayne as he stepped out onto the back porch from the kitchen. "Tell your wife to get off her damn knees and relax."

"Oh, but I love the things she does when she's on her knees," he replied, laughing as he caught the gardening glove Christa chucked at him.

Emily shook her head at her son, tall and strong and way too handsome for his own good. "I'd watch what you say about your wife," she advised. "That girl's got a wicked arm on her."

His hazel-green eyes, the only part of him that wasn't a carbon copy of Luke, were full of mischief when he looked at her. "That she does," he murmured, the Low Country drawl still evident in his voice. He held out a hand to her. "Come on. Time for your appointment."

She groaned. "Already?"

"Yes, ma'am." He tugged on her wrist, his hand so broad and strong compared to hers, but still so gentle. "Come on, don't make me carry you."

And he would too, she thought with another groan, pushing up from the swing and letting her feet touch the gray-painted porch floor. Rayne might not have that same hard edge to him, but beneath the playful image he was every bit the alpha male his father was.

She almost asked him if he'd heard from his father, and how he was doing, but stopped herself. Luke had left a message for her a few days after her surgery, but she hadn't called him back. While in the hospital this last time, she'd finally made up her mind to let him and all her dreams of him go. So far, it wasn't working.

Following Rayne into the house, Emily comforted herself with the knowledge that her son would be a much better husband to Christa than Luke had ever been to her. She'd made damn sure of that while she'd raised him.

# Chapter Two

*Tribal region of Afghanistan, northeast of Jalalabad*

Weak wintry sunlight touched the back of Farouk Tehrazzi's upraised head as he lifted in the midst of his prayers. He faced the south-western sky toward Mecca, and overlooked the rose-tinted valley below. Early morning rays fell on his shoulders and back as he lowered his forehead to the soft nap of his prayer mat. A cold breeze picked up, carrying his words heavenward to Allah over the craggy peaks of the mountains.

When he finished his dawn prayers, he rose without having to put a hand on his belly and barely noticed the tugging sensation around the surgical scars. He was finally healed up from the knife wounds his former bodyguard had inflicted, and ready to move. Thanks be to Allah.

Tucking his prayer mat beneath his arm, he made his way down the steep, narrow trail to the tiny village nestled into the side of the mountain. The men nodded respectfully when he passed, and the children watched him in silence as their mothers shooed them out of the way without looking at him. Eyes lowered modestly, as expected of them.

Uneducated peasants they might be, but they were God-fearing people who eked a living out of one of the harshest environments on earth. Tehrazzi was inextricably connected to them. His ancestors had lived much like the people here did today. For generations they had successfully repelled every invasion that came across the mountains. The Pashtuns had war in their blood, and he was no different. They had adapted and survived centuries of fighting foes far better equipped than they. Yet they remained. And would always remain, no matter how many JDAMs the U.S. and its allies dropped in his ancestral homeland, or how many armies came to these mountains. That was something the enemy did not understand, and it would eventually bring them defeat.

Near the dwellings built of dun-colored rock and brick, chickens pecked in the dirt searching for food and the strong smell of goats hung heavy in the air. Hungry, and waiting for the herding boys to take them into the valley, the goats milled about the bottom of the trail, the tinkle of tiny bells around their necks mingling with their plaintive bleating.

He moved on silent feet to a home hollowed out of the cliff and pushed aside the woven blanket covering the doorway. A single kerosene lamp lit the dim, rough interior. The elder seated next to the ammunition crate serving as a table smiled from beneath his long, gray-streaked beard.

"Blessed morning to you, my son."

"And to you," Tehrazzi responded in Pashto to his guest, sitting cross-legged opposite him. General Aziz was one of the few men he respected. The local warlord had gained a reputation as a tough leader and fighter during the anti-Soviet jihad. That reputation had only gained strength in the years since the Americans had invaded Afghanistan with their NATO allies in a bid to eradicate what they saw as the threat of radical Islam to the rest of the world.

Tehrazzi still couldn't understand how the "rest of the world" couldn't see that America had terrorized innocent Muslims all around the world for generations. They hadn't raised a hue and cry when the Americans withdrew all their financial and military support from the mujahedeen once the war with the Soviets was won. No one had stepped in to help the Afghan people rebuild their shattered lives and country. No help had arrived to stem the bloody tribal wars that followed where various factions fought for control.

Tehrazzi had been fifteen years old when America abandoned him to his fate. He'd barely survived that first winter, spent shivering in the miserable caves dug out of the mountains near an abandoned Soviet outpost. Starving and on the run from another band of mujahedeen that killed all the men he'd served with.

"What are you thinking of?"

Tehrazzi glanced up at the elder, whose dark eyes regarded him with a surprising amount of compassion. "The past." The general would understand. He'd lived through that same dark time.

"Ah." Aziz leaned back a little and rested his hands over his slightly rounded belly. "Do you think it wise to dwell on those memories?"

"Perhaps not. But they serve me well. Forgetting the past would be even more unwise."

Amusement and understanding lit Aziz's eyes. "I remember well what it feels like to burn with the need for retribution."

Tehrazzi did burn. That ceaseless need was a living fire buried beneath his skin. Only the death of one man could quench it.

"You are absolutely sure you do not need anything from me before you go? I have just received another shipment of rifles."

"Thank you, uncle, but no." He had all that he required. What's more, he had new allies in unexpected places that proved to be highly valuable. Not that he trusted them. He would never make that deadly mistake again.

"Your contact will be here soon?"

"Yes." And he would bring the news Tehrazzi had been waiting for.

Aziz stroked his thick beard thoughtfully. "The quarry you are hunting is extremely dangerous."

Yes, he was. His teacher was one of the most dangerous men alive—to Tehrazzi and all his followers.

"I remember him well. He was a good soldier. And a good man."

"He was, once." Before he had disappeared and left Tehrazzi and the others to their hellish fate.

"He had a sincere appreciation for Islam, as I recall. A rare quality among his countrymen."

Tehrazzi's jaw flexed. His teacher had always respected the ways and teachings of Allah. That was the main reason why Tehrazzi had bonded with him so quickly and so hard. He'd barely been in his teens when they'd met. He'd trusted his teacher implicitly. Looked up to him as a kind of father figure. He'd worshipped the man. And then his teacher had suddenly left him without a backward glance.

That original betrayal changed Tehrazzi forever. He'd suffered others since, but that first time had cut the deepest. He still bled from that invisible wound. It was a lesson he would never forget.

"Are you sure it is wise to hunt such a man, my son? Perhaps it would be better to continue your operations here instead, where the people will protect and hide you."

Tehrazzi's hands tightened on his knees, fingers clenching in the loose white tribal-style pants he wore. "You know what he's like, what he's capable of," he said, switching to English. "He won't stop until I'm dead. It's either him or me." Or both of them. Death didn't scare him. Tehrazzi was more than prepared to give his life for Allah. But his ultimate sacrifice would be so much more worthwhile if he took his teacher with him and helped clear the way for his successors to carry out jihad against the western infidels.

Tehrazzi turned his head when the blanket flap opened. One of the village men peered inside. "A messenger has arrived, sir."

"Thank you." Tehrazzi pushed to his feet and excused himself from the general before going outside. A weary-looking Abdu stood near the trail, huddling deeper into the thick down-filled coat he wore.

"Peace be upon you," the young man said. He was somewhere around twenty or so, but he'd lived a hard life. The money he earned from Tehrazzi and from the valuable source on the other end of this information chain would provide him with comforts unimaginable to the villagers who lived here.

"And you." Handing him a wad of cash, Tehrazzi folded his arms across his chest and raised his left brow inquiringly before catching himself and clearing his expression. His teacher had that same mannerism, and Tehrazzi could not break himself of the same habit no matter how much it annoyed him.

After stuffing the cash into his coat pocket, Abdu blew on his hands. "I'm to ask you about the arms dealer you dealt with in Kabul last week."

Tehrazzi almost laughed. That was what they wanted to know? Of all the things they could have asked for, a mid-level arms dealer was what would earn him his teacher's location? Unbelievable. "I'll tell you whatever you wish to know. But first, tell me what you've learned."

Abdu hesitated only a moment. "He is still in the States. But word is he plans to come for you."

*Not if I get to him first.*

He didn't dare say it aloud in case someone was listening back in Kabul via a carefully placed wire. Abdu had proved reliable thus far, but a man willing to play both sides was either desperate or naive enough to think he would be protected by his employers. "Come inside and have some tea before you go. You can meet General Aziz."

The young man's eyes flashed to his. "Aziz is here?"

"Don't they know that back in Kabul?" He clucked his tongue. "Shame, with all their resources and technology." Hiding a smile, he headed back toward the house. "Come on. I'll tell you what you need to know inside." And once the sun set, Tehrazzi would leave this backward village and make his way through the icy mountain passes toward Kabul. When he arrived, he'd personally ensure he got whatever he needed to hunt down his teacher and repay him for all his sins.

****

Luke hadn't been back to Charleston since the day he'd hauled eighteen-year-old Rayne off to the Marine Corps base at Parris Island, the morning after he'd piled Emily's car into a pole. A lot had changed since then.

Driving into the city from the airport in a rental car, a sense of nostalgia hit him. This had been his city once, and his home because Emily was here. Once upon a time it wouldn't have mattered where they lived, so long as she was with him. She was what made a place a home.

When he found out exactly what was happening with

her, he was going to talk with Bryn. He'd already taken her up on her offer to let him use her father's place in Beirut for his staging area.

For the past few weeks Luke had thought about Tehrazzi, and how he'd targeted Bryn and Neveah to get to him. If Tehrazzi thought the women were his team's weak point and he'd already gone after the others, then it only made sense that Emily would be at the top of his list. Up 'til now she'd been safe enough living in Charleston without protection because he'd severed contact with her. But Luke wasn't going to risk leaving her exposed anymore, especially with her health suffering. He might not know precisely what the problem was, but he had his suspicions, and they were burning a hole in his gut.

At Rayne's wedding a month ago she'd been pale and seemed tired. She'd even dropped off to sleep in that damned pullout next to his hospital bed within minutes, telling him how exhausted she was. Throughout their whole marriage, Em had never been a good sleeper, and with all the tension between them at the wedding, there was no way she should have been able to fall asleep.

The silver dollar-sized medallion he wore lay heavy against his heart. The engraved message Emily had added on the back practically burned his skin. *May this always keep you safe from any dangers you will face. Em.*

If he thought he'd been vulnerable before and during the surgery, he was more so now that Emily knew he still wore the thing. She had to know what it meant. Especially after the disastrous phone call back in Basra, when he'd been suffering from an acute concussion and accidentally blurted out that he loved her before passing out. In light of that he supposed he should be grateful she'd stayed in Vancouver until she was certain he was out of danger instead of taking off right away.

Driving along the Battery, Luke passed the stately houses he remembered so well. The historic southern mansions faced Charleston Harbor where Fort Sumter lay, all of them surrounded by lush gardens and manicured lawns interspersed with tall palmetto trees.

Passing White Point Gardens where he'd taught Rayne to throw a ball and where they'd once enjoyed lazy picnic lunches, he took a right onto Emily's street. His chest felt tight already.

A short distance up, he came to the driveway marked by a black wrought iron gate that she always left open. Just another gesture of her southern hospitality. *Closed gates*, she'd once told him, *make people feel unwelcome*. Em would never do that. She was the only person he'd ever known with an endless supply of kindness toward living things, be they human, plant, or animal. She was the one to take in strays and pay for their vet bills. Put her on a public bus and within five minutes she'd have the person next to her spilling the contents of their soul, telling her their deepest, darkest secrets. People sensed her sincere desire to help, and in his opinion, took advantage of that.

Basically, he and Emily were polar opposites. She was sweet; he wasn't. She was outgoing; he was more or less a loner. She liked order and security; he'd always craved the adrenaline rush. She was born into the upper echelon of Charleston society; he'd come into the world in a two room shack on the outskirts of New Orleans. Many times he'd wondered how the hell they'd ever wound up together in the first place.

Pulling up next to the wrought iron fence that marked the antebellum property, he killed the engine and sat staring up at the house for a moment. Em had kept it beautifully since inheriting it from her parents, but that didn't surprise him at all. Family, tradition and history were all vitally important to her. This place was a part of her.

It looked exactly the same as it always had: an elegant brick heritage home with its white columns out front and the wide front and back porches with their wooden rocking chairs just waiting to be filled by a visitor. He knew Em would have a pitcher of sweet tea chilling in the fridge in case company dropped by, and she'd have countless Tupperware containers stuffed full of holiday treats she could whip out at a second's notice. She'd invite them inside or onto the porch and serve them with her best dishes. Crystal for the sweet tea, or in her great-grandmother's antique china if they preferred hot tea, because that's just how she was.

Sitting in the rental car, Luke wasn't sure if he'd get the same treatment, or if she'd even let him in the house, but he was damn well going to find out what was going on. And between him and the backup he'd brought in to guard her, he was going to make sure she was safe. Because Southern hospitality and open gates aside, living here alone she was like a lamb staked out for Tehrazzi if he decided to come after her. It damn near put him in a sweat thinking of it. Em wouldn't last two seconds against that kind of threat.

He got out and pulled his duffel from the passenger seat so his weapons wouldn't be in the car, then closed the door softly behind him. Putting a hand on the intricate, black wrought iron courtyard gate that she'd also left ajar, he spotted Christa bent over working in the garden. When the gate shut behind him with a quiet clang, she looked up.

"Luke!" A delighted smile lit her face. As she rushed over to greet him, Luke was relieved that at least one person was glad to see him.

Christa threw her arms around his shoulders and gave him a hard squeeze, which he returned. "I'm so glad you're here," she said.

"Me, too. Nice hat, by the way."

She chuckled. "Thanks."

He set her away from him and nodded toward the house. "They all inside?"

"Yes." She began gnawing on her lower lip, her robin's-egg-blue gaze swinging up to the kitchen window. "Uh...want me to get you some privacy?"

"I think that might be best, so yeah. I'd appreciate it."

He gestured for her to precede him, and her foot had just landed on the bottom step when the kitchen door opened onto the back porch. Rayne came out with a dish towel draped over one muscled shoulder, his expression guarded. A silent tension built in the cool air. Christa froze in mid-step, glancing between them uncertainly.

Luke met his son's gaze squarely. "Hi, Rayne." He kept the belated Merry Christmas to himself. They weren't exactly close despite the attempt they'd made at reconciliation. Whatever Luke did, he did well. Including his failures. They were all fucking spectacular.

"Hi." The tone was cautious, and Rayne's dark brows pulled together in a hard frown. "What are you doing here?"

"I came to see your mother." *And then drop the bomb about Tehrazzi on you.*

Rayne instantly sent a withering look at his wife. "Is this your doing?"

"Bryn contacted me," Luke answered for her, wanting to spare her the fight that was brewing. Christa didn't deserve that.

Rayne's jaw tightened. "Did she." He cast another fulminating glare at Christa, but she brought her chin up.

"We didn't tell him to come, we just thought he should know," she said. "It was his decision to fly here—I'm just as surprised to see him as you are."

Luke raised an eyebrow at his son. "Got a problem with me being here?"

Rayne held his gaze and instead said to Christa, "Will you go inside for a minute?"

"No. She needs him, and you know it." She went up the steps and laid a hand on his forearm, but Rayne didn't budge. "I'll get Bryn. Just give them a while alone, Rayne."

Rayne didn't answer her, simply kept staring at him with a good measure of resentment swirling in his eyes. When she was inside, Rayne took a step down and put a hand out to rest on the railing, not-so-subtly blocking Luke's way. His hazel stare burned into Luke's. "If you have any intention of leaving her after this, I suggest you turn around and do it right now."

The open hostility coming from his son didn't surprise him. He deserved it and more, and was secretly proud his son was protective of his mother. But now wasn't the moment for this confrontation. He didn't have much time left stateside.

Luke dropped the duffel and folded his arms across his chest. Quite something, to have to look up at your grown son. Rayne had him by at least three inches, and that was without standing on the steps. Craning his head back put a crick in Luke's neck. "You really want to have this conversation out here?"

"Just tell me why you're here."

He nodded toward the house. "I want to make sure she's okay."

"You could've called and asked her."

"I tried. She didn't return my calls, and nobody wanted to talk last night, either."

Rayne shook his head. "I don't know why you came all this way, because there's nothing you can do. You can't help her right now—none of us can."

The dread Luke had been fighting back returned in a rush. "What's wrong with her?"

Rayne lost some of his aggression and dropped his

arm with a sigh. "Ah, Christ, just go in and talk to her yourself, then. But if you hurt her again, I swear to God..." He gave a tight shake of his head, his jaw clenched so hard the muscles stood out.

"Understood." Luke slapped him on the shoulder and picked up his duffel. "You're a good son, Rayne," he said on his way up to the porch. Bryn and Christa were coming out of the kitchen when he reached it, and Bryn gave him a hug. "She know I'm here?" he asked them.

Christa shook her head. "She's upstairs having a nap with Jake."

*Jake?* Luke's stomach dropped like a rock. She'd been single as of a month ago, and with being sick, how had she managed to meet someone so fast?

"Come on, let's get outta here," Rayne muttered, walking toward the gate, and the girls followed him.

"Has she been up there for long?" Luke asked, hating that he was going to meet Emily's new lover.

"Not long, but it's okay, just go on up. She won't mind."

Well, he minded for Christ's sake.

Christa gave him a thumbs-up over her shoulder. "Good luck," she whispered.

Luke nodded. He was gonna need it.

Standing at the back door, a sudden memory flashed through his head. He'd been on the front porch that time, standing in the pouring rain covered with stitches the night he'd come back from the FUBAR he and his team had walked into in Central America. This had been her parent's house back then. He'd dragged his sorry ass up the brick steps and knocked on the door, dying to be let in somewhere safe and familiar. Em had pulled the door open, her nightgown stretched tight across her full-term pregnant belly. She'd thrown her arms around him and held on tight.

This visit he probably wouldn't even get a glass of

sweet tea out of the deal.

Pushing open the door leading into the kitchen and stepping over the threshold was like walking into a time warp. The smell of lemon oil soap scented the air. All the appliances were modern stainless steel instead of white and the countertops were black granite instead of butcher block, but the cabinets were still painted a fresh white and the floor was still black and white tile in a diamond pattern. The furnishings were elegant and tasteful, like their owner.

Looking around him reminded Luke yet again that Emily was in a class far above his lowly station. She was the princess raised in comfort and sophistication and he was the uneducated peon, having clawed his way through a childhood spent dodging his alcoholic father's fists. He'd joined the Navy just to get the hell away from his old man and swore he'd never raise a hand to his children if he had any. At least he'd managed to keep that one promise. Too bad it hadn't extended to his wife.

Sometimes he wasn't sure what Emily had seen in him. She was elegant and refined and intelligent, in a different class from all the other women he'd been with.

A thousand memories assaulted him as he stood in the kitchen, but most vivid was the day he'd been standing at the sink, cleaning his hunting knife to get ready for a fishing trip with eight year old Rayne—

Footsteps overhead alerted him that someone was up. Bracing himself, he went to the kitchen doorway where it led into the family room, and waited. The room smelled like Emily with the faint scent of vanilla perfuming the air. A quiet jingling sound followed by rhythmic clicks made him turn his head to look up the stairs.

Then Emily's distinctive Charleston drawl called out. "Hang on a second, Jake."

A moment later, a black-and-white Border Collie mix

came barreling down the stairs and raced up to him in a wriggling mass of fur. Since when did Em have a dog, Luke wondered above the relief flooding him, and reached down to scratch the soft ears. The animal leaned into him with a deep sigh and started up at him with adoring eyes. "Some guard dog you are."

Emily came into view on the stairs, and when she saw him her steps faltered. One graceful hand fluttered to her throat as she stared at him. "Luke...hi."

His eyes swept over her, heart sinking at what he saw. Even with the laugh lines creasing their corners, her eyes were still her loveliest feature, big and soft and green as emeralds. The mirrors into her beautiful soul. But now they were underlined with dark half circles, and she was thinner than she'd been at the wedding. Too thin. Her skin was so pale it was almost translucent. Yet it was her hair that made him the most uneasy. She'd cut it short, way shorter than he'd ever seen it, into some sort of pixie style where it spiked all over, wisps of it framing her oval face.

Emily hated her hair short.

He found his voice. "Hi, Em." Her hand was still over her throat, fingers covering the scar he'd given her beneath her jaw under her left ear. Shame crawled through him, like worms twisting in his belly.

The astonishment on her face quickly transformed into wariness, tinged with a hint of fear. It damn near broke his heart. They'd been married and had a child together, and yet they were little more than strangers facing each other across the room.

The whole thing made him incredibly sad. They'd held their wedding reception in the back garden after their elopement. Her parents had thrown them a barbecue and dance, with the backyard lit up by paper lanterns and a bright three-quarter moon hanging above Charleston Harbor. They'd been so in love, and so hot for each other they'd only stayed for half an hour before racing off to the historic bed and breakfast he'd booked for their wedding night. They'd only made it as far as the car before tearing each other's clothes off.

He still remembered everything about her. Every vivid, erotic detail. The feel of her silky skin, the tangy-sweet taste of her body and the breathless way she cried his name when she came…

Emily licked her lips. "What are you doing here?" The question wasn't a demand for an explanation, rather a puzzled request.

"You didn't return my calls, so I figured something was wrong." And he'd been right.

She crossed her arms over her breasts defensively. "One of them told you to come, didn't they?"

"No." She still hadn't moved off that bottom stair, so he took a step toward her. "What's going on?"

She retreated up two stairs, never taking her eyes off him. As though she was afraid he'd jump her or something. "Nothing."

"Bullshit." He fought back the edge of temper riding him, but the grinding in his gut needed an answer. "Are you sick?"

Her chin came up, but her gaze dropped. And so did his stomach. "I'm fine."

"Don't bother lying to me. You took off from Vancouver without a word to anyone except Bryn, and only to say you had 'your own demons to face.' What the hell did that mean?"

She flinched, her shoulders hunching. "I didn't want to worry anyone, and you were just out of surgery."

"Well as you can see I'm all healed up, so tell me now." When she didn't reply he maintained eye contact with her and watched her squirm, unwilling to let it go. If necessary, he'd stand there all damn day until he got an answer out of her. He took another step toward her.

"Tell me."

Finally, she sighed and came down the stairs to walk past him into the family room. The sweet scent of her perfume filled the air. "Do you want to sit down?"

Ever the genteel hostess. "No." He wanted a goddamn straight answer. "Just tell me the truth."

Her eyes snapped over to him and narrowed a moment, a spark of anger lighting their depths. "Fine. I have cancer."

For a moment a strange roaring filled his ears, and when he managed to speak, it sounded like his voice came from the other end of a tunnel. "What kind of cancer?"

Her throat moved as she swallowed. "Stage IIIA breast cancer."

The words swam in his brain. Stage three...wasn't that life-threatening? His gaze immediately dropped to where her arms shielded her breasts, covered by that loose T-shirt. He swallowed. She'd had some sort of surgery, but it looked like she still had both breasts—"How bad is it?"

She shrugged and looked away, reaching a hand out to straighten an already perfectly aligned framed photo on the white traditional mantel. Fidgeting, like she always did when she was nervous. That he was the cause of her discomfort twisted the razor blade buried in his heart. And still she didn't reply. Instead her elegant hands continued rearranging the frames until he wanted to scream.

"Em? How bad?"

When she finally lifted her head, her eyes were shadowed with a sadness that made him ache inside. "Pretty bad."

The breath wheezed out of his lungs. For a moment he swore he swayed on his feet. Swallowing, he found his voice again. "Meaning?"

"No one's a hundred percent sure yet. I'm doing chemo to try and kill off any other tumor cells, and the surgery went well, but..." She shrugged again. Like it didn't matter.

"What surgery?" he croaked, though he was pretty sure he already knew.

Her shoulders hunched in a bit, and she cleared her throat as though embarrassed to tell him. Finally she said, "I had a mastectomy."

****

The blood hit Emily's cheeks in a hot rush when she said the words, but the instant they were out of her mouth Luke went utterly white beneath his dark beard. His sharp inhalation echoed in the stillness and his gaze dropped to her chest, covered by her arms. She hunched her shoulders instinctively to keep him from seeing her shape beneath the T-shirt she wore.

"Christ, Em..."

"I'm fine," she snapped defensively, hating the sympathy in his eyes. She felt as vulnerable as if she stood naked in front of him. "Don't worry about it."

He made a scoffing sound. "Like hell."

She turned her back on him and made her way into the kitchen. Jake scrambled to his feet and followed, his toenails tapping on the tile floor. Busy. She had to keep busy. It kept her sane.

Her hands trembled as she took the kettle to the sink and filled it. Tea. She needed some tea to help her calm down and settle her stomach. Without turning around she sensed Luke standing in the doorway, his presence sucking all the air out of the room. It always felt that way around him. Beautiful, unforgettable bastard. The sound of water rushing into the kettle filled the silent void.

"Is that why you left Vancouver so fast?" Luke

asked. “You had surgery scheduled?”

She nodded.

“And you didn’t tell anyone?”

She shook her head, bracing for the lecture she knew was coming.

“Jesus, Em, why? Why would you go through something like that alone?”

Because she had no one to lean on besides her son and Bryn, and they’d both been getting married at the time. She hadn’t wanted to spoil all of that by worrying them because she knew they’d have dropped everything and rushed to Charleston to be with her. Just as they’d done by showing up for Christmas, and Bryn this morning. “I told you, I’m fine. I’m used to dealing with things on my own.” She couldn’t resist the dig.

Luke’s quick footsteps made her swing around in alarm, and the hard expression on his face had her backing up until the hard edge of the granite counter dug into her lower back. He strode over and shut off the tap behind her, caging her in against the sink with his body, his hands on either side of her. Remembering what had happened the last time she’d stood next to him at this very sink made her heart hammer.

As if the ghosts from their past swirled up to haunt him too, he backed off slightly but didn’t move away.

The size and power of him surrounded her, and the subtle spice of his cologne rose up as he held her immobile with the magnetic force of his dark gaze. Emily fought not to react to his nearness, determined not to weaken and let him in, but her senses were going haywire. Whatever she did, she could not let her guard down in front of him. She’d have to be certifiable to open herself up to that kind of pain again. Suicidal.

Staring up into his ruggedly handsome face, she reminded herself how meticulous Luke was about his appearance. He was the cleanest man she’d ever known.

His short beard wasn't as neatly trimmed like it had been for the wedding, and his hair almost touched the collar of his flannel shirt at the back. There wasn't much gray in his hair, but there should have been considering what he did for a living, and his slightly scruffy appearance told her he was getting ready to go back overseas again.

That evidence was enough to put the starch back into her spine and push him away with a hand to his chest. Her palm met hard, warm muscle beneath his soft shirt, and the electric tingles in her fingers had nothing to do with the side effects of her chemo treatments. Snatching her hand back when she had enough space to breathe, she glared at him, heart slamming against her ribs. "Don't crowd me."

He didn't budge. "Then stop shutting me out and tell me what you meant about being used to dealing with it."

His words stunned her. Who the hell did he think he was, barging into her life and demanding answers? He'd been the one to walk away all those years ago, not her. "Let me go." Tense seconds passed while he kept glaring at her. When he finally stepped away, albeit reluctantly, she escaped to the other side of the room and put the rectangular farmhouse table between them. She hated this. Just...hated it.

"Well? What did you mean?"

She raised a brow in challenge. "You want answers?"

"Yes."

"Fine." She tossed her head, even though her hair was too short to swing. "I had breast cancer five years ago and they removed a lump, then because I tested positive for the genetic markers, I had a prophylactic total hysterectomy done. Now the cancer's back and I had to have a breast removed." She said it as matter-of-factly as she could, though it scared her to death.

Luke ran a hand over his face and stared hard at her. "Did Rayne know about this?"

“Not until the other day.”

“Jesus.” He shook his head. “I’m sorry, Em. I had no idea.”

“No one did, because I wanted it that way.”

“You should’ve told him, and Bryn. They would’ve been there for you.”

“And they would have worried themselves sick,” she pointed out. “Besides, it’s not like I was alone throughout all of it...I had Alex.”

At the mention of that name Luke straightened and folded his arms across his chest, the muscles in his forearms shifting beneath the rolled up sleeves. How did he keep himself in that kind of condition at fifty years old?

His eyes delved into hers. “But he’s not here now, is he?”

The sudden burn of tears made her glance away. She would *not* cry in front of him. She’d shed an ocean of tears over him already, and she was done with that. All crying did was make her ugly and give her a sore throat. It hadn’t done a damn thing to ease her suffering.

No, Alex wasn’t here. She’d sent him away, finally, after seven years of complete devotion to her. She’d finally admitted to herself that she’d never feel the same way he did about her, and she’d let him go despite his pleas not to. The guilt still ate at her, as did the memory of his devastated expression the night she’d broken up with him. But she knew she’d made the right decision. He was a good man. He deserved someone to love him back, and she could never do that. Not the way he wanted her to. But she hated that she’d hurt him as badly as Luke had hurt her. She was all too familiar with that kind of gut-wrenching pain.

For better or worse, she’d given her heart away many years ago to the man standing across the kitchen. Much good that had done, because she’d lost him regardless of her efforts to keep him. She'd never wish that kind of pain on her worst enemy.

Gathering her emotional suit of armor around her, Emily faced him. "Well, now you know what's going on with me, and I've told you I'm fine. I can't believe you'd come all this way just to find that out, so is there something else?" Please God don't say he was getting married or was about to become a father again. Her heart would stop right there in the middle of the kitchen.

Her sharp dismissal had his eyes narrowing. "Yeah. Several things."

"Like what?" Fighting always upset her, but it was always worse when it was with Luke. She just wanted this over with so she could get back to her recovery and not torture herself with dreams of him that could never come true.

"You can play this tough cookie act all you want, but you're forgetting I know you better than that."

He thought he knew her? "Not anymore. I'm not the same person I used to be. I'm a survivor now. It's what I do." Because she hadn't been given a choice. When she'd wanted to curl up in a ball and die from the loneliness after he'd left, she couldn't because she'd had a young son to raise. When the cancer came, she'd had bills to pay and a job to be at whether she felt up to it or not. All the money Luke sent her each month had gone into a trust fund for Rayne. She'd refused to touch any of it on principal.

His lopsided smile was so sad it twisted her up inside. "You're also the woman who stayed in a pullout chair next to my hospital bed all night because you knew I wouldn't sleep if you left." He prowled toward her like a panther, not stopping until he was across from her, and leaned his wide palms on the table. "And then you held my hand in your sleep."

She leaned away, a hot blush stealing over her face.

"I did not." Had she?

"Yeah, you did. So don't tell me I don't know you."

But he didn't. He didn't know the first thing about who she was and what she'd dealt with during his absence. Emily swallowed the lump in her throat. "I'm really tired," she said, running a hand through the too-short hair she was likely going to lose. "Is there something else you came to see me about? Because I'd like to lie down for awhile longer."

"Yeah, there is something."

His grim expression made her so uneasy she knew what it must be. "Something to do with your work?"

"It can wait for now." He seemed to measure her with his stare, his eyes stripping through the defensive layers she'd built up. "You're pale. Want me to make that tea for you?"

Damn him, for being this nice to her when she was weak. "No, thanks. I think I'll just go upstairs." *Away from you.*

A muscle tensed in his jaw, but then he straightened to his full height. A tower of strength that she still wanted to lean against more than anything. "All right," he said. "I'll come by later, then."

*Do you have to?* She caught herself before she could say the words aloud. "Fine. Later, then." With as much dignity as she could muster, she walked past him out of the kitchen and up the stairs on unsteady legs with Jake hot on her heels. She was well aware she was running away, but didn't give a damn. Right now the only thing that mattered was getting some distance from Luke, before she fell apart or told him what she really thought of him.

# Chapter Three

Standing alone in the silent kitchen after Emily went upstairs, Luke let out a deep breath and closed his eyes. His head tipped back until it rested against the wall. *Shit.* He felt so goddamn helpless. She was way worse off than he'd feared, and he couldn't do anything for her. She wouldn't let him, even if he could. That much was obvious from her closed up body language and wary expression.

*What did you expect? To walk back in and pick up where you left off last time?*

The derisive voice in his head pissed him off. No, he hadn't expected that at all. But he'd thought she would be warmer, more open. Like she'd been at the wedding a month ago. There she'd made the overture of coming over to dance with him at the reception, and had gone to the hospital to talk through the microphone in the CT scan machine while he'd been in there because she knew he was claustrophobic.

The selfish bastard in him reveled in the knowledge that she'd cared enough to be there, but the hardened, analytical part had known he couldn't encourage her tentative overture. He'd rather die than give her any false hopes of a future with him. He still had Tehrazzi to hunt down. The way things had gone lately, it could be years away from happening, and he might not live to tell about it when it did. No way would he leave her to face that uncertainty again, waiting those endless months or years with little or no contact from him. Never knowing where he was or what he was doing, or if he was okay.

Truth was, he'd never be okay. He wasn't the same man she'd married all those years ago. Hell, after the things he'd seen and done throughout his career, sometimes he wasn't even sure he was human anymore.

He scrubbed a hand over his shaggy face. Emily had been through so much since then. It ate at him that she'd done it alone until Rayne had shown up yesterday. From the way she'd trucked up those stairs, she was glad to be rid of him, so he'd give her a few hours before having the talk he'd come to have with her. This thing with Tehrazzi was too much for her right now, plus he didn't have concrete proof she was in danger. Only that constant unease in his gut that said she might be.

*Like that's not proof enough?*

With a hard sigh, Luke stepped out onto the back porch and walked through the garden to the gate. From out in the driveway, he recognized his son's voice and braced for more tension.

*Christmas is a stressful time of year, haven't you heard?*

Leaning against the rental car with Bryn and Christa, Rayne looked up. "Well? How is she?"

"She's upstairs lying down."

Christa's face tightened. "Is she all right?"

"Yeah. Just tired, and not expecting to see me." He slid his hands into his jeans pockets and put on a smile for her. "Maybe you could go check on her while I talk to these two for a minute."

"Sure," she said, taking the hint and heading straight

inside.

Rayne crossed his arms over his chest. “What’s up?” he asked with a frown.

Luke got right to the point. “You armed?”

His son’s eyebrows flew upward. “Do I need to be?”

“Wouldn’t be a bad idea.” It eased him to know that with Rayne there, Em had a tactical cop staying at the house for the next few days. Just in case.

Rayne scowled at him. “Christ, what now?”

Bryn was pale. “It’s Tehrazzi, isn’t it?”

Luke nodded, then stole a quick look over his shoulder to make sure Em and Christa couldn’t hear them. “He’s on the move, but we don’t know where. Doesn’t take a rocket scientist to figure out he’s been targeting the women of my team members.” First Bryn, then Neveah and Sam, Neveah again... “There’s a certain pattern emerging.”

“So you think he might target them?” Rayne nodded toward the house.

“Your mother, specifically. It’s possible, and even if it’s not probable we still have to take precautions.”

“What about Christa?”

“I don’t anticipate her being at risk, but I’ve already alerted the Team Canada staff to increase security at all venues.”

Rayne’s mouth tightened. “And what about Mom? You think those undercover officers down the road are enough protection?”

It didn’t surprise him that Rayne had noticed the extra eyes. “No. In light of her condition, I think we should move her to a secure location.”

“Meaning?” his son asked.

“For her safety, she can’t be alone here. She needs to be somewhere with good security and a support network around the clock.”

“And that would be where?”

Luke's gaze slid over to Bryn.

"You want to take her to Beirut," she finished for him with a frown. "To my father's house."

He nodded. "Ben and Sam are already over there." Ben was a former Ranger and Sam his CIA communications expert fiancée. "Ben's twin, Rhys, and his other half, Neveah, are flying in tomorrow. He's former Delta and she's a trauma surgeon," he added for Rayne's benefit. "If Emily goes, that'll give her Ben as a medic and Neveah as a physician to oversee her treatment. I checked, and Nev is well qualified and familiar with treating cancer patients. Ben will assist where he's needed, but I'll conference with them and Emily's doctors to make sure we're all on the same page. And if you go," he said to Bryn, "she'll have the support she needs."

Indecision warred in Bryn's dark eyes as she stared at him. He realized he was asking a lot of her. She'd already been through so much, and to go back to Beirut where Tehrazzi had set off the bomb resulting in her kidnapping and ultimately caused her father's death was not something he asked lightly. But Bryn was as brave as they came, and she also loved Emily like a sister. He was counting on that part to win out because she was the obvious key to Emily agreeing to go. Plus, Dec had already approved the idea of her going to her dad's place and was going to call her later on to talk with her.

Luke wasn't leaving anything to chance this time. If he had to stack his deck and manipulate the situation to get what he wanted, so be it.

"Ben's got that whole place re-wired," he added to sway Bryn even more. "He's retained the old staff that passed our security screening, and it's locked down tight."

"Are they setting up headquarters there or something?" she asked.

He nodded. "Coms, mostly."

Rayne's eyes hardened. "So you *are* going back into the field over there," he said accusingly, his scowl telling him what a piece of shit Luke was for disrupting Emily and then walking away again.

Luke tried to ignore the disquiet his son's look caused inside him. "As soon as I get the word I'm waiting for." And it couldn't come soon enough. The urgency grating on his nerves wouldn't go away.

"You want Mom to pull up stakes and fly to the other side of the world so she'll be *safe*?"

"That's right," Luke said, responding to the edge in his son's voice with one of his own. "Things haven't always been easy between us, but I still care about what happens to her. I'm going to talk to someone in the Agency and get all the logistics taken care of. Medication, equipment, all that." He held Rayne's hazel-green gaze. "I think it's the best solution for now." A long, pregnant pause followed.

"Shit," Rayne finally said with a shake of his head. "She's not gonna like it."

"No, she's not," Bryn agreed.

"Maybe not," Luke said, "but it's better than her staying here alone."

Rayne clenched his jaw. "Damn, I wish I could stay with her longer. Maybe I can get a leave of absence and—"

"No." Bryn laid a hand on his arm. "It's all right. You know I'll take care of her."

"We all will," Luke put in.

After a moment's pause, Rayne glanced at him. "Want me to break the news to her?"

"No, I'll do it. But first I've got some calls to make. I'll tell her when I come back later tonight."

Rayne made a wry face. "Well, good luck with that."

****

Emily stared into the fire crackling in the study hearth, curled up into the tufted leather armchair with a throw blanket tucked around her. Her mind was so full of static she couldn't think straight.

Only another few days until her next chemo treatment, and now that she knew what to expect, she dreaded it. The doctors were trying to be optimistic about her chances, but she knew what the probable outcome was. She'd watched her mother suffer endlessly through the same course of treatments nine years ago, dying a slow, painful death. She'd taken every treatment her doctors had recommended in the hopes of a miracle, and died regardless, in the end stripped of her dignity along with everything else.

Was the hell really worth it? The side-effects from the chemo decreased what quality of life she had left, so should she bother? It hadn't done her mother any good. If it merely bought her time and prolonged her agony, she'd just as soon quit now.

The dancing flames soothed her a bit, but couldn't ease the deep anxiety in the pit of her stomach. Luke was due back soon. How sad that she dreaded seeing him again. He'd been her whole world once. Her best friend and her white knight.

The first time she'd met him he'd saved her.

Staring into the flames, she thought about the night that changed her life forever. After a frantic call from the sister she was estranged from, she'd gone to pick her up at a bar in town. To rescue her from her abusive alcoholic boyfriend for the umpteenth time. Emily could almost feel the muggy air on her skin as she closed her eyes and let her mind drift back in time to that humid August night. She still remembered the shock of the hot pavement when the boyfriend had thrown her to the ground in the bar parking lot. She'd brought her hands up to shield her face, bracing to have her teeth and nose broken as he towered over her with a drawn back fist. But the blow never landed.

Coming out of nowhere, Luke had put him into a headlock. And when she'd looked up into his fathomless eyes that first time, something deep inside her had stilled.

*"Go on inside," he told her in a quiet drawl, as though wrestling a man six inches taller and thirty pounds heavier was no more bothersome than restraining a child in the throes of a tantrum.*

*When he came into the bar later he strode right over to her, his dark gaze scanning her face, and she felt its touch all over her body. "You all right, ma'am?" He handed her the purse she'd dropped in the parking lot.*

*"Y-yes." She swallowed, gathering her thoughts. "Thank you so much."*

*"Nothing to thank me for. Just glad I got there in time."*

*He was the most beautiful man she'd ever seen in her life. And those eyes of his, so deep and mysterious. Mesmerizing. He smiled, lighting up the coffee-colored depths of his eyes and revealing a hint of straight white teeth. "I'm Luke, by the way," he said, offering his hand.*

*She glanced down at it, so strong and dark compared to her own, and when she touched him she almost gasped at the heat of his skin. But instead of releasing her, he kept his hand wrapped around hers. His smile widened. "And you are?" he prompted.*

*Her face went red. "Emily." Standing there staring at him, she might as well have been struck by lightning.*

*Luke turned her hand over, his eyes taking in the road rash on her forearm from when Karen's boyfriend had thrown her onto the pavement. "We should get you some ice."*

*She must have nodded, because he set a protective hand against the small of her back and escorted her to an empty table. Her eyes followed his every step as he walked away, admiring the width of his shoulders and the play of muscle across his back beneath his shirt. She was stunned by her reaction. She wasn't like this, didn't respond to men this way. But Luke was...magnetic.*

*He came straight back with a glass of chilled water and a bag filled with ice. He wrapped the bag in a bar towel and took her arm in his big hands, his care of her and the warmth of his touch setting off flutters deep in her belly. She cleared her throat. "Thank you again, for stepping in like that."*

*"It was nothing."*

*It was something to her. "I can't imagine what you must think of me, with that as a first impression."*

*"I think you're real brave."*

*Emily glanced down at her water. "I'm not brave."*

*"Yeah, you are. Bravery's standing your ground even though you're afraid."*

*She wanted to ask him what he did for a living, but thought she knew. "Are you a Marine?"*

*Again, he smiled, his dark eyes full of secrets she wanted to learn the answers to. "Navy."*

*For some reason she couldn't picture him on a ship, sub or aircraft carrier. "Pilot?"*

*Another shake of his head, amusement in his gaze before it dropped to where he held the ice pack against her elbow. "I'm training to be a SEAL."*

*A SEAL? Her eyes widened.*

*Movement in her peripheral vision made her turn her head. A group of men at a table across the room were calling Luke over, and she suddenly realized she'd taken him from his friends. Withdrawing her arm from his gentle grip, she cleared her throat. "Well, I should be going. I've disrupted your evening enough—"*

*"They can wait."*

*Emily met his eyes and stilled. "I feel badly for keeping you away from your friends."*

*"They can wait," he repeated, and for the life of her she couldn't come up with a single excuse to go. "I'll drive you home when you're ready to leave."*

*She laughed. "Do people always do what you say?"*

*His slow smile set her pulse racing. "Usually." He withdrew his hand and settled back in his chair. "Finish your ice water, Emily, and talk with me a while. You're safe with me."*

Even then she'd felt the truth in his words, Emily mused, fingers absently touching the fine scar beneath her left ear. How tragic that the breaking of that promise had wounded him far more deeply than her. That damn tiny scar was an everyday reminder of why she'd lost him. No matter what she'd said or done to convince him otherwise, he was too afraid of what he'd done to her that day in the kitchen, and he'd never come back. She closed her eyes against the sting of tears.

"You still up?"

Her eyes sprang open to find Rayne standing in the doorway. "Yes."

Her son crossed the room and seated himself on the edge of the antique desk. "How you doing, gorgeous?"

She smiled at the charm he wielded so naturally. Like his father did when he put his mind to it. "Fine. Just tired."

"You sure you're up to this tonight?" His eyes were full of concern.

The impending visit, he meant. "I'm sure." She patted his knee. "Where's Christa?"

"Out with Bryn. We thought we'd go out for dinner and give you guys some space."

They were all so thoughtful. "Don't leave on my account."

"Want me to stay?"

His offer touched her. "No-no, I'll be fine." Tilting her head back, she admired him in silence. "I ever tell you how proud I am of you?"

"Once or twice."

"You're an incredible man, Rayne."

"If I am, it's because you raised me to be that way." And he'd stay perched on the desk all night if necessary, ready to intercede on her behalf and protect her from Luke. But she didn't need protection from him, and she never had. Only neither father nor son seemed to understand that.

Emily nudged his leg. "Go. Meet up with your girls and have a good time."

He leaned down and kissed the top of her head. "Call me if you need me."

"I will."

As he left the room he paused, and the slight tightening of his features told her Luke had arrived. She had mere seconds to tuck her feet beneath her and steel herself before he appeared at the study's threshold. The sight of him hit her in the chest like a punch. Larger than life, way too handsome for words, with bittersweet chocolate eyes that had seen too much. The part of her that yearned to heal him filled her chest until it hurt to breathe.

Fighting not to fidget, she forced a smile. "Hi." She could be civil, at least.

"Hi," he responded, glancing around the room for a moment before meeting her gaze. The look in his eyes made her lungs tighten. He remembered what had happened here. The last time they'd been alone in this room was thirteen years ago on the day Luke had shown up to haul Rayne off to Parris Island. They'd made love here, right up against the wall where a beach scene painted in oils now hung.

*Had sex*, she corrected, remembering how fast and ferocious it had been. So much anger and pain and love, all mixed together. Need and apology and that intense, insatiable hunger no one had ever been able to quench in her except Luke.

He'd been her first lover and the love of her life, and no one had ever touched her heart since him. For all the pleasure they'd given, the other two men she'd slept with might as well have not touched her at all. Through no fault of their own. Her body wanted Luke, and would never be satisfied with anyone else's touch.

Staring up at him, she couldn't help but wonder about all the other women he must have been with over the years. Luke was an intensely sexual man. He wouldn't have gone too long between lovers. She pressed a hand to her middle to stem the violent roll of her stomach that thought caused.

While the memories swirled between them in the suddenly heavy air, she couldn't break his gaze. For a split second she caught the unguarded regret in his eyes before he masked it and came to sit on the corner of the desk exactly as Rayne had done. Even their mannerisms were alike.

His dark stare was so penetrating she had trouble meeting his eyes. "How you feeling?" he asked in his low drawl that made her think of sweat-dampened sheets and tangled limbs.

"Fine." It was her standard answer, and all she could say at the moment.

Luke folded his corded arms across his chest. "Rayne talk to you?"

She frowned. "About what?"

"I'll take that as a no," he muttered, regarding her in silence for a moment as though trying to figure out the best way to break bad news to her.

"All right, then you tell me." She braced herself.

He hesitated a moment, assessing whether she was up to it. Then, "You know about the man I've been trying to capture?"

"Tehrazzi."

"Yeah. Know what he looks like?"

"Yes." A handsome man in his mid-thirties with brown hair and green eyes. The farthest thing from what she imagined a fanatical terrorist would look like. She'd sought out everything she could find on the Internet. All part of a pathetic need to know what Luke was up to once she'd found out about the terrorist who had captured Bryn. She'd learned about that incident the same way she'd learned everything else about Luke's work—from seeing it on the news.

Watching her closely, Luke nodded. "You know he targeted Bryn and her father, then Neveah and another of my team members."

She put a hand to her throat. Samarra, Neveah's cousin. "Yes." All women, and all connected to Luke.

"You see what I'm getting at?"

Unfortunately, but she was still incredulous. "What, you think he's going to target me next?"

"It's a logical conclusion, and even though it's unlikely given all the security agencies looking for him across the globe, I can't rule it out. Nobody knows where he is right now, and that's got a lot of people in the business scared shitless. There's a slim possibility he could even be stateside."

Emily stared. He was serious. "Why would he come after me? We've been divorced for almost twenty years."

"That doesn't matter."

It didn't? "If he's trying to get to you, targeting me doesn't make any sense. We didn't even have contact until recently. I'm nothing to you anymore." The words hung in the air between them, and something undecipherable flared in the depths of Luke's eyes. Did he remember blurting out that he loved her when she'd called him in Basra? With the severe concussion he might not have realized he'd said it, but she'd hoped...

"He knows me, Em. Knows me as well as you do, secrets and all." He pulled in a deep breath and let it out slowly, the gold chain around his neck glinting in the firelight. "Believe me, you're at risk."

He still wore the medallion. The surge of hope the words elicited made her heart ache. Was he saying he did care?

*Stop it, just stop it. Are you insane? Don't you dare go there.*

Because it hurt to look at him, she glanced away. "So what am I supposed to do? Get a better alarm system?"

He gave a short laugh. "An alarm system, Em? You think that will keep you safe?"

"You're not seriously suggesting I hire someone to protect me."

"No. I want you to come to Beirut."

She whipped her head around to gape at him. "What?"

"My team's setting up there at Bryn's father's place. She's going, too."

Was he serious? "I can't go to Beirut," she said with a humorless laugh.

"Why not?"

She made an incredulous sound. Wasn't it obvious enough? "I'm sick and in treatment, for one."

"Neveah's a doctor, and Ben was a Ranger medic. I've already arranged for all your medications and equipment you'll need, and cleared it with your doctors. Ben and Nev were on the conference call with them and me. They're all up to speed and ready to make sure you get the care you need."

Her jaw started to fall open, but then she reminded herself who she was dealing with. Luke had more connections and authority than half the generals working in the Pentagon. But going to Beirut? No way. She threw the blanket off her and surged out of the chair, pacing in front of the fire while she attempted to fight the growing panic building inside her. "I can't."

"Yes, you can."

"No." It came out much sharper than she'd intended, but she couldn't seem to get control of her emotions. Too much was happening too fast. What the hell was she supposed to do in Beirut? Most days the chemo had her so tired and sick she slept as much as a cat, and she'd only had one treatment. The next was due in a few days, and the side-effects were bound to get worse. She couldn't handle the thought of being away from the home she loved, staying in a strange place with a group of strangers, vomiting continually but too weak to run to the toilet so she had to crawl. All because the terrorist Luke was after might hypothetically try and target her.

Considering what she was up against physically, she'd rather risk being on a terrorist's hit list and stay home.

Luke stood. "Emily—"

"No!" She shook her head and backed away from him, growing frantic. He couldn't make her. No way was she going anywhere. If she had to suffer through this disease, then she would do so in the home she took comfort from. God knew she had precious little to give her any sense of security anymore. She'd be damned if she would lose this as well.

"Listen to me—"

She cut him off with a curt shake of her head. "You forfeited the right to tell me what to do the day you walked out that door." Luke stiffened as though she'd hit him, and indeed she had. Way below the belt.

Anxiety clawed at her. This wasn't her—she didn't like confrontation and didn't say hurtful things, but her world was spinning out of control and she couldn't stop the words or the terrible pressure forcing them out of her heart. How dare he march in after all this time with the audacity to turn her life upside down yet again? She wouldn't let him do it anymore.

Luke was still as a bronze sculpture, but his eyes seared her like hot coals. He sat back down on the desk. "Maybe I did," he said in a low voice, an undercurrent of anger simmering in his tone. "But you don't know what Tehrazzi's capable of."

"Yes, I do. I know what happened to Bryn."

Luke cocked his head. "Yeah? Did she also tell you we caught people armed with assault rifles and grenades about to kill everyone at Rayne and Christa's reception?"

Emily sucked in a breath. "You did?"

"And that someone tried to kill Neveah that night? When that didn't work, the head of the sleeper cell went after her himself. He was a world renowned neurosurgeon, I might add. Family man, soft spoken and well respected in his community. The last person on earth you'd expect to be caught up in a plot like that."

His eyes bored into hers. "Tehrazzi has a master's degree in political science, from Harvard. He speaks perfect English, without any trace of an accent. He works with anyone who will help him get what he wants—al Qaeda, Taliban, Hezbollah, mujahedeen. He doesn't give a shit about political allegiance or whether they're Sunni or Shi'a. He's got more money and support than most members of the U.S. Senate. Do you get what I'm telling you? Do you understand what kind of a threat he poses? Tehrazzi can get to anyone, anywhere if he wants it bad enough. I want all of you—you, Bryn, Sam and Neveah—in a secure location where I can make sure he doesn't get to any of you ever again."

And for how long was she supposed to stay in Beirut?

Until he got Tehrazzi? He'd been chasing him for six years already. She didn't have that kind of time left to wait. She couldn't go. Wouldn't. He didn't understand. "No."

Luke leapt off the desk, face tight with anger. "Goddamn it, Em, you have to."

"Leave me alone!" She whirled to leave the room, but he shot out a hand and grabbed her upper arm, spinning her around. Facing him, her knees began to tremble. This was awful, so awful. It almost hurt to breathe. Part of her wanted to hit him, and it horrified her. She jerked her arm from his grasp and took a step back, panting, on the verge of losing control and scared to death she might.

"I'm not leaving you alone here," he snarled, jaw tensing. "Not this time."

A bitter laugh escaped her. "Is that right? Well that's ironic," she sneered. "Just when I'm finally able to let you go, you decide to barge back into my life and stand by me."

He stared at her, a muscle flickering in his lean, bearded cheek. "You think I wanted it this way?"

"Oh, believe me, this is the last thing I think you wanted. But I'm still not going." She was being a complete bitch, but she couldn't help it.

"Don't force my hand, Em," he warned.

She closed her eyes, her stomach so tight she thought she might throw up. She couldn't go overseas. He didn't understand the extent of it. Heartsick, she fought to keep her dignity. "Just go, Luke. Take the others and go to Beirut, but leave me alone and give me what little peace I still have."

"Jesus Christ, listen to yourself!" He threw his hands up in frustration. "Peace? You want to stay here and risk sacrificing yourself for a little comfort? For God's sake, since when have you become a martyr?"

Her eyes flew open. She stared at him, unable to stem

the sheen of tears as the knot in her throat threatened to choke her. A tortured sob caught in her chest as she confronted him. “Since I found out I’m dying!”

# Chapter Four

Her words echoed around the room like the report of a high-powered sniper rifle, and for a moment Luke couldn't breathe. He felt like someone had kicked him in the gut with a steel-toed assault boot. He sucked in a painful breath. When he finally spoke, his throat was so tight his voice came out hoarse. "What?"

Emily turned away from him, but not before he saw the tears gathered on her lower lashes. "You heard me! I'm dying." She paced over to the fire and bent her head. As if defeated. "The chemo is going to buy me some time, but that's all."

A vise clamped around his heart, crushing it. He had to remind himself to breathe. *Jesus Christ.* "The doctors told you that?"

She shrugged. "More or less."

He was silent a moment. "Does Rayne know?"

"No, and don't you dare tell him." Her voice was flat.

So she was just giving up? No fucking way. Coming out of his paralysis, he stalked over and grabbed her shoulders to spin her around, ignoring her gasp of protest.

Taking her face between his hands, he put all his resolve into his stare and forced her to meet his eyes. "Screw that, because I'm not letting you quit." Her mouth tightened and her eyes narrowed, but he held her still when she tried to jerk away. "You're going to fight this with everything you've got, every single day for as long as it takes. No matter what it takes, you're going to keep fighting. Got me?"

Raw anger and resentment swirled in her eyes, and they gave him hope. If she had enough spirit to fight with him, then she had enough strength to fight the disease.

"You have no right," she said between clenched teeth. "No right to talk to me like I'm a two-year-old." This time when she yanked her head away he released her, but she nailed him with a look of pure murder. "Do you think I *want* to die?" she flung at him, crossing her arms over her breasts, her hands balled into fists. "Because I assure you I *don't*. I'm doing everything I can to stay alive, but guess what, Luke? Sometimes medicine and will are not enough."

Unacceptable. He refused to even go there in the hypothetical. "Choice is yours, Em. Warrior or coward? Which is it gonna be?"

She shook her head. "You bastard." For a moment she regarded him with utter loathing. "Which one of us is the coward, Luke?"

The words hit him like a knife in the heart, along with an avalanche of guilt. He deserved that, and maybe it was time they finally had this fight. If she needed to rip him to shreds, he was more than willing to be her punching bag as long as it helped her. So he pushed. "Meaning?"

Her eyes, normally full of warmth and kindness, were like bottle-green shards of glass that cut him with a thousand slices. "Which one of us took the coward's way out and took off when things got hard? Which one of us was too scared to stick around and work things out? Which one of us left his wife and eight-year-old son without a backward glance and never came back because he was too goddamn afraid of *himself*?" Her voice shredded on the last word.

A searing pain hit Luke's chest, deep inside his ribs like he'd been shot with a hollow point slug. She was dead on. A fucking bull's eye.

His stomach was so tight it hurt. The fact that she'd sworn twice within the last minute showed him merely a fragment of the unforgivable pain he'd inflicted on her. "And look what happened."

Emily swallowed and glanced away, hurt and sadness replacing some of the anger in her expression.

"You don't think I've regretted what I did to you every single day of my life?" he said tightly.

She met his eyes, and the emptiness in hers scared the hell out of him. "Just proves my point that it doesn't matter how much we want something. Some things are out of our control, no matter how much we wish they weren't."

Because she'd wanted him back, always.

He'd known that since the day he left, and that's why he'd been careful to stay away. And he'd still known it when she'd stubbornly stayed the night in his hospital room in Vancouver, but he hadn't dared take the comfort she so obviously wanted to give him.

Unfortunately, nothing had changed. He couldn't reach out to her now, not after everything else. Tehrazzi was out there, and he wasn't going away. Luke was the only one that could make that happen, and until he did... It didn't matter that he wanted to be with Emily, or that he'd dreamed of it since the day he'd walked out. It didn't matter that his last sight of her had been in his rear view mirror, collapsed in a sobbing heap in the driveway, hands in her hair as she screamed his name. Begging him not to go.

But he'd still gone. Driven by the knowledge that not only was he a threat to her and their son, but that he wasn't good enough for her. She was the fairy-tale princess and he was a lowly soldier, destined to dream about her sitting by the warmth of the fire burning in the castle grate while he shivered outside in the cold, staying out of sight yet remaining close enough to protect her. For more than twenty years he'd done that. But now he wasn't sure he could stay away from her anymore, and that meant he had to go.

He knew he should leave, yet she was so vulnerable standing there with that deep-seated fear in her big green eyes. It killed him not to touch her, not to be able to do anything to ease her. His resolve weakened.

He shouldn't touch her; he knew better. Touching her was both heaven and hell, but tonight even the bittersweet pain it always brought wasn't enough to deter him. Nor was the memory of the last time he'd reached for her in this very room, a few seconds after which they'd both been naked and all over each other. None of that mattered in light of the fear and need he read in her eyes. Right now, no power on earth could keep him away from her any longer.

Luke stepped closer, close enough to catch the warmth from her body and for her light vanilla scent to torment him with a thousand bittersweet memories. She knew what was coming; he could see it in her guarded expression. But she didn't turn away when he lifted a hand to skim his thumb across her cheekbone, light as a sigh. The brief contact sizzled over his skin, and instantly he got hard. She'd always had that effect on him.

His eyes went to the faint scar beneath her left ear. Her pulse beat hard and fast below the delicate skin where he could easily have severed her jugular vein. A few more ounces of pressure or a wrong move on her part and he would have. The knowledge sickened and shamed him. He'd rather have slit his own throat than ever harm her in any way, but it had happened nonetheless. First that accidental nick when she'd snuck up on him in the kitchen.

Right from the start he'd warned her not to startle him, but she'd come up behind him with the intention of being playful. When she'd gone to wrap her arms around his waist, he'd whirled and pinned her up against the fridge with the knife below her jaw before he'd even realized it was her. He still had nightmares about the stricken look in her eyes as she'd stared up at him, like an animal caught in the jaws of a trap. But that wasn't the worst of it.

The whole time he'd pressed his shirt against the wound to stop the bleeding afterward, he'd already made the decision to leave. He'd run from her and the damning knowledge he was a trip wire waiting to be triggered, and broken her heart. The ironic thing was, she didn't seem to realize he'd left his behind with her.

Luke trailed a hand over the velvet softness of her cheek until his fingertips caressed the pale line of the scar. A thousand words of apology crowded his throat but he didn't want to break the spell between them by speaking. His other hand touched her shoulder and crept up to the nape of her neck where the hair lay in silky whorls, and squeezed his fingers around it gently. Her swift intake of breath made him glance up into her face, and the stark desire that made her pupils expand hit him like a body blow. A fine shiver passed through her as he drew her closer to him with the grip on her neck. Her elegant hands fluttered up to rest on his shoulders, making the muscles tense beneath her slim fingers.

Closing his eyes, Luke lowered his head to nuzzle her

temple and fought back a groan when her fingers dug into his skin in response. She was so damn perfect to him, still gently rounded but firm, her scent a heady mix of innocence and sin. His beautiful Em.

He gently rubbed his cheek against hers, careful that his whiskers didn't chafe her smooth skin, and slid the hand at her jaw down her shoulder and arm to her waist. His fingers flexed against that firm flesh, wanting to explore so much more but holding himself in check. Luke dropped his head until his mouth brushed beneath her left ear, right over the scar he'd given her. She tensed in his embrace, a nervous swallow making the muscles in her throat undulate beneath his lips. He paused without moving away, teasing her with that light touch and the warm caress of his breath. When it was clear she wasn't going to pull away, he pressed a lingering kiss there and squeezed his eyes shut.

*I'm so sorry, Em.* He sent the words to her through the caress of his lips and the careful but desperate grip of his hands. *So damn sorry.*

Emily swallowed again, then after a moment slowly tipped her head to the side to allow him greater access. He took it, tightening his hold on her and moving his body in close until it brushed against hers, opening his mouth to let his tongue stroke across the mark, tasting her exquisitely soft skin. His erection pressed painfully against his jeans. A tremor snaked through her.

"Luke," she quavered, her voice full of confusion and need.

He cradled the back of her head with his palm and reluctantly stopped what he was doing, bracing himself for the inevitable moment when she withdrew from him. But she surprised him by threading her hands into his hair and simply holding on, leaning into him.

Luke raised his head, and the breath got stuck in his throat. Emily's eyes were wide and uncertain as she stared up at him, her fingers tangling in his hair to rub against his scalp. Like a kitten flexing its claws. He answered with a low growl of enjoyment and pressed back against the caress, watching her through lowered lids. The hunger was there as it always was, a pool of gasoline waiting for a match strike. It pulsed between them in the quiet and licked over his skin like flames. His gaze went to her lush mouth, mere inches from his. The full lower lip tempted him to bend closer, closer to brush that satin curve...

Emily jerked back with a gasp, squeezing her eyes shut and shaking her head. But her hands remained in his hair, a stark contradiction to her first reaction. She was fighting this, the same as he was. But she was also hungry. She wanted him every bit as badly as he wanted her. God help them both.

Unable to stop himself, Luke touched his lips to hers, a light brushing, both plea and demand. His body was raging hot, the taste and scent and feel of her igniting the inferno inside him. He paused there a moment, his mouth hovering a breath away from hers, then dipped down to taste her. Em made a low sound of protest in her throat and gave a tiny shake of her head, but her hands fisted in his hair, unwilling to let him go. He licked at her pouty bottom lip and settled his mouth completely over hers. A quiet whimper escaped her, and everything dominant in him demanded he possess his female, draw out every sensual response he could from her while he satisfied the hunger raging inside them both.

Angling his head, he firmed his hold on the back of her skull and opened her lips beneath his.

One of her hands went to his shoulder. "No," she whispered breathlessly.

Luke gentled his grip and slid his tongue over the seam of her lips, coaxing and seducing. In response she softened again, tilting her face up to his. Slowly, tenderly, he entered her mouth.

She gave a hungry moan and leaned into his chest, trembling in his arms. Her tongue touched his, caressing, then slid deeper. Needing, the same as he did. Taking over the kiss, he let go of her waist and smoothed his palm up her ribs toward her breast.

On a harsh gasp, Emily wrenched away, stumbling back with one hand over her lips.

The shocking pain in her eyes tore at him. "Em—"

"No," she gasped out. "I can't do this—Oh God, why did I let you kiss me?" She spun around and wrapped her arms around her waist, putting her back to him.

His whole body ached, but not as badly as his heart. "I'm sorry. I shouldn't have done that."

She turned her head and looked at him. Her eyes were full of sorrow and a trace of fear. "I can't go with you," she finally said. "So if that was your way of trying to coax me into it, sorry, but my answer's still no."

She knew damn well that's not why he'd kissed her. He sighed. "Em, if it's because of me—"

"It's not." She shook her head. "It's not."

The hell it wasn't. "I won't be at the house much, but if seeing me makes you uncomfortable I'll stay somewhere else." She started to shake her head again but he stopped her with an upraised hand. "You've been fighting this all alone so far, but it won't be like that from now on. Now you've got people who care about you to help you through this. Let us carry some of the burden for a while."

Tears glistened in her jewel-like eyes, reflecting the flames flickering in the fireplace. Her hands came up to her mouth, and he could see the trembling in them. It made him frantic to hold her, to pull her tight into his arms and against his body so she felt safe and protected. But he didn't dare make a move to touch her this time. She was a second from bolting from the room.

He fought to maintain an impression of calm. "I won't push you about this anymore tonight, but we don't have a lot of time for you to warm up to the idea." Walking past her was damn near as hard as leaving her the first time. He felt worse with every step, like he was deserting her all over again.

"Luke..."

Her broken whisper cut him. "I'll call you in the morning," he said, not daring to look at her. "Sleep well, Em." Rayne was more than capable of looking out for the women for the time being, Luke told himself. Nobody needed or wanted him there anyhow.

Without looking back, he headed out the kitchen door into the cold December night. Nothing had changed. He was still the soldier doomed to spend the rest of his life watching the princess from afar.

****

By the time he updated the undercover officers and drove away from her house, Luke was close to losing it. He drove across the bridge spanning the Ashley River and headed north with no clear destination in mind. He had to drive so he could think.

*Since I found out I'm dying!* He couldn't get the words out of his head, because clearly she believed them. He couldn't take it in. Couldn't deal with it. His hands gripped the steering wheel so hard his bones hurt. She couldn't be dying. Not now, and not like this.

From the day he'd left and through the empty years without her that followed, some subconscious part of him had always held out hope that Em would be there waiting when he'd rectified his mistakes. That she might not be had his mind in chaos.

If only his superiors at Langley and CENTCOM could see him now, he thought derisively, on the verge of having a meltdown. The renowned Mr. Cool had left the building, and all that remained was the screaming void where his darkest fears lay.

It had taken everything he had to walk out of the study and leave her there, frightened and hurting. It made his guts burn like lava to think of how truly afraid she was, how alone she was. He wanted to stay with her. Wanted to step up and be the man she'd always deserved instead of the one who'd run from his own insecurities. But until Tehrazzi was dealt with, he couldn't give that to her. Luke was the only one properly equipped for that job, and he'd made it his life's mission to see it through. And at this point, he was the best shot the world had at bringing Tehrazzi out of hiding.

His cell vibrated against his belt but he ignored it. No way could he deal with anything until he'd calmed down. The blur of headlights whipped past him as he headed out of town through the darkened pastoral landscape into plantation country. The rage and violence followed him, demanding release. He fought them back.

Jesus, he couldn't remember the last time he'd felt this out of control. He'd built his reputation as an operator on the basis of his ability to stay cool no matter what, even if the enemy had surrounded his team and they were taking casualties or he was wounded. He never lost control when he executed a mission. He did what had to be done. Period. But facing the possibility of losing Em was more terrifying than being captured and tortured by the enemy. It tormented him that he was on the verge of the operation that would eliminate Tehrazzi, but it was too late for Emily and him.

He'd lost that precious window of time when they might have reconciled. Instead, he'd spent it hunting the enemy through the deserts of the Middle East. That's the choice he'd made.

At that moment, he'd never regretted anything more.

The phone buzzed insistently against his hip for the second time, and after taking a forced, deep inhalation, he ripped it from its holder. *Ah, Christ*, he thought as he saw the digital display. Reality was calling.

Luke blew out a breath and took the next exit, finding a quiet place to pull over before returning the call. His heart rate was still elevated and his breathing wasn't quite steady, but this might be the call he'd been waiting for. Cutting the engine, he dialed.

After a short delay, Davis answered. "Hey my man, how's it going?"

"It's going," Luke grunted. "You stateside?"

"No, Kabul. Langley's given me this secure number for the time being."

Not good. "We got a problem?"

"Your boy over here is getting help."

He wouldn't have thought it possible, but his stomach clamped even tighter. "What kind of help?"

Another short pause came while the signal reached its destination. "Someone with connections, maybe overseas, I'm not sure yet. All the warlords that were friendly with us are increasingly tight-lipped about Tehrazzi. All of a sudden nobody's seen him or has any idea where he is, and for damn sure nobody wants to help us find him."

With the amount of cash and arms they were waving at the warlords, that said a lot. "Is it him?"

"That's the thing, I don't think it's just Tehrazzi. I already talked to James about it before I called you, but I've got a bad feeling about this. It's like he's getting help from someone either higher up the food chain, or from an inside source. Whatever's going on, he's managed to corrupt sources I've used reliably for over two years."

Luke rubbed at his tired, burning eyes. "Damn." He'd been afraid of this. Afghanistan was complicated enough without this shit. "Jamie's on this already, I take it?"

"Yeah. He wants a meeting with all of us."

"Miller too?" Luke had a long-standing friendly rivalry with the Kabul station chief, so working together was always entertaining. Too bad this meeting couldn't be under less serious circumstances because he could sure use a laugh or two.

"That's affirm."

"I'll fly out in the morning." At least it would save him another encounter with Em. "What's the latest intel?"

The line crackled for a few seconds. "Word is Tehrazzi's looking for you, on the move out of the mountains, but that's all I've got so far."

A rush of energy flooded his veins. "What's Miller's take on it?"

"The same. None of his contacts have intercepted anything useful yet."

Too bad. "I'll be in Beirut day after tomorrow. You staying put for now?"

"Think so. Could change once we talk to James."

"No doubt," Luke muttered.

Ending the call, he pulled back onto the road and headed for Emily's. Stupid, to stay up all night outside her house like a stalker, but he needed to watch over her himself tonight. Probably would be better off driving straight to D.C., but an early flight would get him there soon enough.

Pale moonlight sparkled on the water as he crossed back over the river into Charleston, the city peaceful and calm in the Christmas hush. Whole place looked like a postcard, or an illustration in a children's book. Nothing like the places he would go once he went overseas. He tapped his thumb against the steering wheel.

So Tehrazzi was on the move, trying to find him. Might have left the mountains to head for Kabul. Could be for the best, Luke reflected. He could draw Tehrazzi out this way, lure him to where he wanted him. Anyplace would do, so long as it was far away from Emily, but the less populated the area the better. Things with Tehrazzi always got messy and Luke preferred minimizing collateral damage whenever possible.

The CIA had many sources in Kabul. It would be tough to find out who Tehrazzi's contact was. They needed to find the informant, but for Luke the most important thing right now was Emily. He couldn't stay and protect her now, because suddenly the prey had become the hunter.

So whether she liked it or not, Emily was going to Beirut.

# Chapter Five

Emily collapsed back onto the pillows with a tired sigh and rubbed a hand over her eyes. Putting on a happy face was beginning to exhaust her, but she'd keep up the front if it meant easing everyone's anxiety levels and maintaining the peace between Rayne and Luke. It was a role she was intimately familiar with, and she'd been doing it since the day Luke left. For years she'd kept the reason why he'd left from everyone, including their son, because she hadn't wanted Rayne to grow up hating or fearing his father. And because she'd naively hoped Luke might come back if she guarded that dark secret.

Though Rayne now knew about the incident with the knife, he still harbored a degree of resentment toward his father. Whatever happened, she didn't want any more friction between them, so if she had to smile and pretend everything was fine, and that Luke telling her she had to go to Beirut didn't bother her in the least, so be it.

Not that she would go. Not a chance. But the coming confrontation with Luke wasn't going to be fun. She just hoped it happened after Rayne left for the airport in the morning.

Her throat tightened, and she rolled her eyes at herself. Stupid, to get emotional over him leaving. It wasn't like she wouldn't see him again. She had at least enough time for a few more visits if things went well with her treatment.

Someone tapped on the door. Sighing, she raised up onto her elbows. "Come in."

The door edged open and Bryn poked her head in. "Hey."

"Hi. If you're coming to check on my mental state, I'm fine."

Shutting the door soundlessly behind her, Bryn raised a dark brow. "You sure about that?"

"Yes." And if everyone could let her be for a while, she *would* be fine.

Her friend completely ignored her and came over to sit on the foot of the antique cherry spool bed. "I'm flying out to Beirut day after tomorrow. Dec wants me to go, says he and Luke think it's the safest thing for all of us."

She should have expected them to gang up on her. Emily closed her eyes. "Bryn..."

"I know you don't want to go, and I understand it's because you're in treatment and you're scared."

"I'm not scared."

Bryn stared at her. "Yes you are. I think you're every bit as scared of Luke as you are of the cancer."

"You're wrong."

"Am I?"

*Yes*, she wanted to snap, but kept calm. That was her default mode. Everyone expected it from her. She'd been raised to be ladylike, and no matter how much she wanted to lose it now and again, she usually held it together. Which is why the disastrous confrontation with Luke earlier was so embarrassing. He was the last person on earth she wanted to see her come unglued. In front of him, she wanted to appear rational, serene and independent. Not exactly the impression she'd left him with, was it?

Emily considered the truth of Bryn's statement and figured she'd better explain herself. "Seeing him just reminds me of what I can't have—let alone that I'd promised myself I would let him go before I broke up with Alex."

"Oh, please. You expect me to swallow that?"

"*Yes*." She pushed up onto one elbow and glared at her friend. *This* was the support she needed? "I had to let the idea of being with him go in order to face all of this. Holding on to him that way was killing me."

Bryn's gaze was far too knowing. "It's killed you for over twenty years. You expect me to believe you could just snap your fingers and forget about him one day?"

She didn't expect Bryn to understand. "I haven't forgotten about him, even though I wish I could."

"Do you?"

Emily frowned. "Do I what?"

"Do you really wish you could forget about him?"

"Sometimes." And sometimes she wished he'd pushed that knife deep enough to end her suffering all those years ago. It was cowardly for her to even think it, but in her darkest moments, she had. If not for Rayne needing her so much back then, she didn't know what she might have done to escape the pain. "I can't pine away for him and fight this at the same time." When Bryn merely kept staring at her, she sighed. "What?"

"Since I'm your best friend, do you want my honest opinion?"

Was there another kind when it came to Bryn? She withheld a sigh. "Go ahead."

She laid a hand on Emily's shoulder, her gaze sympathetic. "You're not over him, babe."

"I didn't say I was *over* him," she replied with tried patience, "I said I had to let him go. Meaning the idea of being with him again. And not just in bed," she added, still unsettled by how close she'd come to making that fatal mistake again. "That's not enough for me, and it would do more damage than has already been done." Some part of her knew it would kill her this time if she let her guard down and then lost him again.

A small silence passed before Bryn spoke. "What did he say to you?"

Emily aimed a bland look at her. "Like you don't already know?"

Bryn shrugged, not at all bothered by the comment. "If I hadn't, one look at your son's face when he came downstairs would have told me it didn't go well."

Not entirely true. Parts of it had gone far, far too well. Another reason she couldn't go to Beirut. "I need to stay here while I'm in treatment."

"No, you don't. Neveah and Ben will both take care of you—"

"I'm not going just because there's a small chance a terrorist will come after me." It took everything she had not to shout it, and she placed a hand over the hot ball sitting in her stomach. Why couldn't everyone leave her alone? Couldn't they all see how upsetting it was?

"Em, you don't know this guy like I do. Like Luke does." Bryn's eyes were shadowed with worry. "He can get to you here, believe me."

"I already told Luke that doesn't make sense. Why would I be a target now when I've barely spoken to Luke since he left? I'm not important enough to warrant that kind of attention from a terrorist."

"Apparently you are, or Luke wouldn't be here asking you to go to Beirut with the rest of us."

Asking? That's exactly it—Luke never asked, he peremptorily ordered, and expected people to jump.

Emily glared. "And you're going for sure? Even after what happened to you last time? How does Luke know you'll be safe now?"

"Dec pretty much ordered me to go. And don't forget Ben was head of my father's security team over there. He knows the place and the networking in Beirut better than anyone. Not to state the obvious, but our guys are a lot better versed in security measures than we are. It would be stupid for us not to take their advice." She held up a hand. "And before you remind me that Ben's supervision wasn't enough to prevent Tehrazzi from getting to me the first time, Dec agrees it makes sense to put all of us women together in a secure location, rather than having us scattered around where we can't have adequate protection. Besides, Tehrazzi's in Afghanistan, or at least they think he is. We'll be safe in Beirut."

"Leave it alone, Bryn."

With an irritated sigh, her friend took hold of her hands. "If you won't do it for your own safety and for my peace of mind," she murmured, gazing deep into her eyes, "then do it for Luke's."

Emily's heart squeezed. "What do you mean?"

"Come on, Em...he flew here to see you because I sent him an e-mail—"

"You *what*?"

Bryn rolled her eyes. "It's not important why he's here, the point is he was worried enough to come here and see you. He's tracking the most dangerous terrorist on the planet, and for him to have the added weight of worrying about your safety from the other side of the world is only going to endanger him and everyone else on the team. Including my husband," she finished, her voice catching.

A layer of guilt settled over her already bubbling stomach. "Nice, Bryn. That's just what I needed, a guilt trip on top of everything else."

"Sorry, but it's true."

God, she had enough to deal with without having other people's lives slung onto the yoke around her neck. And to hell with feeling bad about what Luke was going through. Everything that had happened and was happening to him was self-inflicted. She'd done everything in her power to make things right between them. For years. His pride and his job had always won out.

But Bryn continued to watch her with dark, worried eyes, and uncertainty crept in. Maybe her decision *could* affect Luke's frame of mind. He had to care about her to some extent, or he wouldn't have shown up here in the first place.

She looked away from Bryn and started toying with the cuffs of her sleep-shirt. Would it really bother Luke that much if she stayed stateside? Enough to distract him while he was out in the field? She doubted it, but then again, was she prepared to put it to the test? People's lives were at stake here, she couldn't be so selfish. She shook her head at Bryn. "How am I supposed to live in the same house as him?"

"It's a big house," Bryn encouraged. "You don't have to see him if you don't want to, and he'll be out in the field most of the time."

"Oh God, don't remind me." Being there while he was out doing missions would be damn hard on her, regardless of their strained relationship. She didn't want anything bad to happen to him. If she could help him by going to Beirut, she could also give Bryn some support. Because Bryn was going to need it. Being married to an active duty SEAL was hard enough without a strong support network to draw on.

Emily pulled her hands out of Bryn's grip, rubbed them over her face and then through her short hair. She was opening her mouth to say okay when Bryn's gaze shot to the pillow Emily lay on, and her stomach shriveled at the shock on her friend's pretty face. "What?"

Bryn brought a hand up to her mouth, a sure sign something was wrong. "Um..."

Sitting up, Emily swiveled around to find a tuft of hair lying on the creamy pillowcase. Her heart sank. *Ah, damn.* She touched the dark strands, then reached up to find the tiny bare spot on her scalp. *Oh, for—* More hair came out in her hand. "Shit."

Bryn made a strangled sound, almost like a nervous laugh, staring at her with her hand over her mouth.

A smile tugged at Emily's lips. She rarely swore, and in an ironic way it was kind of funny that her hair would fall out in the middle of this conversation. She thanked God it hadn't happened in front of Luke. "The doctors told me I would probably wake up one morning with my hair on my pillow, but this gives the warning a whole new meaning." And right on time, too, almost three weeks to the day since her first chemo treatment.

As an awkward silence ensued, she called on her inner strength. At least she was prepared for this, having agonized about the decision already. Nothing to do now but go through with it. "Well." She smacked her palms against her thighs, mind made up. "Guess it's finally time to shave my head."

Bryn looked at her in alarm, shock clear in her expression. "Are you...sure?"

"Yep. Got my collection of wigs all ready to go." Best to be practical about it and not dwell on the realization that she was going to go bald. Practical, steady, calm. She could do that.

"Of course you do," Bryn remarked wryly, climbing off the bed. "Want me to go?"

"No. I could use a hand, if you don't mind." She marched to the bathroom and yanked open the top drawer of the cabinet beneath the ivory granite vanity, pulling out the electric clippers she'd bought for this purpose. Raising her head, she stared into the mirror. So she was about to be bald. No big deal, most chemo patients had to go through this. What was hair, anyway? Just some dead protein.

She straightened her shoulders, determined to face it with dignity. This damn disease had taken pretty much everything else that identified her as a woman—it might as well have her hair too. "And that's the last piece of me you're getting," she vowed to her reflection in a low voice, a shiver running through her as adrenaline started to flow. She'd be damned if she'd surrender and go quietly.

She narrowed her eyes at her reflection and sent the cancer a silent message. *Fuck. You.*

Behind her, Bryn glanced at the clippers warily before meeting her eyes in the mirror. "You sure about this?"

*No.* "Yes." Em held them out to her. "Here. You do it."

Bryn took them and came to stand at her shoulder. "We don't have to do this right now. We could go have a few glasses of wine first, relax a bit—"

"I want it off on *my* terms, not the chemo's." It was all going to fall out anyway, so better all at once than piece by piece. She jerked her chin at the clippers. "Every damn bit of it so that it's done and I can move on."

"Okay." The clippers made a buzzing sound when she turned them on. Bryn was four inches taller, her height advantage perfect for the task at hand. "Ready?"

Emily nodded and curled her hands into fists, bracing for the first sweep of the clippers. She sensed more than heard Bryn's sigh as she brought them to her head and made the first pass. They drew across her scalp slowly from forehead to nape, leaving a shiny strip of naked skin. Wisps of hair tickled her face and neck as they fell. This wasn't deserving of her grief, Emily reminded herself, hating the lump in her throat. *It's just hair. It'll grow back once this is all over.*

*If you live long enough to see it*, the cancer whispered back.

She forced the ugly voice from her mind. *Bzzzzzz...* More hair fell onto the white tiled floor. Partway through she lost her nerve and looked down at it, the rich brown strands floating through the air to land at her feet. So much of it, though it had been cut short.

*Stop thinking about it. It's nothing. Who cares?* The bathroom fell silent as Bryn finally turned the clippers off, and the fullness of the sudden quiet pressed against Emily. "All done," Bryn said softly, laying them on the countertop. "Why don't you go lie down and I'll clean this up."

Gathering her courage, Emily lifted her chin to confront her reflection. She smothered a gasp. Her naked scalp was a shock, and she forced herself to lift a hand to touch it. Oh, God. She looked ill now. Truly, desperately ill. A convulsive swallow rippled through her throat. Any time now she'd lose her eyebrows and lashes, too.

Bryn put her arms around Emily's waist and rested her chin on her shoulder. "You're still beautiful. You shouldn't be, but you are."

Emily forced a smile. "Spoken like a true friend."

"I'm serious." She studied her in the mirror for a few moments before blurting, "Want me to shave mine, too?"

On a gasp, Emily turned her head. Bryn would do it, too. "Don't you dare," she warned, admiring the gorgeous fall of straight deep brown hair that came to the middle of Bryn's back. "It's sweet of you to offer and I appreciate it, but no."

"Want me to get one of your wigs?"

"I'll get it." On her way to the walk-in closet she looked back at Bryn over her shoulder and searched her mind for something to lighten the mood. "Don't look so worried, I'm fine. And just think—I'll eventually get a free semi-permanent Brazilian out of the deal."

"If you're trying to make me jealous, forget it. I'll keep my bikini line smooth the regular way, thanks."

Emily took the box from the shelf and pulled out a short bobbed wig, in a shade close to her natural hair color. She fitted it on her head and smoothed the ends into place before facing Bryn. "Well? How do I look?"

Bryn's smile was full of genuine pleasure. "Gorgeous. How come you never cut your hair like that before? It suits you perfectly."

"Maybe I will once it grows back." She fussed with the other wigs before replacing the box, eyeing her large pink suitcase set neatly in the corner. After debating it for a minute, she hauled it out and set it on the wide ottoman where she laid out her clothes each morning.

"All right," she relented, facing Bryn with her hands on her hips. "What am I going to need to wear in Beirut this time of year?"

****

*CIA Headquarters Langley, VA*

When Luke arrived mid-morning the next day, Jamie was waiting for him in his office. Luke liked his boss, mild-mannered and only a few years older than him.

Jamie's bright blue eyes crinkled at the corners as he smiled and rose behind his paper-laden desk. "Good to see you, Hutch."

Luke accepted the hand Jamie offered and shook it. "You, too." He seated himself in the wing chair opposite the desk.

"You look like you could use some sleep."

"Nah, I'm good." Other than short snatches when he could grab them, sleep wasn't going to be an option for a while. But he wasn't in the mood for small talk. Lounging back further into the cushy leather, he regarded his boss and cut right to the heart of the matter. "Why didn't you tell me about Em?"

To his credit, Jamie didn't even blink. "I wasn't sure she wanted you to know."

Fair enough, but it still pissed him off. "How much do you know?"

"All of it. The lumpectomy, hysterectomy and mastectomy as well as her chemo regimen." He studied Luke in silence for a moment. "You could've asked me."

Yeah, but he would have looked pathetic, pining after the wife he'd chosen to abandon in the first place. "No, you should have *told* me." All this time he'd assumed Jamie would speak up if something serious happened to Em or Rayne.

"The deal was I would keep tabs on her, not report her private business to you or anybody else."

Luke's hands curled into fists on his tensed thighs. "You knew I would have gone to her."

Jamie inclined his head. "Yes."

"And you also knew she was alone through all of this."

"Not until recently she wasn't." He leaned forward and put his forearms on his desk. "What are you doing about it?"

A hell of a lot less than he'd like. "I'm taking her to Beirut with me, like we discussed."

Jamie's eyebrows went up. "She agreed?"

"As of this morning." He'd received the e-mail from Bryn when he landed in D.C. "She's not happy about it, but at least she's going."

"Good." His boss steepled his fingers and regarded him for a long moment. "Anything else, or shall we get on with the business of the day?"

Luke tossed the copy of *To Kill a Mockingbird* on the desk. Jamie glanced up at him. "Still think it means he's coming after you?"

"I don't think it. I know it."

His boss sighed. "Shit. Guess we'd better find out what the hell's going on, then."

When Luke nodded, Jamie got on his desktop and connected through to the Kabul office. Luke rounded the desk, taking a seat on the corner of it. Within moments, Davis and Miller appeared on screen.

"Tell me what you've got so far," Luke said to Miller, who pushed up his rimless glasses with his forefinger. He looked like the analyst geek he was. Miller was a detail freak. Very little got past him, which was why he was so good at his job.

"Nothing solid yet. Some chatter that Tehrazzi's moving southwest, but we can't confirm it. Without the help of the locals, it's near impossible to corroborate."

"And you, Davis?" Jamie asked.

Davis leaned in closer, the live feed from the webcam making the video appear jerky and digital. The former Green Beret's dark coloring and beard made him look like an Afghan. His average stature and features made him an ideal covert agent, perfectly suited for his role in counter insurgency operations. Luke had seen him change like a chameleon to suit whichever tribe or cultural nuance was needed for a mission. He could be a Taliban leader one day and a Serbian arms dealer the next. And he was damn good at what he did, capable of blending in seamlessly with a group in order to infiltrate a tribe or organization. The ultimate operative for Foreign Internal Defense.

Davis's keen dark eyes looked into the screen as he

spoke. "The tide's turning out here, and not in a good way. Sources I've been able to count on for the past three years have dried up like the Great Salt Lake." He snapped his fingers, his expression and demeanor remaining calm. Yet another trait Luke loved about the guy. He never got rattled about anything. Exactly the kind of guy a man wanted at his back when things turned ugly. "Let's just say I'm not exactly welcome where I used to be." Davis's expertise and ability to earn people's trust was a winning combination, so him having trouble said a lot.

This shift in loyalty only made their job tougher. If someone as superbly trained as Davis couldn't gain access to the warlords on the CIA payroll, then things had indeed iced up on the information highway. "But y'all are sure Tehrazzi's still in country?"

Miller nodded. "As sure as I can be."

Jamie laced his fingers behind his head. "How do you want to handle this, Hutch?"

"I'll be in Beirut tomorrow afternoon local time. I'll conference you both when I get everything set up."

Miller's eyes narrowed. "You think he might be headed for Lebanon?"

"Possibly. Or Syria." Those were the most likely places because of his connections there. And if it was Lebanon, Luke would make damn sure he led Tehrazzi away from Beirut. As far away from Emily as possible.

"Have you got a security team in place?"

Worry from Miller? Since he had expected some kind of a jocular comment instead, Luke couldn't keep the sardonic edge from his voice. "I'm touched by your concern, but yeah, I'm set up there."

Rather than let it go, Miller edged Davis out of the way and moved in closer, a deep frown forming under his carefully styled, but thinning bangs. "You know he's looking for you. I mean actively hunting."

"Yep. And I'm counting on him finding me, too. Just haven't decided where that showdown's gonna happen yet. I'll let you know when I do."

"You're planning on coming to Kabul to bring him out of hiding," Miller said incredulously. "Jesus, do you have a death wish? I thought the whole idea was to draw Tehrazzi away from his supporters—"

Before Luke could reply, Jamie jumped in. "I think we all agree Luke's the bait we need to catch this particular shark. Once we have more intel he'll put together a mission plan and brief you all. Now, we all have work to do, so let's get back to it. Hutch will contact you once he's overseas." He ended the conference and the screen went black. When he looked at Luke, his expression was deadly serious. "You watch your back over there."

The stark warning surprised Luke. "Will do."

"Why do I always feel like I'm wasting my breath with you?" Then his boss sighed and regarded him almost fondly. "Who do you want?"

"Davis." And a dozen more just like him. Pity that wasn't going to happen.

"That goes without saying. Anyone else?"

"I've got my crew assembling over there now, for support and logistics. Would be nice to have a little muscle for backup, though."

Jamie's lips curled upward. "Why do I get the feeling this will involve me pulling some strings?"

"I want Dec McCabe's SEALs on standby."

"You got it," his boss replied instantly. "Anything else?"

"Yeah." Luke pulled an envelope out of his jacket and tossed it on the desk. "I've made you executor of my will. If something happens to me, I want you to make sure Em and Rayne are looked after. I don't want them left dealing with red tape and security clearances."

"Understood." Jamie took the envelope to a safe in the wall and entered the combination on the keypad.

"Jamie."

"What?"

"I want your word you'll take care of them."

Unflinching blue eyes met his. "I will."

Some of the tension bled out of his body. There was no one he trusted more than Jamie to look after his family in his absence. "Thank you."

"You'd do the same for me."

"I would."

Jamie placed the envelope in the safe and locked the door, then crossed the room to his chair and sank into it. His eyes narrowed. "Don't do anything stupid out there, Hutch. Killing yourself getting Tehrazzi won't fix anything. I'd hate like hell for you to wind up a nameless star on the wall downstairs after all these years."

Luke's mouth twisted in the semblance of a smile. "Thanks for the pep talk."

"I mean it." His searching expression made Luke believe Jamie could see into the darkest part of his soul. "I'm saying this as your friend, not your boss. It's not too late to get your life back."

The words sent a shiver down Luke's spine. He immediately rose and headed for the door. "I'll be in touch," he said over his shoulder.

He didn't give a shit anymore if he died, so long as he took Tehrazzi with him. It didn't matter that he'd once loved him damn near as much as a son. It didn't matter that he was to blame for what Tehrazzi had become. All that mattered was making things right. A chance at absolution before he gave his last breath. The end was close, he sensed it, and he didn't much care how it would happen. He almost looked forward to it, in a way.

Having lost his last remaining shot at a future with

Emily made death a hell of a lot more appealing than another twenty-odd years of this bleak existence. Without her, he had nothing. And God knew he had no desire to stick around and watch her die. Even he wasn't that much of a masochist.

****

*Mountains of Afghanistan*

Tehrazzi's sandaled feet left deep imprints in the snow as he walked at the front of the line of his men. The mountains rose steep and sharp against the eastern sky at his back. To his right, the hillside plunged away into deep canyons of snow-covered rock. The straps of his heavy pack dug into his shoulders mercilessly, but he ignored the pain and the cutting wind that sliced down the steep gorge.

Behind him, eight men trudged wearily along the slippery trail. All but a few of them had only a light woolen blanket to keep out the freezing air. Their clothing was threadbare, their footwear pitiful for the conditions. He kept them moving, never letting them stop because the temperature was dropping fast. Staying still for too long in this weather was a death sentence. He forced them onward.

In another day or two they'd reach the foothills and meet up with the convoy to take them into Kabul. The final pieces of intelligence he'd been waiting on would be ready. Then the hunt would commence.

In the distance behind him, the continued braying of a donkey rose over the punishing wind. Tehrazzi paused. The animal was frightened and in pain. He could hear it in its cries. Turning, he looked back up the trail, at the end of the column where the pack animals were. None of them moved, but the donkey's cries soon became screams. The hair on the nape of his neck stood up. The plaintive sounds raked over his spine like icy fingernails until he couldn't bear it. They reminded him too much of his beautiful mare, Galliyah. She had made those same horrific noises when she'd died in the desert outside Najaf.

Because of his teacher.

She'd been weakened by a bullet to her shoulder his teacher had fired from a high-powered sniper rifle, and fallen over the edge of a cliff because of a careless handler. His own fault, Tehrazzi reminded himself as he rushed back up the trail. He had let someone handle her because he'd been too weak and battered to do it himself, and she had paid the ultimate price for his decision. He'd had no choice but to go into the ravine and slit her throat to end her suffering because it was the only humane thing to do.

The donkey's cries continued to reverberate in his skull, spurring him onward. A deep, burning rage took hold. Whoever was torturing that animal would regret their actions.

His men got out of his way when they saw him coming, the tight expression on his face making their eyes widen in fear as he passed. Up the trail, he finally caught sight of the struggling animal. It was laden down with hundreds of pounds of equipment, nearly lost beneath the mountain it carried on its swayed back. Its head was reared back, ears flattened against its head, eyes rolling white as the chilling cries tore from its open mouth. A man beat its rump repeatedly with a lash. His arm raised and sliced down repeatedly, cruelly. He beat the animal until its hind legs gave out and it dropped to the snow. Spatters of blood marred the pristine blanket of white around its shivering body.

Tehrazzi flung off his pack and started running. He was so enraged he didn't feel the bite of the wind or the numbness in his feet. His sole focus was riveted on the pathetic excuse for a man wielding the whip.

The man looked up when he heard Tehrazzi coming, and his eyes went wide with surprise and alarm. The donkey tried to get up, its forelegs trembling weakly, sides heaving. Dark red stripes stained its soft grey coat along its flanks and rump. Ruby red and glistening, like Galliyah's blood when it gushed over her skin. The edges of his vision blurred.

The man dropped the lash but Tehrazzi didn't stop. He lunged forward and caught him by the throat, tackling him onto his back in the snow. They skidded through it, ending up inches from the edge of the cliff. The man's eyes bulged from the pressure Tehrazzi exerted on his throat as he tried to claw the gripping hands away. *One push*, Tehrazzi thought. One push, and he could shove him over the side to his death. Leave him there bleeding out, listening to his own screams of agony as he died.

Reining in his anger with effort, Tehrazzi kept one hand anchored around his victim's neck and ripped the loaded pistol from his waistband. He shoved the muzzle against the man's forehead and held it there, breathing hard. Before, he'd never been comfortable killing people by his own hand. He preferred to have others carry out his orders, and that's why he'd kept his dangerous bodyguard for as long as he had. But since the day he'd put Assoud down like a rabid dog, something had changed inside him. Taking a life was no longer the burden it had once been. And he trusted no one. He was more than capable of killing to protect himself.

"Please," the man begged, wheezing beneath the pressure around his throat. "Please I beg you, do not."

"I should kill you," Tehrazzi snarled. He was barely aware of the men gathering behind them, of a few of them trying to soothe the traumatized animal.

“N-no...the donkey...he would not move...”

“So you chose to beat it to death?” Tehrazzi fought the urge to smash the man’s darkening face with the butt of the gun.

He tried to shake his head, face turning from red to purple. “No...had to get it...moving...”

Tehrazzi’s hand shook slightly around the grip of the pistol. The hazy edge around his vision began to clear. His breathing slowed. With a warning snarl, he jerked the man to his feet by the hand on his throat and shoved him toward the shaking animal. He landed face first in the blood-spattered snow, and when he raised his head, the mix of it created pinkish rivulets that dripped down his face.

Without another word, Tehrazzi put his gun away and carefully approached the wounded donkey. His other men backed away and watched him in silence, some of their expressions making it clear they thought he was crazy. He wasn’t. Few things disturbed him anymore, but the suffering of horses was one of them. This donkey had not deserved such hideous treatment.

The beaten animal regarded him fearfully as he neared it, crooning in Arabic. He got on his knees before it and held out his palm. The flared nostrils blew against his callused skin, its sides still heaving with a combination of exhaustion and pain. Tehrazzi knew exactly what it felt like to be betrayed by someone you trusted. He recognized the anguish in the wide brown eyes staring up at him. Just as he understood why the animal kept its ears flattened against its skull and tensed its muscles. A lesson like that was never forgotten. Once someone learned not to trust, it stayed with them every waking minute. It turned them wary and mistrustful, even around people they once considered friends.

Tehrazzi gently stroked the velvety muzzle and continued speaking. The animal’s thickly-lashed eyes regarded him warily. He scratched its forehead and behind its ears, sliding his hand down over the thick, soft winter coat covering its neck. The donkey shuddered beneath his touch and heaved a groan.

Rising, he went to its side and undid the straps and buckles that held the loaded equipment in place. Two other men rushed to help him. The animal let out another deep groan as he relieved it of its burden, then shakily climbed to its feet. Tehrazzi praised it with soft words and continued the gentle strokes over its neck until it pricked its ears up and stood calmly. Running his hands over its forelegs, he lifted each hoof and found a walnut-sized stone lodged in one.

Lips pursing in disgust, he picked it out and set the animal's hoof down. Holding up the stone, he faced the man who'd lashed the beast so cruelly. "This is why it wouldn't move," he ground out, wanting to hit him all over again. He had no tolerance for that kind of stupidity.

Still pale, the man nodded. "Yes. I see that now. I'm sorry."

He would be sorrier yet. Tehrazzi threw the rock over the side of the canyon. It made a high-pitched crack when it hit a boulder partway down. The sound seemed to echo in the vastness of the canyon below. He stared hard at the man.

As if reading his thoughts, the man backed away and raised his hands when Tehrazzi approached him. "N-no—"

He grabbed the offender by the scruff of the neck and dragged him, letting him think he was about to be thrown over the edge. Tehrazzi held him at the lip of the gorge while he struggled and squirmed, staring down into the deep abyss. But then he shoved him back down the trail and nodded to the massed supplies lying in the snow. "You will carry this down the mountain."

The man stared back at him in incomprehension. "A-all of it?"

"All of it," Tehrazzi snapped. It would take him at least five trips to get it all down the trail, maybe more unless the others helped him. Tehrazzi would never give that order. If they helped, so be it, but he suspected they would let the man face his punishment alone. "I know every last item in this pile. If you show up at our base camp with any of it missing, I'll kill you."

Leaving the man to his fate, Tehrazzi walked back to the donkey, now shivering in the wind. Without a word to anyone he picked up the halter lead and led the animal down the trail himself. Behind him, the others got back into line, as he'd known they would. They would follow him anywhere, even to the afterlife if he asked them to. Because every last one of them knew the rewards waiting for them once they reached Kabul: more money than they would make in a decade of back breaking labor in some opium farmer's field.

And for Tehrazzi, he'd find the intelligence he needed to complete his final mission. From this moment on, his teacher's days were numbered.

# Chapter Six

*Beirut*
*Two days later*

Emily followed Bryn up the Jetway to the gate, the weight of her carry-on and purse dragging at her shoulder.

"I see Ben," Bryn called over her shoulder.

"Go on ahead," she urged. "I'll catch up." Emily held her pace while Bryn rushed ahead. The long flight had left her in a kind of fog, and her body felt heavy and sluggish.

Rounding the corner at last, Emily caught sight of Ben wrapping Bryn up in a hug and lifting her off the ground. For some strange reason, finding out Luke wasn't there was both a relief and a disappointment. She wanted to slap herself. Did she want a repeat of the argument from the other night? What was wrong with her?

Setting Bryn down, Ben smiled when he saw her. "Hi, Emily."

Before she could do more than return the smile, he

took her bags from her and gathered her up into a hug as well. For a moment she leaned into his hard shoulder, grateful for the warmth and strength of his arms around her. But secretly she'd have given anything for them to be Luke's.

"You feeling okay?" he asked as he released her, his pale green gaze running over her. "You must be tired." His South Boston accent erased the 'r' in the last word.

She liked Ben, had from the moment she'd met him at Rayne's wedding. He'd chauffeured her around town because Luke didn't want her taking a taxi. "A little," she admitted, "but I'm okay." She dug into her purse. "Here, I brought you something." She pulled out a box of the Big Red gum he chewed all the time and gave it to him.

Ben grinned. "Hey, thanks. You're such a sweetheart."

Emily waved the thanks away. "It's nothing. I just wasn't sure you'd be able to get it here, and I'm not sure how long we'll be here, so..." She reached for her bags, but Ben stopped her.

"I'll get them." He swung the straps of the bags over his shoulder as if they weighed nothing at all, then took Bryn's on the opposite shoulder.

Bryn laughed at him. "You look like a pack mule."

He grinned and shrugged his wide shoulders. "That's already the second time today someone's called me an ass."

"What, Rhys beat me to it?"

"Nope. My own darling Sam did."

"Oh God, Ben, please say the wedding's still on."

He rolled his eyes at Bryn. "Of course it's still on. You think I'd let her go?" He set a brawny arm around each of them. "Shall we?"

Emily lengthened her steps to keep up with their long legs. The airport was crowded and the noise bombarded her over-sensitive ears, so she tuned out as much as she could on the walk to the luggage carousel. When they stopped to wait for the rest of their baggage, Emily was aware of the way Ben's gaze kept scanning the crowd. Though he carried on a light conversation with Bryn, he maintained constant vigilance. And that slight bulge under his thin jacket wasn't her imagination, it was a shoulder holster. He probably had another gun tucked into his waistband. She met Bryn's eyes briefly, and Emily read the increased tension in her friend. And little wonder. Bryn had been through hell the last time she'd come here.

An answering prickle crawled over Emily's skin. She was suddenly all too aware that the threat hovering over them was real.

Exhaling, she forced herself to calm down. Ben was more than capable of protecting them, or Luke would never have hired him. Provided she stayed close to him, she'd be fine. Or Bryn for that matter, who could inflict plenty of damage with her hands and feet if she needed to. Thanks mostly to Ben, who'd trained her for her black belt. Emily suddenly wished she'd had some sort of martial arts training, too.

Ben snagged the luggage from the conveyor belt and pulled out his cell phone. He put it to his ear and said, "We're coming out." There was a short pause, then, "Roger that." Putting it back on his belt, he smiled at them. "Ready?"

She half expected him to drop the bags near the door and usher them out with his gun drawn, but he simply led them out to the silver Range Rover idling at the curb. The driver leaned over to pop the passenger door open, and she recognized Ben's fraternal twin, Rhys.

His navy blue eyes twinkled at them. "Hi ladies."

"Hi," they answered. More of her tension dissolved. Rhys was former Delta. If he was relaxed, then everything must be okay. And she couldn't have wished for two more formidable bodyguards.

Bryn climbed into the front seat to hug him, and Ben waited until Emily got in the back before putting the luggage in the trunk and sliding in next to her. The moment the door shut, Rhys pulled away from the curb into traffic.

"Is Nev back at the house?" Bryn asked him.

"Yeah." He glanced in the rear view mirror at Emily. "You need anything before I take us back?" Unlike his brother's, Rhys's deep voice held no trace of an accent.

Emily wondered if the Army had trained it out of him. Time in black ops changed everything else about a man, why not his accent too? "No thanks, I'm good."

He refocused on the road. "Nev and Sam have got everything set up for you. Trust me, you won't want for anything."

She smiled. "That was sweet of them."

Ben laid an arm across the back of the seat, his hand resting near her far shoulder. "You'll be in good hands while you're here."

"I'm sure I will." Luke wouldn't have brought her here otherwise, but with the twins she felt safe enough.

"Anyone heard from Dec?" Bryn asked.

"Luke has," Ben answered. "But I don't know the details."

Emily's stomach tightened. "Luke's here already?" She wasn't sure she was ready to confront him again so soon.

"Yep. Got here last night with our marching orders." Ben winked, his dark brows and lashes a startling contrast with the pale green of his irises. "We have to keep you guys safe, happy, and entertained, in that order."

"You being the entertainment," Bryn remarked dryly.

"You got it, sweets. I'm a one man show. What more

could you ask for?"

"Earplugs," Rhys responded, earning a shot in the arm from his brother.

Out her window, Emily stared at the unfamiliar city, but the reality of the culture shock wasn't as bad as she'd expected. Beirut was a cosmopolitan city, and had once been called "the Paris of the Middle East". The road signs were in French and Arabic, but the shop signs were mostly in English. Sleek, modern buildings rose above arabesque Ottoman-style architecture. As Rhys wound them through the congested traffic, she spotted churches and mosques nestled side by side and wished people could coexist as peacefully. Why was it so hard for human beings to get along?

The temperature was cool, but the shops and cafes they passed on the palm tree-lined streets were still busy, and the clubs would be busier yet come nightfall. How surreal to think Luke had spent many months here over the years. He'd told her once how much he hated the place, but that was because of his combat experience here.

"What do you think, Em?"

She looked over at Bryn. "It's beautiful. I wasn't expecting it to be after what Luke had told me and because of the 2006 war."

"That's because most of the city has been rebuilt since Luke was deployed here," Rhys said. "And we know which areas to stay away from."

"Such as?" If she went out, she didn't want to go to the wrong area.

"Like the Palestinian refugee camps," Ben answered. "And the southern regions, which are mostly Shiite and controlled by Hezbollah. Some areas down there are still covered with land mines."

"Those are not fun," said Rhys.

Emily's gaze travelled to the thin tracks of surgical

scars on the right side of his head, barely visible now that his thick black hair had grown in. He was lucky to have made it, let alone recover to the extent he had. "I'll bet not. I can hardly see the scar now, though."

"Yeah, Nev and the neurosurgeon did a good job on me."

"How is she?" Bryn asked. "Healing up okay?"

"For the most part. Her thumb still gives her trouble, though. She's pretty hard on herself. Keeps pushing with the rehab."

"Hmm, sounds like someone else I know," Bryn said, poking him in the ribs.

Neveah was fortunate to have function in her hand at all considering the knife wounds she'd sustained. Luke's words about the incident came back to Emily, and that Neveah's attacker had been a world famous neurosurgeon Tehrazzi had enlisted. Thank God she and her friends had Luke and the twins to protect them while they were here.

They passed neighborhoods filled with shops and markets, and when they stopped at a military checkpoint, she saw the first indicator of war in the bullet holes and crumbling exteriors on houses and buildings. She hated to think of Luke being here while those bullets and shells flew. That deployment was one of the longest of their marriage, and one of the few when she'd actually known where he was stationed.

She still remembered with vivid clarity the day she'd found out about the Marine barracks bombing. When she'd flipped on the TV, her knees had given out and she'd collapsed onto the couch. For hours she'd watched the frantic efforts of the men digging wounded and dead out of the rubble, praying Luke wasn't somehow among them. She hadn't slept for two days until he'd finally called one night to tell her he was okay.

Once the soldiers waved them through, the Rover's

powerful engine hummed as Rhys got them to the outskirts of Beirut, into the hills that cradled the city.

"Home sweet home," Bryn murmured a few minutes later.

Emily peered out the windshield as a tall, white wall came into view. Beyond it sat a large Mediterranean-style villa surrounded by manicured lawns and gardens. "Wow." If she had to be locked up somewhere for the foreseeable future, she couldn't have chosen a nicer place. "It looks like a country club."

"My father would have loved you for saying that," Bryn said, and Ben reached out to give her shoulder a squeeze, completely comfortable with her and the easy affection between them. That's partly why Emily liked him so much. He was amazingly warm and caring underneath that prankster image.

"He'd love that you were staying here again, safe and sound until everything's taken care of," he said to Bryn.

"Yeah, he would." Bryn swiveled in her seat to smile at her, her long shiny hair gleaming in the weak rays of sunlight streaming through the windows. "You ready for this?"

"Absolutely." What other choice did she have? Might as well stay positive and make the best of it for everyone. Now all she had to do was gear up for the possibility of seeing Luke.

When Rhys pulled up to the house and parked next to a marble fountain, he and Ben popped out to get the luggage. The surprisingly warm, fresh air felt good on her face when she climbed out of the vehicle, and the welcome rush of water from the fountain soothed her because it reminded her of her own back garden.

The massive front doors opened a moment later, and a beautiful redhead rushed out. "You're here!" she cried, running over to Bryn and throwing her arms around her. "It's so good to see you. Nev and I have been dying for some company."

"What's wrong with mine?" Ben demanded, dragging her close when she released Bryn and kissing her full on the mouth.

She laughed, a full-throated sound of delight. "You know I love you, but sometimes you bug the hell out of me." Once she'd pulled away, she met Emily's eyes. "Hi, you must be Emily." Waves of auburn hair swept around her shoulders in the light breeze as she approached. "I'm Sam."

"It's nice to meet you," Emily replied, offering her hand, but Sam ignored it and hugged her instead. They were around the same height, and she smiled at the warmth Sam showed her.

"Thank God I'm not the only short-ass around here anymore," Sam whispered, and Emily laughed.

"Maybe it's just that everyone else is freakishly tall."

"Exactly." Her soft brown eyes glowed with warmth. "We'll stick together, you and me."

"Sounds good."

"Come on." Ben lugged the bags inside behind his brother, who also had his hands full. "Let's get you guys squared away."

Stepping over the threshold onto the mosaic tiled floor of the foyer, Emily gazed around in wonder. The twins headed up the stairs and she followed with Bryn. The upper hallway was a dark, exotic hardwood with an elegant, expensive looking carpet runner in the center. The hall was long, with four carved wooden doors on either side. Ben stopped at the second from the end on the left and opened it.

"This is your room," he said to her, stepping back to let her in. "Bryn's across the hall. Rhys and Nev are to your left, and Luke's on your right."

Trying her best to ignore the pang in her chest at the mention of his name, Emily looked around the exquisitely furnished room. The walls were papered with black fleur-de-lis on an ivory background. The floor was polished mahogany with a cream Aubusson carpet anchoring the ebony king-sized, four poster bed. Black-and-white vertical striped silk drapes framed large picture windows that overlooked the garden, a comfortable-looking window seat perched beneath them. A perfect spot for curling up to read a book when she wanted some privacy.

"There's a TV in the armoire over there," Ben added, pointing to the far wall across from the bed. "And the fireplace is remote controlled." He picked up a remote from the nightstand and demonstrated how to turn it on. In seconds, a soft whoosh sounded and an instant later orange flames licked at the fiberglass logs behind the glass inset.

"I could get used to this," Emily said with a smile.

"Jamul was big on comfort."

She sensed a slight change in Ben, a tightening, as he said the words. She wondered if he still blamed himself for Jamul's death.

"Anyway," he continued. "Go ahead and get settled, then come down and have something to eat if you want."

"Thanks." When he left she checked out the bathroom, also done in a Parisian theme of black and white. Cream marble and crystal, with crisp white tile and ebony accents. A glassed-in shower and Jacuzzi soaker tub finished the room, perfect for easing the aches out of her muscles. Lovely.

Pulling herself away, she unpacked her things and passed Luke's room on her way down to the kitchen. It was a huge, sunny room with creamy walls and deep charcoal gray granite countertops, with commercial grade stainless steel appliances. Grand enough for a gourmet chef to work in. Emily looked forward to cooking in here. It had been too long since she'd had anyone to cook for, and besides, it would make her feel useful.

"Feel like some tea?" Sam asked, standing by the white apron front sink.

"That'd be great."

"I love your accent, by the way."

"Oh, thanks." But to her ears, Sam was the one with an accent.

Sam opened a glass-fronted cabinet and pulled out some china cups. "Let's see, what've we got?" Another cupboard was full of stacked tea boxes. "You like chai, right?"

Startled, Emily blinked. "Yes. How did you know?"

"Luke told me. He left this for you." Sam pulled out her favorite brand, and a sharp pain jolted Emily's heart as she stared at the familiar box. The whole reason she'd started drinking the tea in the first place was because it reminded her of Luke. Years ago she'd read about the Afghan and Pakistani preference for chai tea, and drinking it was a tiny link to Luke because she knew he'd have drank it during his time overseas. Stupid and pathetic, but there it was. And she still drank the stuff.

When Sam handed her a steaming, spicy cupful, Emily had to swallow the lump in her throat to say thank you. Such a small thing, for him to remember her favorite tea, but it meant a lot to her. The question was, did it mean anything? Or was he just trying to be nice because he felt bad about dragging her here?

After three sips, she couldn't stand it anymore. "Is Luke here?"

Sam's wide brown eyes flashed up. "No, he's out...working."

Ah. "In Beirut?"

"And elsewhere."

Okay. She apparently wasn't going to learn anything more about Luke's whereabouts here than she had when they'd been married. Emily was disappointed, but not all that surprised. There was no reason for her to know the details, was there? She had no claim on him, and she wasn't part of the team. She and Bryn were merely guests during their time here.

"Listen." Sam laid a hand over hers and squeezed. "I'm not privy to all the details either, but I can promise you he's safe."

Was he? He hated Beirut, and the whole reason he'd brought the rest of them over here was because of a credible threat against them. Knowing he was out there hunting Tehrazzi and putting himself in danger had her stomach in knots.

"There she is."

Emily turned at the familiar female voice and turned to smile at Neveah. "Hi," she said, hopping off her stool to hug her. Nev was nearly as tall as Luke, and Emily had to reach up high to put her arms around her neck.

"How are you?" Nev asked, assessing her with those gorgeous lake blue eyes.

"Good." She was getting sick of saying that and "fine" all the time. "How about you?" She glanced pointedly at Nev's right forearm, and the wicked scar that marred the length of it.

"Almost healed up." She rotated her thumb. "This still gives me trouble sometimes, but don't worry, I can handle IVs well enough that I won't cause you any damage when we do your next treatment."

The mention of it filled her with dread. "Are you really all set up to do this?"

"Do what?" Bryn asked, wandering back into the kitchen and helping herself to some tea.

"The chemo," Emily said.

"Oh." Bryn's gaze sought Neveah's. "Where are you planning to do it?"

"Wherever Emily's most comfortable. In her room,

the family room or out by the pool. It's up to you," she said to her. "We'll make it work."

"Thanks." Though all Emily really cared about was doing it someplace private. She didn't want anyone watching while that poison pumped through her veins for three hours. Nor did she want anyone to see her if the nausea hit her again this time. The first week after the last treatment had been the worst, and the second week she'd been wiped out. Right now she felt almost normal except for some lingering fatigue. Shame she had to repeat that cycle a few more times over the next couple of months.

"Want the grand tour?" Bryn asked, and Emily knew she'd said it to change the subject.

"I'd love to see the rest of the place." She followed her friend while the two cousins trailed behind them. The family room was bright and beautifully furnished with cozy leather couches, and it had a spectacular view of the mountains and manicured grounds through the tall windows. "It really is beautiful."

"Yeah, it is," Bryn agreed. "My father had good taste." She led the way through the main floor, pointing out all the amenities and finishing with the study. Pausing in the doorway, she was silent as she stared at the large mahogany desk.

The faint scent of cigars still permeated the air, and from the way Bryn stared at the tufted leather chair behind the paper-strewn desk, Emily knew she was thinking about her father. The room was intensely masculine with its dark leather and woodwork. The bookshelves were full of leather-bound legal volumes, along with several framed pictures of Bryn at various points throughout her life.

Sam cast an anxious glance at her. "We put Luke in here so he could work in peace. Is that okay?"

Emily's stomach tensed at the same time Bryn said,

"Sure. My dad would have liked that, I think."

She rubbed a comforting hand on Bryn's back. Jamul had met Luke back during the Lebanese civil war and they'd maintained contact over the years, but it was damned eerie that Luke was occupying his dead friend's study. She could picture Luke here, bent over the laptop sitting on the desk or talking on his phone in any number of languages he'd mastered during his career.

"Why don't we take you downstairs and show you the gym?" Nev offered, obviously trying to give Bryn some time alone.

"I'll take her," Bryn insisted, but her eyes were moist as she turned away from the study.

Emily followed her down the polished hardwood stairs to the lower floor. The gym was state-of-the-art, boasting all the equipment one would expect at a health club, plus a large area of floor covered with a thin sort of mat.

"I imagine Ben and I will go a few rounds while I'm here," Bryn said with a fond grin. "My dad used this for kickboxing, but it works for martial arts, too. It's been way too long since I worked out like that."

"I'm looking forward to watching that by the way," Sam told her with a conspiratorial smile. "It's not every day Ben gets his ego knocked down to size, and usually that's Rhys's job."

"Duty and privilege," Rhys corrected, emerging from the back room. He came up to wind a long arm around Neveah and pull her tight into his body.

Her expression tightened. "Going somewhere?"

He smiled, but the motion of his lips was slight, as though they were unused to it. "Damn, you're smart."

"Yeah, yeah," she muttered, tilting her head back to look into his face, which said a lot considering how tall she was. Rhys was a giant of a man. "So? What's going on?"

"The mother ship called with my orders."

Luke, he meant. The tension in Emily ratcheted up another few notches. Was something dangerous already happening?

Rhys kissed the top of Nev's head before releasing her and striding over to a locked cabinet at the end of the gym. "Ben's going to stay here while I take care of this," he said, taking out a pistol and what looked like a sniper rifle. Nev's dark blue eyes fastened on the weapons and she flinched. "Nothing to worry about," he assured her. "Just some recon."

"With loaded weapons."

"Unloaded weapons aren't much good to me, sweetheart. Be back in a while." He kissed her gently before he left them standing there in the expanding silence. From the back room a radio crackled, but other than that they were quiet, staring at the doorway Rhys had walked out.

"Well." Nev folded her arms beneath her breasts as she sighed and changed the subject. "Who's hungry?"

Emily stepped forward and laid a hand on her shoulder. "You don't have to do that." She looked at the others. "None of you do. I know exactly what y'all are going through, so please don't cover up what you're feeling for my sake. I've been there, trust me. Many times."

Nev's brave facade slipped a notch. "God, how did you do it for as many years as you did?"

Emily swallowed. She owed them the truth so they understood they could come to her for support while she was with them. "Honestly? I'm still doing it. And unfortunately, it doesn't get any easier, which is why it's a good thing we've got each other to get through this."

"That's right," Bryn agreed, holding out her arms to gather them up into a circle. They looped their arms over each others' shoulders, four women linked by shared fears for the men they loved and their own traumatic experiences. Survivors, all of them. Kindred spirits, and then some.

"Oh, Christ."

They turned their heads to find Ben standing where his brother had just been.

He shook his dark head in apparent disgust. "You're starting with the girl bonding stuff already? Listen, the only time I want to see a circle of women hugging is if they're naked or I'm in the middle of it," he said, pushing his way into the center of the knot they'd formed. He raised his brows and stood there looking at them expectantly for a moment, and Emily couldn't help but laugh. She hugged him and then the others joined in. Like the ham he was, Ben sighed in contentment, clearly eating up their attention. He reminded her of Rayne that way.

The first to pull away, Sam shook her head at her fiancé, but her eyes were alight with laughter. "You're hopeless."

"I know, but you love me anyway." His smile said he wasn't the least bit repentant, and Emily laughed again.

"How about I wipe that grin off his handsome face for you, Sam?" Bryn offered.

That devilish smile of his widened, showing straight white teeth. "You and what army, sweets?"

"Uh-oh," Sam said, taking her cue and breaking loose. "Here they go. This should be good." She grabbed Emily and Nev by the arms. "Come on, let's get a seat so we can watch the show."

Ben was already pulling off his shirt, baring the rippling muscles of his torso in a completely unself-conscious display of male power. Sam rolled her eyes. "God, you are such a show-off."

"Yeah, and you love looking at my pecs," he replied without missing a beat. He hitched up his cargo pants as he raised his brows at Bryn in challenge. “Sure you want to do this with an audience? I bet you’re rusty. Wouldn’t want to embarrass yourself in front of your girls.”

Bryn’s eyes narrowed to slits. “Neither would you, mouthpiece.”

Emily snickered, loving the distraction, which was exactly what Ben had intended. He’d managed to lift everyone’s mood in the space of a minute. He was entertainment indeed, and God knew she could use the diversion right now.

She watched with a pang of envy as Bryn went at him, rolling effortlessly when he threw her to the mat, and jumped to her feet. Their movements were fluid and beautiful to watch, almost choreographed. The satisfied gleam in Bryn’s eyes told Emily how much her friend enjoyed her workout, and though Ben made her work hard, he tempered his strength in consideration. Then Bryn went on the offensive. Ben laughed in delight as he blocked a rather vicious kick to the kidney.

Emily winced, but Sam yelled out, “Get him, Bryn!”

Fending off another attack, Ben shot a betrayed look at his fiancée. “*What*?” he demanded in a shocked tone, lunging over to grab Sam. Bryn stood off to the side and smiled, shaking her head at the two of them.

Sam shrieked and hung on as he lifted her over one shoulder and carefully tumbled her onto her back on the mat. He kept her pinned there for just a moment before kissing her soundly on the mouth, then Nev jumped in with a playful shout and grabbed him around the waist from behind. In less than a second, Ben had her on the floor next to her cousin, laughing as he tickled them.

When Emily snickered, Ben turned his head and locked his gaze on her. She held up her hands in self-defense and opened her mouth to protest but he came at her anyway. She let out a yelp and clutched at his wide shoulders as he hauled her into the air and spun her, his arms controlling her descent when he laid her down beside the other two. By the time her back touched the mat, she was laughing so hard she could hardly breathe. She couldn't remembered the last time she'd had this much fun. It felt wonderful.

"That's right, ladies," Ben remarked, towering over them with hands on hips while they tried to catch their breath. "Don't mess with the master." He surveyed his handiwork for a moment before grinning. "One more to go," he said, wiggling his eyebrows at Bryn.

"I dare you to try," she taunted, going back into her fighting stance.

Emily and the others scooted out of range while the next round got underway, laughing and cheering Bryn on. For the first time in days, she wasn't thinking about Luke or her cancer and the upcoming chemo treatments. Right then, she didn't feel sick at all.

****

Later, when the others left to go up to the kitchen with Ben shooting snide remarks about Bryn's rusty martial arts skills, Emily stayed behind. Her heart pounded. Watching those two grapple and punch and kick away their frustrations made her want to do the same. God knew she had an overload of tension and anger to unload. The inexplicable urge to hit something rose hard within her. She eyed the heavy bag hanging in the back corner and the pair of boxing gloves lying beneath it. Biting her lip, she took another glance around. She was all alone here, so if she was going to do it, now was the time.

The closer she got to the bag, the more her heart pounded. She'd never hit anything in her life, but she needed to now. She was sick and tired of feeling like a victim, of having no control over anything. The stockpiled memories played in her mind like a movie on fast-forward, and she let them build. Luke deploying for missions. Losing her mother. Losing her father less than a year later. Luke leaving. Raising Rayne without a father. The damned cancer and the operations that had carved her femininity out of her. Being dragged to Beirut.

But the worst of all was a vision of her dying in a lonely hospital bed, terrified and in agony.

*No more.*

The words echoed in her brain, resonating within the deepest part of her heart. Starting right now, she was taking back control over her life, and her body. The cancer was there and she couldn't do more about that than she already was, but if she had to go down, she was going down fighting. Like a heavyweight champion.

She picked up the thick gloves. The left one went on easily enough, but the right took some maneuvering as she held it between her knees and pushed her hand into it. Her fingers automatically curled into fists as she raised them toward the bag. No one was around. No one was there to laugh at her poor technique. She could vent all the ugliness inside her. Right now, without being embarrassed or having to explain herself to anyone.

*Hit it.*

Her breathing came faster as she visualized the way Ben and Bryn had punched, feet spread apart to give them balance, weight thrown forward as they struck. She imagined how it would feel, throwing her fist into the bag.

*Hit it.*

Hell yes, she would. She gave it an experimental shot with her right glove, testing the way the impact traveled up her arm.

*Hit it!*

Face twisting with all the rage and hurt bottled up

inside her, Emily let loose on the heavy bag. Her blows slammed into the leather sides, one after the other, the impact jolting right up to her shoulders. But it felt good. It felt *right*. Damn near addictive. She might not know what the hell she was doing, but that didn't matter. Channeling her energy into her fists was exactly what she needed.

Switching her lead foot to get better balance, Emily put her full weight behind the punches. The chain hanging the bag from the hook in the ceiling rattled as she upped the ferocity of her attack, the muscles in her arms and shoulders burning with the effort. She started panting, and a delicious sense of power rushed through her battered body. She was *not* weak, and she was no quitter, no matter what Luke thought. She'd show him, her body, and everyone else what she was made of. Just frigging watch her. Goosebumps broke out over her skin.

The bag jerked as she threw her fists at it, angry growls ripping from her throat. When that wasn't enough she got her knees into it too, ramming into the leather until her legs quivered with fatigue. Sweat beaded on her face and between her breasts, but she kept going, loving the sense of freedom. When she was gasping for breath and her arms were too weak to put any force behind the punches, she stopped and staggered back to put her gloved hands on her knees.

But the room began to spin.

*Oh damn...* Emily shook her head to clear it, but it didn't help. If anything, the movement made the disorientation worse. Her breaths turned raspy and shallow. Oh, shit, she wasn't going to pass out, was she? In the middle of the floor after her first try at boxing, where anyone could stumble upon her?

In case she was about to hit the floor, she got onto her knees before collapsing on her butt. Encouraged that she was still conscious, she lay down on her back and lifted her feet in the air, resting them against the heavy bag to push more blood to her brain. Gradually her breathing slowed and the awful chill left her, but she didn't dare risk getting up yet. She stayed that way for an unknown amount of time, feeling like a complete ass with her legs up in the air until she heard heavy footsteps coming down the stairs.

Cringing, she swung her legs down as she opened her eyes and looked toward the stairway. The treads were too heavy to be one of the girls, so it had to be Ben. Ah well, at least it wasn't Lu—

"Em?"

Her heart almost stopped at the sound of Luke's deep drawl. Before she could move he appeared in the doorway, and his dark gaze locked on her.

"Jesus Christ," he muttered, rushing over to hunker down beside her. "Are you okay?"

No. No, this couldn't be happening. God wouldn't do this to her on top of everything else.

He put a hand on her damp face. "Em, are you hurt?"

She tried a smile. "You should see the other guy."

Luke didn't smile back. "Are you *hurt*?"

"No. Just a little dizzy." And mortified. If she was going to pass out, now would be a good time.

In silence, his gaze took in the boxing gloves on her hands. "What were you doing?"

*Knitting*, she wanted to snap. Wasn't it plenty obvious? "Exercising."

"Can you sit up?"

"In a second." She wished he'd just go away and let her collect herself.

Instead, Luke tugged the gloves off, and the air suddenly felt cold against her damp palms. Unfortunately, the burning in her face continued. She avoided his gaze, but he knelt and took her face between his broad hands. Electric tingles shot through her nerve endings where he touched her skin, but when she dared to look into his eyes she found only concern, and maybe a bit of annoyance. Then she realized the pressure of his fingers beneath her jaw wasn't a caress. He was taking her pulse.

She pushed his hands away and sat up, but he immediately steadied her with a hard arm across her back. She couldn't look at him. He'd been a SEAL for a long time. They respected strength and the ability to take physical punishment in silence. She detested that he saw her as weak and helpless.

"Okay now?"

"Yep." To prove it, she shifted onto her knees with the intent to get up, but he simply slid his other arm beneath her legs and lifted her into the air. With a startled gasp she grabbed his wide shoulders. "No, put me down."

"Nope." He strode to the stairs, carrying her as though she weighed nothing. And oh, he smelled good. Her body went a little weaker.

"I'm not hurt, I just overdid it—"

"Damn right you did." The annoyance in his tone stopped her from protesting any further, made her set her jaw. "You just got off a long flight," he reminded her, "and I bet you haven't eaten since you left London, have you?"

She scowled at the middle of his wide chest. "No."

"You're a nurse for God's sake, so you should know better."

Any satisfaction she'd gained from exorcising her demons was long gone. All that remained was the sinking feeling in her stomach. She'd managed to make herself appear pathetic and feeble in front of Luke yet again.

"You could have given yourself a concussion if you'd fallen down there alone. Ever think of that?"

She clenched her teeth until her jaw ached, his words putting the match to her usually dormant temper. "Okay, so I got carried away!"

His arms tightened around her as he went up the stairs. "You need to take better care of yourself. You just had a chemo treatment a few weeks ago, and you're going to have another one tomorrow. You know you're anemic, same as you know you'll bruise easily now—and that makes me wonder why the hell you'd decide to go at a heavy bag within an hour of arriving on an intercontinental flight."

Since any argument she came up with would be a complete waste of time, she bit her tongue and suffered his achingly familiar embrace while he carried her into the kitchen. The second they entered the room, Ben and Sam both stopped chopping vegetables at the granite island and stared at them.

Luke ignored them, taking her straight to the family room to set her on the couch, placing a few pillows under her feet as though he worried she might pass out still. As if his skin burned her, Emily yanked her arms away from his neck. And then Ben was standing next to them, inadvertently adding to her misery.

"You okay?"

She gritted her teeth. "Yes." But now she wanted to hit something again.

Sam came in and tugged on Ben's arm. "Can you come into the kitchen for a minute?"

"In a sec. I just want to make sure she's—"

Emily nailed him with a glare that promised bodily harm if he finished that sentence. "There's nothing wrong with me. But thanks for your concern," she added to soften her hard tone.

Ben's eyes widened a fraction, and he threw Luke a "good luck" look as he turned to leave.

Now her face burned with shame on top of the

humiliation. Ben was only trying to help, and she shouldn't have snapped at him. Her anger should be directed at herself, not at anyone else. Luke was right. She should have known better.

She brushed at a spot of lint on her black pants, wishing he'd go yet praying he wouldn't. His nearness made it hard to breathe. "Thank you, but I'm fine now. I can take care of myself."

"That's not how it looks to me. So far I'd say you're doing a piss-poor job of it."

An outraged gasp came out and her eyes snapped to his. "Who the hell do you think you are, to talk to me like that?" she demanded. "I got my ass on the plane and came here like you ordered, did I not? What the hell else do you want from me?"

His eyes smoldered with annoyance. "I'm getting Nev."

Her mouth tightened. "I told you, I'm fine. Don't bug her."

"Yeah, I'll believe it if she tells me you're fine." He walked out of the room, leaving her to stew.

She closed her eyes and took slow, deep breaths to calm down. What was happening between them? They'd never sniped at each other this way, not even when they were married. Stress, she decided. It was the stress of everything. Him planning out the next mission, knowing she was terminal, and still trying to take control of everything.

Quiet treads had her opening her eyes. Neveah walked up and studied her. "What's going on? Luke said you fainted."

Emily rolled her eyes. "I didn't faint. He's being an overbearing, controlling…asshole."

Nev burst out laughing. "Oh, is that all? Well, get used to it, hon. All the men in the house are like that. Us girls are going to have to stick together if we want to stand a chance against them."

# Chapter Seven

Next afternoon, Nev found her in the kitchen staring out at the patio. “You ready to do this?”

Emily just wanted the treatment over with. “Yep. Where do you want me?”

“Wherever you feel most comfortable.”

Not in her room. She felt too closed up in there. Maybe it would help to be out in the open somewhere. Outside, the sky was clouding over but the breeze was light, blowing the edges of the shrubs occasionally. And she’d be out of everyone’s way there. “By the pool, I think. Maybe under the pergola there.” The wooden beams dripped with grapevines. Maybe she’d pick some leaves to make those Lebanese roll-ups later for dinner if she felt up to eating.

“Sure. I'm going to give you the diphenhydramine first, to make sure you don’t have a hypersensitivity reaction, then I’ll start the Taxol. Do you want a sedative or anything?”

“No, just some Gravol if you’ve got it.”

Nev snorted. “Of course I do. You think I’d agree to do this if Luke didn’t have all the meds and equipment I might need brought in?" She put an arm around her shoulders and started for the French doors.

A seating area was arranged beneath the teak pergola, and Emily chose the padded chaise lounge, settling into it before pulling the cozy throw blanket at its foot over her body.

"I'll go get everything and bring you a coat."

When she was alone, Emily laid her head back and sighed. Despite how tired she'd been last night she hadn't slept much. Some part of her was still too aware that Luke was in the house, in the study on the main floor. She knew he'd been in there all night, and had probably only taken a couple of fifteen minute combat naps at most. How he could function on that little amount of sleep she'd never know, but he seemed to manage beautifully. When they'd first been married she'd never really noticed it, but after Rayne was born it had amazed her. The man was a total rock.

Through the whole of her torturous twenty-two hour back labor he'd held her hand or rubbed her back, keeping her calm and not letting her panic when the pain got so bad she thought she would die—and then worse until she *wanted* to die simply to make it stop. He'd stayed next to her and talked her through it, one horrific contraction at a time. He never broke a sweat, never even yawned though he'd been up for almost two days without sleep. And when she'd come home with the baby, so exhausted she'd occasionally burst into tears for no reason, Luke took over. He brought Rayne to her for feedings so she wouldn't have to get up, and sometimes fed him a bottle so she could get some extra sleep.

A lot of those early nights when he was home at their bungalow near the base he took the night shifts, but he didn't catch up on his sleep during the day. He just kept going, which shouldn't have surprised her because he was a SEAL, and a man couldn't attain that status without being able to handle sleep deprivation. It also should have told her about the strength of his will. Once he made his mind up to do something, he'd do it or die trying. Little wonder he'd never come back after he left.

"Feel like some company?"

Emily opened her eyes and held out a hand to Bryn. She wasn't the only one hurting right now. The waiting was a killer. "How are you doing, sweetheart?"

Bryn sighed. "Coping as best I can. You?"

"The same. Nev's coming back to give me a treatment. Sure you want to stay?"

"Yeah, I thought we could play Scrabble, just like old times."

Emily smiled. "I'd like that." And it would make the time pass far more quickly than watching each torturous drip fall into the IV tube.

All too soon Nev returned, and while Emily got her coat on and buttoned up to the waist, Nev got her long thick rubber gloves on. They came almost up to her elbows. "Careful," she warned Bryn as she got everything hung up. "This first stuff's not so bad, but if the Taxol gets on your skin we're gonna have to scrub you down before it burns you."

Bryn cast a disbelieving glance at Emily. "Good to know, since that shit's going directly into her *veins*."

"Hence the Brazilian effect," Emily quipped.

Nev let out a short laugh. "That's about the only good side effect."

"I'm trying to focus on the positives."

Nev's eyes were full of empathy. "I know you are, and I know it's not easy. I'm going to do everything I can to make this okay for you. Just promise me you'll speak up if you need something."

"I will. You've got an amazing bedside manner, by the way," Emily told her. "I've worked with doctors over the years who never should have been allowed into medical school, let alone in a hospital working around sick people. Your patients are lucky to have you."

A faint trace of red stained Neveah's cheeks, and it wasn't from the cool December breeze. "Thanks, but I'm mostly known for my, uh...blunt way of speaking."

"Sometimes that's what's needed. The difference is, you know when you need to be kind. Trust me, that's a winning combo." Things got quiet while Nev hooked up the preliminary drug to the subclavian port in her chest and boosted it with a push of Gravol. Within minutes Emily's lids felt heavy.

Bryn paused in the midst of setting up the Scrabble board. "Maybe you should sleep for awhile instead. I can come back later."

"No, it's okay. I'd rather have a distraction if you don't mind."

"Of course I don't mind. I'm all about distractions right now."

Nev glanced between them as she took off her gloves. "You guys need anything else? I could really use another job around here, before I go nuts."

Because she was worried about Rhys, same as Bryn worried about Dec and Emily worried about her ex-husband. "We could use a third player," Emily offered. "So long as you can handle how competitive Bryn gets."

"Me?" her friend said in a shocked tone. "I'm not the one who stayed up late studying the dictionary every night for two weeks last time I visited just so you could beat me."

She shrugged. "I like to keep my brain active. Well? You in?" she asked Nev.

"I'm so in." Nev tugged her sweater on and took a seat across from them. "I should warn you I did a minor in English lit before I got into medical school. My vocabulary's pretty good."

"Talk is cheap," Bryn said. "Prove it."

Emily had the lead when it was time for the Taxol, and watched with dread as Nev hooked it into her line. The now familiar burning started up, bringing with it a rush of anxiety that made her breath shorten and her feet tingle. Nev watched her carefully as she took her vitals. "How you doing?"

Focusing on staying calm, Emily merely nodded. Nev added more Gravol, then resumed the game to take her mind off it. It was a strange feeling, to be hooked up to a tube and know poison circulated throughout her entire body, every heart beat sending more of it into her bloodstream. The nausea started up, but thank God not as strong this time.

"Em?" Bryn asked. Nev pulled out a bucket she'd brought from one of the bathrooms.

"Gimme a sec," she said, tilting her head back and taking a few slow, deep breaths. The cool air did seem to help, as did the fact she wasn't alone, and after a few minutes the worst of it seemed to pass. Wiping a sleeve over her damp face, Emily blew out a breath and put on a smile for her friends. "I hate that part."

Bryn squeezed her free hand in answer. "Just so you know, that excuse isn't going to cut it. I'm still taking you down."

She smiled. That was the beauty of having a friend who knew her so well. Bryn knew exactly when to push and when to support. "Have I told you lately that I love you?"

"Ditto, lady. Now come on," she gestured impatiently to the letter tiles resting in the holder. "Quit stalling."

They played for another hour or so, and when Nev stopped to check her vitals again, Emily could barely keep her eyes open.

"You need to sleep," Nev said gently. "Want to go inside now?"

She shook her head. "I like the fresh air."

Just then the French doors to the patio opened and Luke stepped out. The nausea she'd managed to keep at bay came back with a vengeance. Emily swallowed hard, her pulse leaping beneath Nev's practiced fingers.

He crossed the tiled surface and acknowledged them with a nod, and Emily had to fight the urge to check that her wig was on straight. "Phone call for you inside," he said to Bryn.

She leapt up like she'd sat on a thumb tack. "Is it Dec?"

"Maybe."

Bryn tore into the house without a backward glance. In the ensuing silence, Emily avoided Luke's gaze though she felt it resting on her face.

"I'll be inside if you need me," Nev suddenly blurted.

A spurt of panic flooded Emily's veins as her buffer left, but she couldn't tell her not to go without looking like a coward. Without waiting for an invitation, Luke sat in the chair Nev had vacated and looked straight at her. "Doing okay, sunshine?"

The endearment took her completely off guard. Luke hadn't called her that in over two decades, and him using it now confused the hell out of her. If he'd said it because he felt sorry for her, she didn't want his pity. "Yes, thanks." Why did he have to show up every time she was at her most vulnerable? She tucked the blanket around her shoulders and huddled beneath its folds, but she couldn't get warm and her eyelids were so heavy...

"You're tired," Luke murmured, his gaze drifting over her face with careful scrutiny. His lashes were thick and black, and when he lifted his gaze, his irises were the exact color of melted bittersweet chocolate.

"A bit."

"And cold." He tucked the edges of the blanket more securely around her legs. "Want me to take you in?"

Didn't he know how it hurt her to be next to him like

this? Couldn't he see what it did to her? She closed her eyes, afraid of what they might reveal in her current weakness.

"Em?" The deep syllable flowed over her like a caress, then the edge of his hand brushed her cheek, pushing some strands of the wig away from her face.

She grabbed his wrist. "Please don't."

Torment swirled in the depths of his eyes, but he dropped his hand. "You're exhausted, Em. Let me get you inside where it's warm, then you can sleep."

She stared at him. Why was he doing this to her? She was an inch from tears, and dying to reach for him. But she couldn't.

Luke got up and sat on the edge of the chaise with her, so close his hip pressed against her thigh. Ignoring how stiff she was, he reached for her hand. He curled his long fingers around her palm and rubbed gently.

If he truly wanted her to be comfortable, the quickest way would be for him to leave her the hell alone.

She sat stock still, gazing at the pool. Its turquoise water was clear and calm. Exactly the opposite of what she felt. Yet she couldn't make herself pull her hand away from his.

To fill the void, she stared out at the water and asked, "So how are things coming?"

He flicked a sharp look at her before replying. "Nothing concrete yet. Still waiting."

His answer surprised her so much that she looked at him. She hadn't thought he'd talk about it at all. "Oh. Sorry to hear that." The fingers of her free hand sought the edge of the blanket and fidgeted with it. "The girls are fantastic by the way, and the twins are really sweet."

"Sweet?" He chuckled. "I bet they've never been called that before, except by their mother and significant others."

She shrugged. "They are to me."

His hand tightened around hers. “I’m glad. I want to make this as easy on you as possible, but more importantly I want you to know you’re safe here.”

*You’re safe with me.* The echo from their tragic past weighed heavy on her heart.

She dropped her gaze to their joined hands. Strange to see them that way when she’d ached for that simple pleasure thousands of times. And it hurt because it didn’t mean as much as she wanted it to. Not on his part, anyway. And it shouldn’t on hers. Couldn’t. “You don’t...you don’t have to do this, you know.”

“Do what?”

“Feel obligated to check in on me. I know you’ve got more important things to do.”

Luke captured her jaw in one wide palm and turned her face toward him. “Nothing’s more important to me than making sure you beat this.” His eyes delved into hers, bottomless and magnetic. “And if you think I’m checking in on you, you’re right. But I’ve got a damn good reason. You won’t tell anyone if you need help, and you never did.”

Something stilled inside her as she stared at him. Is that what he thought? “That’s not true.”

“Yeah it is. You’re so determined to take care of everything by yourself that you won’t speak up, not even if you’re in pain.”

Emily pulled away from his grasp. Exactly, and why did he think that was? “Because I’ve had to.”

“Because I left?” he said pointedly. “Uh-uh, sweetheart. You were like that when we got together. Right from day one when you showed up at that bar to rescue your sister, facing down a guy twice your size.”

“Excuse me—”

“And you did it throughout our marriage. You never once asked for help with anything important, even when I knew you needed it.”

"Well that's because you'd always take over! And I thought it was my job to take whatever stress I could off you. I wanted to pull my own weight. I wanted me to be strong, and thought you admired that about me."

His eyes softened. "Em, of course I did. But I'm a hell of a lot stronger than you ever gave me credit for."

He thought she'd seen him as weak? She wanted to laugh at the absurdity of it. "I never *ever* doubted how strong you were, not for a second."

"No? Well then why didn't you realize I didn't need you looking after every minute detail so everything was perfect when I came home, and then killing yourself to make it stay that way?"

A burning lump settled in her throat. All those times she'd been on pins and needles waiting for him to come home, making sure the house was spotless and the yard work and laundry was done, that his car was washed and waxed. Having Rayne dressed in his best clothes and ready to race up and hug his daddy with a smile on his face. Nothing wrong in their world. Everything was sunshine and roses.

The times when she'd known he was arriving home, she'd meticulously ensured every homecoming was as perfect as she could make it. She'd always been careful to keep her own problems and worries from him. Never saying or doing anything that might upset him, so their time together would be as peaceful and comforting as she could make it. She'd wanted their home to be a haven for him. And he was telling her now that he hadn't needed her to do any of that? That he didn't appreciate it?

"Don't you think I knew what kind of stress you were under when I was gone?" he said. "That I didn't know how hard that life was on you?"

She twisted her fingers together. "I just wanted to make you happy," she said in a small voice.

"You did. You and Rayne. I never needed anything else."

*Then why did you go?* She almost said it, had to choke the words back along with the tears building up. She didn't have the energy or the will to tackle that topic right now. Her nerves were ready to snap as it was.

Turning away from her, Luke leaned forward and put his elbows on his thighs. As he spoke he stared out at the garden, still lush and green despite it being winter. "You know what I think? I think the real reason you felt obligated to do all that is because you were afraid I'd come home and snap over something stupid one day. Which I did."

She squeezed her eyes shut. "Luke—"

"No, it's the truth. I was subconsciously afraid of the same thing, but you saw the truth of it before I did."

Words of denial died on her tongue. Had she known somehow? Was that why she'd always been so tense for the first few days when he came back from a long deployment? She didn't know what to say.

"So if I tended to take over where you were concerned, that's why. And that's why you think I'm a heavy-handed asshole right now for dragging you here while you're undergoing chemo."

She didn't deny it.

His lips quirked in a wry grin. "You'd never ask for help, let alone mine, so the only thing I can do is be proactive."

Rather than make her mad, his words touched her. A tremulous smile quivered on her lips. "A pre-emptive strike."

He smiled back. "Exactly." Then his face grew sober. "I want you to know…I'd take the cancer myself in a heartbeat if it meant healing you."

*Why?* she wanted to cry. Why would he say that when he'd stayed away for so many years? Guilt?

Trying to make up for what he'd done? She couldn't understand.

"Em," he sighed, his Louisiana drawl becoming more pronounced. "You're tired and scared whether you want to admit it or not. So be a doll and take some stress off my shoulders for old times' sake. Lay your head back and close your damn eyes."

She wanted to. She was so desperately tired. And worried. But no matter how tense and unresolved things stood between them, it bothered her that she might have inadvertently hurt him in the past. She swallowed. "I didn't know. I never meant to shut you out. I'm sorry if I ever made you feel that way." Was part of the reason he'd walked away because he'd thought she didn't need him? The idea wounded her. She'd needed him more than anything.

"I know you didn't do it intentionally." He sighed, an ironic smile on his lips as he shook his head at her.

It killed her to know he'd felt that way during their marriage and she hadn't known. Why hadn't he said anything?

"Now get some sleep."

Before he could get up, she gathered all the courage she could find and captured his hand with hers. Stilling, he looked down at her questioningly. She bit the inside of her lip, struggling to put the truth of what she felt into words. He wasn't saying he loved her or that he wanted another chance. But he still cared enough to stand by her and do whatever he could to ease her. It shredded her heart.

"You know," she began, looking down at his hand beneath hers. Large and tanned. Strong, yet capable of incredible gentleness. He wanted her to speak up when she needed help? *I'm scared. I'm hurting. I miss you.* "I think I'd sleep better if you stayed here with me. If you don't mind."

When she raised her head, his eyes showed surprise and a sad kind of recognition that she'd reached out to him in that small way. "I don't mind at all." He tucked the heavy blanket around her tightly and then sat in the chair next to her. "Sleep, Em," he murmured. "I've got the watch."

Fighting the need to reach for his hand and hold onto him, she closed her eyes to hide the tears. She wanted his arms around her so badly. *Hold me.*

She bit the words back, too afraid to say them. It was enough that he was beside her. The gentle sighing of the wind filled her senses, along with the knowledge that nothing would hurt her while Luke kept watch. She was safe with him. Always had been.

****

Luke peered over Sam's shoulder to look at the satellite link she'd pulled up. It'd been hours since he'd sat with Em out on the patio. Though he wished he was still with her, duty had called. "How long ago did this activity start?" he asked, noting the stockpiled ammunition crates being offloaded into the caravan of trucks.

"About nine hours ago, best we can figure. I can't get in any closer than this. Can you make out what it says on the crates?"

He squinted at the screen, waiting until the man in the foreground moved out of the way. "Some Chinese RPGs there." He tapped a forefinger against one crate. "The others aren't marked, far as I can tell. Could be mortars or mines. Whatever they are, at least they're small."

"There sure are a lot of them," Sam murmured with a frown, chewing on her bottom lip as she tried a different angle.

Yeah, there were. "All the trucks going to the same

drop off point?"

"So far. I've tracked two of the convoys to the same location where the caves are."

He was so sick of caves. The ones the enemy used in the Syrian Desert weren't as big as their counterparts in Afghanistan, but they still guaranteed to be a major pain in the ass. Not to mention it was gonna be damn cold out there. He was tired of freezing his ass off, too, but it had to be done. Luke straightened. "Keep monitoring this and advise me of any changes."

"Of course." Sam swung her brown gaze up to his. "You going out tonight?"

"Looks like tomorrow afternoon, unless something changes drastically. It's going to take Davis some time to get there."

Ben walked in and joined them, peering at the on-screen images. He let out a low whistle. "We got human eyes there yet?"

"Dec's SEALs are humping in now," Luke answered. He looked at Sam. "What's their ETA, do you know?"

"Dec's aiming for seventeen-hundred Lima. He'll contact us with the radio link once they're up and ready."

Five o'clock local time. Six hours from now. Plenty could change in that amount of time. It ate at Luke that he couldn't pull the trigger and go now, but they had to time this right. Everyone had to be up in position and updated on the latest intel. Still no word if Tehrazzi was there, but these were definitely his men. He had strong ties with the locals in this part of Syria, through blood and the threat of shedding it. Murdering civilians tended to be an even better motivator than U.S. greenbacks. Luke's team wouldn't get any help from the villagers there.

"Forecast still calling for snow?"

"Yes," she said bitterly. "Accumulation's going to

depend on the next front that's coming through. Wind speeds keep changing."

"We'll just have to wear plenty of layers." The chance that Tehrazzi might be holed up in one of the caves was reason enough to execute the op, but something had to be done about the stockpiled ammunition. No doubt that would come back to bite them all in the ass if they didn't destroy the weapons. "Air Force is going to drop some JDAMs in the area, see if they can't soften these guys up before we hit them." His stomach rumbled, grinding in protest because he hadn't eaten since... He couldn't remember when he'd last eaten.

Heading to the kitchen to search for leftovers, he hesitated when he heard Emily humming in there. Things between them were awkward enough without him compounding it, and he didn't want to add to her stress level. She was dealing with too much shit already.

"You might as well come in," she called out, and he hid a smile.

"How'd you know I was there?"

"My sixth sense kicked in."

Dressed in a cream knit sweater and snug jeans, Emily stood at the island kneading dough, her hands covered with it. The dark brown wig she wore was long, coming to her shoulders in waves, and it made her look almost as young as the day they'd met. She was still beautiful enough to tie him in knots. "Biscuits?"

"Yeah, I was in the mood for some." Her hands continued to work the dough, and since she was focused on that it gave him time to get a good look at her. Dark smudges lay beneath her eyes though she'd tried to cover them with makeup, and she was still pale. He didn't like the flush that rode on her cheekbones or the hollows beneath them. His immediate instinct was to go over and put a hand on her forehead, but he held himself in check. He didn't want to make her even more uncomfortable.

"You running a fever?" he asked instead.

She looked up, and her vivid green eyes were slightly glazed. "A little one. No big deal."

Dammit, why wasn't she taking better care of herself? She'd just had a frigging chemo treatment. She should be in bed, or at least lying down someplace with a blanket on her to stop the chills. "Should you be making biscuits right now?" He kept his voice even, but he caught the answering spark of anger in her eyes.

"I feel much better than I did after the first treatment. Besides, I'm tired of lying around and wanted something to do. I'm used to keeping busy, and it helps pass the time."

That's how she'd always coped with stress, by puttering and cleaning. She always needed a project to work on, as though having a physical task to complete helped keep her mind occupied. Crossing to the island, he sat on a stool at the far end to give her some space. "I know this isn't easy on you." And it was getting increasingly hard on him, too.

Rather than answer him, she tossed some flour on the granite surface and began rolling out the dough with practiced ease. "These'll be ready for the oven in a minute," she said. "You can stay and have some if you want."

The tentative overture almost broke his heart because the offer wasn't merely an effort to be polite, though Em didn't have it in her to be rude. She was trying to ignore all the unfinished business that lay between them, plus she was worried as hell about him finishing this mission. He hated leaving her to face everything on her own, but she wasn't letting him in and he couldn't stay behind on this one.

He waited in silence while she cut the biscuits out

with the rim of a glass and arranged them in a pan before brushing them with melted butter. It had been so long since he'd seen Em at work in the kitchen that he'd forgotten how much he enjoyed watching her. She seemed much more relaxed when she popped them into the oven and set about cleaning up that he didn't dare break the spell by speaking or offering a hand. She wouldn't let him help anyway.

She'd never know how much it had meant to him when she'd asked him to stay with her during her treatment. The whole time he'd sat in the chair watching her, he'd ached to pull her into his arms and cradle her while she slept. But he hadn't.

Em was wiping the already gleaming countertop for the second time when the timer went off. She exhaled almost in relief and pulled them out, and the heavenly scent had his mouth watering. She slid a few onto a plate and set it in front of him. "Want some butter?"

"No, this is perfect." The tentative truce between them was starting to grate on his nerves. There was so much left unsaid and too many questions filling his head. What he'd said to her out by the pool was merely the surface of what he needed to. He chewed his biscuit slowly, savoring the familiar, delicious flavor. Maybe he should just get this over with and put it out in the open once and for all. Like lancing an infected wound. He watched her carefully controlled expression as he ate his second biscuit, the warm, fluffy layers melting on his tongue. "These are great, Em."

"Thanks," she said without looking up, concentrating on her food. She barely picked at it. Was she uncomfortable about how exposed she'd been a few hours ago? Or was she feeling sick to her stomach? His fingers itched to reach out and touch her flushed cheek and see how hot it was. He suspected she felt a hell of a lot worse than she let on, but at least she was attempting to eat so maybe the nausea wasn't bothering her as much as it had the first time. His gaze lowered to her chest, the outline of her breasts beneath the heavy knit of her sweater. Had she had a reconstruction done or was she wearing a prosthetic bra? He hadn't asked her and wasn't about to now.

Emily swallowed the last bite of her biscuit before glancing at him, and the impact of her gaze hit him like a bullet to the heart. "So. How are things...coming?"

"Operationally speaking?"

She nodded. "Any good news?"

"Some. We're following up on some leads right now, but we'll know more when I'm on the ground tomorrow."

Her shoulders tensed. "You're going out tomorrow?"

"Maybe sooner."

"Oh." She lowered her lashes, picking at one of the biscuits. "For...for how long do you think?"

"Not sure. Couple days, maybe."

"By yourself?" She pushed the plate away as though she'd suddenly lost her appetite.

"No, with Rhys and another team." When she nodded and started plucking at her cuffs, something she always did when she was agitated, he wanted to reach for her. "I'll be fine, Em."

She nodded again, an anxious frown creasing her pale brow.

He knew she was thinking of all the times he'd deployed on a mission without being able to tell her where he was or when he might be back. This time the mission wasn't classified and at least she'd have an idea of where he was. Not that he could tell her everything, but he could tell her more than he used to. Damn, he didn't want to leave her now. Especially not after this afternoon. "It'll be different this time. Sam and Ben will be monitoring everything, so they'll be able to reach me if something comes up."

"And update me if something happens to you?"

His heart squeezed painfully. She was scared for him, and he didn't want that. He didn't want to cause her any more worry. "Nothing's going to happen to me. I'm too mean and stubborn to die." The second he said it she went white beneath her fevered flush and he cursed. "I just meant—"

"God, I can't believe I'm doing this again," she muttered, tilting her head back to look up at the ceiling. "It's like I've been thrown back in time." Her lashes fluttered when she blinked fast, and it hurt Luke that she battled tears.

Because she still cared that much about him. Even now. The knowledge burned like a red-hot coal beneath his sternum.

She shook her head, the ends of the long wig swinging around her shoulders. "I swore I'd let you go."

A deep ache settled in the middle of his chest. "Em..."

Her head righted, and the pain in her eyes stabbed him. "You wanted me to be more authentic, right? That's what you meant earlier. You hated that I put on an 'everything's fine' front when you knew it wasn't. Well, careful what you wish for."

She seemed to be working up a head of steam, her anger rising palpably. He could only watch and wait to see what would happen.

A moment later she nailed him with that vivid green gaze. "You want to know what's really going on with me? Fine, here it is." She punched a forefinger into the air at him. "I want to forget you and move on, but I can't, not even now when I know I might only have a few months left. How pathetic is that? What's wrong with me that I can't let you go?"

*Aw, fuck.*

She didn't give him the chance to respond, just kept on with words that tore him up inside. "You'd think my heart would finally realize it's over, but it doesn't care. It doesn't care that you walked out and never came back, and it doesn't care that you don't love me anymore—" She covered her face with her hands.

Luke stood, pulse pounding in his ears. This was his penance. Having to watch her suffer and not be able to hold her or make it better. But the fight brewing was way overdue and she needed to get this out. Question was, how much should he tell her in return? If he spilled his guts now and something happened to him out there tomorrow, she'd be in even more agony than she already was. He owed her the truth, but could she handle that right now?

More importantly, could he afford to take the chance to wait?

"It would've been easier if you'd died," she told him as she lowered her hands, bottom lip trembling slightly. "At least then I could have grieved and learned to live with the loss eventually. But having you leave when I knew damn well you still loved me? How the hell was I supposed to live with that loss?" She tossed her head, cheeks alight with building anger along with the fever. "For God's sake, Luke, we barely ever fought because you weren't home enough for us to get on each other's nerves. You know what? I'd have loved the chance to *get* sick of you. Life as I knew it ended when you walked out."

Years of buried regret, love and anger rose up in a dark tide. Pushing out a ragged breath, he shook his head. "I gave you every chance to make a new life and find someone that would make you happy, but you wouldn't. Why, dammit?" The words were torn right out of his soul.

Her eyes glittered with fury. "Same reason I never

changed my last name or signed those damned divorce papers you had your lawyer send me. I wasn't ready to give up." The suppressed rage pulsed around her like an aura. "Too bad you weren't man enough to stick around and fight for us," she flung out. "But oh wait, I forgot—you only do that for your country, so I guess Rayne and I didn't count."

He was around the island and facing off with her without even being conscious of moving. Of all the things she could have said, that was the worst. "You'd rather I'd stayed after what I did? I almost slit your throat!" Their gazes clashed.

"Sometimes I wish you *had*."

He reeled back, a cold wave sweeping over him. "What?"

A fresh sheen of tears glistened in her beautiful eyes. "If I'd known then that you'd never come back, if not for Rayne I would rather have died than go through the next twenty years without you."

He couldn't believe she'd said that. It horrified him that she'd ever thought it. "Christ, you don't know what you're saying."

"Is that right? Well, what about your lofty statement you left me because you wanted me to find happiness? Like some pathetic version of 'if you love something set it free'? That's bullshit, and you know it." She thrust her finger at him. "You left because you were too frigging scared to face what was happening to you, and because you didn't know how to handle it. You thought I'd just move on and find someone else? For God's sake, Luke, it took me over nine years to date anyone, and the first time I slept with him I cried the whole time."

Every muscle in his body stretched taut, ready to snap. "Did he hurt you?" The words came out a low growl.

Emily threw him a look of disgust. "No he didn't *hurt*

me. I cried because it wasn't *you*. Even after all that time I still felt like I was cheating on you. After that horror show, I didn't date anyone until Alex."

He covered a flinch at her ex's name. "I know he treated you well." He almost strangled on the words. He'd been so sure she'd marry the guy and settle down again, much as that would have ripped his guts out. Being a wife and mother was what Em had been born to do. "Why did you break it off?"

"Because I didn't love him, and it wasn't fair to keep him hanging. So there's my love life over the past twenty years, Luke. What about yours?"

Her question threw him. "What about mine?"

Em folded her arms across her chest and glared at him. "Yeah, how many women have you slept with since me, Luke? I'll bet it's more than two."

He gripped the edge of the countertop until his knuckles ached, fighting the need to roar his response. Did she expect him to admit he'd screwed his way through a long list of women he couldn't even remember the names and faces of? Not frigging likely. "What the hell does it matter now?"

"It matters," she said venomously, "because it proves how easy it was for you to get over me."

Fuck this. "You think it was *easy* for me? That I just flipped some sort of fucking switch and turned my feelings off?"

"Yes."

The haughty eyebrow she raised set his blood boiling. "I regret what I did every single day of my life," he said through clenched teeth, "but I knew leaving was best for you and Rayne."

Her shrill laugh was full of disbelief. "You did *not* just say that to me."

Luke folded his arms and glared right back. "I didn't want to hurt you anymore, can't you see that? It hurt you every time I went on a mission or a training exercise, let alone when I was home and you having to be afraid your husband might come after you with a knife. I didn't want you to have that kind of life. Rayne, either."

"It wasn't your place to make that choice for us." Her voice shook. "I was prepared to deal with long absences and watch CNN every day in case it might tell me where you were. I was prepared to deal with all the baggage that came along with being married to a SEAL officer. I was even prepared for the fact I might lose you to combat or training, but I was *not* prepared for you walking away because you didn't want me anymore."

"Not *want* you?" The tenuous hold he had over his temper snapped. He stalked over and grabbed her hand, ignoring her gasp as he brought it to cover the aching length of the growing erection straining against the fly of his jeans. "*Wanting* you was never the problem."

They were both breathing hard, bodies caught up in the maelstrom of sexual hunger and the pain they'd suffered for too long. Then Emily wrapped her fingers around the length of him and squeezed. "This isn't what I'm talking about. I meant *this*," she cried, laying her other palm over his heart.

"So did I," he fired back, wanting to back her up against the sink and kiss her until she couldn't breathe, then tear her clothes off and bury his throbbing cock inside her. "Because with you, they're connected." There, he'd finally said it. "I'm *not* over you, and I never will be. Got that?"

Em sucked in a breath, shock igniting the depths of her eyes. "Then why won't you—"

"Because I can't! I want it more than anything, but I *can't*." His heart tried to pound its way out of his chest as he tore away from her. "I have to finish this mission, and until I do I can't give you what you deserve."

"Yes, you can."

The aching whisper undid him, had him wrapping his arms around her back, bringing their bodies flush against each other as he stared down into her eyes. "I don't want to hurt you again, Em." But he was so scared of losing her if he didn't act.

"Then don't." Her answer was so simple it broke his heart.

He closed his eyes, praying for strength. When he opened his mouth to tell her he still loved her, voices from the hall stopped him. He turned his head and when Rhys saw him holding Emily he stopped so fast Neveah smacked into him.

"What the hell, Rhys," Nev grumbled as she tried to push past him. Rhys stopped her by throwing an arm out and corralling her into his side.

Her eyes went wide when she saw them. "Oh. Sorry."

"You looking for me?" Luke asked as he released Emily.

Rhys nodded. "Sam needs you. Something new just came in."

"I'll be there in a minute."

A few awkward seconds passed while Nev and Rhys did an about face and headed back the way they'd come. With the moment for life-altering declarations gone, Luke stepped back and thanked God he hadn't completely laid his heart on the line.

When he didn't make a move to touch her again, Emily turned away and put her arms around her waist. "You should lie down for a bit," he told her. "I have to take care of this."

She nodded, every line of her body radiating defeat. "Sure."

Feeling like he was ripping off his own skin, Luke walked away for what seemed like the thousandth time.

# Chapter Eight

That night after dinner, Emily was too tired to visit with the girls, so she headed upstairs.

"Hey, wait up," Nev called, jogging after her.

She waited at the top of the stairs, and when Nev grabbed her hand, followed her into one of the guest baths. The elegant chandelier threw off a warm light that made the white marble floors and vanity glow.

"Got something for you," Nev said. She pulled a drawer on the vanity open and withdrew a small paper bag, and when Emily opened it her eyes popped wide.

*Oh my God.* "Lube?"

Nev gave an amused laugh. "Just in case."

Emily stared at her, her face flaming. She didn't have any idea how to respond.

Nev shrugged. "After I saw you two in the kitchen, I thought it might be a good idea because of the side effects of the chemo," she said in her matter-of-fact way. "You're already blushing, so do you want me to go into this more?"

"*No*."

Nev let out a strangled chuckle. "Well, like I said,

just in case. Have a good night." She winked.

Standing alone in the bathroom, Emily closed her eyes on a hard sigh. So everyone else could see the sparks between her and Luke too. She hadn't seen him since that confrontation in the kitchen because he'd been holed up in Jamul's study and hadn't even come out to eat.

Her body still tingled all over when she remembered the heat in his eyes as he'd stalked toward her. And when he'd grabbed her hand and pressed it against—

*Nope. Not going there.*

Crushing the paper bag in her hand, she turned off the light and went to her bedroom, passing Luke's along the way. She had the fleeting thought she should climb into his bed and wait for him, and see what he'd do about it. But she quickly came to her senses. He'd probably stay downstairs all night working, so that would be a waste of time. And why should she be the one to make that move? If he wanted her just as badly, this time it should be up to him.

Closing her bedroom door behind her, she turned on the bedside lamp and went into the bathroom to undress, keeping that light off. She didn't want to see the disfiguring scars where her right breast had been as she removed the prosthetic bra, or the IV port plugged into her subclavian vein beneath her right collarbone. She hated looking at all of it, and her background as a nurse didn't make it any easier to bear. Sometimes she regretted her decision not to have a reconstruction done, but at the time she'd been thoroughly sick of hospitals and uninterested in undergoing another surgery. She'd been more worried about getting rid of the cancer than she had about her appearance. Besides, she could do it at some point in the future if she wanted.

*If you survive.*

Blocking the oily whisper in her head, she pulled on

her favorite pale pink nightie and walked across the cream, silk carpet to the bed. Pulling back the thick down duvet and sliding in, she eyed the paper bag she'd left on the nightstand.

*You don't have the guts.*

No, she didn't. She couldn't stand to make herself that vulnerable to Luke again, and cringed at the thought of him seeing her naked. How sexy was she right now? One breast carved away, wearing a wig, brows penciled on with cosmetics, and having to use lube because the chemo dried her out even more than the total hysterectomy had. Yum, what a prize.

Rolling onto her side she flipped the lamp off and shut her eyes, going over the fight she'd had with Luke earlier, analyzing his words. *I'm not over you, and I never will be.* He'd seemed so sincere when he'd said it. Was he really staying away because of his job, or was he using that as an excuse? Not that it mattered. Point was, he intended to keep his distance, regardless of his feelings for her.

Yet the more she thought about it, the more pissed off she got. Her time was running out, and he was going on a mission into hostile territory tomorrow. Just how many chances did he think they were going to get to be together in this lifetime? She lay there stewing about it until someone came up the stairs. Her heart tripped, but the footsteps passed by her room and the door to Rhys and Neveah's room closed. Soon after, heavier treads followed, but they too passed by and carried on to next door. Rhys, joining Neveah. His deep voice seeped through the wall between their rooms, and a husky feminine laugh followed. Then everything got quiet and there was no doubt as to the reason why.

She was about to get up and go back down to watch a movie with Bryn when she heard someone else coming up the stairs. The treads came down the hallway, slowing as they approached her room, then stopped in front of it. All her muscles tensed and she held her breath. Seconds ticked past while her gaze stayed locked on the doorknob, waiting for it to turn. Willing it to. But the steps went in the other direction instead, and a few moments later a door shut down the hall. Luke. Had to be, since Bryn was staying in her father's old room at the opposite end of the hall. Sighing, Emily flopped onto her back. He'd walked away yet again.

Disappointment gave way, transforming into resentment. She lay in the darkness, alone, while Nev and Rhys made love in the next room and Luke remained alone in his on the other side of the wall. He'd be in the shower, because he never went to bed without showering first, and though things might have changed over the years, she was sure they hadn't changed *that* much. Images of his naked, muscular body beneath the spray of water had her squirming around an ache of arousal until she wanted to snarl in frustration. This was exactly why she hadn't wanted to come here. She was going to go insane before this was over.

When the blue digital display of the clock on her nightstand flipped to two in the morning, Emily gave up any hope of sleeping and turned on the bedside lamp. *To hell with this*, she thought, riding a wave of anger as she ripped open the bag and grabbed the bottle of lube. She might feel less than sexy, but she was still a woman and still had needs of her own. Life was too damn short to waste an opportunity to be with Luke because of insecurity and hurt feelings. Once again, it was up to her to reach out.

Fine. She couldn't stand leaving things this way between them for another minute anyway. Something had to give. Maybe once this happened she'd be at peace, or be able to get some closure. Something.

Pausing at her door, she smoothed the wig into place

and quietly turned the handle, careful not to make any noise as she stepped into the hall and tiptoed to Luke's room. She felt ridiculous for having to sneak around like she was doing something illegal, but she didn't want an audience for this. Facing him was hard enough without drawing anyone else's attention. Especially if he turned her down and she had to slink back to her room in a few minutes.

A moment's indecision hit her when she stood in front of his door, and she lowered the hand she'd raised to knock. She wasn't going to knock, for God's sake. She was going to march in there and take what she wanted. Tossing her hair back, body humming with anticipation and desire, she turned the knob and pushed the door open, striding into the room as if she belonged there. Which she did. Her rightful place was with Luke, even if he was determined to fight the idea of them being together.

"Em?" Luke sat up in bed, the covers falling to his waist and revealing the mouth-watering contours of his muscled chest and arms. She stalled out halfway to him, growing unsure of herself under the intensity of his gaze. "You okay?"

"Yes." Her voice was hoarse and tentative instead of full of authority like she wanted it to be.

In the soft light coming through the filmy drapes, his eyes glowed like agates as he stared at her.

Breaking free of the paralysis holding her, Emily prowled toward him. She might not have control over her life or what was happening to her body, but she damn well was going to have control over this, even if for only one night. Right now she was going to take care of business on *her* terms.

He must have sensed the predatory vibe coming from her because his eyes flared and a muscle jumped in his lean, bearded jaw. "Something on your mind?"

"I don't want to talk," she informed him, pleased when his brows rose in surprise. *That's right. I'm not here to answer any of your questions.* He sat up even further as she reached the bed, the muscles in his arms and shoulders tensing. Good. She wanted him on edge, wondering what she would do.

Before she could over think the situation, she leaned against the edge of the mattress, took his gorgeous face between her hands and kissed him. Luke sucked in a sharp breath and pulled back, but she held on and kissed him harder, deeper, sliding her tongue into his mouth. He broke away.

"Em—"

"Shut up," she muttered, furious and desperate, and sealed their lips together once more. This time he responded, his hands sliding up her back and into her wig. Though she couldn't feel his fingers in the strands, she felt the pressure of his hands against her scalp and that was all she needed because it told her how much he wanted her. The pressure increased as he leaned up and brought her closer, trying to take over, but she wouldn't allow it. Not this time. Tonight, *she* ran the show. And she proved it by nipping at his full lower lip and breaking his hold.

Luke's head jerked back and he stared at her, chest rising and falling with rapid breaths. She ran her hands through his thick hair and buried her face in his throat, relishing his clean masculine scent and the frantic beat of his pulse. Soap, dark spices and aroused male. The smells that haunted her dreams.

Broad hands traveled up her back, his arms holding her gently. So strong and warm. He nuzzled her temple. "Tell me what do you want, Em."

She drew in another deep lungful of his scent and exhaled slowly. "You." That's all she'd ever wanted.

Before he could answer she kissed him again, slower

this time. Slow enough to savor the exquisite softness of his lips and the brush of his beard against her skin. The silky softness of the inside of his mouth and the velvet nap of his caressing tongue. The lingering hint of spearmint from his toothpaste.

The throb of arousal grew to a hot ache that centered low in her belly and between her thighs, shocking in its ferocity. Sliding her hands down his neck to his wide shoulders, Emily followed the path with kisses, gliding her lips over his smooth skin while she reacquainted herself with each curve and line of his powerful physique. She could feel the sheer strength of him pulsing beneath her touch. Her tongue darted out to glide over his collarbone, then lower over the pad of his pec to the flat, deep bronze nipple in the center. Rubbing her cheek against him, feeling the pounding of his heart, she licked it.

Luke hissed and grabbed her head but she shook free and kept going with her sensual exploration. Apparently done with being passive, he seized her waist and swung his legs around to the side of the bed so that his feet touched the floor. She braced herself against his chest and pushed back, shaking her head. After a tense second he let go, watching her with blazing eyes. The sheet was pushed down to his hips now, so she trailed a hand down his chest and over his clenched abdomen, over his tensed thighs to lightly brush over his rock hard erection straining against the thin covering. It kicked against her hand, but he didn't move otherwise. The silence expanded, magnifying the heated rush of their breath.

Closing her eyes, Emily rested her forehead against his sternum and wrapped her hand around the length of him, squeezing and stroking until a deep rumble of pleasure came out of his chest. She felt the vibrations against her cheek and smiled in satisfaction. She would have him writhing and begging before she took him, she vowed, releasing him to peel back the sheet in a slow, teasing manner. Then she went to her knees before him.

Giving herself a few inches of space to look up at him, the breath caught in her lungs. His chest rose and fell with rapid breaths, those dark eyes glittering down at her. Below the ridged outline of his abs, his thick penis lay stretched out across his belly, dark and swollen with need. Oh God, she needed him. More than he knew.

But when she nuzzled her way down his abs, Luke took hold of her head and stopped her. When he spoke, his voice was deeper than normal, ragged. "Em, don't force this. You don't need to—"

Ignoring him, she curled her fingers around his and pulled them free of her head. She wasn't nauseated from the chemo treatment, which was a miracle in itself. She was going to make the most of that right now. Placing his hands on the bed on either side of his hips, she pressed on them so he understood she didn't want him to interfere with this. This was about pleasure; his to receive and enjoy, and hers to give. She needed him like this. Raising her eyes, she let him see both her hunger and her entreaty. In answer Luke's nostrils flared, something dark and knowing entering his eyes. But he left his hands where she'd placed them, giving his silent consent.

Taking the beautiful, hard length of him in her hand, she let her other caress his inner thighs and gently trail over his scrotum. He inhaled sharply. Her breathing grew ragged along with his, her body preparing itself to take him deep inside and hold him there, finally, after all these years. A shudder ran through her at the thought.

"Baby," he whispered, breaking her request to keep his hands on the mattress as he stroked her hot cheek with questioning fingertips.

Emily closed her eyes and leaned into him, resting her head on his thigh as she stroked him from base to tip, base to tip, then swirling gently around the head with her fist until his low growl shot around the room. Beckoned by the rising need she sensed in him, she lowered her head and rubbed the hot velvet length of him with her cheek. He pulsed beneath her touch, thigh muscles twitching beneath her palms. *Yes,* she thought as she nuzzled him more. This was how she wanted him. Hungry. Waiting. Wondering if she would take him in her mouth.

Rubbing him gently with her face, she dared to look up into his eyes. Staring down at her with naked longing, he brought his hand to her nape and cradled the back of her neck as he shifted forward on the edge of the mattress and spread his thighs. She was caught in the dark depths of his eyes, unable to look away.

Holding her gaze, he lifted his hips in a subtle motion and rubbed the head of his engorged cock against her lips. She licked her lips, swiping away the silky drops that wept from the tip, salty on her tongue.

His long fingers contracted ever so slightly around her nape, holding her in place. “Suck me, Em,” he rasped, half command and half desperate plea.

Everything in her went hot and soft. *God.* He knew exactly what he was doing to her with that display of tender dominance. She’d always found it sexy as hell. He knew precisely what turned her on and how much to push her to increase her excitement. Kneeling before him in this submissive posture while still having control sent a thrill coursing through her.

Staring into his eyes, she parted her lips and pressed a tender kiss to the glistening tip of his cock, loving the way he jerked in her grasp. He lifted against her again, a silent plea, and she tenderly slid her tongue around the head, tasting the salt and the heat of him. Luke drew in a harsh breath and clenched his jaw. She teased him with tiny flicks, feathering over the sensitive spot beneath the tip and down the shaft, underneath to his sac. Flattening her tongue, she gave him a slow, gentle stroke that made him moan out loud and widen his thighs while she leisurely pumped him with her fist. Nestling deeper between his trembling legs, she let her eyes close and got lost in the bliss of pleasing him.

The pressure on the back of her neck increased subtly. “Suck me, baby.” His voice was ragged, pleading.

*Yes.* Her heart thundered in her chest. She’d fantasized about this forever.

Moving upward, she opened her lips and closed her mouth around the plump head, applying tender suction as she twirled her tongue in a slow circle. A low, agonized moan ripped from Luke and his head fell back, every muscle in his magnificent body drawn taut, his back arching while he fought to keep from shoving deeper into her mouth. She felt the pressure of his hands on her head and knew he clenched his fists in the wig. Tears burned the backs of her eyes as she pleasured him, but she refused to let them fall. She was going to savor every second of this time with him, milk every bit of enjoyment from it.

“Oh, God, baby, that feels so good,” he groaned. “Yeah, right there…” The words dissolved into a delicious moan.

A soft whimper issued from her own throat, her body pulsing with desire. She loved him with her mouth for long minutes until he was panting and his skin was damp with sweat. But then he took hold of her head in both hands and gently pulled her away.

Blinking up at him, she met Luke’s stare. The wild, desperate pleasure was there for her to see in his molten eyes and the tense lines of his expression.

“Come up here and take me,” he said, his voice hoarse with need and erotic promise. His hands tugged at her gently.

She hesitated.

His thumbs rubbed her temples. “Are you sore inside?”

Swallowing, she shook her head. Early menopause and the chemo’s side effects had dried her out, but didn’t have any sores like she’d had after the first treatment. That’s not what was holding her back. The thought of him seeing her scars—that was enough to kill any tingles of pleasure she’d been feeling. She didn’t want him to see her body, and wasn’t sure she could take him inside her even with the lube. The little bottle lay cool against the flushed skin of her right calf. It was humiliating to have to use it so she could have sex with him, especially when she was more thoroughly aroused than she’d been in forever.

“Want a condom?”

She stiffened. God, she’d been so caught up in what they were doing that she’d completely forgotten to consider that he’d been with other women since her. No doubt numerous ones. She forced the thought away and found her voice. “Do we need one?”

Luke’s touch was gentle on her face. “Would I have let you go down on me if we did?” He shook his head. “I’m clean.”

She let out the breath she’d been holding. *Thank God.* “Then we don’t need one.” Gathering her resolve, she reached down and picked up the lube before rising to her feet, hunching her shoulders a bit so her missing breast wouldn’t be as obvious beneath her thin nightgown. Why hadn’t she thought to wear her robe?

Her legs shook and her hands were unsteady when she reached for his shoulders to balance herself. Luke took hold of her waist and lifted her effortlessly as he leaned up for a slow, sensual kiss, arranging her thighs on either side of his hips. The ridge of his erection pressed against her abdomen through the thin satin she wore, hard and searing hot. With one hand he took the bottle from her, and she felt the blush of embarrassment staining her face.

"It's the chemo," she explained in a whisper, cringing at how unsexy she felt. She didn't want to ruin the moment, but she wanted to make sure he understood it wasn't his fault she wasn't wet. "It's not that I don't want you—"

"Shhh," he soothed against her lips, gliding his hands over the satin covering the small of her back. "It's okay. I'll take care of you."

Her lower belly tightened in reflex. He would. Luke could and absolutely would see to her pleasure, but that's not how she wanted this to go. She was too nervous to enjoy what he might do to her anyway, and besides, this was for him. Her pleasure was going to come from ensuring his. She couldn't wait.

Pushing at his shoulders, she took the bottle from him as he lay back against the pillows and scooted up so she'd have better access to him. Trying to cover the awkward lapse she'd caused, she uncapped the thing and went to pour some of the clear liquid into her hand but Luke took her wrist and held out his other palm instead. It pooled in the center of his hand and she could only watch, mesmerized by the sight of that broad palm as it wrapped around the swollen length of him, strong fingers curling around the shaft, surrounding it with a seductive caress.

Her mouth went dry when he dragged his fist over himself, up and down, squeezing with firm pressure in a slow, hypnotic caress. His swollen cock was all shiny, the quiet, slick sounds of his hand moving over it sending another wave of heat through her. When she glanced up into his face, his eyes smoldered as he watched her reaction, completely uninhibited in his sexual response. Unembarrassed by his body and his desire for her.

Like the sensual creature he was, he lowered his eyelids until he looked up at her through his lashes, and really got into it. A few seconds into the incredible show she tried to replace his hand with her own, but he shook his head, knowing it would drive her nuts, and groaned roughly when he twisted his fist around the head of his slippery cock. He kept it up until she panted along with him, a tidal wave of desire roaring beneath her skin, building the ache between her thighs to a relentless pitch. She was ready to jump him when he finally released his cock, baring the slick, glistening length of him to her rapt gaze as he lifted his fathomless eyes to hers. She gazed back, helpless under the power of that stare.

"Ride me, Em." The low, velvet command made her shiver.

Moving without conscious thought, she slid up to straddle his hips. She gasped as she settled the hot, pulsing length of him against her bare folds and rubbed gently, lubricating her tender flesh. He reached for the hem of her nightgown, but she immediately grabbed his hands. "No." She didn't want him seeing her.

"I want to look at you."

She shook her head. She couldn't handle that yet. All she wanted was to hold him inside her while she took him to the absolute pinnacle of ecstasy. To steal this time with him and hold onto the memory of it in the hard days and weeks ahead.

Reaching down between them, she seized his rigid flesh in one hand and stood him up, bringing the thick head against her entrance. Luke gripped her hips to steady her and she sank down slowly, carefully, allowing her body to stretch around the blunt invasion. A soft moan escaped at the scalding heat of him pressing deep inside, but she took him without pain, easing down until his entire length was buried in her. Seated above him, fully connected with him, a rush of emotion hit her and brought a stinging lump to her throat. She'd ached for this for so damn long. She could hardly believe it was happening.

Beneath her, Luke growled low in his throat and gripped her hips tighter, his head tipping back in pleasure. Rising up on her knees, she laid her palms on his hard pecs and lowered her body again, watching his face. His jaw tensed, mouth tightening as she worked him, eyes locked on hers. The grip on her hips eased, then he reached up to her throat, trailing his fingertips down the sides to her shoulders and over her collarbones—

Like a bucket of ice water, the touch made her freeze. She seized his hands. "*No*," she said emphatically, ready to jump off him if he touched the port or her scars.

"Baby, let me touch you—"

"Don't." She pushed his hands away, pinning them to the bed.

Frustration glittered in his eyes, but he didn't break her hold, allowing her the illusion of control. "I want to touch you."

*No, you don't.* "I don't want you to. Just this," she whispered, bending to kiss him as she began moving her hips again. "Please, I need just this."

Suppressing a growl of irritation, Luke lay back against the sheets and let her move how she wanted. With the threat of him seeing her scars behind them, Emily focused on making love to him, tightening her body around him as she rocked and undulated. The incredible heat and friction of it sent tiny ripples of pleasure echoing through her, and soon she had him at the same place she'd taken him to while he was in her mouth; panting, muscles twitching, head kicking back into the pillow. So incredibly beautiful she could have wept.

His hands crept up to her hips and then to her waist, fingers biting into her flesh. “Goddamn, Em,” he moaned, lifting into her rhythm. “It’s so good, don’t stop...”

No, she wouldn’t stop. Not until he was helpless with pleasure, then she’d pause for a few moments to let him wonder if she would leave him that way before riding him fast and hard until he exploded inside her.

Currents of pleasure zinged over her skin, the ache in her body increasing. As though he sensed it, Luke’s hands caressed her through the satin nightgown, over her stomach and hips to her thighs, moving lower to where the hem kissed her bare skin. She wavered at the tingling sensation his fingertips wrought. Her body craved his touch, her clit throbbing, begging for attention. She gasped at the erotic caress as his fingers slipped beneath the edge to tease the sensitive skin of her inner thighs, higher, moving slowly toward where she ached so badly, to her flesh slicked by the lubricant.

“So good, Em,” he groaned, surging gently beneath her, filling her perfectly, stretching and caressing the delicate nerve endings inside her. She parted her thighs more, leaning back as she opened to him, her eyes drifting closed as the incredible, unexpected pleasure built. She hadn’t thought she’d want this, but now she was desperate for it.

His fingers trailed higher, so close. Inches away from where she was dying to be touched. “Luke...” He would take care of her. He wanted to. She was already so aroused one touch was all it might take for her to come.

“Yeah, open for me just like that,” he coaxed. She was trembling, caught in the spell they’d woven, frantic for his touch and the unbelievable pleasure it would bring. Her internal muscles clenched in anticipation and he sucked in a breath, his jaw clenching, almost there—

Someone knocked on the door.

Emily froze, a cry of denial locked in her throat. Please say she'd imagined that sound.

Then, "Luke?" The loud whisper was muffled by the door.

A mortified gasp came out of her. Luke's hands tightened on her hips, but she yanked them away and slid off him. His head snapped toward the door with a frustrated growl while she frantically straightened her nightgown and backed away from the bed.

"What?" he snarled, yanking the sheets over his lap.

The knob turned and Bryn stuck her head in. "Sorry, but I can't find Emily. She's not in her room and she's not downstairs—"

"She's right here," he bit out.

A shocked silence filled the room. Even in the darkness Emily saw her friend's eyes widen when she noticed her standing by the bed. "Oh, God," Bryn muttered. "Sorry." Then she disappeared from view and shut the door fast.

Luke flopped down onto his back and rubbed a hand over his face with an aggravated sigh. Looking over at her, he gave her a rueful smile. "Any chance we can pretend that interruption never happened and pick up where we left off?"

It took a moment for his words to register through the haze of mortification because all the blood had rushed out of her brain into her face. Feeling like an idiot, she crossed her arms over her lopsided chest and stared at him. "I'm sorry."

"Don't be sorry." He lifted an arm in invitation, the muscles in it rippling as he moved. "Come back over here and I'll make you forget—" He didn't get the chance to finish because his cell phone rang. His arm hit the bed with a thud. "God dammit," he snapped, rolling to his side to grab it from his nightstand. For the first time she noticed the gun laying there, and had no doubt it was loaded.

She swallowed as he checked the number during the third ring. It stopped, presumably going to voicemail, but she already knew their time together was at an end. People didn't call at this time of night—morning, rather—unless it was urgent.

Luke's eyes were full of regret when he looked back at her. "Em, I—"

He had to answer the call to duty. "It's all right, I understand." Her legs felt wooden as she started for the door. And her heart? She wasn't sure, but she suspected the crushing sensation in her chest was her heart realizing it was over. At the door, she stopped and turned around to face him. She wasn't leaving like this. Not like a coward.

Instead, she walked over to the bed and cupped his chin in one hand, then bent and kissed him with all the love and tenderness in her. When she pulled away he grabbed her wrist to hold her there, and she saw the fierce yearning mirrored in his gaze. "I wish I could stay."

A hesitant smile quivered on her lips. It was enough that she'd shown him how she felt, and to know that he wished things were different. "Be careful out there," she whispered. Because she was on the verge of tears she didn't give him the chance to reply, and rushed out of his room and down the hall to her own, where she crawled into her lonely bed and let silent tears flow into her pillow.

# Chapter Nine

*Kabul, Afghanistan*

"There's a problem."

Tehrazzi ignored the obvious stress in Abdu's voice and stared out the hotel room window into the crowded city streets below. A fine dusting of snow covered the ground, nowhere near as much as had fallen in the mountains last night. He was happy to be in a warm room with indoor plumbing and fresh-smelling soap. "And that is?"

"We are risking exposure if we go forward with this. Davis is getting suspicious already. He's asking too many questions and I don't think he believes my answers."

"Imagine that." It didn't surprise Tehrazzi in the least. His teacher was the best and, therefore, only worked with the best. For Davis to have attained the position of right-hand-man, he would have to be every bit as formidable as his teacher. Tehrazzi and his men would simply have to act more carefully from here on out.

"What if he finds out about us?"

He suppressed an irritated sigh. Davis would, it was only a matter of when. In a few hours Tehrazzi would board a helicopter waiting to take him to the place where he would begin the hunt for his teacher. Time was running out. He didn't have the patience to deal with any more "problems".

The cell phone on the table behind him rang. He glanced at Abdu for a moment before giving him permission to answer it. The phone was secure. They couldn't track his location with it, and though they needed him to draw out his teacher and kill him, Tehrazzi wasn't naive enough to believe the young go-between wouldn't sell him out.

No. When he left this life, it would be on *his* terms. His, and no one else's.

Abdu answered it, and finally said, "What do you want me to do?"

Tehrazzi watched the younger man's face as he spoke to the contact on the other end. He was agitated, kept running his free hand through his freshly washed hair. "He wants to talk to you," he finally said, holding out the phone.

Tehrazzi shook his head. "No." He was far too paranoid to talk to the man personally. Using Abdu as a liaison was as close as he wanted to get. Abdu gave him a long-suffering look and went back to his conversation. When he hung up, his eyes were tormented. "So what am I supposed to do now?"

"Take care of it."

Abdu ran his hands through his hair again. "That's what he just said."

No doubt. Because the man on the other end of that phone call wouldn't want loose ends left to trip them up any more than they did. "Everything's already in place. Now we must execute the operation discussed."

His choice of wording wasn't lost on Abdu. The man's eyes flinched, as though he had just realized he was in too deep to get out. Tehrazzi handed him a handwritten note he'd prepared in advance and smiled grimly. "I'm sure you'll think of something." The decision had already been made for him. And with it came a permanent solution.

****

Icy cold air rushed in through the Black Hawk's open door, hitting Luke in the face like an arctic blast despite the protective goggles he wore. Below the cruising helo, the stark Syrian desert spread out as far as the eye could see. Across from him, Rhys checked his equipment one last time.

"Good to go?" Luke asked him over the headset.

He glanced up from adjusting his assault vest, indigo eyes steely with resolve. "Yep."

"Thirty seconds," the pilot announced.

Rhys went back to checking his gear, then went onto one knee on the deck to secure the last holster around his left thigh. He was a deadly shot with both hands, but Rhys was obviously concerned about his perceived lack of coordination on his right side and wasn't taking any chances. As far as Luke was concerned, the only way someone could tell Rhys had been injured was by the scars on the right side of his head. As an operator Rhys was as good as they came, and though he might not be at a hundred percent in his own mind, Luke had absolute confidence in him.

The helo banked and descended fast, the rotors kicking up sand and gravel from the desert floor. Reaching out, Luke slapped Rhys's shoulder. "See you at seventeen-thirty if the weather holds." If not, they could be in for a long, cold night. Or several.

One corner of Rhys's mouth turned up in his version of a smile. "Roger that."

The moment the wheels touched down he jumped out and went into a defensive position while Luke covered him from the chopper. Satisfied the LZ was cold, Rhys took off in a loping run, his long legs eating up the ground, and Luke gave the pilot a thumbs-up. The pitch of the engine rose to a shrill whine as the pilot pulled back on the collective and took off into the clear, wintry sky. A patrolling AWACS forecasted possible flurries at the edge of the primary operational area with a chance of high winds, but Luke couldn't hold off because of the weather. Recent intel that Tehrazzi had been sighted near his grandparents' village was perishable, and they had to act before the trail went cold. And there was also Davis's call, which had cruelly killed any chance of finishing making love with Emily last night. Bastard.

Davis had uncovered suspicious evidence that Tehrazzi might be on someone's payroll at the CIA. Following up on it, they'd found regular, substantial amounts of U.S. currency had been funneled into an offshore account, and it carried all the earmarks of how Tehrazzi operated with his other financiers. At first Luke had refused to believe it, but after listening to Davis, he hadn't been so sure anymore. Was someone inside the Agency helping him? Wasn't Miller. He didn't have the balls to pull something like that. So who else could it be? Jamie had launched an internal investigation this morning, but had given the go ahead for the operation to follow up on the human intelligence report that Tehrazzi was in the isolated Syrian village.

If Tehrazzi was there, it wasn't to visit with dear old gram and gramps. He'd had his bodyguard decapitate them for leaking Bryn and her father's location back in September.

Settling back against the bulkhead, the aircraft's

rhythmic vibrations relaxed him while his mind kept busy. This could be it. This might finally be the day he made amends for what he'd done. He shouldn't let himself think farther ahead than that, but he couldn't help imagining the future he and Emily could have together. After last night he felt a renewed urgency to finish this so he could get on with living the life he'd denied himself for so many years. A life with her.

"Three minutes."

Luke opened his eyes at the pilot's warning and checked his watch. Once he landed, he had a three hour window to make it to the rendezvous point outside the village. There he'd link up with Rhys, Dec's SEALs, and Davis, who was transporting in from Kabul. Until then, they all had to get visual confirmation of enemy targets and relay coordinates for the Air Force to clear out some of the caves with their ordnance payloads. The SEALs had an Air Force combat controller with them, but thanks to their advanced training and skill sets, he and Rhys were almost as proficient in calling in air strikes on enemy positions.

Once on the ground, he tugged his scarf up further around his face to shield him from the wind as he made his way over the rugged terrain. Overhead the sky was an ominous gray, the clouds swirling and thickening with the promise of snow. So long as the wind stayed down and he could maintain reasonable visibility, he didn't much care.

Working his way toward the RV point, he kept out of sight while scanning for any sign of the enemy. Two hours in, the wind had picked up and the first fat snowflakes drifted down. He contacted Sam via the radio, keeping his voice low. "What's the status on the weather forecast?"

"Still iffy," she replied in her calm, steady voice. "Storm's starting to affect our visibility from the satellite feeds."

*Wonderful.* "I'm coming up on the first cave. ETA seven minutes."

"Roger that."

The wind stung his cheeks above the line of his beard. He thought about donning his cold weather gear, but held off. He needed to keep moving. Just over a klick away to the east, the first cave awaited him. Hidden behind a low rock formation, he pulled out his Leopold binoculars to get a better look. From this distance he could only make out the mouth of the cave, but there didn't seem to be any enemy targets guarding the entrance and he couldn't see any smoke that would indicate a warming fire. "Any heat signatures registering?"

"Affirmative," Sam responded. "Looks like five contacts around what could be a fire."

"Stand by." Holding his rifle at the ready, he crept to the base of a small cliff and climbed up to get a better look. Once at the top, he pulled out his map and compass to double check the location and took another peek at the network of caves with his high powered binoculars. The caves here might not be as intricate or as large as the ones in Afghanistan, but they could be just as deadly. He verified the bearing on his compass, and Rhys's deep voice came over the radio earpiece, saying he was in position and then relayed coordinates. Setting his binoculars aside, Luke added his own, then asked, "Anyone heard from Davis yet?"

"Negative," Sam answered, then Ben came on. "Cobra team is reporting enemy activity in their sector," he said. "Team leader has given coordinates for air strike. Aircraft standing by."

Dec and his SEALs. But it bothered Luke that Davis hadn't checked in yet. "Copy that. Scorpion One out." He got busy camouflaging himself amongst the rocks and maintained visual on the target, aiming an infrared laser at the cave's entrance while he transmitted the coordinates to the Air Force combat controller working with the SEALs. Somewhere above the thick cloud cover, a B52 bomber and an AC130 Spectre gunship patrolled, waiting for clearance to unleash their onboard arsenals. At the SEALs' location, the CCT would have the aircraft in a holding pattern until he called them in for the strike. Handy guys to have on a mission.

Sam came back on the radio. "Be advised, pilot has been cleared to drop his JDAMs."

"Roger that." Should be a hell of a show, he thought, huddling deeper into the crevice he lay in. The wind raked over him with icy claws, the temperature dropping with each minute. Snow fell in a filmy curtain, already accumulating on him and the ground. So much for any hope of the weather cooperating. Those bombers better drop their payloads before conditions worsened to the point when poor visibility and wind speed made the air strikes impossible. The minutes stretched out as he lay there shivering, his hands growing numb.

In the distance, streaks of light lit up the night sky, then a series of big, hard explosions shook the ground, the shockwaves rippling through the earth. Geysers of dirt and rock spewed up into the air near the SEALs' location. Any minute now Dec would lead his assault team down to take care of any enemy survivors in the area.

Another light show, then a massive set of explosions a few clicks away toward Rhys's position. Even at that distance the concussion pounded against Luke's eardrums and rattled his teeth. Shouts came from below as the men in the cave ran out to see what was happening. They pointed to the huge clouds of debris rising into the sky, their voices both awed and frightened. Luke held the laser steady and waited, bracing for the inevitable impact. Seconds later he caught the high-pitched scream of the 2,000 pound JDAMs and shielded his eyes from the incendiary flash.

The initial explosions knocked him backwards and slammed the breath from his lungs. The massive shockwaves blew out, hitting his body like a tidal wave, then a series of secondary explosions followed, telling him they'd hit the ammunition stores. Luke gritted his teeth and rode it out, the pressure squeezing his skull and ribs. In the sudden stillness that followed, his head rang, and it took a few moments to hear anything but the throb in his ears. Bits of debris rained down on him, covering him with dirt and pieces of gravel. Snatching out his binoculars, he checked the area. The cave was gone. All that remained was a black crater and the colossal tower of smoke boiling into the air. No sign of the enemy, and he wasn't surprised. JDAMs were goddamn powerful weapons.

"This is Scorpion One, confirming target destroyed."

"Roger that," Sam said. Rhys reported the same. "Cobra team leader confirms the same," Sam added, meaning Dec and his boys had taken care of business on their end.

Good. All they had to do was link up and clear out any remaining enemy forces. "Copy that. Checking target area now." Using the face of the cliff for cover, Luke got down the rock face as quick as he could and closed in on the smoking, blackened hole. There was nothing left. The only signs he found that anyone had been there were the torn pieces of clothing he passed, their owners blown out of them from the concussive force of the strike. Nothing moved around him, the only sound the crackle and snap of flames burning what was left of the cave and everything inside it. He found scorched mortar tubes and some twisted RPGs, but no other weapons. No sign of Tehrazzi, or whether he'd been there at all.

Stepping out into the open, the wind howled around him, stealing the breath from his lungs. Snow lashed at his face despite the scarf and goggles. Leaning forward to battle the force of the wind, Luke trudged onward. A few hundred meters outside the mouth of the cave, a blackened corpse lay on its back, startling white teeth standing out in its open mouth, like the man was screaming at heaven for allowing him to die this way.

*Sucks to be you, buddy.*

His radio crackled to life. "Signals interceptors report enemy radio transmissions confirming heavy casualties," Sam said. "Also, the aircraft are returning to base due to low visibility."

At least they'd been able to get the strikes in first. "Roger that. Moving to RV point now." If he could see, that is. He only had a few klicks to cover, but if this blizzard kept up it would take him half the night to make it there.

Minutes later his teeth chattered and his muscles shuddered in an effort of keep him warm. Already he couldn't feel his toes in his boots. The snow came down so thick it was like a white sheet. Turning his back to the wind, he pulled out his map and compass, though he was rapidly losing the ability to make out exactly where he was. Best he could do was head southwest toward the general vicinity of the RV point and hope the weather cleared up so he could find the rest of the team. As he stuffed the map into a pocket of his assault vest and started to pull out his cold weather gear, he caught the faint sound of nearby voices and got into firing position. He raised his rifle, finger ready on the trigger. He couldn't see shit right now, but someone was out there. Was there another cave out here they'd missed?

"Over there!" someone shouted in Arabic, the disjointed voice floating eerily out of the darkness.

Luke tensed. Had someone spotted him? Unwilling to take the chance that they hadn't, he edged closer to the cliff in the hopes of cutting the wind so he could hear better. Only the howling of the wind came back.

He keyed his radio. "Th-this is S-scorpion One."

Ben's voice came across loud and clear. "Go ahead."

"C-can you c-confirm enemy con—"

A sudden blast close to him knocked him to the ground. Cursing, he dropped the radio and covered his head while debris pelted him. When it was over, he raised his head and squinted into the darkness. He hadn't heard a goddamn thing, which could only mean one thing.

Someone had a good idea of his location and had fired a mortar round at him.

Shit. He hated mortars. Couldn't hear the fuckers coming, and if he ever did he was dead because it would be too late to get away.

Ben came back over the radio, asking for clarification, but Luke didn't answer. Last thing he needed was to break radio silence again and give his position away if the enemy was close enough to hear him.

Another round went off to his left, closer this time. It knocked him back into the rock hard enough that he let out a growl of pain. Two more landed near the same spot, in rapid succession. Luke's heart hammered in his chest. How the hell could they see him in this shit?

He couldn't move without being sighted, and no telling how many fighters were out there waiting to welcome him with a spray of bullets from their Kalashnikovs. Hating that he had no other option, Luke felt along the base of the cliff until he found an opening large enough for him to fit in, then dumped his heavy ruck and squeezed his body into it. He wedged himself in good and tight, the rocks digging cruelly into his flesh.

The wind shrieked through the crack he'd just come through, cutting into his body like icy knives. Every so often, more mortar rounds went off, shaking the cliff. No way Dec's team could reach him in this, and he wasn't going to get any help from the Air Force until the storm died down. For now he was stuck here alone in this freezing stone sarcophagus, but it was either this or get blown to hell.

Trapped in the cage of rock, he fought to calm his racing heart. He'd always hated being confined, especially in the dark. Probably due to how his father had locked him in the broom closet as punishment when he was a kid.

The blackness closed in on him, fueling the claustrophobia that threatened to suffocate him. Closing his eyes, he took slow, shallow breaths because his chest was squeezed too tight in the tiny space to get a full one. Back when he'd first joined the SEALs, the shrinks had informed the cadre of this deep seated fear, and they'd done everything humanly possible to capitalize on it in an effort to either get him past it, or make him ring out. SERE training had damn near killed him—two days and three nights shut up tight in a windowless room too small for him to lie down in. But when he'd come out he'd done everything he could to make them think he was unaffected. From there, he'd finished at the top of his class and risen quickly through the ranks.

Though he'd never liked locking out of a sub after that, he'd managed to control his physical and mental reactions to being trapped in a confined space. The trick was to think of something else until it was over.

Staying still with his arms at his sides, he let his mind drift to a happier time and place. He had to go back more than twenty years to find one, but he still had them all, tightly locked away in the tiny corner of his heart still capable of feeling emotion. They were all of Emily and Rayne. He filed through them, and settled on one in a warmer setting. Emily, on their honeymoon in Bermuda.

They'd spent the morning playing in the azure water, snorkeling while he'd showed her the wonders of being underwater. She'd been delighted and curious about every single thing he'd pointed out. He'd loved watching her enjoyment, and knowing that she felt completely safe because he was with her. As a SEAL, he was most at home in the water, but he couldn't remember the last time he'd gone in for pleasure. His mind played back the memory of that day like a movie on a screen. Em had worn a silver bikini that showed off her cleavage and taut stomach with devastating effect.

She'd climbed out of the water after their snorkel and splashed through the waves, tossing him a mischievous smile over her sun-kissed shoulder, her eyes as green as the palm fronds swaying in the breeze along the beach. Drops of water gleamed on her naked skin and in her hair like jewels. She'd led the way to a secluded spot tucked against the cliff, and sank down onto the thick towels she'd spread out. When he'd stretched out next to her and pulled her into his arms to kiss her, she'd melted like ice cream in the sun. He could still taste the salty-sweet flavor of her lips.

Outside his stone prison, the wind rose to a screaming crescendo, the force of it pounding mercilessly against his eardrums until he thought they might explode. Uncontrollable shivers wracked him, so strong he felt like he was having a seizure. Damn, he couldn't move enough to rub his limbs, and he couldn't reach the extreme cold weather gear in his ruck. Even if he could it wouldn't do much in these conditions. He needed to find shelter and build a warming fire before hypothermia set in, but until those mortars got quiet he couldn't even do that.

At least Emily was okay, securely locked into the compound with Ben and the security team. She was probably reading somewhere right now. Doubtless she'd still be awake, no matter how exhausted the chemo made her, because he knew damn well she wouldn't go to bed until she found out he was okay. Luke huddled deeper into the crevice and held on, shuddering so hard his bones hurt. Whatever Em was doing, at least he could content himself that she was safe and warm.

There were countless things he wanted to say. So many things he wanted to ask her. They filled his head in a screaming crescendo of regret and pain. He remembered lying next to her in his hospital bed in Vancouver, listening to the sound of her soft breaths, fighting the need to reach out and draw her close as he'd imagined countless times over the years. One embrace would tell her much more than his words of apology ever could. She'd always been able to read him. If he touched her that way again, she would understand what it meant.

*Please let me get another chance.*

He vaguely realized someone was trying to reach him over the radio. Struggling to focus, he grabbed it with his shaking hand and lifted it the few inches the rock wall allowed so he could key it. Sam's voice came through, urgent. "Luke? Luke, do you copy?"

He was shaking too hard to be coherent, but he had to answer her somehow. He had to make sure Emily knew he was alive so she could be at peace. And if these were his last words to anyone, at least he'd die knowing he'd given her this last measure of comfort.

# Chapter Ten

Almost three in the morning and Sam and Ben were still monitoring their equipment in the other room. Seated next to Bryn in the media room watching a chick flick, Emily snuggled up beneath the throw blanket she'd pulled over them. She didn't hear a single thing the actors said; she was too full of turmoil. She didn't know where Luke was and no one had told her, but she was terribly afraid something was wrong.

*You're just being paranoid. You always felt like this when he got called out on a mission.*

She angled a glance at Bryn, who was staring at the screen, but Emily knew she wasn't paying attention to the movie either. Wherever Luke was, Dec was out there, too.

Bryn had apologized profusely for her untimely interruption the night before, but Emily wasn't mad. She was starting to wonder why she'd ever thought her and Luke could take a crack at reconciliation. The universe sure as hell wasn't supporting the cause any.

Bryn shifted beside her, covering a yawn. She laid

her head back against the couch. "God, I'm so tired. You must be done in, too."

She was, but she'd never sleep with this feeling of dread crawling around in her gut. "Go on up to bed," Em told her.

Her friend shot her a "get real" look. "Not until I know they're okay."

Craning her neck around, Emily checked the coms room. The door was closed but the bar of light coming from under its edge told her the others were still up. Were they working on anything, or were they just monitoring the situation? Even if they didn't have direct contact with Luke, they must know what was going on.

"I'm going to find out if there's an update," she announced suddenly, and when she rounded the couch, Bryn was right behind her.

They stopped at the closed door and shared a silent look. Emily swallowed. "Ready?"

"More than," Bryn responded.

Ben answered her knock, looking exhausted. "Hi," he said, shifting so Sam could see them. She sat at her desk with a headset on, and her eyes were full of strain when she looked over at them.

"What's happened?" Emily demanded, heart sinking.

"Look," Ben said gently, and her whole body stiffened at his tone. "Now's not the best time—"

"We just want to know if everything's okay," she interrupted. But they clearly weren't okay, were they? One look at Sam's face told her that.

A radio hissed and crackled in the silence, and then Luke's unmistakable voice came over the line. "I c-copy."

Sam swung around so fast her hair swished around her shoulders, and Ben immediately strode over to peer at the computer in front of her. Beside her, Bryn gripped Emily's hand. Hard. They stood frozen like statues, staring at the couple examining the screen.

Sam's fingers raced over the keyboard as she typed, her brow creased in a worried frown. "Give us status, Luke."

More crackling came, then a loud whistling noise, as if the wind blew into Luke's radio. "P-pinned d-down... M-mortar f-fire..." A clacking sound followed.

Emily's hands flew to her mouth. Jesus, that was his teeth chattering, wasn't it? He was freezing to death. Bryn gripped her shoulder to steady her.

Something came up on the screen in front of them. "Shit, he's alone," Ben muttered, grabbing the radio from Sam. "We've got your position. Can you move to a more secure location?"

"N-negat-tive... Wh-where are o-others?"

"Rhys linked up with Dec and the others. They're holed up in a cave three klicks to your southwest."

Behind her, Emily felt Bryn sag a little, but was too afraid to feel relief on her friend's behalf. Luke was all alone facing enemy fire, and slowly freezing to death.

The radio crackled again, but Luke didn't say anything else.

"Luke?" Ben's voice was sharp. He raised a hand at her and Bryn to wave them away, but they didn't move. "Come back," he said to Luke urgently.

The howling of the wind filled the room for a moment before Luke replied. "Em-m-m..." he said clearly.

"Emily?" Sam finished. Both Ben and Sam's heads whipped around to stare at her.

"Sh-she ok-kay?"

Swamped with pain, Emily stared back into Sam's sympathetic brown eyes when she answered him. "Yes, she's fine."

"Sh-she h-has to g-get bet-ter..."

"She will."

Emily moved without conscious thought, focused solely on the radio with Luke's voice coming from it. "Let me talk to him." Her own voice was nearly unrecognizable, hoarse and strangled.

Then Luke came back on. "W-weather rep-port?" Sam swung around, shifting into work mode.

"Storm should clear substantially within the next few hours."

Hours? Dear God, he'd be dead by then. Emily raised her hand toward Ben, fingers shaking as she held it out for the radio. "Give it to me so I can talk to him."

Ben's mouth tightened for a moment and she was sure he was going to say no, but then he held out the radio and keyed it for her.

She grabbed onto it like it was a lifeline. And maybe it was. "Luke? Luke, it's me."

"Em-m-m..."

"I'm here, sweetheart." She didn't give a shit if they had an audience for this. She needed to make him hold on. "You told me I couldn't quit, do you remember that?"

"Y-yeah."

Tears clogged her throat. "Well then I'll keep fighting if you promise to do the same." She bit back the ragged sob that wanted to explode from her aching chest. "Hear me? Don't you give up. You have to stay awake and hold on—"

"B-Ben," Luke rasped, "g-get her out-ta th-there...N-now..."

Emily jerked and clenched the radio when Ben tried to pull it away. "No, I—"

The wind shrieked in the background. "I'm-m out…" The radio fell eerily, awfully silent.

A loud roaring filled her ears. Hot tears spilled down her cheeks. She was barely aware of Ben taking the radio from her numb fingers, or of Bryn's words of reassurance as Ben lifted her into his arms and strode from the coms room. Emily covered her face and hid against his wide chest, swallowing the scream of denial crowding the back of her throat.

Up in the warm, brightly lit kitchen, Ben set her down in a chair and crouched down at her feet. "Okay, you need to look at me," he said in a low voice.

She focused on him with blurry eyes. Luke was alone. Suffering. Dying. No one could get to him to help. "He's hypothermic."

"Not yet, and he's going to be okay. The weather's going to lift and the temp will go up. As soon as it's clear enough, Rhys will be going to him with Dec and his team." He took her chilled hands between his and rubbed them, sending a glance at Bryn. "Get her some tea, will you?"

"I don't w-want tea." She wasn't going to sit in a warm, comfortable kitchen and drink hot tea while the man she loved was freezing to death out in the desert.

Her mind spun. Did Luke believe he was going to die and hadn't wanted her to know when he did? Is that why he'd cut communications?

"Luke's a tough sonofabitch," Ben added. "He's been through worse than this before, I promise you."

*Oh God.* She curled her fingers around Ben's, so warm and strong. "They'll get him out, right?"

"Absolutely." His voice rang with conviction. "As soon as the storm clears enough the others will find him, and we'll send in a chopper. The crews are already standing by, waiting for conditions to improve."

It helped a bit, but not much. Bryn set a cup of chai tea next to her despite her refusal, and the sweet, spicy aroma brought a flood of fresh tears. Luke had bought that for her. And now he was dying out in the cold while a cup of it steamed in front of her. The thought of drinking it turned her stomach. No way in hell would she take a single sip. She pushed it away, wanting to throw up. "He didn't want me to know."

Ben caught her hands again. "He didn't want you to hear him like that. Because he knew it would upset you, and he's already worried about your health. I'd have done the same thing if it was me out there and Sam on the other end of the line." He looked to Bryn for help, and her friend slid into a chair beside her.

"Go on back downstairs," Bryn said to him. "I'll stay with her."

But Emily grabbed his arm when he got up. "Swear to me you'll tell me if something happens. Good or bad. Please."

He nodded. "All right, but at least go upstairs and try to rest. That's what he'd want you to do."

Bryn placed a comforting arm around her shoulders and Emily leaned into her embrace. "I can't stand it," she confessed.

In answer, Bryn wrapped both arms around her and held on tight. "Yes, you can. We both can. And we will."

Closing her eyes, Emily sent up a prayer for Luke. Sitting together in the silent kitchen, all she and Bryn could do was wait for one of their men to re-establish communications and let them know what had happened.

****

Blurred thoughts and fragmented sounds swam through Luke's head. Shuddering, he pried his heavy eyelids open and listened. He had the vague impression of a lightening around him, and that he couldn't feel his body anymore. And someone was talking to him.

*Luke...*

Fighting to keep his eyes open, he focused on that far away voice calling his name.

*Luke...come in...*

His breathing was shallow and fast. His heart beat sluggishly. He peeled his lids wide open and shook his head, feeling like he was coming out of a general anesthetic. *Desert.* He was in the desert, crammed into this dark hole in the rocks because of enemy mortar fire.

Jesus, had he lost consciousness? He'd never been so fucking cold in his entire life. His limbs didn't respond when he tried to move them. Damn he wished he'd have put on the cold weather gear before inserting.

"Luke!"

He grunted at the shout in his earpiece, fighting to bring his arm up in the tight space. Couldn't feel his fingers. They were like lumps of ice as he fumbled for the button on the squad radio.

"Luke, come on you ugly bastard, say you copy." Dec. Dec was talking to him.

His body shuddered uncontrollably as he managed to key the mic. His brain was sluggish, slow to turn over. Like a computer coming back online after a power outage. "I c-c-copy," he managed, speaking into the boom mike.

"'Bout friggin' time."

He was too cold to smile. His limbs were numb, but everything else ached like a bitch, and his teeth were rattling so hard he wondered if he'd broken them all. The wind was calmer now, and he didn't hear any rounds going off. How long had he been asleep? Another few minutes and he could have died.

"Storm's lifting, buddy. We've got your coordinates. Any action where you are?"

"N-ne-g-gative." Not yet, anyway.

"Can you move?"

No, but he had to. "Y-yes-s-s." If he didn't get moving he'd freeze to death. He had to keep his blood circulating. *Move, dammit.*

"Make your way southwest, and we'll find you."

"W-wilc-co."

"Cobra Team leader, out."

Luke gritted his chattering teeth and pulled upright. His legs were like lead weights attached to his torso and he couldn't feel his feet at all, but he forced himself to shuffle painfully out of the rocks toward the opening. At the entrance he paused, listening for signs that the enemy was still close, but only the wind answered him. It was still stiff, but nowhere near what it had been, and the snow had almost stopped. The eastern sky showed a line of turquoise lightening the indigo horizon. Had to be close to dawn.

Struggling to raise his forearm, he squinted down at his watch. He'd been trapped in there for almost three hours, and he'd been asleep for probably twenty minutes or more. It scared the hell out of him to know how close he'd come to succumbing to hypothermia. His thighs would be covered with bruises because he'd kept pinching them to stay awake, but he'd fallen asleep anyhow. He was lucky to still be alive.

*Move, you dumb bastard.*

Staggering because he couldn't feel his feet, he dug his ruck out of the snow and finally put on some cold weather gear. Already a bit warmer, he managed to get the ruck on after struggling with the straps. Then he contacted Sam back at the compound to let her know he was still kicking and intended to link up with the rest of the team. All except one. "Any w-word from D-Davis?"

"Negative, and the Agency can't confirm his location either."

"T-tell Em to g-go to b-bed." He knew he'd scared the shit out of her with that radio call and hated it. As he disconnected, a wave of uneasiness washed through him. Davis was a pro. He'd never missed a rendezvous yet. Until now. What the hell had happened? The blizzard hadn't blown up until after his scheduled insertion time.

Shifting his slung rifle around, Luke shuffled ahead for the first few meters until he got a renewed sense of balance. His movements were wild and jerky at first, but soon his respiration evened out and warmth returned to his core. The sky lightened enough for him to push the NVGs up onto his helmet and slog forward. If the enemy was close by, there was no way they could miss the tracks he left in the snow. Sensation slowly came back to his arms and legs, bringing a stinging rush of blood, but his hands and feet remained numb. Thawing them out was not going to be fun, and it'd be a miracle if he didn't have frostbite on at least a few of his digits.

Moving toward the original RV point in the growing light, he hugged the base of the cliffs to maintain what cover he could. Since the snow and wind had died down, he was able to make out the topographical landmarks and match them to the terrain detailed on his map. The worst of the shivering seemed to have subsided, but he was still wracked with occasional shudders. He thought again of Emily talking to him over the radio during the night. Shit, he wished she hadn't heard his transmission to Sam. Sure as hell she'd been up all night waiting for word about him, worrying herself sick. *Sicker*, he corrected himself angrily.

A few minutes later Dec came on the squad radio. "We've got you in our sights."

*Good.*

"No enemy contacts observed, but we'll keep you covered. We're six hundred meters from your present position, south-southwest behind the rise."

"R-roger that." With friendly eyes on him and their weapons covering his movements, Luke pushed his body into a jog, his bones feeling brittle enough to shatter like glass with each step. About twenty meters from the rise, Dec appeared at the bottom, his white teeth a slash in the middle of his camouflaged face.

He grabbed Luke's shoulder. "Glad you could make it."

A rusty laugh was all he could manage. Dec led the way to a more secure location where the others hunkered around a small warming fire, apparently convinced the enemy had left the field otherwise the SEAL platoon leader would never have allowed it. Rhys stepped out of the shadows, a towering figure holding a steaming mug. "Coffee," he said as he handed it to him.

Luke let out a low chuckle. "I'm out th-there f-freezing my a-ass off while y'all're h-hav-ving a f-fucking tea p-party?"

Rhys cracked a grin. "Pretty much."

*Nice.*

Holding the metal mug with both hands, some of it spilled as he brought it to his mouth. The coffee burned his lips and scalded his mouth, searing right down his esophagus to his stomach. He chugged it down anyway and gave a heartfelt groan of appreciation. Dec helped him pull off his ruck and the SEAL medic came over.

"Better sit by the fire, sir."

"D-don't mind if I d-do." He squatted down in front of it and held his gloved hands out to the flames. The warmth against his frozen face was bliss, and stemmed the shivers that continued to plague him. After a few minutes feeling came back to his nose and lips. The medic pulled the Nomex gloves off and examined his hands. They were pure white, but at least the skin wasn't hard and waxy.

Rhys draped a blanket around him, then the medic took Luke's hands between his and held them there, and soon warmth registered. The younger man's gray eyes held a sardonic glint. "Just frost nip. But this is still going to hurt like a bitch, sir."

And holy hell, it did, as soon as the blood began flowing to his fingers again. The fiery burn made it feel like he'd stuck his hands in the fire rather than between the young SEAL's palms. As it warmed, his skin throbbed and turned bright red, but at least the pain meant he hadn't killed any nerve endings, so he could still shoot if he needed to. Inside his steel-toed assault boots, his toes were like icicles. As soon as he was able to move his fingers, he unlaced his boots and pulled off his damp socks. Someone handed another pair to the medic and they set about warming up his feet.

When the familiar burn started up in his feet, the medic stood. Dec ambled over, his golden eyes assessing the situation. "Well? What's the verdict?"

"No need to amputate, sir," the medic replied with a grin. "He's good to go."

"Damn right," Luke growled, and Dec clapped a hand on his shoulder as he squatted down next to him.

"We've already scouted the village," he said, and from his tone Luke already knew what he was going to say. "No sign of Tehrazzi, and nobody's saying anything."

"Any evidence to suggest he was in one of the caves during the air strikes?"

"None."

Luke clenched his jaw. It was possible the HUMINT Davis had received from their source was false, but Luke had never known him to be wrong before. Something else that made him uneasy. Even if he'd been caught up in the blizzard, Davis should have checked in by now. "Any word from Davis?"

"No, but the TOC confirmed his arrival at the insertion point twenty-five minutes prior to you. I've got some of the boys out looking for him."

He wouldn't have gotten caught up in the air strikes. Davis was way too good at what he did to make a mistake like that, and he was a superb navigator. If he was out there wounded too badly to make radio contact, they'd have to resort to using the infrared cameras on an aircraft or satellites to scan for him. The temperature was rising, so if he'd survived the cold this long, he'd probably make it until they found him. He swiveled around to grab his ruck, but Rhys was already there, handing him a satellite phone.

"Thanks." Rising, he dialed using the secure connection and Jamie answered on the second ring. "No word on Davis," Luke told him. "Miller know anything?"

"He dropped Davis off at the airfield yesterday. Hasn't heard from him since."

Well, they weren't leaving until they found him. "Keep this line free."

"You know it."

Luke tucked the phone away into one of the pockets of his assault vest and pulled on his gloves. "Let's get moving," he said to the others.

They doused the fire and grabbed their equipment, then Luke and Dec consulted their maps. Using Davis's insertion point, they established a search area radius between that and the RV point, then split everyone up into two groups. Dec updated the SEALs already out looking for Davis as they left the shelter. The sky grew brighter, layers of stratus clouds breaking up and letting in rich golden rays of early sunlight. Moving around in enemy country during daylight hours was not a covert warrior's ideal operating conditions, but the only other alternative was to hunker down until nightfall. Not an option. They needed to find Davis and regroup until another lead on Tehrazzi came along.

Luke, Rhys and two SEALs humped it out to their designated are and fanned out, still maintaining vigilance for any of the insurgents, or whoever the hell had lobbed those mortars last night. His heart was heavy. He didn't want to find his friend's body out here. *Don't do that to me, Davis.*

They combed the snowy terrain at the insertion site, moving steadily toward the original RV point. Less than a klick away from the village, Dec came over the squad radio, saying they'd found evidence of tire tracks leading away from there.

Luke and the others hustled over to meet them, and when he got close enough to see Dec's grim expression, his stomach sank. "Find him?"

Dec nodded, and Luke knew Davis was dead. "This way."

*Ah, Christ,* Luke thought, wanting to bow his head and close his eyes for a minute. But he followed Dec to where two of his SEALs hunkered beside a body laid out in the snow. Tire tracks showed in the sandy soil beneath the melting snow, leading up to his friend.

Davis was on his back, dark eyes half open and staring sightlessly into the blue sky. Luke knelt next to his friend, jaw clenched so hard it ached. Part of his skull was missing on one side, and on the other, two round bullet holes marked the skin behind his temple. A double tap to the head. Done at close enough range to leave powder burns. Whoever had shot him had been up close and professionally trained. One of *them*.

Luke had seen death enough that it didn't affect him much anymore. This time was different. This hurt. It always hurt when he lost one of his own, but Davis had been the closest thing he'd had to a friend out in the field. They'd gone through variations of hell together, and they'd made an incredible team. One of the best.

Luke took Davis's hand. His facial muscles were already stiff with rigor mortis. The motionless fingers were still bendable, but the elbow and shoulder were fairly rigid. Rigor mortis wasn't a reliable thing to use for estimating time of death, but it gave Luke some clues. Maximum effect occurred anywhere from twelve to twenty-four hours post mortem. Rapid cooling of the body could delay the onset, but it always occurred upon thawing. Like the sub-freezing temperatures of last night's blizzard, and the comparatively warm temperature now. *God dammit.* Forcing aside his anger and sadness, Luke glanced at his watch, then up at Dec and Rhys. "They had to have shot him right after he inserted."

Rhys's expression remained calm, but his navy eyes hardened like shards of steel. "Someone he knew."

*And trusted.* The words hung in the air between them all. Was it the contact? Davis had trusted his murderer. Otherwise he never would let someone that close with his back turned.

Dec looked at Luke. "Any hunches?"

Yeah. He had a few. Each as ugly and hard to believe as the next. But unless he found more evidence, he couldn't prove a damn thing.

A molten anger boiled in his gut as the pieces clicked into place. He didn't want to accept the conclusion he'd come to, but it had to be dealt with. As soon as he calmed down enough to make the call. While Dec got on the radio to request an extraction, Luke and Rhys went over Davis's body to examine it more closely. No blood soaking the ground, so he must have been dragged and dumped here after the killing shots. Pulling off his friend's web gear and vest, something crinkled beneath Luke's gloved fingers. He stilled an instant, then opened Davis's coat and BDUs. A wrinkled piece of paper lay against his cold, bare chest.

Pulling it out, Luke opened it and read while Rhys and Dec watched him closely.

*Betrayal is the deepest wound of all. Let us finish this in the place where it all began. Allah's will awaits us both.*

The handwritten Arabic blurred before his eyes for a

second. He knew that writing. Would recognize it anywhere.

*Tehrazzi.*

"Jesus *Christ*," Rhys growled, looking up at him. "You think he did it?"

Luke's heart leapt. Had Tehrazzi been here after all? He could have captured Davis somehow, though Luke didn't think that was likely. But shit, had Tehrazzi done this and managed to escape from under their noses?

Betrayal. It could mean so many things, but his gut said his first reaction was the right one.

Luke fished out the satellite phone and contacted Jamie.

"Ah, shit," his boss sighed when he heard Davis was dead.

"Double tap to the head, along with this note." He translated it, and after a shocked pause on the other end said, "You need to get over here, now."

"Yeah. I'll be on the next flight to Beirut. I'll contact Miller and let him know."

A lethal rage began to build, cold and bitter. "Tell him you want a meeting with him in Beirut. I want to talk to him face to face." Before Jamie could respond, he ended the call and stood. "How long until the chopper gets here?" he asked Dec.

"Fifteen minutes."

Luke looked at Rhys. "I want to talk to some of the villagers."

"Absolutely."

"You'll stay with him?" he asked Dec, nodding to Davis's still form lying in the snow. *I won't let this go unanswered*, he told his friend silently. *You have my word.*

"I'll personally load him onto the helo."

"And tell command that I'll be the one to inform his parents." A retired couple living out their golden years in southern Florida. Luke was already dreading that call.

"Roger that."

With Rhys at his back, Luke started for the village. He didn't expect to find Tehrazzi there, nor any trace that he had been. Bastard was much too clever for that.

But Luke was going to get some answers to the question foremost in his mind.

Had that note been shoved into Davis's uniform by friend, or foe?

# Chapter Eleven

Voices outside her room woke her. Emily jerked awake and rubbed at her eyes before glancing at the clock. Almost eight. She'd been awake until after three waiting for Luke to return but had eventually dragged herself up to the bed because Ben had threatened to carry her there. That she'd fallen asleep at all was a miracle, but she'd been exhausted. Sitting up, she strained to make out who was in the hallway, and recognized Bryn and Neveah's voices. Were the guys back? After shrugging on her robe, she tore her door open. Bryn stopped in her tracks and gave her a tired smile.

"Are they back?" Emily demanded.

Nev nodded. "On their way."

Her knees went weak, and for a moment she sagged against the door frame. Bryn came over and put her arms around her. "They're all okay. Why don't you take a shower and get cleaned up? Sam said they won't be back for another hour at least."

But Dec wasn't coming back with them. He'd be either in the field with his men, or back at his base, wherever that was. Her heart went out to Bryn. "It'll be over soon," she said to her, returning the embrace. "He'll come back to you."

"Yeah," Bryn sniffed, struggling not to cry. "He knows I'll kill him if he doesn't."

They shared a smile, then Emily pulled away. "I'll meet you downstairs in a bit."

Once she was showered, dressed and ready to face everyone, she smoothed her wig into place and headed downstairs. Everyone was in the kitchen, and they all looked as tired as she felt. Sam and Ben were both filling big mugs of freshly brewed coffee when she came in.

"Hey," Sam said, and reached into the cupboard to pull out another mug. "Want some?"

"Please." She looked at Ben. "Long night for you both."

"Yeah," he said, "for all of us." He narrowed his pale green eyes on her. "Nev look you over recently?"

"She just saw me upstairs. Why, do I look that bad?" She'd spent extra time getting her make up just right to cover the dark circles beneath her eyes.

"I've seen you look better." Sam elbowed him, and he flinched before glaring at his fiancée. "Well, it's true."

"I'm just stressed out," Emily said.

Sam nodded, throwing her long red hair over one shoulder. "That's understandable. Personally, I think you're a trooper."

She was glad someone did.

They were all milling about the kitchen when Rhys walked in the front door a half hour later, his desert fatigues covered in dirt, and his face streaked with camouflage paint and grime. Nev let out a glad cry and ran over to him, leaping into his outstretched arms. His wide smile completely transformed the hard lines of his face and warmed his frigid blue eyes. Looking away to give them some privacy, Emily's heart pounded against her ribs. Luke had to be here. Was he outside still? How she'd love to be able to run up and throw her arms around him like that, but she couldn't. He wasn't hers anymore.

He'd been thinking of her out in that desert last night though, while he'd frozen waiting for an extraction. And the way he'd looked at her the night before he'd gone when she'd kissed him goodbye— like he wanted to pull her back into his arms more than anything. That had to mean something. He'd nearly died out there last night. Did he finally realize they should be together while they could? She prayed he did.

Ben was uncharacteristically grim as he watched his brother reunite with Neveah. The instant they separated, he spoke up. "Need you downstairs for a few minutes."

Rhys slid an arm around Nev's waist and tucked her into him, his expression sobering. "Be right there." He murmured something into Nev's ear that Emily couldn't make out, then kissed her and nodded at Ben, who followed him down to the coms room. Emily glanced at Sam, who bit her lip.

"What's happened?" she asked.

Sam looked down into her coffee. "We...lost a good teammate yesterday."

Her stomach sank. "One of Luke's?"

"Yes. One of his favorites."

There was something more to it than that, Emily was positive, but she wasn't going to ask because she wouldn't get any more information. That much was clear from Sam's closed expression.

A door shut down the hall. Drawn to it like a magnet, Emily's head turned, her eyes going to the study. "Is Luke..."

"Looks like." Sam met her gaze. "It's not my place to stick my nose into your business, but… You might want to give him some space for a while. Until he sorts some...things out."

*What sort of things*, she wanted to ask, but thought better of it. "Thanks for the warning."

Though her heart demanded she go to him straight away, she took Sam's advice and went to sit outside with Bryn on the patio instead. They chit-chatted to kill some time, but Emily couldn't focus. She kept thinking of Luke. Despite what had happened the night before he'd left, he'd come in, gone straight into the study and shut the door. He hadn't so much as come to say hi, or even let her know he was back.

Whether it was because he didn't want her there or because he was working on something, clearly he wanted to be alone. For now she'd respect his wishes and give him that space.

She passed the next hour with Bryn staring at the house's reflection in the pool. After a few attempts at conversation that fell flat, they gave up and sat together in silence. When she couldn't stand it any longer, Emily excused herself, went back inside and walked quietly down the hallway. The study door opened and the twins came out, both looking grim. Emily stopped when she saw them and almost turned around, but Ben left the door open and moved aside to let her pass, giving her shoulder a quick squeeze on the way by. Taking a deep breath, she paused for a moment outside the room before peering around the corner. What she saw drew her stomach into a hard knot.

Luke sat in the tufted leather chair behind the wide desk, his elbows resting on the blotter in front of a laptop, his hands buried in his hair. He'd obviously made an effort to wash his face, but traces of camouflage paint and dirt remained around the edges of his hairline and beard. He stared at the screen, his eyes looking almost sunken in his face, lines of strain radiating out from the corners of his eyes and bracketing his mouth. He looked haggard. Beyond hope. It scared her.

Gathering her courage, she knocked softly.

His head came up, those dark eyes zeroing in on her instantly. Then he stilled, as though she was the last person he'd expected to find in the doorway.

"Hi," she ventured, unsure of her welcome.

"Hi, Em." He sounded tired, spiritless.

"Can I come in?"

He scrubbed a hand over his face, looking ready to drop. "Sure."

Sitting up straighter as she approached, he closed the laptop. Part of her was glad, because she had a feeling she didn't want to know what he'd been looking at. Standing near the desk, she wrapped her arms around her waist. "I'm glad you're back safe and sound."

Luke lifted his dark stare, and the haunted expression in his eyes made her heart lurch. She'd seen him like this only once before, years ago when he'd first been in the Teams. He'd shown up on her parents' doorstep in the middle of the night while she was full term with Rayne, shivering and soaked to the skin from the pouring rain, face covered in bruises and stitches. *They left us all there, Em. Just left us there to die...*

A shiver of foreboding snaked down her spine. What else had happened out there last night? Her arms ached to enfold him, to have him lay his head on her shoulder and let her hold him. To tell him without words that he wasn't alone and that he was loved. Her hands clenched into fists at her sides so she wouldn't reach for him. "Luke—"

"It was my fault."

His raw whisper made the hair on the back of her neck stand on end. "What was?"

He shook his head and looked away. "I should have seen this coming. It was about me. It's always been about me," he said, and his confusing words alarmed her. "He wanted me to feel betrayed, and all along I've known what the point of it is. I've read about it, seen movies about it, heard stories from the Agency in the Cold War, but I never thought it would happen to me."

What did he mean?

His ragged sigh tore at her. "Shit I'm tired," he muttered, rubbing at his eyes as though they burned.

Helpless to ease the raw pain she sensed in him, she reached out with tentative fingers and brushed a lock of his too-long dark hair away from his cheek. "What can I do?" she asked, bracing for the inevitable moment when he shut her out and retreated from her. But then he stunned her by folding his hand around hers and leaning his scruffy cheek into her palm.

"Stay," he whispered, closing his eyes and pressing harder. "Just...stay."

Her heart turned over in her chest.

Emily closed the gap between them and he pulled her right into his lap. She wrapped her arms around his back and fought the rise of tears when he locked his arms tight around her waist and buried his face in her throat. Giving him the wordless comfort of her embrace, she smoothed his hair and leaned her weight into him, resting her cheek on his hard shoulder. In answer he pulled in a ragged breath and gripped the back of her sweater with his fists, holding on like she was his anchor in the middle of a hurricane. She squeezed her eyes shut.

Whatever pain he was in, words couldn't ease him now. She swallowed them all and held him fast, willing him to find solace in her arms. Luke took several deep breaths and exhaled hard. The muscles across his back were rigid. She stroked them with her fingertips, consciously slowing her breathing. He was hurting, but at least he was home safe, in her arms. She kept waiting for him to let her go and pull away, but time stretched out and he didn't move except to release his grip on her sweater and slide his hands to the small of her back. Their warmth penetrated to her skin, sinking into her flesh. The weight of his head on her shoulder grew heavier and his breathing deepened. Her fingers paused on his back. Was he asleep?

Shifting her head slightly she peeked at him.

His thick lashes were down and his facial muscles were relaxed. His hands at her waist jerked slightly, but he didn't stir otherwise. He was dead asleep in his chair with his head on her shoulder. He was that exhausted.

It touched her that he trusted her enough to let go and slide into sleep. He rarely slept at all, and it was usually a light combat-ready sleep. But he was out hard. The knowledge filled her with pleasure and pride, because Luke trusted very few people. And from the sounds of it, he'd lost one of them in last night's operation.

His breathing stayed slow and even in the quiet room. With his defenses down and him vulnerable in her arms, a fierce protectiveness rose within her. It sent a shiver over her skin. More minutes passed. The muscles along her spine ached with the need to move, but she wouldn't. Not if shifting meant waking Luke. She'd stay like that all damn day if he needed her to, no matter how uncomfortable she got. Thinking of how cold he'd been out there alone last night, she wished she had a blanket to wrap him in as she cradled him. She never wanted him to be alone and cold again.

Footsteps out in the hall made her tense and glance over her shoulder, but Luke didn't even twitch. That in itself told her how wiped out he was. Luke had hearing like a bat's.

Rhys poked his head in and stopped when he saw them. Emily gave a tiny shake of her head, giving a silent warning not to wake him up, but he didn't leave. Suppressing an irritated sigh, she returned his stare and raised her brows in question. Whatever he needed, was it really important enough to warrant waking Luke out of the only real sleep he'd had in days?

Rhys's somber expression said it was.

*Sorry, sweetheart.* Regretting their closeness was about to come to an abrupt end, she woke him.

All she had to do was shift and Luke came instantly awake, head jerking off her shoulder and his eyes snapping open, focusing immediately on Rhys. Still sharp as ever, from sleep to complete alertness in the blink of an eye. He gently set her away from him as he addressed Rhys. "What's up?"

"Ben just went to pick up James at the airport. We're supposed to link up with them at the meeting location," he said, gaze swinging to her.

She felt like rolling her eyes. Did he really think he needed to be so secretive with his words? She'd been married to Luke for almost eleven years without spilling any sensitive information to anyone. And she'd lived with his dark secrets far longer than that.

Feeling awkward, she slid off Luke's lap and headed for the door so they could discuss their business in private.

"Em, wait."

Surprised, she stopped and looked over her shoulder at Luke.

"Thanks. I needed that." A rueful grin tilted his mouth.

She smiled back. "Anytime." Before she said something she shouldn't, she slipped past Rhys into the hall.

****

Luke crossed the hotel's parking lot and opened the front passenger door of the Agency-loaned black

Suburban. As he slid into the seat the scent of cinnamon reached him, from Ben chomping on his Big Red. He popped it once, a sure sign he was lit.

Pale green eyes focused on him. “Well?” he prompted. “Good to go?”

“Yep.” Luke swiveled around to look at Jamie, sitting next to Rhys in the back seat. “Miller’s flight get in on time?”

“Landed ten minutes ago.”

He should arrive at the hotel within the hour. Luke settled back into the leather seat and closed his eyes, imagining what would happen when Miller got there. He wasn’t worried. Nope. He was seething inside, pushed to a deadly cold rage. It took a lot to get him there. He had a reputation for having a long fuse and never losing his cool when he worked, but right now he was as close as he’d ever been to wanting to kill with his bare hands.

“You want us to sit this one out?” Rhys asked from the back seat.

The idea had its merits. “No. I want all of you there.” In case he was tempted to let the darkness in him out of its cage.

A long pause followed before Ben said, “Sure you don’t want me to rig up a few cameras in there?”

“I’m sure.” He could feel the anxious tension coming off Jamie in waves, and his own heart rate responded by quickening. A fog of testosterone filled the SUV. They all wanted to avenge Davis.

“So you’re going to wait and follow him in when he gets here?” his boss asked.

Luke consciously relaxed the muscles in his shoulders, forcing the anger deep down where he could lock it away. Whatever happened, he would keep a clear head. “I’m going to give him some time to relax and get comfortable first.”

“Why? He doesn’t know we’re coming—”

“He will,” Luke interrupted, staring unseeing out the windshield through the gray drizzle. “I left him a message.”

# Chapter Twelve

After placing his sidearm in the drawer of the bedside table and checking for electronic bugs or cameras or wires that might be hidden in his hotel room, Hank Miller went into the clean, modern bathroom, stripping off his tie and wilted dress shirt. The armpits were damp with the sweat he'd shed over the past nine hours. Ever since he'd been told Luke and the SEALs had found Davis's body with the betraying double tap wounds in his head.

Dumping his clothes on the marble counter, he ripped back the shower curtain and turned on the spray, waiting for a few seconds until it warmed before stepping beneath it. The instant the water hit his skin he released a deep sigh. The grinding in his stomach eased somewhat. His boss had called him here for a meeting, and that was all. There'd been nothing in James's voice to suggest he suspected anything. No urgency or accusation in his tone. Miller had played back the recorded conversation several times looking for signs of vocal stress, but hadn't found any. Maybe he was still okay.

Pushing the voices of doubt from his mind, he took

the soap and scrubbed at his chest and pits. He detested feeling dirty. Hated that he couldn't control his body's reaction to stress enough that he'd stained a good dress shirt with cold, greasy sweat. He already had his story set in his mind. Once he dressed in fresh clothes and got himself together, all he had to do was hold fast against whatever accusations they threw at him. If they had any.

The hot water flowed over him in a cleansing rush, easing the tension out of his stiff muscles. He'd spent over twenty years with the Agency, and more than half of that working counterterrorism. He hadn't worked this long and this hard to have his career blow up in his face.

*They have no proof.*

That was his mantra. James didn't have any hard evidence. Couldn't. Still, it was going to be tough facing his boss for this. Facing Luke, however, was another matter. The idea of having those x-ray eyes boring into his while he defended himself had nausea churning in his belly. Luke scared the holy hell out of him. Thank God James would be there as a buffer. Whatever happened, Miller didn't want to wind up alone in the same room with Luke. Not until he'd cleared his name and they backed off enough to let him breathe again.

He shut off the water with one hand and reached out blindly for a towel hanging on the rack. Couldn't see shit without his glasses. Damn weak eyes. He'd thought about laser eye surgery a few times, but what was the point? It's not like he needed it for his job. If he'd been out in the field doing ops, that would have been one thing. But sitting at a desk, his glasses were all he required for perfect vision.

It still irked him that he'd wound up a glorified desk jockey. All he'd ever wanted was to make it into paramilitary ops. He glanced down at himself, his unfocused vision still able to see the soft belly protruding at his waist, big enough that it obscured his view of his genitals. He could barely make out the ends of his toes sticking out from beneath his navel. God, how had he let himself go like this? Up until a few years ago he'd been in good shape. Not as good as Luke, but still decent for a desk jockey.

A wave of self-disgust washed over him. He was soft and fat and his hair was thinning, and his close quarter battle skills were so rusty he probably couldn't even disarm a mugger anymore. Sure as shit he wouldn't be able to hit anything long range with a rifle. Luke on the other hand, was still sharp as a razor and every bit as lethal. All anyone had to do was look into the man's eyes to see that. The guy was fifty-freaking-years-old, five years older than him, and Luke's body fat percentage was low enough to make most Olympic athletes jealous. It made him jealous, for Christ's sake. They'd joined the CIA at the same time, but Luke had gone on to become a living legend both there and in the Spec Ops world.

Miller frowned as he toweled off. Had his Agency handlers and superiors known back then that he simply didn't have what it took? He'd come out of the FBI's Counterterrorism Unit one of their top agents, but they'd never put him into the field. What had they seen lacking in him? The relentless drive that Luke had? Or had they known he'd wind up old and fat before his time?

Didn't matter now. He'd taken the path offered to him and reached the pinnacle. He was the Kabul station chief, for Christ's sake. He was just as focused, just as driven as Luke, but they'd spent their time in the Agency directing their energies in very different ways.

Squinting, he groped along the vanity for his glasses and put them on. They were steamed up, so he cracked the bathroom door open and reached up to wipe the towel across the foggy mirror—

He leapt back with a strangled gasp.

Outlined by condensation on the mirror, the word *Traitor* stood out in a silent accusation.

His heart galloped inside his ribcage. Beads of sweat broke out on his skin. They'd *been* here. Earlier, before he'd checked in. Someone had written this on the mirror with their finger, knowing he'd find it. Miller cast a frantic look around the bathroom. Christ, had he missed a camera in here? Were they watching his reaction right now? No. Impossible. He'd been thorough when he'd checked for eyes and ears.

They could be waiting for him outside that door, he thought, glancing at the flimsy deadbolt and chain. He stared at the brushed nickel knob, mind racing with wild thoughts. What if they'd sent a hit team after him? The next person at his door could be waiting with a silenced pistol in their hand, ready to pull the trigger.

His gun. He had to get his gun. He'd left it in the drawer of the night table.

Naked, he flung open the bathroom door and raced into the bedroom. His eyes fastened on the table and the little drawer inside it. He tore over and ripped the thing open. And stopped dead.

The gun was gone. But the hotel bible lay there, open to the book of Luke.

His skin prickled and crawled. *No*.

A passage was underlined. Chapter 11, Verse 23, and he couldn't stop himself from reading it. The words swam before his eyes.

*Whoever is not with me is against me, and whoever does not gather with me scatters.*

His mouth went dry. *Oh my God...* Luke was coming for him.

"Looking for this?" a deep voice drawled.

"Shit!" he cried, whirling around with a hand over his thudding heart.

Luke's penetrating dark gaze seared his naked skin as

he lifted the loaded SIG Sauer and aimed it at Miller's head.

Miller stumbled back against the night table, knocking the reading lamp over with a crash. "Jesus," he gasped, dizzy from the flood of adrenaline roaring through his bloodstream. He couldn't hear anything but the rush of blood in his ears.

Never taking his eyes off him, Luke tossed him a hotel robe. Miller caught it and threw it on to cover himself, his movements jerky and uncoordinated. "This is all a misunderstanding—"

"Shut. The. Fuck. *Up*."

He did, throat constricting as he swallowed. Oh Christ, what was Luke going to do to him?

The door flew open and two huge guys strode in, the twin hit men he'd met in Kabul last time he'd seen Luke. They were dressed in jeans and black leather jackets that no doubt concealed a holster or two. Their shoulders were so wide they blocked out the light coming in from the hall and their eyes were concealed beneath wraparound shades. Miller locked his knees to keep them from shaking, his gaze swinging between the two assassin-types and Luke. The sheer intensity of the dark stare coming back at him shriveled his insides.

He was a walking dead man.

Luke lowered his weapon and took a menacing step toward him. "Jamie's waiting downstairs for us. You coming quietly, or do the boys and I get to make this interesting?"

****

Luke might have believed Miller was unaffected by the interrogation except for the frantic way his pulse throbbed in the side of his throat and the faint sheen of sweat on his upper lip. His eyes, though, were cool as ever. Ice blue and devoid of emotion. Flat. This wasn't going to be easy. Miller was a slick bastard. Wouldn't give up information without a fight. But that was fine. Luke still had his trump card to play.

Across the table from his up until now stellar Kabul station chief, Jamie regarded Miller calmly as he finished his questions. Positioned near the door, Ben and Rhys lounged against the wall with their arms folded across their chests, giving just the right impression of menace and authority. They both appeared to be waiting for the word to take over the interrogation using less subtle methods. Which was exactly the kind of threat necessary when dealing with a bully like Miller. Bullies only understood intimidation, and the twins had that air of silent menace down to perfection.

Listening to Miller's answers and the absolute lack of inflection in his voice, Luke felt a shred of admiration underneath his disgust. Kinda had to admire him, the way he was playing this. Miller was a shark. Coldblooded and instinctive. No surprise he'd thought he could get rid of Davis and not get caught. Luke didn't doubt for a moment he'd never intended things to go so far. Miller wasn't the type to sabotage his own career. But in his efforts to siphon his own intelligence and use it to nab Tehrazzi so he could be the Agency's new darling, he'd crossed an unforgivable line.

Without the trap Luke was itching to spring, they might never have nailed the bastard. Miller had been damned careful. Almost perfect in his duplicity. They hadn't been able to trace a single cell or satellite phone call that incriminated him in any way. Just the odd one from Tehrazzi using Pashto code words to a contact in Kabul. Without the other prisoner Luke had brought in, the whole investigation would have hit a brick wall.

Miller answered another question in that flat voice of his. His eyes remained cool, but he couldn't quite mask the disdain in them.

Jamie turned to Luke. "I'm done here. Go ahead."

Oh yeah, he was more than ready to do this. He came away from the wall, his stare pinned on Miller's.

Miller paled when their boss got up to leave. Considering how lethally pissed off Luke was, the show of unease reinforced just how intelligent Miller was.

Luke prowled toward him, stopping short of the chair Jamie had vacated. He would stay standing for this. "Great story you've got," he remarked, the anger bubbling up despite his efforts to stop it. "I especially like the part where you deny having any contact with Tehrazzi leading up to Davis's death."

Miller's cool blue eyes regarded him frostily from behind the rimless glasses. Empty and lifeless. A shark indeed. "Glad I could entertain you. Want me to tell it again? Because you're not going to find any inconsistencies no matter how many times I say it." He cast a glance over at the twins. "Even if those two get involved."

*Don't you challenge me, you piece of shit.* "No, I don't want to hear it again, because if I do I might puke. Instead I think I'll tell you my version of the story. Know how I think things went down?"

Miller arched a challenging brow. "I'm on pins and needles."

Damn right he was. He might be putting on a good show, but Luke knew if they took his vitals his BP would be through the roof along with his pulse. Slimy son of a bitch wouldn't last five seconds if Luke got physical with him. He didn't need the twins' help, and Miller knew it. If anything, he should be praying they stayed in the room to safeguard him from Luke's wrath.

"You used one of Davis's informants on the Agency's payroll as a go between to get to Tehrazzi," he said to Miller, curling his hands into fists to keep from going at his throat. "You paid him American cash to keep his mouth shut and learn how Davis operated, and it was perfect because Davis had worked with him for over a year. You knew he trusted him." And that degree of manipulation was what sickened Luke the most. "See, I already know how this whole thing worked. To keep us one step behind, you looked the other way when intel about Tehrazzi came in, and in exchange he rolled over on the occasional drug trafficker or arms dealer, which you got the credit for. He stays safe in the mountains, and you earn the reputation as the guy who helped clean up Kabul. A win-win situation, until Davis got suspicious and started looking into it."

Luke placed his palms on the cool metal surface of the desk and leaned forward. Miller shifted back in his seat almost imperceptibly, but held his ground when Luke continued. "You got scared because you knew Davis was the kind of guy who wouldn't let it go. You knew he could blow your cover. So you brought him in and planted the HUMINT that Tehrazzi was visiting dear old gram and gramps' village in Syria. Then you sent Davis, and the informant you both used, to rendezvous with us. You even accompanied them to the airfield like a concerned boss. Only Davis didn't realize you'd paid the Afghan kid ten times what his entire family makes in a year, to kill Davis when they inserted. And to cover your ass, you'd already paid someone in the village to take out the informant."

Miller shook his head. "You're so full of shit. What about all the times you got within an eyelash of getting Tehrazzi, huh? I think you purposely let him go because you love the thrill of the hunt and the fact that each operation makes you an even bigger legend in your own mind."

*Don't take a swing at him. It's not worth it, no matter how great it would feel at the moment. Just let him screw himself into the ground with his lies, then bring in the other prisoner and walk away from this whole fucked-up mess.*

Drawing in a calming breath, Luke continued. "And the reason it might have worked was because you knew Tehrazzi killed that IT kid in Peshawar with the telltale double tap to the head a month ago. So making us run a wild goose chase to follow up the sighting of Tehrazzi was perfect. Informant shoots Davis, plants the note Tehrazzi had given him, and heads for the village where he never suspects a bullet is waiting for him from one of his Muslim brothers he thinks will take him in from the cold." A wintry smile spread across his face. "Too bad the blizzard fucked that part up."

The first edge of fear crept into Miller's eyes, but he masked it instantly. "Interesting story, but I'm sick of the accusations. Prove it, or let me go."

The rage in him expanded, sending a ripple through his muscles. He stared hard at Miller. "Last chance."

"*Fuck* you."

Clenching his jaw, Luke turned his head and nodded at the twins. Ben pulled open the door for Rhys, who disappeared down the hall.

"What are you doing?" Miller demanded, his voice betraying a hint of unease.

Luke ignored him, pinning him with an unrelenting glare until Rhys returned, pushing a handcuffed and battered-looking Afghan male into the room. Still staring at Miller, Luke knew the instant Abdu stepped through the door. Miller's face lost all its color.

*Gotcha, you pathetic son of a bitch.* "Gonna come clean now? Because I've gotta tell you, I'd dearly love to beat the truth out of your fucking sorry excuse for a body."

Miller's throat bobbed as he swallowed convulsively, staring at the other prisoner like he was seeing a ghost.

"How..?"

Standing up, Luke jammed his fists beneath his armpits to keep from smashing them into his former colleague's slack face. "You shoulda checked with the AWACS patrolling the area before you dropped them off at the airfield. Blizzard moved in too fast and too hard for Abdu to make it to the village. We found him freezing in the middle of the desert after locating Davis's body on our way to the village. He was so relieved to see me, Rhys and the SEALs, he promised to tell us the whole story if we took him with us. Funny enough, his prints were on the hand-written note from Tehrazzi we lifted from Davis's body."

Though he didn't admit his guilt, Miller dropped his eyes to the table. "I want my lawyer."

Luke glanced over his shoulder at Jamie, who stood in the doorway looking tired and very pissed off. Finding out one of your men had gone rogue was not a party, let alone a station chief who had been doing an outstanding job until this ugly incident. "We done here?"

"Yeah. I've got what I need."

"Let's get outta here," he said to the twins, brushing past the forlorn-looking Abdu on his way out the door. If he had to look at Miller's lying mug for one second longer he'd wind up facing assault charges.

# Chapter Thirteen

Stepping into the front foyer of the house, Luke rolled his head from side to side to ease the tension in his neck and shoulders. Damn, he was wiped. He felt hollow inside, like someone had scooped out his guts with a dull spoon.

He'd missed things before in his career. Important details he should have noticed, and times when he'd acted too late. But of all the things he'd seen and done in his years in the field, he'd never expected to have to deal with what Miller had pulled. Never in a million years would he have believed the guy would be so traitorous. Conniving and opportunistic? Yeah. Willing to protect a terrorist to enhance his own career and have one of his own men killed to cover it up? Luke hadn't seen that coming.

To top it all off, tomorrow he and Rhys were going back to the hellish mountains of Afghanistan with Dec and his SEALs. Landlocked in those frozen, hostile peaks where friend and foe changed allegiances on a whim or whenever a better offer came along. All the analyst reports and intelligence pointed to Tehrazzi being there. They couldn't be sure where exactly, since Miller had fed them false information all along. Hopefully something more would come in before Luke and the others landed at Bagram tomorrow.

His tired gaze strayed unerringly to Jamul's study down the hall. After tonight he didn't feel like working anymore, but he should at least check his e-mail one last time in case Davis's family had contacted him again. Families always wanted more information about their loved one's death. Details of their final moments. Whether they'd suffered or not. At least when Luke told them their son hadn't suffered, this time it would be the truth for a change. Davis hadn't known what hit him, and that was the only blessing Luke could think of.

His steps were silent as he made his way down the hall. A faint glow came from the edge of the doorway, where the door was opened a crack. Had he left the light on before he'd gone? He couldn't remember.

Reaching it, he pushed it open slowly, peering around the room. He stopped dead, aware of a peculiar sensation in his chest, as though his heart had just rolled over.

Emily was curled up in an armchair in the corner across from the desk, sound asleep with a cup of tea resting on the table next to her elbow. No steam curled from its surface. Her pale pink lips were parted slightly, and she had a thin blanket tucked beneath her chin. Her neck was tilted at a bad angle, her head resting against the wing of the chair. The awkward position had knocked her bobbed wig askew. Tenderness welled up, swift and painful. She'd been waiting up for him, knowing something was wrong. *Ah, sweetheart.*

How long had she been in here? Probably for hours, and she had an appointment tomorrow with a local oncologist she needed to be rested for. He shook his head at her stubbornness.

Careful not to make any sound, he walked over and

touched the tea cup. Cold. He was willing to bet it had been that way for some time, too. He watched her for another few minutes, tracking the slow, even rise and fall of her chest. One dainty bare foot poked out from beneath the blanket. Her toenails were impeccably polished with a shade of brilliant red. A true lady to the core.

*What am I going to do with you, Em?*

Luke fought with himself as he stared down at her. The sight of her fragile and fighting for her life, yet curled up in that chair in an uncomfortable position because she'd been worried about him... It choked him up. He was so damn tired of all of this. Tired of living with nothing but regret and responsibility, chasing shadows across the globe. And he was tired of living with the guilt of what he'd done to her and Rayne. He'd hurt them both so badly.

And yet she'd never once given up on him. Emily had always believed in him, no matter what. And now he'd dragged her here despite her wish to stay in the home she loved and found comfort in, all because he'd failed to get Tehrazzi.

He'd stayed away for so long, but...he couldn't maintain the distance between them anymore. The consequences were too terrible. He hated to admit the possibility, but Em might have only months left. Tomorrow he returned to Afghanistan. Chances were, he wasn't coming back this time. Tehrazzi was good enough to kill him when they crossed paths again. Whatever else happened, Luke owed it to Emily and himself to give them the goodbye they'd never had. She needed to know he loved her, had never stopped loving her. He was tired of holding back.

Dropping to one knee, he lifted an unsteady hand and brushed a lock of hair away from her flushed cheek. The instant he touched her soft skin her eyes flew open and her head came up. That vivid green gaze focused on him and she sat up with a relieved gasp. He kept his hand where it was. "Hey, sunshine."

"Luke," she breathed, grabbing him around the shoulders and holding him tight.

He squeezed his eyes shut and fought the sting of tears. She felt tiny in his embrace when he gathered her close and pressed his face into the side of her neck. Small and delicate, yet she loved so fiercely. He pulled in a deep breath, filling his lungs with the vanilla scent of the lotion she always used after a bath. His chest tightened further. Damn, he was an inch away from losing it.

"Are you okay?"

"Yeah." He was now.

Sighing sleepily, Emily cuddled in tighter and stroked his hair. "I'm so glad you're okay."

*I'm not okay*, he wanted to say. *I can't take losing you again.* But she pulled back and took his face in her slender hands, and her smile was serene as a Madonna's. "I couldn't sleep until I knew you were home safe and sound," she whispered.

He swallowed. "And here I am."

"Hmmm," she sighed, laying her head on his shoulder and closing her eyes. Her body seemed to melt into his, growing pliant and supple. Because she trusted him, even after everything he'd put her through.

Luke slid his arms beneath her and scooped her up, blanket and all. In response she settled against him with a contented sound and laid her head on his chest. Beneath her cheek, his heart thudded hard against his ribs. She felt perfect in his arms. He wanted nothing more than to take care of her, be there for her through her illness. To hold her and cherish her for whatever time they had left. The sudden lump in his throat made it hard to breathe as he strode down the hall and up the stairs to Emily's room. Pausing next to her bed, he glanced down at her. Her eyes were closed and she didn't stir when he shifted his grip. Sound asleep because she was so exhausted from the chemo and waiting up for him two nights in a row.

Knowing it was probably for the best that she kept sleeping, he eased her onto the bed and pulled the thick duvet over her robe, removing the blanket from the den. The wig moved slightly. She immediately shot a hand up to grab it, her eyes snapping open to find his. Trepidation and fatigue filled her gaze. Worried he'd seen beneath the wig.

"Don't worry it's still there," he whispered, and her hand lowered slowly to her pillow. He couldn't remember the last time he'd cried, but he was damn close.

He wanted to crawl in next to her so badly his muscles knotted. Instead he knelt next to the bed and gently rubbed her back through the covers, hoping to soothe her. She brought one hand up to take one of his and kiss it, then twined her fingers through his and laid their joined hands on her pillow. Her eyes drifted closed again. The quiet spread throughout the room while he continued to stroke her back, dying to give her so much more, but he hated to wake her when she obviously needed to rest. When he was sure she was asleep again, he reluctantly withdrew his hand from hers and stood. For several minutes longer he watched her, memorizing every precious detail of her face. Then he made himself leave the room.

Shutting his own door behind him, he went into the bathroom and fired up the shower. When the water was hot as he could take it, he stripped and stepped under the spray, leaning one hand against the tiled wall. He closed his eyes and let his head sag on his shoulders while the water ran over him. His brain was full of dismal images.

In a few more hours he'd be in a chopper on his way back into the mountains of north-eastern Afghanistan. The snow would cover the barren terrain, and the temperature would be bone chilling even without the razor-sharp winds that scoured the Hindu Kush. After tonight God knew when he'd ever get another hot shower, or a hot meal for that matter. For the foreseeable future he'd spend what little time he got for rest huddled and shivering in some dug-out abandoned by al Qaeda or the Taliban during the carpet bombing performed by the US at the start of the war on terror. The knowledge depressed the shit out of him.

Once he'd soaped and scrubbed himself clean, he got out to towel off and caught a glimpse of himself in the mirror. God, he looked like a mountain man with his shaggy hair and beard sprinkled with far more gray than there'd been a few months ago. He was still in good shape, but the years were starting to catch up with him. Back in his twenties and thirties, fifty had seemed goddamn ancient. Now that he'd reached the milestone, it didn't seem very old. His body didn't feel old, except for the usual aches and pains that came from everything he'd done to his body over the years, and neither did his mind. Yet the years had crept up on him without him noticing. He was halfway through his best-case scenario life span, and his life was a pile of shit.

God. *Had* he wasted the best years of his life? The question scared the shit out of him. Because the honest answer was he suspected he had. And there was nothing he could do to get those years back.

Reflected in the mirror, his eyes were time-worn. Weary. He thought of Emily asleep in the next room, curled up alone in that big bed. He thought of her unrelenting loyalty and devotion to him and everyone she cared about. She gave it without reservation, even if she never received it in return. Even if he and a lot of others she'd given it to didn't deserve it.

Luke exhaled deeply, urgency building inside him. Shit, he couldn't stay away any more. He needed to go to her and at least hold her against him for the few hours he had left. Needed it more than he needed air to breathe.

Wrapping the towel around his waist, he left the bathroom and headed for the door. Something in his peripheral vision caught his attention. A lump lay curled up beneath the covers on his bed. He swallowed, heart turning over in his chest. *Em.*

She was on her side with her hands tucked under her cheek, innocent as a child in the snowy white sheets. And too beautiful for words.

The bed dipped beneath his weight when he settled a hip on the edge of it, but she didn't waken. He admired the hell out of her quiet courage. Coming in here again couldn't have been easy for her. Yet exhausted as she was, she'd dragged herself in here and climbed into his bed to be with him, whether for comfort or something more. How the hell could he not reach for her?

When he touched her shoulder her eyes flickered open, the luminous moss-green almost disappearing as her pupils expanded in the dimness.

"Hi," she murmured, pushing up onto one elbow. She tucked her blood-red robe around her legs as she looked up at him, eyes full of a quiet hunger that made his guts clench. "I didn't want to sleep alone."

A blast of heat flooded him, chasing away the chill in his soul. It swirled through his bloodstream to his muscles before settling in his groin. His cock lengthened and swelled beneath the confines of the towel, growing tight and painful. Wanting in her, now.

The faint light coming through the windows from the security lights across the yard illuminated her ethereal features. She looked like an angel staring up at him. A very nervous, uncertain angel. Wondering if she was welcome in his bed.

When she continued gazing at him without moving, he understood what she was waiting for. She wanted him to take the decision about what would happen next out of her hands. To seduce her into letting go. She'd always loved it.

Worked for him. He preferred controlling things, in and out of bed. But knowing she was unsure of herself wasn't okay. After the other night, she had to know he still wanted her. Didn't she know she would always be beautiful to him? How ultra-feminine and outrageously sexy he found her? She needed to accept her body the way it was now and not be ashamed of it. Luke vowed to take any and all fears from her tonight.

He would erase the doubt and pain embedded in her eyes, and replace it with pleasure until they both went blind from it. He needed to do that. For himself as much as for her. Every touch would give pleasure and restore her confidence, give her the comfort she so obviously needed. She'd trusted him once. Deeply, and without reservation. He could reach her on that same level again, if she'd only let him in that far. Would she?

Planting one hand next to her head on the pillow, he bent over her and trailed his index finger across her cheek, watching her eyes. The green depths flared with instant arousal before she lowered her eyelids and leaned into his touch. Softness and deceptive strength in a powerful combination that never failed to turn him inside out.

Luke dipped his head to brush soft kisses across her eyelids and cheeks, down her straight nose to hover over her mouth. He feathered over the seam of her lips, teasing and tempting until she threaded her fingers into his hair and pulled him down. Her mouth parted beneath his, opening for the tender stroke of his tongue. She was like warm silk, and he couldn't get enough.

Her soft moan made his whole body hard, but he forced himself to take things gentle and slow. Leaning farther over her, his hands took his weight while he sank into her more, losing himself in the feel and taste of her. Emily stirred beneath him, her robe parting slightly as she stretched out to twine her calves around his. Her hands slid down his neck to his shoulders and arms, pausing to squeeze his muscles before moving to his back. The delighted moan she made at touching him had him sliding his hands beneath her back to bring her closer. He'd always loved that his body turned her on. She made him feel powerful and masculine while managing to pull out all the tenderness in his soul.

*Oh God, touch me. Hold me.*

He kissed her harder, angling his head while he lowered his weight atop her. He shuddered at the feel of her beneath him. Growing impatient, Emily gripped the edge of the towel around his hips and pulled. Luke traced a damp path with his tongue down her long, lovely throat. She shivered in his arms, tilting her head back like an offering. He inhaled the intoxicating scent of her skin and took what she exposed, finding the most sensitive point where her neck met her shoulder and gently scraped his teeth against it. She jerked, and he laved away the little sting with his tongue. Her hands tightened on his back. He sucked the spot firmly. Her quiet gasp was full of anticipation, and all the reassurance he needed that she was as into this as him.

Kissing her throat, he reached for the neckline of her robe where the two halves came together and caressed the skin over her sternum. She tensed and brought her hand up to grab his wrist, but he anticipated the move and circled hers with his fingers, pulling it away to her side. He wasn't going to let her be ashamed of her body. Not for one second.

Her other hand went to the front of his shoulder and

pushed. "Luke—"

Hearing the fear in her protest, he captured her other wrist before pressing a soft kiss to the spot where his fingers had been, right at the notch between her collar bones. "Shhh." He nuzzled just inside the neckline, breathing in more of her heavenly scent.

She tried to break his hold on her wrists. "Luke, no."

Fear. He sensed it in her, growing, threatening to break through her arousal. So afraid he might reject her because of her scars. How could she ever think he would? Luke lifted his head to look into her face. Her jaw was tight, eyes pleading with him not to uncover her. "Roll over, sweetheart," he whispered, watching as surprise filled the depths of her eyes.

She hesitated a moment, then allowed him to help her onto her stomach. Luke paused to sweep the ends of the wig away from her cheek and nuzzle at the thin scar beneath her jaw. Her pulse leapt against his lips, but the remaining tension in her body told him she was still wary of what he intended. He was going to take care of that. "Relax for me, Em. Give yourself to me." A shudder sped through her muscles, but she took a deep breath and let it out slowly, her body softening by degrees.

Luke praised her with low murmurs while he eased the robe off one shoulder, following it with his mouth, hands moving over her satin skin with loving propriety. He ached to fill her, to wrap around her tight enough that she'd feel safe enough to let go.

When he had the robe pulled down as far as he could without removing it from her entirely, he took her chilly hand in his and slid the sleeve off her arm. Then he did the same to the other. With his fingertips he caressed the silky soft skin along her spine from nape to the tempting swell of her hips before sliding up to blanket her with his weight. She gasped at the contact and stretched out beneath him. His painfully hard cock nestled between the cheeks of her softly rounded ass. Closing his eyes on a growl, Luke surged gently against her, loving the feel of her naked skin against his sensitive flesh. In answer Emily moaned and pushed back against him, more at ease in the new position. Her arousal building again because she felt secure.

Luke eyed the bottle of lube she'd left on his bedside table the other night. He'd use it to ensure she was as ready as he could make her, and to guarantee there would be no chance of discomfort for her. He wished she wasn't self-conscious of her body. There was so much he wanted to do to her, but he couldn't until he'd taken her to the place where pleasure overrode thought. Before he could love all of her the way he wanted to, he needed her lost in a haze of sensuality, all her shields down. Damn. He wanted that so badly he shook. But he had to go slow. Seduce her into that place.

"Ohhh, you feel good," she whispered, arching up like a cat.

"Not as good as you." Nibbling and kissing her neck and shoulders, one hand cupped the front of her left shoulder before sliding down toward her breast and moving right. Instantly she stiffened again but he kept going, careful not to pause when his fingers found the IV port embedded below her collar bone. His touch moved left again, and she released the breath she'd been holding.

He stroked the side of her breast, moving inward until he cupped it, her hardened nipple stabbing into the center of his palm. Emily bit her lip, watching him in her peripheral vision. His aching cock slid deeper between her cheeks as he shifted his weight, allowing his hand enough freedom to rub against her straining nipple. She sucked in a sharp breath and arched her back to give him more room, but he didn't change what he was doing. He kept sliding over that sensitive spot while she gasped and moaned, her legs instinctively parting to let him ease between them. So damn perfect.

Luke nudged one of her thighs with his and pressed outward until she bent her knee, exposing the softness of her sex to him. She hissed in a breath when the head of his cock pressed against her, wriggling to get him closer. "Easy." He slid his hand out from beneath the weight of her breast and grabbed the bottle of lube. When his fingers were coated with it, he used his knee to push her thigh up higher and reached under her hip. He took the time to caress her inner thighs and as first, all around where she wanted him to touch, but never quite there.

"Luke," she groaned, curling her lower back to give him access. "Please touch me."

"I will, pretty baby," he crooned against her nape. "You're so soft."

The skin of her mound was completely naked. Satin smooth against his searching fingers, the tender folds already damp with her arousal. He bit back a moan at the feel of her bare flesh. At least he could make that side effect of the chemo good for her, he thought, sliding his slick fingers over the exposed, delicate folds, up, up. She trembled and cried out, but he kept his touch slow and gentle as he aroused and moistened every inch of sensitive flesh before gliding his fingers down and pausing at the entrance to her body. Emily pressed her hips into his palm, demanding more. He kissed the nape of her neck. "Easy, Em. Let me take care of you."

He slid one finger into her carefully, then two, enjoying the feel of her body stretching around him, hugging him in a tight grip. Another moan left her lips. After a few gentle strokes he pulled out and followed the delicate folds to the hard bud of her clit, circling that fragile flesh.

"Ohhh," she moaned breathlessly, opening her legs

wider and straining back to bring the aching length of his cock into her. But he moved away, circling his fingertips around her taut clit before easing into her body again, searching for and finding the sweet spot inside. The broken cry she gave almost made him come.

Tensing his jaw, he pressed and stroked with firm, slow pressure before withdrawing and feathering around her clit again. Softly. Just the way she liked it, the way she loved him to use his tongue there. Over and over until she breathed in shaky bursts and a fine sheen of perspiration dewed her skin. One of her hands grabbed the forearm he was braced on, fingers clamping tight.

"Let me see your eyes," he whispered, straining to hold back the need to plunge into her. His cock throbbed in agony between her thighs, the tip already drenched with her silky juices.

On an unsteady breath, Emily opened her eyes and lifted her head to look at him over her shoulder. Heavy-lidded from pleasure, but not quite blind. Not yet. "Please..." she gasped.

"Feel good?" he asked, slowing his touch, her intimate flesh warm and slippery beneath his caressing fingers. So damn hot and wet it tied him in knots. His lips teased the edge of hers before he leaned to the side and penetrated her mouth with a slow, erotic glide of his tongue at the same time his fingers pressed deep into her.

Gasping, she tore her mouth away and squeezed her eyes shut. "God—Please push into me..."

Damn he wanted to go down on her. Turn her over right then and put his mouth between her thighs. He was dying to taste her again, the exotic-sweet flavor of her a haunting memory. She would feel so good against his mouth, his tongue gliding over her smooth, slick folds while she writhed and begged for more...

His cock pulsed in agony, screaming at him to slide

into her. He growled at the thought, struggling to hold on. She needed to be able to trust him in this. Needed to know he had complete control of himself before she could let go. She had to consciously trust he would take care of her needs first when she was helpless in his arms. She already knew it on a subconscious level, because she'd come to him. Now he had to prove he was worthy of it.

Relishing her uninhibited response, Luke petted and teased and stroked her softest flesh until she strained back toward him and whimpers of frustration tore from her throat. When she was finally ready, he fitted himself to her entrance and pushed slowly and firmly into her. She gasped and curled her spine, crying out as he filled her and retreated. Luke closed his eyes. She was so tight around him. So goddamn hot and wet he wasn't sure if he could hold back. "Em..."

"Don't stop," she begged, squeezing his wrist tighter.

"I won't." Not even if it killed him. He had this one night with her. He was going to make it as loving and memorable as he could.

He gave her more. All of him. Long, slow strokes that stimulated every nerve ending possible. He took her higher and higher, caressing her clit with his fingers as he kept up with the gentle pumping. She was almost there. His own pleasure grew and expanded until it threatened to take over, but he held on for her. Her breathing turned shallow, then a long, liquid moan spilled out and her head went back, eyes closed in rapture.

*There.* This was where he wanted her. Lost in the pleasure he bestowed. Helpless to do anything but feel.

He kissed the top of her left shoulder, fighting back the need to thrust until he came. So close now. "Almost there, Em." And once she got there, they were both going to die from the pleasure.

****

Emily wanted to yell at him, but didn't have the breath. He had her balanced on the absolute precipice, on that razor's edge of pleasure, but he wouldn't let her fall. She needed to. Her body was dying for the release. What was he waiting for? She lay still beneath him, trembling, willing him to give her that final caress that would hurl her over the edge. "Luke..." Her voice was ragged and desperate.

He smoothed the wig away from her face with one broad palm, his other fingers stroking where she was wet and aching and desperate for his touch. His lips brushed her ear, the faint prickle of his beard forming goosebumps over her violently sensitized skin.

"Yes, baby, so good..." His voice was like black silk sliding over her. The low, velvet murmur wrung another shiver out of her.

He pressed tight against her back, an unyielding wall of hot, hard muscles, the thick length of his erection buried deep inside her. Stretching and filling her beyond bearing. The heat of it stole her breath. His fingers stayed torturously close to her throbbing clit. Near enough to tease, but not close enough to give her the final caress she needed to send her flying. She was mindless, focused on nothing but the orgasm that hovered maddeningly out of reach. But he took her yet again up to the pinnacle before stopping his caressing fingers at the critical moment that would have detonated the charge inside her.

A soft cry escaped. She couldn't take any more.

"Shhh," he whispered against her damp temple, the passion-rough edge of it raking over her senses. "You know I won't leave you like this."

*But you will leave. It's only a question of when.* She

shook her head to erase the thought. God, she needed to come. Just a little more pressure, something. Please.

But Luke maintained that slow, steady rhythm with his hips and fingertips, at once soothing and devastating. Her fingers dug into his wrist like talons. "God—"

"Mmm. You there, sweetheart?"

At insanity? *Yes*. She nodded, desperate, beyond caring how she looked or that she was begging for release. "*Please...*"

His low, erotic growl of approval vibrated in her ear, then his hips drove hard against her. His fingers continued their torment between her thighs as he thrust strong and deep. The air locked in her throat. Too intense. She couldn't bear it.

"Ah yeah," he whispered. "There it is, sweetheart..."

She was going to die from it. The pleasure was too deep, too huge. Her mouth opened in a silent scream.

Luke anchored her firmly to the mattress. "Let yourself go, Em. I've got you."

She didn't have a choice. Her body clamped down around his burning cock with a hard spasm. A high, choked sob escaped. Lightning gathered and seared her nerve endings. Brilliant colors exploded behind her eyelids, and she screamed as the orgasm finally hit. Wave after wave of unrelenting ecstasy roared through her. And the whole time Luke's arms were tight around her. She teared up.

When it was over she lay sweating and gasping, her eyelids so heavy she couldn't lift them. Aftershocks rippled through her inner muscles as she clenched around Luke. He was scalding hot inside her, still thick and hard because he'd waited to ensure her pleasure before seeking his.

Out of nowhere, a lump formed in her throat, expanding until it threatened to choke her with the pressure of the unshed tears burning her eyes. It was as though her orgasm had ripped away any hold she had on her emotions and torn down her protective shields. A quiet sob ripped out of her, and she covered her face with her hands. Trust her to come unglued at such an intimate moment.

But Luke wouldn't let her hide. He pulled out and turned her onto her back, then gently pushed back into her to join them face to face. Instantly her arms encircled his muscular back. She tucked her face into his throat and prayed he hadn't seen the terrible scars on her chest.

Luke was still hungry for her, lodged deep inside her body, but she felt the difference in him when he closed his eyes and rested his forehead against hers. His protective shields were down too. It choked her up more. She'd needed that, even more than his lovemaking. To hold him as close and hard as she could while he gave himself to her in return. But now that she'd gotten it, the tears wouldn't be stopped.

Another sob came, harder than the first, but she couldn't cover her face and her mastectomy scars at the same time when he raised his head. When she tried, Luke merely caught her wrists and lightly pinned them on either side of her head.

"It's all right, baby. Tears are part of this," he whispered, bending to kiss them away. He moved gently within her, a tender caress that soothed as much as it stimulated. It broke the seal on the dam of her tears. They came out in a quiet rush while he stayed above her, eyes on her face as he murmured soothing things she didn't quite catch. When the tears slowed, she looked up into his handsome face with a sniffle and the smile he gave her filled her heart to overflowing. Dear God she loved him. Had always loved him and would never love another man but him.

Her heart had known it all along. And so had her body.

Still, she tensed when he released one of her wrists to touch the skin beneath her right collarbone. Luke shook his dark head, those liquid eyes looking right into her soul. “I won’t let you hide from me. Or from yourself.” Embedded deep inside her, he raised his upper body to gaze at her, and all she could do was close her eyes in resistance. “Look at me.”

After a long hesitation, she did.

He stared down at her with a powerful mixture of tenderness and hunger. “You think a scar’s going to change how I see you? Feel about you?”

She swallowed and struggled to find her voice. “It’s ugly.”

“You’re fucking *beautiful* to me, Em. Always.” She opened her mouth to say something but he leaned down to kiss her again. “Give me your hand,” he coaxed, his voice a seductive whisper. She did, tentatively, and his fingers closed around hers in a warm grip. Strong and reassuring. “Accept who you are. Be proud of your body. It’s fighting a war for you.”

He brought her hand to his mouth, nibbling at the base of each of her fingers, sliding his tongue between them as he rocked his hips against hers. Emily gasped and arched her lower back, bringing him deeper. Already the pleasure was building again. How did he to this to her? He was the only man who ever had, and he still knew just how to touch her. Holding her breath, she waited to see what he’d do next, steeling herself for the inevitable moment when he touched her scars.

Holding her gaze, Luke lowered their joined hands to her right collar bone, gently opening her palm before bringing it flush against her hot skin. “You’re so beautiful,” he whispered. The deep, approving tone of his words stroked over her in another caress, buoying her confidence. Using his hand to guide hers, he slid her palm downwards over the flat expanse of her chest where the scars lay. She flinched when she touched them, not because they hurt, but because she hated him seeing them. The surgeon had left the skin and pectoral muscles intact, but the incision site was still disfiguring.

Luke ignored the way she stiffened, bending instead to her other breast. His mouth was a warm, sweet bliss against her rigid nipple. The lazy glide of his tongue as he curled around it sent shocks of sensation between her thighs where he moved in and out. She moaned and slid her free hand into his hair, lifting into the caress. Then he sucked gently, rubbing his tongue over the tip, making her crave the velvet oblivion that awaited them both. She bit down on her lip and let her body relax.

This was the difference between Luke and the other men she'd been with. Right from the start, Luke had taken the time to find out what she liked, committing every detail from that very first time to memory. And he enjoyed giving her what she liked. Genuinely loved giving her pleasure. He got off on that almost as much as he did reducing her to quivering, mindless need with his unique brand of sexual dominance. It showed in his touch and in the care he took to make sure he satisfied her. Every single time. Like now, when he was slowly killing her with her body's response to his seduction. And obviously loving every minute of it.

Drowning in sensation, she barely noticed when he released her hand and settled his warm palm over her racing heart. His fingers traced every inch of the scars on the right side of her chest while he pleasured her left breast. After one last slow suck, he pulled free over her protests and leaned down to press kisses in the wake of his fingertips. Emily wrapped her arms around him and buried her face in his neck, trembling all over. He was so tender with her. It broke her heart.

The touch of his mouth on the scars brought a lump to her throat. Oh God, she'd missed him. Missed this explosive passion and the intimacy between them. What she felt was too deep for tears, or words. He was healing her with his touch and kisses, and she understood that's exactly what he'd set out to do. But she wanted more of the blinding heat she could only find in his arms.

She turned his head toward hers and kissed him, teasing his tongue, pouring everything she was into it. "Love me," she breathed against his lips.

"Always."

Her heart stuttered for an instant but then he made a dark, hungry sound and kissed her with ravenous need. Slow and deep and so erotic she felt her belly clench. Had he meant what he'd just said? She couldn't answer him. She was too blind with need.

Luke moaned into her mouth and settled back atop her, moving with greater power while he surged in and out of her greedy core, breathing roughly. Then he shifted onto his knees and drove even deeper.

Craving more, she guided his head back to her breast and hummed in approval as his mouth lavished more wicked attention on her nipple. Her hands trailed over his back and shoulders, luxuriating in his strength and the loving concentration he gave her. *More.* She never wanted this to end. He shifted his weight and gently laid his thumb over her swollen clit, and the pleasure intensified so fast that in seconds she was gasping and whimpering. He was so good... So amazingly good. "Luke..."

"Yeah baby, come for me again," he growled, thrusting deep as he licked and sucked her sensitive nipple and his thumb caressed her slick nub. So perfect.

Sighing, she widened her thighs and wrapped them high around his waist, urging him to take more, give more. That familiar tide of ecstasy rose within her, climbing higher. Against her breast, Luke's head tipped back on a tortured moan. So close to the edge of release she could see the beautiful agony of it on his face. She clung to him, urging him on with her cries of pleasure and her nails in his back. In response he stretched out on top of her and lengthened his thrusts, stroking every nerve ending inside her aching core. The orgasm exploded and forced a low wail from her, and only Luke's heavy weight kept her safely grounded as she soared outside her body for a moment.

When she came back to earth, his hips drove deep one last time and a growl ripped out of him as the wrenching pulses of release coursed through his big body. He finally stilled and dropped his head against her shoulder, breathing hard. The smooth skin on his back was damp with sweat.

Smiling contentedly, Emily cradled him in her arms, stroking his soft, thick hair. For the first time since the hysterectomy and mastectomy, she felt whole. Feminine and desirable. Beautiful, even. Because of Luke. In less than one night he'd managed to make her feel like the sexiest woman alive.

*But you're still dying.*

Her fingers froze in his hair. She shoved the thought from her mind before it could take hold and ruin the fragile intimacy of the moment.

Rising up on his hands, Luke gave her a slow, sexy smile and leaned down to kiss her. His lips were tender, his tongue caressing hers with lazy movements. Her eyelids drifted down as she savored the sweet contact. She didn't open her eyes when he pulled away, but her mouth pulled into a pout when he withdrew.

He let out a low chuckle and kissed the tip of her nose. "Be right back." He drew the covers over her.

"'Kay," she sighed, rolling onto her side. She must have drifted off, because the next thing she knew a cold draft touched her skin. Then Luke slid in beside her with a warm, damp cloth. He gently wiped her face and neck, moving down to her chest. She didn't protest when he touched her scars, merely turned onto her back and let him stroke the cloth over her body. This was another thing she'd missed about him. Luke always took care of her after they made love because her comfort mattered to him as much as her pleasure did. He was the most amazing and considerate lover any woman could wish for. Adding in the depth of her love, was it any wonder she'd never gotten over him?

He washed slowly down her abdomen and between her thighs before leaving the bed. When he came back he shifted her onto her side and spooned up tight against her back, tucking his thighs beneath hers to hold her in the cradle of his body. She couldn't stop the groan of enjoyment from escaping when the hard planes of his muscles pressed against her. Her body was warm and sated, boneless. After more than twenty years, she was finally where she'd always wanted to be, secure in Luke's loving arms. And she intended to savor every second of it for as long as it lasted.

If she could only stay awake.

Luke nuzzled the back of her neck, arms holding her tight. "Let yourself go, sweetheart."

"You too," she mumbled, already sliding into sleep, reassuring herself she'd have plenty of time to tell him how she felt in the morning.

# Chapter Fourteen

Waking up the next time was like drifting through layers of fog. Her brain was sluggish, having trouble coming online, and her limbs were leaden. Between her thighs a lingering dampness made her smile and snuggle closer to the powerful body that had cradled her all night.

Except Luke wasn't there.

Her eyes sprang open. She turned over and sat up, taking in the indentation in the pillow next to hers. What time was it? Bright light seeped through the edge of the roman blinds on the windows. She glanced at the clock. Stared. That couldn't be right. Did it say one seventeen? As in, early afternoon? She had an oncology appointment soon.

"Shit," she muttered, swinging her legs over the side of the bed and grabbing for her robe at the foot of it. Something caught around her neck as she drew it on. Her fingers touched the chain snagged on the robe. Stomach knotting, she looked down. Luke's St. Christopher medallion hung from her neck. He must have put it on her before he left.

As a goodbye.

*No.* She refused to believe it. Scrambling from the bed, heart in her throat, she rushed to the connecting bath. The door was open. "Luke?" she called. But it was empty.

He wouldn't have left without saying goodbye. *But he already said goodbye*, that whisper in her mind pointed out. *It's hanging around your neck.*

*Screw that.* Emily tore out of his room and checked hers, but it was empty also. Running down the stairs, she called his name, fighting to stay calm. He might be in the study.

She raced into the kitchen, and skidded to a stop when Nev looked up at her from her seat at the island, a cup of coffee steaming at her elbow. Her pretty blue eyes were red and swollen. Emily's heart sank like a rock.

"Hey," Nev said.

Emily swallowed. "Where's Luke?"

Nev tilted her head, frowning at her. "They left hours ago."

Her heart drummed loud in her ears. "Left for where?" He wouldn't go without telling her. Not after last night. He wouldn't do that to her.

"A meeting of some kind and then the airfield."

A hole opened up in her gut. She was afraid she already knew the answer to her next question, but needed to ask it anyway. "Where are they going?"

"Afghanistan."

Emily swayed and grabbed the edge of the island. "God," she whispered, sick to her stomach. It pitched and rolled beneath her ribs, clamped up so hard it hurt.

"I thought you knew."

She managed to shake her head. "He didn't say anything." And she hadn't asked. Why the hell hadn't she asked him?

"They got fresh intel after the meeting they had last

night. Luke didn't want to risk missing Tehrazzi again."

She couldn't believe he hadn't told her. Her gaze wandered around the room, her brain unable to process that he'd gone. The St. Christopher medallion seemed to singe her skin where it lay over her breaking heart. "Did—did he say when they'll be back?"

Nev's face scrunched as she looked down into her coffee. "No."

Emily wanted to wail from the pain. Luke had finally admitted he still loved her, but she hadn't said the words back. Now it was too late.

*No.* She straightened her spine. The hell it was. The goddamn *hell* it was.

She rushed down the hall, took the stairs to the lower floor and shoved the coms room door open. Ben wasn't there, but Sam sat at one of the computers. She partially turned her body toward her without looking up. Emily waited while she finished whatever she was doing and Sam finally turned her head and smiled. "Hi."

Emily put a hand to her tight throat. "Can you still reach Luke?"

Sam's smile disappeared. "He was in a meeting last I heard, but I can try."

Relief swept through her. He hadn't left yet.

Sam grabbed a phone from the corner of the desk. "Everything okay?"

*No.* "I just need to talk to him for a minute."

"Sure, hang on." She dialed and adjusted her headset, waited a few moments. "Just his voicemail," she said as she disconnected. "Let me try Ben." Buttons clicked, then another pause. "Hi, Ben, it's me. Could you get Luke to call in when you guys are through? Thanks. Love you." Sam eyed her. "Want to leave one on Luke's voicemail?"

"No. I have to tell him something, and it can't be left as a message." Unless it was a last resort.

A hint of sympathy crept into Sam's mahogany eyes. "I'll come and get you when he calls. Probably on their way to the airfield."

"Okay. Thanks." Disheartened but still optimistic she'd get her chance to say what she needed to, Emily went back upstairs.

Bryn and Nev were in the family room watching the huge flat screen TV mounted above the marble fireplace. A cable news channel was on, broadcasting footage of combat in Afghanistan. A female reporter stood before the camera wearing a helmet and armored vest, talking about American military casualties in the latest offensive launched by the Pentagon.

"We are receiving reports that a team of America's elite Navy SEALs engaged the enemy in the mountains northeast of Jalalabad again last night," the woman said. "Sources say that at least a dozen militants were killed in the most recent operation, and the enemy is said to be hunkered down in the region behind me, anticipating more attacks..."

"For Christ's sake," Bryn hissed, looking daggers at the screen. "How the hell do these idiots expect the SEALs to get the job done when the media tells the whole world they're there? She's going to get them fucking *killed*."

Emily went and sat beside her, setting a hand on her shoulder. The muscles beneath her palm were rock hard. She perfectly understood her friend's outrage. SEALs and their families deeply resented the media prying into their operations because it put men's lives at risk. For a band of covert commandos who worked best under cover of darkness using the element of surprise, unwanted attention was a bad thing. "No she won't. They're isolated up in the mountains, and no reporter's going to get up there."

"Yeah, well I bet someone will try to get a couple of

them to do interviews or some stupid thing." Bryn shook her head. "God, why do they do that? Can't they understand how dangerous these reports are?"

Oh, guaranteed they did. But it also increased ratings because the public loved anything to do with commandos and their secret operations. She squeezed Bryn's shoulder. "Think Dec's out there?"

Bryn rubbed her eyes. "I don't know. Luke told me yesterday he was close to here, but they could have been dropped in Afghanistan overnight."

And if Dec hadn't been, he certainly would be heading there now with Luke and Rhys. Emily glanced at Nev, who watched the footage with haunted eyes. "You okay?"

The surgeon nodded, staring at the screen for a moment before replying. "Just takes me back. I keep thinking about what happened out there. To me and Rhys. And my friends..."

Emily's heart ached for her. "Should we change the channel?"

"No," both women answered at once. Emily wasn't surprised. Part of her wanted to see what was happening, too. Luke would be there sometime later today.

Behind the reporter's shoulders, the rugged peaks of the mountains rose sharply into the sky. What Emily could see of them in the shot was covered with snow, and the wind blew hard enough to interfere with the reporter's audio equipment. Whenever they got there, Luke and the others faced their upcoming operation in what appeared to be bone-chilling conditions. It made her want to cry, thinking of them enduring more of it.

"I'm going to take a shower." The others nodded but didn't look at her, and Emily didn't bother trying to pry them away from the TV.

Upstairs she pulled off her wig and placed her robe on the counter before taking a good long look at herself in the mirror. She barely recognized herself, but somehow the scars on her body didn't repulse her the way they had before. Luke had touched them all. Kissed them. He still thought she was beautiful. Her eyes went to the gold medallion resting in the center of her chest. All these years Luke had worn it. Had he put it on her because it was meant to be some sort of protection for her? Or because he didn't think he'd be coming back?

Forcing the thought away, she showered and dressed, trying to decide what to do with herself until it was time to leave for her appointment. She wasn't up to socializing right now, and she didn't want to watch any more disturbing footage coming in from Afghanistan. Instead she went to the study with a book she'd brought along, and curled up in the chair where Luke had found her. But a few pages in, she hadn't retained anything about the plot or characters. As usual, her mind refused to be distracted when she had something weighing on it. Sighing, she got up just as Bryn knocked on the door and cracked it open. Her friend had dark shadows under her eyes Emily hadn't noticed before.

"Feel like some lunch?" Bryn asked.

"Not really, but I guess I should eat something." Maybe that would take care of the acidic rumble in her stomach. Together they made up some grilled cheese sandwiches with a Greek-style salad and took it downstairs to eat with Sam and Neveah. Sam pulled herself away from her computers for a few minutes and joined them on the couch outside the coms room.

"We need to find something to do," Nev said between bites, "or we'll go nuts."

Sam's phone rang and she jumped up to answer it using her headset. The three of them watched her disappear into the coms room, and the tension in the air was palpable. She came back out a minute later and stopped when she saw them all staring at her. "None of the guys," she said. "Sorry. But isn't it time for you to get going to your appointment?" she asked Emily

"Yeah, soon."

"I'll call the security guys out front. Anyone want to go with her?"

"No," Nev said.

"Me either," Bryn said, giving Emily an apologetic smile. "Sorry, hon. I want to hang around in case something important comes in to Sam."

Emily nodded. "I understand. I could use some time alone anyhow."

"What if Luke calls?" Sam asked.

"And what if he doesn't?" She already knew he wouldn't. He hadn't the last time he'd walked away.

Sam tossed her hair over one shoulder. "Take my cell then," she said. She went into the coms room to get it and brought it to her. "It's got a GPS tracking chip in it so I'll know where you are, and when Luke checks in I'll have him call you. If you need to get hold of me, just press and hold the number two."

"Thanks."

Bryn called down to the gate house and asked one of the guards to drive her into the city, and Emily walked with her down the driveway. "Be back before you know it," she said, desperate to get away from everyone and their whole situation. Who'd have thought she'd ever look forward to an oncology appointment?

Bryn hugged her tight. "If I wasn't so frantic for information about Dec I'd be going with you whether you wanted me or not. Just so you know."

"I'll be fine."

Bryn pulled away, her dark eyes delving into Emily's. "You're still in love with him, huh."

She sighed. "More than ever."

"You at least get to be with him last night?" Her expression must have answered for her, because Bryn gave her a sad smile. “Oh, honey... This whole damn thing sucks.”

Tears welled up. “I didn’t know he was leaving. He didn’t say goodbye.” She took a deep breath. “And I didn’t tell him I love him. God, I’m so stupid.”

Bryn smoothed a hand over the long wig. “I’m sure he knows.”

“I hope so, but I... I’m scared he doesn’t think he’s coming back. He put this on me.” She lifted the medallion from beneath her sweater. “You know how he is with Tehrazzi. He’s obsessed. Won’t stop until he gets him or dies trying.”

Bryn shook her head. “Don’t think like that. You can’t. We’ve all got to be strong and stay positive.”

Emily wasn’t sure she could anymore. She’d been hoping and praying for him forever, but now she was at her breaking point. She wiped her damp cheeks. “If Luke calls and I’m not back yet, have Sam tell him I’m going to light a candle for him.”

“A candle?”

“He’ll understand what I mean.”

“Sure.”

The guard nodded at them, and a minute later another pulled up with the silver Range Rover. Stepping out of the gatehouse, the first guard held the door open for her.

Bundled in the back of the Rover, Emily waved once to her friend. The driver took her to her appointment, escorted her into the building and up to the fifth floor office. When she came out forty minutes later, he was there waiting to escort her back to the vehicle. She asked him to drive her to a place she’d seen on the way in from the airport. Closing her eyes, she laid her head back against the leather seat for a moment, willing herself to calm down. Her blood counts were good. Luke wasn’t gone yet. She might still get the chance to talk to him before he left, tell him she loved him and would be waiting for him when he got back.

She needed to hear him tell her he was coming back.

The driver stopped at a security checkpoint before driving through traffic into the downtown area. They had to stop a few times because of congestion, and when they came to a standstill the third time, Emily was feeling anxious. Through the windshield, she spotted the Christian church nestled next to the mosque a few blocks away. She'd go into the church and light a candle, then maybe go to the mosque and offer up a prayer there as well. Hedge her bets. Why not? Couldn't hurt.

"I think I'll get out here and walk," she told the driver.

His dark eyes met hers in the rear view mirror. "You're going to the church?"

"Yes, that one," she said, pointing. "Then the mosque, I think. Will they let me in if I'm not a Muslim?"

A smile quirked his mouth. "Just make sure you cover your hair and take off your shoes before you go in. Someone will see you and tell you what to do."

"Thank you."

"Not at all. I'll pick you up outside the doors."

"You don't have to wait. I'll call you—"

"I'll wait," he said firmly before putting the vehicle in park and coming around to let her out. "Go ahead. This is a safe area."

As she slid out the passenger door, the cool, damp air washed over her, thick with the promise of rain. People crowded the sidewalks, heading for shops and cafes or businesses. She caught the tempting scent of pastries when she passed by one of the shops, weaving through the pedestrian traffic as she cut across the street. The spire of the church and minaret of the mosque were her beacons, guiding her through the unfamiliar streets. The comforting weight of Sam's cell phone rested in her hip pocket. A gust of chilly wind plucked at her jacket, and she wrapped the pretty red velvet scarf Bryn had given her for Christmas higher around her face.

The old brick church welcomed her with a breath of slightly musty air when she pulled the heavy front door open and stepped inside the dimly lit interior. She wasn't particularly religious, but she'd been baptized and raised an Episcopalian. Growing up, she'd attended St. Michael's Church in Charleston every Sunday with her parents. Though she might not attend services regularly anymore, her faith was a gift that had seen her through many hard times throughout her life. And St. Michael's was where she'd always lit candles for Luke.

Her gaze immediately went to the altar, still decorated with the advent candles from Christmas celebrations, and the table filled with flickering votives close to it. Walking toward it and the elaborate manger scene set up on a dais, her heartbeat settled.

Feeling calmer already, she silently recited the Lord's Prayer as she approached, and selected a candle for Luke. Lifting the lit taper, she closed her eyes and asked for his protection, then chose a votive and touched the flame to its wick. The instant it caught fire something inside her eased, yet she still gripped the St. Christopher medallion tightly with her free hand. She had performed this same rite every time Luke had gone out on a mission or training exercise she'd known about. Sometimes she went in between those times to light another candle just in case. Over the years they'd been apart she'd gone once a month without fail to do the same.

And every time he'd come back alive. Maybe he hadn't come back to *her*, but he was still alive.

Kneeling before the flickering votive, her gaze went to the statue of Jesus suffering on the cross, suspended above the altar. It didn't seem right for her to ask anything more of Him than she already had. Too selfish somehow. But staring up at that icon, another prayer formed.

*Please let him come back to me. Let me live. Give us the rest of our lives together.*

Bowing her head, she sent up one last prayer for Luke's protection, and rose. She felt lighter, as though some invisible weight had been lifted from her shoulders. She breathed deeper and easier than she had in a long time.

Leaving the church, she walked the short distance over to the mosque, paying careful attention to what the other people did. Everyone seemed to be leaving. She must have just missed afternoon prayers. She didn't see anyone going inside, so she waited until the crowd thinned out.

Remembering the guard's words, Emily lifted the ruby velvet scarf and covered her wig, carefully tucking the hair inside it before tying the ends under her chin. Beneath her coat she wore a long-sleeved turtleneck and dark jeans, so she was modestly covered. Approaching the entrance hesitantly, she stopped in the foyer and took off her shoes, glancing around. A large fountain graced the center of the room, and, unsure what protocol she was supposed to follow, she didn't dip her hands in the water. The last thing she wanted was to offend anyone.

A white-bearded man saw her as he appeared from another room and approached, making eye contact. She put on a smile and waited until he came close enough that he could hear her lowered voice.

"May I go in?" she asked.

A pleased smile broke over his grizzled features, and he bent a little at the waist, holding a hand out to an inner doorway. "Please." She followed behind him at a respectful distance. "Is this your first visit to a mosque?"

"Yes."

"You are American."

"Yes." Which likely didn't raise his opinion of her any, but he seemed friendly enough.

"In here," he gestured, indicating an open prayer hall. Its rows of carpets were broken only by ornate white pillars that anchored floor and ceiling. A reverent hush filled the cavernous room. "You may stay at the back," her guide instructed in a whisper, "away from the men. Be mindful not to walk in front of someone who is praying, out of respect."

She nodded. When he left her, she gazed around with a growing ache in her chest. From what she'd read about Islam, it was a beautiful, gentle religion. Emphasizing charity and tolerance and peace. The mosque fit with that image. The radicalism Luke and his team faced did *not*.

Every religion had its dark side, she wasn't stupid or naive enough to believe otherwise. But how could men twist the teachings of God until they actually believed they would go to paradise for killing innocent people? How could they wage what they considered a holy war, looking for any excuse to blow up those they regarded as "unbelievers"? She'd never understand it.

But that's not what she'd come here to think about. God was God. She wanted to kneel here and pray for Luke, showing Him the fight Luke waged was not a crusade to crush Islam. It was about doing what was right and defending the world from those who would do harm in His name. No matter what faith they practiced.

Moving quietly, she slipped along the back wall to find some privacy, stopping when she spotted a man in white robes kneeling off to the left facing an embellished wall, his forehead touching the carpet as he prayed. Walking away from him, she picked a spot and knelt down on the prayer carpet. The nap was soft and worn from age, a bit threadbare in spots, clear marks upon it from countless knees, hands and foreheads touching it.

Closing her eyes, Emily laid her palms on her thighs and bent her head, clearing her mind of everything but her prayer to keep Luke safe from harm.

When she was done, a feeling of peace filled her, like a warm weight in her heart. It brought a smile to her lips and made her eyes sting. Wherever he was, she hoped Luke was safe.

*He'll call. Stop worrying.*

No he wouldn't. She knew better.

Exhaling deeply, she rose and brushed off her knees. Raising her head, she saw the man over by the wall turn to look at her over his shoulder. Her heart skipped. Had she disturbed him? Done something wrong?

She would have lowered her eyes and walked away, but something about him was familiar. He was young, maybe in his early thirties, with light skin and a neatly trimmed mink-brown beard. His shoulders were broad, the robes merely hinting at the muscular build. He watched her with an unnerving stillness. Unblinking. Alert, as though waiting for something.

She took a step backward, instinctively touching the medallion that hung around her neck. His gaze followed her hand, and even from where she stood she saw the sudden tension grip him.

When he raised his eyes their gazes collided. Her pulse beat frantically in her neck. This didn't feel right. She should leave. Taking another step back to do exactly that, he suddenly surged to his feet, staring at her with an eerie focus. Like he was a hunter and she was his prey.

*Run.*

She stumbled, bracing herself against the wall to steady her feet and threw a frantic glance over her shoulder. He came toward her, his expression intent. But when she realized she was staring into a pair of green eyes, the air exploded from her lungs in a gasp of startled recognition.

*Tehrazzi.*

Whirling on her heel, she ran.

# Chapter Fifteen

Luke hefted his heavy ruck higher onto his back and headed toward the C-130 waiting on the tarmac. In the cockpit the pilots were well into their pre-flight checklist. Rhys strode beside him, his long legs eating up the distance.

"How long until Dec and his boys get here?" he asked.

Luke checked his watch. "Another forty minutes maybe. Could be less." All he knew was, the instant that bird took off, he would be out for the entire flight. Wouldn't get much sleep in the coming weeks, and he intended to get what he could on the trip to Bagram.

He'd only slept a few ten minute snatches last night. He hadn't been willing to lose what little time he'd had to hold Emily against him. It shook him up, how much he was still in love with her. More than ever, if that was possible. Making love to her last night had been the most intense, shattering experience of his life. No matter what happened after today, she owned him, body and soul. If he got Tehrazzi and lived to tell about it, he was never leaving her side again.

He didn't want to think about what awaited him in Afghanistan. Dwelling on it would only depress the hell out of him. But his mind wouldn't shut off. His life with Tehrazzi had finally come full circle. He was going back to the place where it had all begun for them, just like the hand-written note had said. In the mountains where he'd taken that gangly, pissed-off kid and inadvertently turned him into one of the greatest threats that existed to western civilization. A man who had learned enough from his teacher to avoid capture by the most powerful agencies in the world these past six years.

But no more. Tehrazzi's days of threats and terror were all but over. Luke would get the bastard this time, or die trying.

Nearing the aircraft, his cell vibrated against his hip. Stopping, he pulled it out to check the display. "Hey, Sam. What's up?" *Please don't let her say something's wrong with Emily.*

"I left Ben a voicemail hours ago. Didn't he give you the message?"

He frowned. "No, what was it?"

"Emily wants you to call her."

Luke looked down at his steel-toed assault boots. He'd been dreading that request. He didn't want to make any promises he couldn't keep, and he didn't want to hurt her anymore. It would tear him apart to hear her on the other end of the phone right now, even if she didn't cry. Because he wasn't sure what he could tell her to make it any easier. That's why he'd left without saying anything. "Okay. Is she there?" When he'd left her curled up in his bed that morning, she'd been dead asleep, hadn't so much as stirred when he'd kissed her cheek and put the chain around her neck. Still, he felt like a bastard for not being honest with her. And for sneaking out before she woke up because he was too much of a coward to watch her face crumple when she found out he was leaving.

"No, she's still out, but—"

He stiffened. "What? Her appointment should have been over by now." A while ago, actually. What if she'd gotten bad news?

"She said she was going to light a candle for you."

He closed his eyes. *Ah, damn, Em...* Barbs pricked at his heart. He couldn't believe she still did that for him. Rubbing his tired eyes, he sighed. "Please tell me she's got a phone with her."

"I gave her mine, and the number's already programmed into yours. I've got her on GPS now, but as far as I can tell she's inside a mosque."

"A mosque?"

"Yeah, it's the big one right next to a church downtown. Know it?"

He did. Knowing Em, she'd gone into both places to plead her case for his soul with God and Allah, on the off chance either one of them would intercede on his behalf. Maybe she knew he could use all the help he could get. "I'll call her," he promised.

Hanging up, he took a deep breath and found Sam's cell number in the menu. There wasn't a damn thing he could say that would make this any easier on Emily, but he was willing to try. She at least deserved to hear him say why he hadn't told her he was leaving. And she deserved to hear that he loved her. Apart from that, there was dick all he could give her until this thing ended.

****

Her perfume gave her away. Nothing ever disturbed him when he was in prayer, but that light note of vanilla in the air had alerted him a woman was nearby. The tingling between his shoulder blades had made him glance behind him once he was finished. He might have only frowned in disapproval had he not seen her grab the pendant around her neck. Then her face became clear to him, as did the significance of the jewelry she wore. He'd recognize it anywhere.

His teacher's cherished medallion.

Tehrazzi took a step toward her, his heart thudding hard against his ribs. Her eyes were green, almost the same shade as his, and they widened in apprehension. He could not believe she was standing there. She had willingly entered Allah's house. Because Allah had brought her to him.

Triumph soared through his blood. Everything was clear to him now. This was the way it was meant to happen. She was the instrument with which Allah wanted to draw his teacher to his death.

He knew the instant she realized who he was. Her face went utterly white, her nostrils flaring as she gasped. She spun to flee, but he followed. Not at a run, for it would be disrespectful to cause a scene in the musalla.

Near the door she bent to snatch up her shoes, casting a quick glance over her shoulder as she ran. He came closer and she fled, running into the courtyard. The blood red scarf she wore over her hair made her easy to follow in the crowd. He raised a hand to signal two of his men, and they intercepted her. She got out one tiny shriek before one of them clamped a hand over her mouth and dragged her quickly toward the waiting vehicle.

His blood raced through his veins. The surge of triumph was harder and more potent than a hit of heroin. The end was finally here. He was ready.

****

Emily tossed her head and screamed beneath the

meaty hand covering her mouth. Two men had her in a tight grip, and practically carried her as they rushed away from the street to an alley. Hadn't anyone seen her? She kicked and struggled, managed to knock one of them in the face with her elbow, hard enough that he grunted and loosened his grip. She jerked away and whirled, pulling to escape the other man's hold as she grabbed for the phone in her pocket. The number two, Sam had told her. She had to press and hold the number two. Yanking it out, she clamped her thumb onto the button and held it down.

A split second later Tehrazzi was upon her, knocking it out of her hand with one swipe of his arm. It clattered to the cobbled street. Enraged, she rammed an elbow into her captor's stomach. "Let me go!" Another hand clamped down over her mouth, staying there no matter how hard she thrashed her head back and forth. Had she held the button long enough? Maybe the signal was transmitting right now. When she didn't answer, Sam would know something was up. But then Tehrazzi walked over and smashed the phone under his booted heel, shattering it on the cobblestones. He twisted his foot for good measure, the sound of grinding plastic and electronic components loud in the empty alley.

Fear threatened to choke her as he approached again, his eyes holding an unearthly glow. If Sam hadn't received the call, then no one would know she was missing. She would die by Tehrazzi's hand.

Someone shouted behind them.

Emily wrenched against the arms holding her and caught a glimpse of her driver running flat out toward them, a weapon raised in one hand. He fired once. She flinched and screamed louder beneath the hand, fighting with all she had to get free. But then Tehrazzi's other man pulled out his pistol and fired twice. She jumped at the muted pop of the silencer and cried out when the guard crumpled, two bloody wounds blooming on his chest. His hands grabbed at his shirt as though he couldn't believe he'd been hit. His eyes bulged and his back arched upward, fingers clawing at his throat for air. Scarlet froth bubbled up from the holes in his ruined lungs and gushed out his mouth and nose.

Tehrazzi said something to the others in another language and they dragged her away, the guard's awful gurgling ringing in her ears. She wanted to cry. That poor man was dying a hideous death because he'd tried to help her, and now no one would know what had happened to her.

Hard hands shoved her face first onto the back seat of the waiting Mercedes SUV. She yanked her head up and lunged for the door, but Tehrazzi slid in beside her and caught her wrists, yanking the scarf off her head and using it to lash her hands behind her back. The doors slammed shut, the engine roared to life, and then the vehicle shot down the alley. He trapped her flailing legs with one knee and pushed her bound hands up. The sudden flare of pain in her shoulder joints wrenched a cry out of her.

"Let me *go*," she cried.

"Lie still."

The hell she would. She wriggled and fought, an animal growl tearing from her throat. Was this really happening? Everyone thought he was in Afghanistan. Luke and the others were going there to get him. A sob of fear shook her.

"Be easy." Tehrazzi's low voice was without an accent, eerily soothing. Almost kind. She shivered. "My fight is not with you."

"Then let me go!"

"You're going to bring my teacher to me."

Did he mean Luke? Because he'd trained him? "No," she managed. "H-he's gone to Afg-ghanistan for you."

Tehrazzi grabbed her upper arms. He raised her off the seat and jerked her jaw around with one hand. "What?"

The rage burning in those green eyes withered her insides. "H-he's going there—"

"How do you know this?" She flinched when he shook her once. "He told you this? When?"

She didn't dare tell him she'd heard the information from another source. "Th-this morning."

His eyes flared. "Is he still here? In Beirut?"

Emily swallowed. She wasn't going to tell him anything that might jeopardize Luke's safety. Maybe she'd said too much already.

His hand tightened painfully on her jaw. "Is he?"

"I-I d-don't know..."

He released her with a snap of his wrist and her cheek hit the leather, hard enough to make her flinch. Then he spoke rapidly in another language to the driver.

"Please let me go," she begged, squirming against his hold.

"No. You are the key to this."

What was he talking about? "I have nothing to do with this."

One of his hands grabbed the chain around her neck. "If you're wearing his medallion, you have everything to do with this."

"It doesn't mean anything," she cried.

"It means *everything*. He would only give that to you. Because you matter to him more than anyone."

Tears burned her eyes. "Don't do this. Please, he's been through enough."

He said something else to the driver, completely ignoring her pleas. She wanted to scream from the pain clawing at her. If Luke came charging to her rescue, Tehrazzi would be waiting to kill him.

****

Luke's call immediately went to an electronic message saying the owner was either out of range or unavailable. Was she still in the mosque maybe? Instead of turning it to vibrate, she might have turned it off out of respect.

Frowning, he hung up and dialed Sam back at the compound. "Her phone's not on," he said as soon as she answered.

"*Luke.*"

His blood chilled at the fear in her voice. Sam was always calm when she worked. Even when she'd been facing an attack from an approaching enemy force alone in a cave in Afghanistan, she'd held it together. "What?"

"The signal went dead about two minutes ago. Just stopped transmitting... Hold on."

*Shit.* Luke's hand tightened around the phone. He made out an urgent male voice in the background speaking in rapid Arabic, but couldn't hear what he was saying. Was Emily okay? Rhys strode over, his eyes locked on him.

Sam came back on the line. "Oh God, Luke, the guard who drove her reported in that three men were chasing her. He was pursuing on foot, but we can't reach him."

Luke's blood congealed in his veins. Couldn't be coincidence. No way.

*Let us finish this where it all began...*

The bottom of his stomach dropped out. Oh, fuck, he'd screwed it up.

Not Afghanistan. *Beirut.* Where Tehrazzi had first been recruited by a radical militia.

"I'm calling Ben," he said, fighting the undiluted fear streaking through him. "Get Dec on the line for me." Ben answered on the first ring. "Emily's gone. I think

Tehrazzi's got her." He could barely get the words out of his tight throat.

"Shit. The police just called me. One of my guys was found dead in an alley downtown beside a mosque."

"Come get us. We'll start there."

"I'll be there in five."

Luke shoved the phone into its holster, struggling to get his heart rate under control. All he could think about was that Tehrazzi had Emily.

At one time he could have guaranteed Emily would be safe until he showed up, because Tehrazzi didn't like to kill his victims himself. But no longer. He was increasingly unstable, had killed at least one man himself in the past few months. Tehrazzi was paranoid and unpredictable now. He didn't trust anyone and was finally taking matters into his own hands. He wanted Luke, and knew damn well Emily would guarantee him coming after her.

But until Luke got there, there was no telling what he'd do to her. Luke's stomach lurched sickeningly. He was going to kill that fucker.

Without a word he and Rhys ran back to the hangar to wait for Ben.

# Chapter Sixteen

Emily's heart was in her throat when the SUV finally stopped and the engine turned off. She couldn't lift her head enough to see out the window. Where were they? Was he going to hurt her? Torture her for information she didn't have?

Tehrazzi said something to his men and then dragged her out of the vehicle, forcing her to walk in front of him as they approached a darkened industrial building. The air was heavy and damp, carrying the salty tang of the sea. They must be near the waterfront.

It was growing darker outside, and the oppressive shadows deepened as he pushed her inside the empty room. The metal door shut behind them with a bang, echoing off the concrete walls. She shivered and snuck a glance around. A single barred window in the far wall let in the fading light. No other doors. She had to get out the way she'd come. Tehrazzi wasn't looking at her. His back was to her as he moved purposefully around the barren room while he gathered things and stuffed them into a backpack. The SUV was parked out on the street.

If she could get outside and run in the opposite direction, maybe she could get enough of a head start to lose them and get help.

Her heart thudded against her ribs. She had to try. She couldn't stay here and let Tehrazzi use her as bait to trap Luke.

Luke might be gone already. Airborne, well on his way to Afghanistan. She didn't know. Sooner or later, Sam and the others would realize she was missing and start looking for her. They'd find out about the guard who'd died trying to save her. The police would be alerted. Were they out looking for her now? Every major security agency in the world wanted Tehrazzi, yet he'd made it into Beirut without arrest. Did he have someone protecting him from the inside? The idea made her sick with despair.

Careful not to glance over her shoulder, she watched Tehrazzi stuff clothes, money and some ammunition into his bag. Wincing inside, she slid one foot back and slowly transferred her weight from toes to heel. Then the other, while her fingers twisted in the scarf binding her wrists. He'd tied it tight enough that it cut off the circulation, and she couldn't get a good enough grip on the velvet to loosen it. She took another step backward, sensing the door at her back. She'd have to ram it with her shoulder and run for it. And pray she could find some kind of cover before they shot her in the back.

Another step. Beads of sweat broke out over her upper lip. Then Tehrazzi paused and looked back at her. She froze.

His forest green eyes pinned her like an insect. "Don't."

The look on his face, the quiet warning frightened her. The door was right behind her. Only a few feet away. Tehrazzi was on the other side of the room.

*Now or never.*

She spun and lunged for the door, slamming her shoulder into the release bar with a heavy clang, but her head snapped back and she fell to the floor, one hip and elbow taking the brunt of the impact with the cold concrete. Cool air washed over her bald scalp. She scrambled onto her knees and faced Tehrazzi, preparing for the beating she feared was coming. He stood above her, her long wig dangling from his fist.

His expression transformed from buried rage to astonishment as he stared down at her. “You’re ill,” he said softly.

Body tensed, she glared up at him and gritted her teeth. She would not let the bastard see how afraid she was.

He took a step toward her and she flinched despite herself, but he merely placed the wig back on her head and moved away. She would have sworn his eyes filled with sympathy, but that was impossible. He was a twisted, hate-filled terrorist and wouldn’t care about anything but his perceived duty to Allah.

“I’m sorry that you’ve suffered so much in this life.”

His softly spoken words sent a chill rippling down her backbone. He spoke as though he planned to send her to the afterlife to ease her. And what did he know of her suffering? The look in his eyes was all wrong. It confused her. Why would he feel sorry for her? He must hate her because she was a non-believer, an American, and worse, Luke’s ex-wife.

Then he surprised her again by reaching out a broad, strong hand. She flinched, but he merely grasped her upper arm gently and helped her to her feet in an almost chivalrous gesture. He was shockingly gentle with her, even adjusting the wig before he moved away. She pulled back, almost more afraid of this oddly tender side of him. Was he clinically insane? That would explain his polar personality shifts.

The unexpected kindness in him tangled her up. Jesus, what was going on with her? It was way too early for some stupid rendition of the Stockholm syndrome. "Please let me go." Her voice was breathy and weak-sounding, but she had to try to make him release her.

Tehrazzi shook his head, the faint light coming through the window behind him illuminating his rich brown hair. It formed a kind of halo around his head, transforming him into the angel of God he believed he was.

"I cannot. I'm sorry." True regret colored his voice.

Her heart sank. What was she supposed to do? She didn't have a prayer against him physically, and no way could she outrun him.

"Now stay there and don't move."

The snap in his command jolted her, but still she edged toward the door when he became swallowed by the shadows. She turned to flee again but he emerged pulling the hem of a black knit sweater over the waistband of his dark jeans. He had something on beneath it. A bullet proof vest?

He picked up a pistol from the table and slung his pack over his shoulder before stalking toward her. "Let's go." His gentleness was gone, as if it had never happened. There was no trace of kindness in his face or his eyes. Just the hardened warrior, back in control of everything.

He grabbed her bound hands and shoved her out the door.

****

Luke lowered his phone and braced himself as Rhys took a sharp right turn. The Suburban's tires squealed when it did a controlled skid around the corner. "Dec and his boys are on the ground. They'll move in from the south." Through the most dangerous part of Beirut, the stronghold of Shiite Hezbollah. Was that where Tehrazzi was headed?

His gut said no. Tehrazzi would find people willing to hide him there, but it was too obvious a destination. Too predictable. Luke bet he had other plans in mind, and was working things out on the fly. No way could he have known Emily was in Beirut. The only person who'd known besides him and his team was Jamie, and Luke was absolutely sure he'd ended the treachery with Miller's arrest. There was no way anyone could have found out about the doctor's appointment today. No, Emily running into Tehrazzi's path was pure, shit luck. The question was where the hell to start looking for them. Every second mattered.

"No sightings at the airport or borders, but the alert's been issued," Ben said as he hung up his phone. "Police are out looking for them now."

Rhys hit the brakes and muttered under his breath when he had to stop for the traffic, then laid on the horn.

Luke wasn't wasting any time. "This is good enough," he said. "Pull over and we'll start here."

He couldn't believe Tehrazzi had gotten Emily. Here. Where he'd forced her to come because he'd been sure she was at risk back in Charleston. If she'd stayed put at home, she would still be safe. The damning knowledge tied his guts in knots. He wanted to kick his own ass. This was all his fault. All of it.

*Hang on, Em. Please hang on.*

Wherever they were, Tehrazzi would be ready for him. Luke just prayed he wouldn't hurt Emily before they had their final confrontation.

****

The alley was shadowed and quiet, exactly what he

needed. He had to move quickly. If Emily was here, his teacher wouldn't be far away. And he'd be coming for him. They had to know about the dead bodyguard by now.

Tehrazzi's blood hummed. So close now. He could almost feel his teacher's breath on the back of his neck, coming closer with each minute. The eerie sensation of being followed spurred him to move faster.

Ignoring Emily's protests, he propelled her along in front of him, away from where the truck was parked. He'd destroyed the tracking device in her phone. She didn't have any others, he'd checked her over when he'd hauled her into the vehicle. There wouldn't be anyone following them with electronic eyes, and if either of his men tried to follow, he'd kill them. He'd learned the hard way never to trust anyone, and he wasn't about to put his life in anyone's hands but Allah's.

She dug her small feet into the ground to slow them down, and he forced down his irritation. He understood her fear, but there was no help for it. "The faster you move, the faster this will be over."

"Screw you," she snapped, flinging her head back to bash him and he narrowly got his jaw out of the way in time. Her outrage radiated off her in waves, so strong he could practically see them, like flashes of red fire.

"I won't help you hurt him. I'll die first!"

Her courage impressed him nearly as much as her fierce loyalty did. Loyalty was as rare as it was precious. At one time, he'd been as loyal to his teacher as Emily still was. At one time, Tehrazzi would have killed for him. Died for him without hesitation. He shook the memories away.

"Let me go!" She lashed out at him with her foot, but he ignored the shot. She was breathing hard, and not solely from fear. She was tiring rapidly. Weakened from either the disease attacking her body or the treatment of it. A hint of guilt crept in. He was uncomfortable harming an innocent woman. But what other choice did he have?

"Be quiet or I'll gag you," he warned, shifting his grip on her wrists. She continued struggling, gasping now, her increased body heat rising up through her clothing. "And stop fighting before you hurt yourself."

With a snarl, she whipped her head around to bite his shoulder.

"Enough," he barked, pulling out his pistol and pressing it to the small of her back. She stilled instantly, freezing in place. When he forced her to keep walking, her movements turned stiff and jerky. "Why were you at the mosque?" He needed to know.

At first she wouldn't answer him, but he gave her a tug and she looked up at him with pure venom in her eyes. "I was praying for someone."

"Your husband."

"Ex-husband," she said through gritted teeth.

Semantics. The medallion told him the real story between her and his teacher. They might be divorced, but she still cared enough to pray for him. And she'd gone to the mosque to ask for Allah's help. Had removed her shoes, covered her hair and knelt quietly at the back of the musalla. Respectful of Islam, though she was a Christian. So much like his teacher.

"I want to know why," she suddenly demanded in a half-whisper.

"Why what?" he answered, stopping to make sure the next alley was deserted before pushing her onward.

"How could you do this? You're a man of God."

"I'm a *soldier* of God," he corrected coldly. "And I take my responsibilities very seriously." Unlike others he knew.

"Damn you, stop dragging me," she snarled, struggling though she must have known how futile it was. “Why Luke?”

His stomach seized at the name. He hated hearing it. But was it possible she didn’t know? Perhaps, since his teacher had left her before meeting him in Afghanistan. “We have a shared history.”

“Why?” Her voice was filled with such pain, such sorrow, it made his skin prickle.

“Because he betrayed me,” Tehrazzi said in a low rasp. “He abandoned me, the same as he did you.” And that made them kindred spirits of sorts, didn’t it? How odd the workings of Allah were.

She inhaled sharply at his words, and again her pain radiated out to him. Jagged and fresh. “Don’t...don’t hurt him anymore. He’s suffered too.”

His jaw tensed. He was not interested in his teacher’s so-called suffering. Anger rose hard within him. His teacher had been a fully grown man when the anti-Soviet jihad ended. Tehrazzi had been a scrawny teenager left in the desolate mountains of his ancestors when the Americans suddenly withdrew their support for Afghanistan. Leaving him forgotten by the man who’d been the closest thing to a father he’d ever known.

He thought of the trigger switch hidden in his left coat pocket. His heart responded with a desperate throb. The mortal body, weak and fearful. But not his soul. He was a soldier of Allah, and devoted to His cause. All Tehrazzi had to do was take his hostage to a more secure location and arrange plans for him and his teacher to meet one last time. But time was running short. Someone must have noticed the woman missing by now. His teacher would be alerted. If Tehrazzi was lucky, his teacher was indeed heading back to Afghanistan. That would give him time to find a better position and plan his final strategy.

The briny scent of the water grew stronger as he wound them through to the waterfront. The cry of gulls increased. His hostage was stiff but unresisting in front of him, the muzzle of his SIG pressed against her spine. They emerged between two industrial buildings near a small fishing dock, a place he knew would be all but deserted this time of night. He needed a boat. A fast one. And he needed time to think. He could almost feel those intense, dark eyes watching him right now from the shadows. His teacher would come. Tehrazzi didn't question that for a moment. The chain around Emily's neck guaranteed it.

He needed to be ready.

Her feet slipped as he pushed her onto the dock, the surface slick with the mist rising off the surface of the gray-green water. She shook her head, the ends of her hair whipping in the cold breeze. "N-no," she gasped when she realized his intent.

He ignored her and pressed on, heading for the end where a fleet of fishing boats and pleasure craft bobbed in the tide. Voices came from behind him. He whipped around, cutting off Emily's gasp with his free hand, and stared through the film of fog toward the street. He relaxed. Merely some fishermen, heading home for the evening.

The prickle between his shoulder blades didn't let up. He felt as though someone had him in the crosshairs of a sniper rifle. Was his teacher already here?

Tehrazzi searched the darkened rows of shops and offices at the far end of the dock. Nothing moved. No lights, no reflections of a camera or binocular lenses.

He took two steps backward, scanning warily before turning her and propelling her toward the boats.

*You're not ready.*

The whisper in his head sent a bolt of fear through him. Sweat popped out on his upper lip and beneath his arms. Doubt crowded his mind. He wasn't prepared for this. He'd never expected to have the woman dropped into his hands, nor to have to face his teacher so soon. His fingers itched to grab the switch in his pocket. If his teacher was here, the switch and the woman he held were the only things capable of buying him time to escape and regroup. He had to plan this carefully. It had to end up with just him and his teacher. No one else.

More voices floated toward him. Disjointed because of the fog obscuring the speakers. Every muscle in Tehrazzi's body went tight as a cable. He listened intently, trying to ascertain the source of the words. Then he heard it, and his belly drew up hard.

"...reported seeing them...moving toward docks..."

English. The hair on his nape stood on end. He shot a fervent glance behind him. The boat he wanted was a short sprint away. So close. He could still make it.

The muscles in his thighs twitched, ready to run. Then Emily gasped and stiffened in his hold. A shiver of foreboding snaked up his backbone.

"Don't move," a deep voice warned in Arabic.

He knew that voice. Slowly, Tehrazzi turned his eyes to the end of the dock.

Out of the fog, two men emerged, armed with assault rifles. One was huge, almost a head taller than the other.

The shorter one moved closer, his movements practiced and stealthy. Expert in their precision. The man moved another step closer, then another. Tehrazzi edged backward. Were there snipers already in position waiting to take him out?

Fear rose up hard and fast, threatening to choke him. He brought the pistol up and locked his forearm around his hostage's throat, then grabbed the device from his left pocket with his other hand. "Don't move or I'll blow it," he replied.

Through the fog, the man's face came into view. Unmistakable dark eyes stared back at him, the intense hatred in them threatening to make his knees shake.

His teacher had come for him at last.

# Chapter Seventeen

Emily grabbed at the thick forearm cutting into her windpipe and dug her nails into his skin, rising on tiptoe to keep from choking. Tehrazzi was frozen in place behind her, his muscular body rigid as the men approached. He grabbed something from his pocket and raised it, then growled some sort of warning she didn't understand. The approaching footsteps stopped.

Her eyes went to his hand, poised next to her head. What was he holding? Another gun? Unable to move her head, she strained to see it in her peripheral vision. Not a gun. Something small. His thumb was pressed on the top of it. A trigger of some kind?

He jerked her backward, cutting off her air for a moment. Beneath his sweater she felt the hard lines of the vest he wore and the truth froze the blood in her veins.

He had some sort of suicide vest on him, and was holding the switch for the detonator. If he let go...

Fear paralyzed her. She shook with the effort of holding still, taking shallow breaths so she wouldn't jostle him. Afraid to move her head, she turned her eyes to stare through the fog toward the men before them. Was it the police? The military?

Then their faces appeared through the thin veil of fog. A broken gasp tore out of her. "Luke!" His name wrenched from her throat as her heart leapt in relief, then in stark fear. Tehrazzi would kill them all. "No, stay back! He's got—"

Tehrazzi clamped his arm tighter around her throat, cutting off the words and her air. She clawed and gasped. Any second now he'd release his hold on the trigger of the vest and detonate it. Luke and Rhys were close enough that the blast would kill them too. The bitter, metallic taste of fear filled her dry mouth. She stared into Luke's fathomless eyes, pleading for some sign of what he wanted her to do.

He didn't move a muscle, his gaze locked on Tehrazzi, rifle raised and aimed. He said something to him in what must be Arabic, his deep voice eerily calm in the stillness. Tehrazzi replied, inching her backward with him toward the row of boats behind them. Her legs were stiff and unresponsive as he dragged her with one arm. She was too afraid to move.

*I don't want to die, I don't want to die...*

A hot wash of tears scalded her eyes. God couldn't let this happen. They'd all been through too much. She had no idea what they were saying to each other, but beneath the words she picked up the low timbre of Rhys's voice speaking English. She hoped he was calling for help.

Tehrazzi hauled her back another few feet, the muscles in his forearm like tempered steel beneath her grasping fingers. She kept waiting for a shot to ring out, was braced for it until she realized they couldn't shoot him without setting off the explosives. Tehrazzi had tied Luke's hands as much as Tehrazzi had tied hers. The only way Luke could kill him was if he was willing to sacrifice them all to do it.

"Stay still, Em."

His low voice brought a fresh rush of tears. She gulped, the motion painful against Tehrazzi's iron hold on her throat. She wouldn't dare move any more than he was making her. He was still walking backward, away from Luke and Rhys, and they weren't moving. Were they waiting until she and Tehrazzi put them out of range of the vest before shooting? Her stomach dropped as she finally understood what was happening.

Tehrazzi was a high value target. Important enough that he warranted Luke and his team hunting him down to the ends of the earth. She didn't even register on that value scale. Luke couldn't let this opportunity pass by. He had to kill him. Even if Tehrazzi took her life in the process. Even if it would kill Luke to lose her this way. Nothing mattered but getting Tehrazzi.

As she stared back into Luke's dark eyes, a tear slipped over her cheek. She understood, but the thought of dying here and now terrified her. *I understand*, she told him silently, helpless to do anything, let alone ease the burden for him. But God, she was terrified. Her legs began to quiver. They trembled until the weakness spread throughout her body and made her teeth clatter. The muscles in her face felt stiff, like hardened wax. Another convulsive swallow rippled through her constricted throat. Would it hurt? She thought of the blast wave. She was right up against him. The force of the explosion would rupture her organs and tear her flesh. She trembled. The heat would burn her. Would she feel any of it? It would happen so fast, but...what if it didn't kill her instantly? Another tear fell.

*Oh God, Luke.* She wasn't brave enough to face this. She wanted to close her eyes and retreat somewhere in her head, but she couldn't let go of Luke's stare. She loved him so much. She didn't want him to die too. *Oh God, I'm so scared...*

Thoughts raced through her panicked brain. She was dying anyway. Even if she'd never stumbled upon Tehrazzi in the mosque the cancer would have eaten her from the inside out. She would have died a slow, agonizing death, just like her mother. At least this would be fast. Little, if any suffering.

The sound of water lapping against hulls grew louder as they reached the edge of the dock. Neither Luke nor Rhys had moved yet. And they weren't going to.

Luke said something else to Tehrazzi she couldn't understand, his tone low and full of buried rage. Tehrazzi ignored him, pulling her backward. She was his only insurance. If she hadn't been standing in the way, she knew without a doubt Luke would have taken the killing shot despite the blast radius of the vest killing him too. Tehrazzi needed her to make his escape work. And Luke...

She sucked in a quick breath. What if he didn't have to die to get Tehrazzi?

Tehrazzi wanted on a boat. He wanted to get away. If he did, Luke would have to come after him. But if she could get Tehrazzi to detonate the vest once they were out on the water, Luke and Rhys would be clear. The thought crystallized in her mind. She could end this for him. With Tehrazzi gone Luke could hang up his guns for good. He could have his life back.

She desperately wanted that for him. Wanted him to be free to live again. Even if it wasn't with her. Her life was fading anyway. This way she had control over her destiny. And she could save Luke in the process.

Gathering her courage, she took one last look at him as Tehrazzi stepped up onto the bow of a boat. Through the tears that almost blinded her, she forced a smile on her trembling lips. "It's all right," she told him shakily.

"I love you."

His eyes were tormented when he met her gaze for that instant. "Em..." She could hear the edge of raw helplessness in his voice.

"It's okay," she forced out, the words distorted from the pressure around her throat.

The unbearable pain in his expression tore her to pieces. "Em, I—"

The pressure around her throat vanished. Caught off guard, she fell to her knees on the damp dock when Tehrazzi suddenly released her. What was happening?

"Emily, get *down*!"

She raised her eyes to Luke's. He was running flat out toward her. The confusion in her brain made it seem like he moved in slow motion. His rifle was up, his legs moving in a blur. Rhys was a step behind him. Then the roar of a motor filled the air.

Luke came nearer, still not firing. She cast a glance over her shoulder. Tehrazzi leapt over the seats of the speed boat, one hand on the vest trigger and the other reaching for the steering wheel. He couldn't get away. Her head turned toward Luke.

"Dooowwwnnn!" he yelled at her. He wasn't shooting because she was still too close to Tehrazzi.

She pushed to her feet. Her heart slammed wildly, echoing in her ears. She couldn't let Tehrazzi get away. She had to do this. Had to. Luke would die if she didn't.

A surge of power hummed through her body. Goosebumps raced over her chilled skin. Her leg muscles bunched. Pushing off the dock with every ounce of her strength, she kicked off hard and dove through the air as the boat pulled away from the dock.

****

Luke saw the intent forming in her eyes. *No*, he

silently begged her, quads burning with strain as he sprinted flat out down the dock toward her. For whatever reason, Tehrazzi had let her go. If she stayed still, she'd be safe.

But she didn't. Casting one last glance at him, she pivoted and launched herself onto the stern of the boat. His knees threatened to buckle.

"Emilyyyyy!" he roared, heart in his throat. What the fuck did she think she was doing?

She bounced hard on the stern but held on as Tehrazzi shot the boat away from the dock. Luke choked back a howl of denial. He couldn't take a shot now, not with Emily there. The blast from the vest would kill her.

"Christ," he snarled, slinging his rifle across his back and charging to the closest speed boat he could find. Rhys leapt over the bow a second after he did and within a few moments had it hotwired. The inboard motor came to life with a deep-throated growl.

Luke immediately went to the side and threw a leg over. He had to stay out of sight to have any chance in hell of saving Emily. He hadn't clung to the gunwales of a boat moving through the water at top speed in years, but he wasn't taking any chances of being spotted. "Make sure you get her clear," he barked at Rhys, who expertly maneuvered the craft after Tehrazzi. "No matter what happens, you get her clear."

"Understood," Rhys shouted back, his short hair whipping back in the wind.

Luke flattened his body to the hull and held on as the icy cold spray of water pelted him. His only chance at saving Emily was to get onto that boat and grab the trigger before Tehrazzi let go.

# Chapter Eighteen

Tehrazzi jumped when someone landed on the stern of the boat. Holding the trigger tight in his left hand, he cast a disbelieving glance at his teacher's wife as she dragged herself up the slick white fiberglass surface. His mouth tightened. He didn't need this!

He yanked the steering wheel sideways. The boat veered and her legs whipped out to the side like a flag in the wind. But she didn't let go, and when he righted the wheel, she rolled into the interior with a hard thud. Tehrazzi suppressed a growl of frustration. He was prepared to martyr himself, but on his terms. Not because of this woman, and not until his teacher was within range. Why hadn't the damned woman run when she'd had the chance?

He had only a second's warning after he heard her enraged cry, and staggered back with the impact when she launched herself at him. She caught him in the chest with her shoulder, and the unexpected force threw him backward against the instrument panel. He'd knocked the throttle back, and the boat came to a plunging stop as he struggled to hold onto the vest's trigger and get her off him. Her slender fingers wrapped around his like a claw, trying to pry his thumb off the release lever.

"Stop!" he shouted, pulling his hand out of her reach as he dodged her fist. Her enraged attack stunned him because she was half his size and ill with cancer. What was she doing? He would not die like this. He would not let his death be wasted.

"Blow it!" she screamed at him, her eyes wild in her pale face.

He should shoot her. Put a bullet in her skull and toss her overboard. His hand itched to do just that. Something stopped him. It was not his place to take her life. But he was tempted, catching her fist in his and twisting it behind her back.

The sound of another motor broke through the lapping of the waves against the hull. Tehrazzi stilled and stared out through the fog into the encroaching darkness. His teacher. Coming after him.

His mind churned frantically as he fended off yet another attack from her. Maybe he should stay here. Suppressing a roar, he flung the woman off him. Others would be coming for him. Soldiers and police, Coast Guard. He didn't have much time. If he was going to destroy his teacher, he might not get another opportunity. His hand hesitated on the throttle as he stared down at his new adversary. He hadn't wanted her to die, but perhaps there was no other way. This woman had again put herself in his path. Perhaps he should detonate the device once his teacher came within range. That wasn't how he'd intended it to go, but it would serve his purpose well enough.

As she pushed to her feet, he saw the rank hatred in her expression, and knew she would attack him again. Letting go of the throttle, his hand closed around the butt of the pistol in his waistband. One shot. His teacher was coming for him, for her or her dead body, it didn't matter.

Again, something held him back. Her suffering, and her undying loyalty that touched a deeply buried part of him. A part he'd thought was gone forever.

She lunged at him again, going for his face with her nails. Biting back a curse, Tehrazzi caught both her wrists in his free hand and squeezed the bones together, thwarting an attack between his legs from her knee. He pinned her hard against the edge of the boat and met her tear-bright green eyes.

"I won't let you kill him!" she half-sobbed, struggling in his grip. "You want to die? Do it now!"

Her bravery in the face of death sent an unwelcome pang of admiration through him. Only one who knew death was at hand could be this brave. Or one of great faith.

The other boat drew nearer, emerging through the fog. Its driver was the big man from the dock, one of his teacher's men. Tehrazzi couldn't make out anyone else in the craft. Was his teacher hiding in it? Or had he stayed ashore in the hope of getting his wife back before coming after him?

This could still happen on Tehrazzi's terms. All he had to do was release the woman and escape, prompting his teacher to resume the chase. The bomb he wore would ensure he got away. They would not jeopardize her life by killing him before she was safely out of range.

She glared up at him, trembling from the cold and the fear he could see eating through her resolve. Willing to die to save her ex-husband, but so very afraid of the moment it would happen.

He could not kill her and snuff out her magnificent spirit. It would be wrong. She was innocent of any wrongdoing and killing her would be unforgivable. She deserved to live after fighting so bravely for what she believed in.

Tehrazzi loosened his hold a fraction, his mind made up. "You are not meant to die here," he said through gritted teeth. "Allah will take you in His own time."

****

A frustrated sob caught in Emily's chest. She shook so hard she could barely stay on her feet and her heart smashed against her ribs. She'd never been so afraid in her life as she stared up into those laser-like green eyes. They seemed to burn through her, brimming with anger and resolve. And maybe even a hint of respect.

Tearing her gaze away, she refocused on the device he held. The blood pounded in her head, filling her ears with a roaring noise. His will was every bit as strong as his powerfully built body, but she couldn't give up. She had to keep fighting.

Somehow she had to get his hand off the detonator. She had to do it before Luke arrived or she chickened out. And she was damn close to losing her nerve. Exhaustion pulled at her, the fierce determination she'd come aboard with waning in the face of her own death. God, what if she couldn't do it?

*You have to. Or else Luke will die because you were a coward.*

Tehrazzi's grip was too strong. She couldn't break it and get to the trigger he still held.

Then she heard it. Another boat. Twisting her head, she stared in horror at the speed craft coming toward them through the fog. *No!* she wanted to scream. *Not yet.*

Spurred by desperation, she reared up and sank her teeth into Tehrazzi's hard shoulder. He let out a bellow and backhanded her across the cheek with his free hand.

She let go, stars exploding before her eyes and then her knees hit the deck with a thud.

Dazed from the blow, she got to her feet to try again, but Tehrazzi seized her arm and twisted it behind her at a sharp angle. Emily cried out and arched up to relieve the pressure, afraid her shoulder would pop out of its socket. Then he dragged her to her toes and shoved her against the side of the boat again, hard enough that the low metal railing cut into her thighs.

Her gaze cut to the other boat. Rhys was at the wheel, and brought it to a bow-plunging stop some distance away. Luke was nowhere to be seen. Her throat tightened. Had he stayed behind? She was torn between relief that he was still safe and grief because he'd left her on her own to face her fate with Tehrazzi.

Tehrazzi's hand cranked down on her forearm. "Where is he?" he shouted over her head.

Rhys raised his hands, showing he was unarmed for the moment. "Just give me the woman."

"Where *is* he?"

"Getting ready to kill you once I take her ashore."

"No," Emily cried, bowing back and lashing out with her leg. Tehrazzi pinned her even tighter, paying as much attention to her futile struggles as he would a bothersome insect. Yet through her fear, Emily swore Tehrazzi shuddered at Rhys's words.

When he spoke again, his voice was frighteningly soft and calm. "I've already activated the trigger. It can't be diffused. If you shoot me, the bomb will kill you both."

"I'm not going to shoot you," Rhys replied in the same calm tone. "That's going to be Luke's privilege. I'm here for her. Then you and Luke can face off."

Tehrazzi hesitated for another instant, then shoved her over the side of the boat.

Emily only had time to utter a short scream before

hitting the surface face first. The pain punched her hard. Icy, dark water closed over her head, forcing the air from her lungs. The shock of the cold and the blackness disoriented her. Twisting about, she couldn't tell which way was up. Panic flooded her. She couldn't breathe. Couldn't see. Didn't know how far down she was.

The long strands of the wig wrapped around her face, suffocating her. Her heavy wool sweater and jeans were lead weights against her body. Her waterlogged shoes were heavy, dragging her down into the cold depths. Frantic, she ripped off the wig and kicked, clawing toward what she prayed was the surface. How far down was she? Her lungs burned, desperate for air.

Her legs scissored hard. Her hands reached above her to push the water away, propelling upward. *Please, please let it be upward.* Fire scorched her aching lungs. No air. They were going to burst from the pressure before she ever reached the surface. Instinct took over. Her tired limbs blindly clawed and kicked at the water. Faint light. She was sure she rose toward the light.

Battling with all her strength, she fought not to draw a breath. Not to let her mouth gasp open against the fire in her lungs. Her depleted body made the decision for her. Salt water rushed into her nose and mouth, burning, singing, choking her. Her eyes rolled back in her head, panic overtaking everything. Drowning. She was drowning. A silent scream erupted from her soul.

Her legs kicked in reflex and she finally broke the surface for an instant. Air rushed over her wet face and head. Her starving lungs sucked in a gulp of sweet air. Choking, coughing up mouthfuls of water, she mindlessly fought to keep her head above the surface and dimly made out the sound of a motor in the distance. Another raw breath of air went in. Finally, she could open her watering eyes.

It was pitch black except for the faint lights coming

from the distant dock, all but obscured by the thickening fog. Her limbs floundered as she treaded water, head whipping back and forth to find the boat Rhys had been on. She couldn't see anything but the waves before her and the fog rolling on its surface. Helplessness flooded her. Oh Jesus, had he gone after Tehrazzi anyway? Her hands and feet were numb from the cold and her strength was failing. The sodden clothes were like a heavy hand pressing her back into the water.

"Help!" she cried, choking on another mouthful of water when her head dipped beneath the low waves. Flailing weakly, she broke through the surface once more but knew she didn't have the strength to stay afloat. She fought back a sob. Luke. She'd failed to detonate the bomb, and now he would die getting Tehrazzi.

She turned onto her side and tried to pull her exhausted body through the water. The numbness spread up her arms and legs, her breaths frantic and choppy. The rhythmic pump of her limbs turned to uncoordinated thrashing as she lost control of her muscles. The water closed in over her head again, a frigid, dark embrace pulling her down toward her death. And it wasn't peaceful at all. Not like the stories she'd read about by people who had almost drowned. She wasn't calm and filled with warmth. This was terrifying.

Panic flooded her, sharp and vicious as the blackness took hold.

Strong hands grabbed her. A muscled arm closed around her ribs, and then she shot upward. Rocketing toward the surface.

Luke, she thought blearily, fighting to stay conscious. He'd come in after her. Her head and shoulders exploded through the surface. Her starved lungs sucked in a tiny amount of air between wracking coughs. The arm around her never wavered in its hold.

"Just lie still," a male voice shouted to her. Not Luke. She jackknifed in his hold, choking and sputtering. The arm around her ribs tightened and began towing her backward. When she finally got her first full breath of air, her head fell back against a hard shoulder. "You're okay."

Rhys. Of course it was Rhys.

Emily was too cold and weak to help him when they finally reached the boat. He heaved her over the side and climbed in after her, rolling her onto her back. She blinked up at his shadowy face. Rivulets of water poured off his tall frame, splashing around her on the deck.

"I need to get these clothes off you," he said, voice calm and full of authority as he stripped her down and wrapped her in a towel. All she could do was lay there and shiver, a million questions racing through her brain. His chilled fingers pressed against the side of her throat to take her pulse. It felt sluggish even to her.

Her teeth were chattering, lips so cold she could barely move them. "L-Luke," she mumbled. "W-where—"

"I'll have you ashore in a few minutes." Rhys ignored her question and stepped over her to fire up the engine.

Emily rolled to her side and weakly pushed up on an elbow, barely able to hold her head up. "Luke," she repeated. Where was he?

Rhys didn't look at her as he turned the boat around and made for the dock. "He asked me to get you clear. The sooner I drop you off, the sooner I can go back and help him."

Go back? "G-go b-back wh-where?"

"To Tehrazzi."

# Chapter Nineteen

Beneath the waves, Luke slid through the water like a knife toward his target. Under the surface it was quiet and still. The claustrophobia never came. The water was his second home. Working beneath the surface in the dark, he was in his element as he sliced beneath Tehrazzi's boat and came up soundlessly on its starboard side.

Breaching the surface, he barely made a ripple and reached for the side edge when he heard Emily's scream a second before she splashed into the water. His whole body tightened, wanting to dive under and save her, but he couldn't. If Tehrazzi saw him, they'd all die. Em was a strong swimmer. He knew Rhys would already be in the water going after her. Luke had this one chance to get Tehrazzi and make sure Emily got clear.

Locking his jaw, he gripped the edge of the boat. As Tehrazzi fired up the engine, Luke threw one leg over the lip, flipping over the side when Tehrazzi opened up the throttle. Driven by pure instinct, Luke lunged at him. Tehrazzi turned his head at the last second, a flare of surprise registering in his expression as he pivoted, knocking the throttle back. The bow plunged down and Luke hit him straight in the chest, the abrupt stop adding to his momentum. Like lightning, Luke's right hand lashed out to grip the detonator in Tehrazzi's fingers before he could let go. They crashed against the dashboard and for an instant Tehrazzi sagged forward with a grunt of pain. Luke took a blow to the kidney and blocked another, clamping down with cruel force on his adversary's fingers.

The familiar green eyes boring into his were full of fanatical glee. And relief that it was finally about to end between them.

Luke strained to keep Tehrazzi's thumb pressed down tight on the lever. In the distance he heard the sound of a motor starting up, and the hollow ache in his chest receded. Em was safe. Rhys had her, would take her to shore. Luke's arm trembled with the effort of keeping Tehrazzi's arm and hand still. Just a little longer. He only had to hold it a minute longer until Em was well clear. Then it didn't matter.

Except he didn't want her to see him die.

He didn't want to leave her again. Needed to be with her.

Tehrazzi's lips peeled back from his teeth with an animal snarl. The bastard was fucking strong, juiced by the thought of his impending martyrdom and taking Luke in the process. He jerked his wrist, nearly breaking Luke's hold. Luke felt his fingers slipping. Beads of sweat broke out over his chilled skin. He was soaked with cold seawater but he didn't feel it. Inside he was raging hot. And lethally pissed off.

At one time, Tehrazzi had been like a son to him. Following him like a fucking shadow with worshipful puppy dog eyes in the bleak Afghan mountain camps. Doing everything and anything to please his teacher. The slightest amount of praise Luke gave him lit the teenager's lean face with a brilliant smile. So desperate for approval and guidance that Luke had ached for the kid.

He'd gone out of his way to protect and train him, thinking it would help Tehrazzi survive when Luke inevitably got pulled out by the CIA. Instead, he'd created a monster, and it had finally come down to this. Hand to hand, locked in a death struggle. The teacher and the student, once almost as close as father and son, now facing each other in mortal combat.

Luke growled low in his throat, pouring all his strength into holding onto Tehrazzi's hand, his left crushing his opponent's right wrist as it moved down and back toward his waistband and the pistol Tehrazzi had tucked in it. Luke's knife sheath dug into the quivering muscles of his right calf, the weapon so close but completely out of reach. If he let go of Tehrazzi's right wrist for even a split second, he was a dead man. Tehrazzi was too fast for Luke to be able to snag the knife and get a clean stab in before he got shot. And Tehrazzi knew it. The taunting gleam in his eyes said so. The bastard was certain of his victory.

Then a malicious smile twisted Tehrazzi's lips. "I let your wife live," he ground out in Arabic, forcing Luke's white-knuckled hand toward the gun inch by agonizing inch despite his full resistance. "She is a woman of God."

Luke didn't respond, just kept his gaze pinned on Tehrazzi's, fighting with all he had to hold on. His muscles burned with the effort, locked against Tehrazzi's unrelenting strength. The tendons beneath his fingers flexed as Tehrazzi's fingers opened, reaching for the gun, shifting around the grip. Fuck, he couldn't hold him, Luke realized. His resistance was futile against the inexorable movement of Tehrazzi's arm as it crept upward. The muzzle of the pistol raised infinitesimally. Up, up. Turning toward him.

Luke's heart pumped so hard it felt like it might burst. His muscles tightened to the point of pain, determined to hold that gun away from him.

"She suffers," the bastard continued, raising the pistol despite Luke's steely grip. "Her body and soul."

Luke clenched his jaw until he thought his teeth would shatter, trying to ignore the words. Every muscle in his body quivered, struggling to break the stalemate. He could not let up. Had to find a way to disarm him and still hold on to the detonator.

As he glared up at Tehrazzi, those green eyes flashed with hatred and then a shocking vulnerability. "You left us both."

The accusation hung between them, and the truth of it hit Luke in the heart like a red-hot knife. And finally he truly understood his enemy's motivation. Betrayal. That's what his note had said on Davis's stiffening body. This had all been about perceived betrayal. All of it. Tehrazzi blamed him for the hardships he'd suffered after the CIA had pulled Luke and the others out after the Afghan-Russian war. Luke had suspected it as a cause, but had never guessed it was the whole motivation for Tehrazzi turning to radical Islam.

Guilt jolted through his rage, momentarily weakening him. "I had no choice," he bit out, sweating and straining. God, he'd caused all this. So much suffering and rage and pain. So much death. But he could end it here and now. He still had that power.

His death grip on Tehrazzi's fingers eased a fraction. He could end this so easily. All he had to do was let go. Release the pressure on Tehrazzi's hand and less than a heartbeat later they'd go up in a ball of fire together. His sacrifice would be his last act of penance, a chance at atonement for all his sins. Tehrazzi would never take another life again.

But a picture of Emily's face swam before his eyes. Green eyes so similar to Tehrazzi's held his, but they were soft, and filled with tears of desperate hope. Of love. So much love it hurt to breathe. *Hold on*, she begged him in his mind, her voice so real he could hear it. *Please hold on. I need you.*

In that moment Luke knew he couldn't desert her again. Not by choice. She wouldn't make it without him. He knew her too well. Without him she'd stop fighting. That couldn't happen. He wouldn't let that happen.

The only way he would leave her to face the future alone this time would be through death. And he wasn't going there without giving everything he had first.

Iron resolve swept through him, giving him a renewed surge of strength. Luke forced Tehrazzi's arm down with a throttled growl, using his whole body to put more power into it. All the while he kept his other hand curled over Tehrazzi's on the lever, the relentless pressure turned his bloodless fingers numb.

Sweat trickled down Tehrazzi's face, the muscles in his cheeks twitching. Time seemed to stop. The pistol stayed where it was, hovering at waist level, muzzle pointed away from them both. Locked in a lethal standstill of life and death combat between their iron grips.

They both panted hard, chests heaving like bellows. No chance they were both walking away from this. Luke could see the deadly intent in Tehrazzi's eyes. He was more than ready to die and go to paradise to be with Allah. But Luke had unfinished business here on earth. "Not going...with...you," he ground out.

"Yes, you are," Tehrazzi snarled. "And your death…will mean *nothing*." A low laugh rumbled in his chest. "Others are waiting…to carry on the…jihad I've waged."

Luke knew it was true.

"It's Allah's...will."

"Last...chance," he bit out.

Holding his gaze in defiance, Tehrazzi began praying, the eerie Arabic monotone raking over Luke's skin with icy fingers. He knew the prayer by heart. A martyr's prayer. And Tehrazzi followed it up by reciting, "Allah-uh-aqbar...Allah-uh-aqbar..."

*God is great.* A death chant. Over and over. Luke's hand shook on Tehrazzi's forearm. His grip slipped. Muscles gave way. He dug down for his remaining strength, but the gun came up regardless. Slowly, inexorably. Turning toward him. Closer with every heartbeat. The fingers gripping Tehrazzi's wrist loosened.

*No. You won't let go, Hutchinson. SEALs don't quit and they don't give in.*

He had only seconds left until Tehrazzi gained the leverage he needed to twist the gun up and shoot him. Refusing to give up, Luke gathered his remaining strength and spun, risking letting go of Tehrazzi's gun arm for a split second before ramming him back against the dashboard with the full force of his body, simultaneously grabbing the trigger with his left hand. His other seized Tehrazzi's right wrist, twisting the muzzle down and away.

Tehrazzi's outraged cry rang in his ears and Luke pushed back with all the strength in his legs, mashing his spine into Tehrazzi's chest. Crushing him against the dashboard. The hard edge of the explosive vest dug into Luke's back. He glanced at their left hands, locked around the detonator. Luke couldn't feel his fingers, but he was still holding on. His shoulder and arm muscles burned with the strain. Tiring fast.

And still the gun came up. Shit, he couldn't hold it anymore. Couldn't stop it no matter how hard he tried.

Up, up it inched, the muscles in their arms bulging, shaking. Luke stared at the little black hole at the end of the muzzle as it cleared his waist. Seconds now. That's all he had left.

His arm slipped. His heart missed a beat, eyes riveted on the muzzle of the pistol as it swung up toward his chest.

****

Emily lay shivering on the floor of the boat when Rhys got to the dock. He lifted her and jumped ashore, running flat out toward the street. His booted feet made a hollow thudding sound as he pounded over the damp wood. She tried to raise her head to see over his shoulder, but couldn't. She was too weak. Too cold. "L-Luke," she muttered. She'd heard the other boat quit a few moments after Rhys started them back to shore, but there'd been no explosion. No way Tehrazzi had given in. Had Luke gotten aboard? Or was he alone in the dark sea, left to find his own way back to land?

Noises brought her heavy eyelids open. Rhys shouted something. She heard more voices, all talking at once until she wanted to cover her ears. Then Rhys handed her to someone else and she looked up into Ben's pale green eyes. "Wh-where's L-Luke?" she repeated, wanting to scream it at him. Why the hell wasn't anyone telling her what was happening?

*Because they don't know anything.* The knowledge chilled her even more.

"Rhys is going after him," Ben finally said, jogging over to a black truck. He yanked open the passenger door and put her in the seat, belting her in before racing around to the driver's side and sliding behind the wheel. "Dec and his boys are on their way."

Like that was supposed to reassure her? Luke was

alone out there. How long would it be before any reinforcements arrived?

Ben gunned the engine and took off. Reaching over, he aimed the vent at her and turned the heat on full power. The hot air blasted over her chilled skin but didn't touch the ice encasing her heart and lungs. Inside she was frozen solid with fear for Luke. A ragged sob built up.

"Hang in there." Ben took a sharp turn before hitting the gas once more. The powerful engine revved as the vehicle raced over the pavement. "We'll get you warmed up and dry when we get back to the house."

The sob worked free. She didn't care about getting warm and dry. Tears of fury and pain tracked down her cheeks. The medallion lay heavy against her chest, reminding her that Luke had woken up that morning expecting to die.

# Chapter Twenty

Luke's heart lurched as the pistol came up to point at his chest. Tehrazzi gave a shout of triumph. It reverberated in Luke's head like a gunshot.

*Fuck. This.*

Pressing his lips together, he reached down inside him for his last ounce of strength. In one final burst, he shoved the gun upward, catching Tehrazzi by surprise for the split second he needed to bring the weapon up high enough. Luke angled the pistol and steeled himself against what was coming, praying the angle was right so it wouldn't trigger the vest. His thumb reached down to curl around the curved trigger. He closed his eyes. Stopping the sudden jerk of Tehrazzi's arm, he squeezed down. The shot rang out above the hideous, burning pain in his left shoulder, so strong his hand loosened on the detonator. His own scream shattered the night.

His fingers spasmed around it and he held on with all his will, fighting to stay above the pain as Tehrazzi slumped behind him with a terrible wheeze. Releasing the gun to grab the vest's detonator with his right hand,

Luke's legs gave out and they crashed to the floor. He bellowed as the raw wound in his shoulder burned like fire, stealing his breath and making him light headed. His hand spasmed on the detonator.

*Don't let go. You can't let go.* He wanted to live. Had to look after Emily.

Clamping down, he managed to firm his grip around Tehrazzi's slackening fingers. A terrible gurgling filled his ears. Fighting through his agony, Luke jerked the gun from Tehrazzi's limp hand and turned it on him with his ruined arm, fighting to maintain his hold on the trigger as he turned painfully toward his former protégé.

Through the haze of pain, he stared down at Tehrazzi's pale face and the ragged, bleeding hole in his throat. The bullet had missed the spinal cord, passing out the side with a baseball-sized exit wound. Severing the jugular vein and carotid artery on the right side of his neck. Mortal wounds, even if there'd been an equipped medic standing by.

Tehrazzi's body corded, his hands going to his throat, clawing at the hideous wound. Luke shook, the pain and fatigue combining with blood loss and shock. He clung to the desperate will to survive, somehow holding fast to the vest's trigger.

Wide green eyes stared up at him beseechingly. Tehrazzi's lips moved. Froths of scarlet blood bubbled from his mouth and nose. He choked on it, gagging and heaving, eyes rolling into his head for a moment.

Gasping, Luke looked into that young, handsome face, only a few years older than his son's. A sound wheezed out amidst the choking noises.

Luke leaned closer. "W-what?"

The lips moved again, rapidly turning blue beneath the hideous gush of blood. Tehrazzi's eyes bulged. "F-finish...m-me..." The English words were slurred, nearly unintelligible.

Ice congealed in Luke's gut. His hand tightened around the grip of the pistol. He could do it. End Tehrazzi's earthly suffering and release his soul to Allah. Would be a kindness. One final gesture of mercy for the boy he'd once loved.

But he couldn't do it. Couldn't make himself take the shot. All he could do was tremble and pant through his own pain as he stared down into those pleading eyes.

"A-Allah's...will..." Tehrazzi rattled out, blood flowing from his mouth and throat, pooling around them in a warm, sticky pool. The metallic smell of it coated the back of Luke's throat.

Before he knew what he was doing, Luke dropped the suddenly heavy pistol and reached up with his injured arm, dragging it up despite the roar of agony tearing from his lips to grasp one of Tehrazzi's blood-slick hands. Luke tightened his grip and clung to it fiercely, holding his gaze.

Tehrazzi stared back, his fingers closing around Luke's weakly. Hardly more than a twitch. But the gratitude was there, along with the fear. A sheen of tears filled his frightened eyes. "S-stay," he wheezed, clutching with the little strength he had left.

Luke nodded once, fighting to hang on. "I won't…leave you…"

"S-swear…"

The raw vulnerability in that plea made tears burn his eyes. He'd loved the son of a bitch. "I swear." He squeezed harder.

Tehrazzi's hand contracted around his and he bowed up, thrashing as he choked on his own blood. Gritting his teeth to stay on his knees and keep the detonator pinned down, Luke held tight to that hand. It seemed to take forever for the rattling gasps to stop and for Tehrazzi's body to still.

Those green eyes remained open, staring up at Luke's

face even in death.

Exhausted, overwhelmed by the white-hot fire in his shoulder, Luke finally allowed himself to slump down and roll onto his back. Rising above the pain, all his focus remained on holding the trigger. He held that directive in his consciousness while he sucked air through his nose in shallow bursts. Where the hell was his backup? Surely to Christ someone was on their way to him. He couldn't hold on forever.

His fingers twitched spasmodically around the metal lever. He was too far gone to attempt disarming it himself. The blood loss and shock already had him shaking and queasy as hell.

Then, finally, he made out the sound of a distant motor coming toward him.

*Thank Christ.*

His left hand twitched again. *Don't you fucking let go.*

He cranked down on it, the abused muscles in his hand and forearm exhausted. He didn't want to die. Emily was back at the house by now. She needed him. And dammit, he needed her. The goddamn vest was the only thing standing between them now. He'd taken care of Tehrazzi. Had redeemed himself for past mistakes. He wanted it to be over with. Once and for all.

Because he still had to find a way to make up for what he'd done to Emily.

The steady hum of the approaching boat grew louder. He recognized the pitch of it. Knew the skimming sound the distinctive rubber hull made as it skipped across the tops of the waves. A zodiac. Relief slid through him. The SEALs had finally arrived. Dec and his boys would take care of the bomb.

*Hold on. Almost over.*

Luke forced his eyes open when someone climbed aboard and the beam of a flashlight blinded him until they hunkered down beside him. The light illuminated Dec's golden brown eyes like topazes in his camouflaged face.

"G-gotta...hold th-this..." Luke rasped.

Dec grabbed the trigger from his numb fingers. "I've got it," he said in a low voice, glancing up as three of his men climbed in. With a shudder of relief, Luke shut his eyes and let his left arm flop on the deck, his fingers still frozen in their curled position.

God, he was going to puke. The pain was merciless, all consuming. The warm, sickening smell of blood made his stomach roll.

Someone knelt next to him and ripped his BDUs open. Luke bit back a howl as the medic probed the wound with his fingers. "Don't think you clipped the artery, sir," the man said, ripping open his ruck. "But I bet it's gonna need surgical repair."

Luke didn't care. All he wanted was the bleeding stopped and the pain to go away so he wouldn't pass out. The medic put a steadying hand on the ruined shoulder and someone else pinned his other arm and legs.

"Brace yourself," the medic said. "This clotting powder's gonna hurt like a bitch."

Luke gave a curt nod and clenched his teeth, but when the powder hit the raw wound he bowed up like he'd been electrocuted. "Fuuuuuck!" he roared, almost welcoming the blackness hovering at the edge of his vision. His whole body was instantly covered in sweat and he jerked against the hands holding him when the medic packed the wound and pressed down hard to stop the bleeding.

"Hang on. Here comes the morphine."

Luke didn't even feel the syringe go in, but all of a sudden his body felt lighter, as though he was going to float away. The pain receded. Vanishing into nothing more than a memory. He faded in and out for a few minutes until he lost all concept of time. He was vaguely aware of the men around him speaking in low tones, and of the snipping sound of wire cutters. Knowing he was safe in their hands, Luke let himself go. The words "We're clear" registered briefly before he began to sink under. The last of the tension in Luke's gut dissolved. *It's over*, he thought blearily. *It's finally over.*

But there was no elation. No sense of satisfaction that accompanied the thought. All he felt was weariness and relief. And a lingering hollowness that Tehrazzi's cooling body lay beside him.

"Ambulance is standing by," Dec said from above him. "Let's haul ass and get him to shore."

"He's lost a lot of blood, Lieutenant," the medic said. "Pulse is thready."

"He'll make it," Dec replied. "He's a tough motherfucker."

A moment later the big inboard engine came to life and then the boat sped across the water. Luke lost consciousness sometime during the trip back to the dock. He came to as they were loading him into the ambulance on a stretcher. They'd hooked him up to a saline drip to increase his blood volume. The paramedic was busy checking his vitals.

"A-positive," Luke mumbled from beneath the oxygen mask strapped to his face.

The man looked down at him in surprise. "Your blood type?"

Luke nodded and closed his eyes again. Em had once joked his blood type matched his personality type. A-plus alpha male, she'd said.

Was she all right? He hoped she was sitting next to a warm fire with the other women gathered around her. He wanted her safe and warm. She was going to need someone's shoulder to lean on. Especially when she found out about him. Ben would handle everything.

Neveah would make sure she was okay. And Bryn was there to comfort her.

He still couldn't believe Tehrazzi had let her go. A lump settled in Luke's throat as he remembered Tehrazzi's words before he died. The conflicting emotions rolling through him made his eyes sting. Somewhere in the hardened shell of a man Tehrazzi had become, a streak of human decency had still existed. A glimpse into the soul of the wide-eyed youth he'd once been.

He'd recognized Emily's pain. He'd seen that she'd suffered enough, both from what Luke had done to her and from the cancer. So he'd granted her mercy.

In return, Luke had taken his life.

*Stay...*

He had. In the hours of darkness ahead of him, Luke could hold onto that. And maybe, just maybe Tehrazzi's spirit was already with the God he'd loved more than his own life.

The wail of the siren faded into the background. The paramedic's voice receded. Releasing his tenuous hold on consciousness, Luke let the darkness take him.

****

In the great room, Emily surged to her feet and faced Ben, knocking Bryn's restraining hand off her forearm. "Wounded? What do you mean, wounded?" Her heart throbbed painfully.

Ben's light green eyes were somber. "He's in surgery."

"What?" One hand went to her throat. "How bad?"

"I don't know all the details yet—"

"Jesus, just tell me what's wrong with him!"

"Gunshot wound," Ben replied evenly.

But at least it wasn't from the suicide vest. Emily

swallowed hard. "Where?" Head? Thorax? One of his limbs?

"I don't know."

"But...he's okay? He's stable?"

"Yes. Rhys is at the hospital. He'll give us an update when he can."

*Okay. Take a breath. He's okay. He's a fighter.* "I want to go there."

"No."

His flat refusal made her hackles go up. "I'm a nurse."

"Not today."

"He's my husband," she argued, not caring that she was stretching the truth, "and I want to be there."

"No. You're in no shape to go anywhere, and we're still trying to figure out if the threat's over. You're staying put."

Bryn rose and set an arm around her tense shoulders. "It's what Luke would want, Em."

Barely resisting the urge to throw her friend's arm off, she choked down the snarl rising in her throat, never taking her eyes off Ben's. "And what about...Tehrazzi?" She could barely get his name out.

"Dead."

Emily sagged. *Thank God.* "Is that how Luke was hit?"

Ben nodded. "Then Dec and his boys diffused the vest."

She remembered the feel of it against her shoulder blades, and shivered despite the thick sweater she had on and the fire crackling in the hearth.

And yet he'd let her go. Twice.

Shoving the thought from her mind, Emily tore away from Bryn and began pacing the room, rubbing her hands over her suddenly chilled arms. God, she wanted to go to Luke so badly. Needed to tell him she loved him.

"Em."

Raising her head, she met Bryn's steady gaze. "Ben's just doing his job."

"I know, but *dammit...*"

"I'm going back downstairs," Ben announced.

When he'd gone, Emily turned back to her best friend. Her worry was mirrored in Bryn's dark eyes. Apart from what Ben had told them, there hadn't been any word on Dec, either.

Emily opened up her arms. "I'm sorry," she said as Bryn moved into the embrace.

"It's all right. I understand perfectly."

But there was no excuse. "We'll wait it out together. Deal?"

"Deal."

With a firm grip on her emotions, Emily followed Bryn downstairs where they parked it on the couch outside the coms room. Neveah followed them down a few minutes later.

"Ben pulled rank and won't let me go to the hospital. Any more details?" she asked.

"None," Emily answered, moving over to make room for her. She appreciated that they'd come down to be with her so she didn't have to wait alone.

They sat in silence together, every so often glancing over at the closed door of the coms room. But neither Sam nor Ben came out to give them an update. After a while Nev broke the silence. "You really should sleep for a bit," she said to her. "That dip in the Med isn't going to help your immune system any."

Emily shook her head, determined to stay awake though her eyelids felt like they weighed a hundred pounds each.

A heavy sigh followed. "All right, then as your doctor I'm ordering you to have a nap. Being this sleep deprived isn't doing your body any good."

She couldn't possibly sleep now. Not when she didn't know what was happening with Luke.

"Rest your eyes, at least. Ben or Sam will come get us if anything happens."

Emily didn't want to rest her eyes, but when another hour went by without any further updates, her lids slowly drooped despite her best efforts to keep them open. By way of a compromise she allowed her head to fall back against the leather couch cushions. She was vaguely aware of Bryn's deep, even breaths beside her, and the way Neveah curled up to lay her head on the armrest.

The next thing she knew, Sam was shaking her awake. Emily's head snapped up as the others stirred. "What?" she whispered hoarsely, brain fuzzy with sleep. "What's happened?"

Sam's eyes were lined with fatigue, but she was smiling. "Luke's going to be okay."

"Oh God," she whispered, covering her face with shaking hands. The sheer relief of knowing that almost sent her to her knees on the floor. She felt Nev and Bryn's hands on her back. Then she heard footsteps overhead.

"Ben's up in the kitchen making coffee," Sam added. "You guys want some?"

"Come on," Bryn said, hauling her to her feet. "You need some caffeine in you so you can argue with Ben about letting you go to the hospital."

They were all up drinking hot coffee and tea when a vehicle pulled up outside. Everyone looked at Ben, but he merely smiled and shrugged.

"Is it Rhys?" Nev asked, jumping off her stool to run for the door. Emily and Bryn stood as she threw it open, then Nev let out a squeal.

A moment later Rhys came through the door,

carrying her like a monkey. She was plastered to the front of him, arms wound around his shoulders, her legs around his waist. His answering deep chuckle squeezed Emily's heart. He walked into the middle of the kitchen, his big arms locked tight around Neveah, and over the top of her head smiled at Emily and Bryn. "Got enough coffee for the rest of us?"

"Rest of us?" Bryn squeaked, and raced to the foyer. Her eyes popped wide. "Dec!" she yelled, leaping on him as he came in. Dec twirled her around for a moment, then set her down and captured her face between his hands, kissing her breathless. "How—what are you doing here?"

Dec shrugged. "Some guy I know pulled a few strings on my behalf."

Emily gave the happy couples a minute to say hello, then demanded, "How's Luke? Is he okay? What happened?"

Dec's golden brown eyes twinkled. "See for yourself."

"He's here?" She couldn't believe it. There was no way, she thought, rushing past the others. No way would the hospital have discharged him so soon. But when she rounded the corner and crossed the threshold, she came to a full, hard stop.

Luke really was there. He closed the truck's back door, his left arm immobilized in a sling.

"Luke!"

His head snapped around, and the instant he saw her a weary smile lit his face.

Emily tore over the damp pavers in her bare feet. Mindful of his bandages, she flung her arms around his waist and held on for all she was worth.

# Chapter Twenty-One

The gnawing pain in his newly repaired shoulder disappeared the moment Emily touched him. His right arm went around her back to hug her as she squeezed the breath out of him. Her sweet scent drifted up and her soft curves molded to his body. Part of him couldn't believe he was holding her. He'd never thought he would have the chance again. She was a gift he intended to cherish for the rest of his life.

"Oh my God," she whispered, voice choked with tears. "Oh thank you God."

"Hi, sunshine," he murmured against her temple, holding on as tight as she was.

Emily pulled back and gazed up at him. Her beautiful green eyes were wet with tears. "I love you. I've always loved you."

Damn, he was already on the ragged edge, but that put him a second away from crying. "I love you too," he told her, cupping her velvety soft cheek.

She took his face between her palms and lifted on tiptoe to kiss him. "I was so scared," she muttered between kisses, raining them over his face.

Luke stopped her, setting her away from him, battling the tears that wanted to come. "Christ, Em, I almost had a fucking heart attack when you jumped on that boat." He still couldn't believe how brave she'd been. How selfless.

"I thought I could save you. But I made it worse."

*Aw, fuck.* Knowing she'd been prepared to die in order to save him rocked him to the core.

He couldn't talk about it yet. He'd be having nightmares about it for months to come. "Baby, you scared the living shit out of me. I've never been afraid like that. Not ever." And he'd seen some scary-ass things in his life.

She hugged him again, laying her head on his uninjured shoulder and stroking his back. "Me neither."

He buried his face in her hair. Wig, rather. In that instant, the awful reality of the cancer hit him like a body blow. Oh Jesus, he couldn't lose her now. Couldn't. He squeezed her tight. "Say it again."

Emily titled her head back to look into his eyes. "I love you."

Shit, he was shaking all over.

"Are you okay?"

He forced a nod and found his voice. "Be a while until I can use my arm again, though."

"What happened to you?"

"Had to take a shot through my shoulder to get him." The words hurt his dry, tight throat. "Surgeon patched me all back together though."

Her eyes delved into his. Spring green, clear and gentle. Full of love and acceptance, though his soul was permanently stained by the things he'd done. She slid a steadying arm around his waist. He wanted to laugh because she barely came up to his chin and he had seventy-plus pounds on her, but he was afraid if he opened his mouth only a sob would come out.

Emily stayed pressed tight against his side and tugged on him. "Come on. Come inside."

He followed her into the house, unsurprised that no one else was around. All the others were no doubt having their own romantic reunions, and he thanked God because he was too raw for an audience. All he wanted was Emily, and he didn't want anything to get in the way of that.

She led him upstairs to his room and closed the door before turning back the covers and helping him in. With brisk efficiency she arranged him on his right side and propped some pillows around and under his injured arm. By the time she lay down beside him, he teetered on the brink of losing control. Hating the weakness, he tried to think of something to say. "You're a good nurse."

"Thanks." But her smile was sad when she smoothed his hair back.

He was acutely conscious of the length of it and how grubby he felt. He was still covered in dried salt from the water and sweat, plus his beard itched. He couldn't wait to shave the fucker off.

"Can I do anything?" she asked.

"Yeah. Help me clean up?"

"Sure." She set an arm around his back and he let her pull him to his feet. In the en suite she filled the tub and helped him strip down. Her eyes went right to the blood seeping through the bandages. "You could've hit your lung or heart so easily," she whispered, shaking her head.

"But I'm okay, baby." And he would hold it together for her. He didn't want to scare her any more by losing control and breaking down.

She held his free hand when he stepped into the tub. Luke sighed as he hit the hot water, wishing he could sink up to his chin. He laid his head back against the marble edge and closed his eyes while Emily used a washcloth on him. The instant it touched his bare chest his dick went rock hard, but he ignored it, focusing instead on the simple pleasure of her touch and the fact he was alive to enjoy it. When she dampened his hair and rubbed shampoo into it, he groaned at the feel of her fingers massaging her scalp. "Oh *God* that feels good..."

Her husky chuckle made him even harder, until his heartbeat pulsed in his cock. She took her sweet time, drawing the erotic bath out for him, then kneaded the knotted muscles in the back of his neck and right shoulder. After she rinsed him off, he grabbed her hand and stepped out of the tub. Catching sight of his reflection, he grimaced.

"Shave this thing off me," he said, stroking a hand over the beard.

She hesitated. "Are you...sure?"

"Yes." He reached out to touch her, his hand trembling against her face. "It's over." The words came out a low rasp.

"Really over?"

"It's over," he repeated quietly, gathering her close. She melted into his hold for a moment, then looked up with an impish gleam in her eyes.

"You sure you don't want me to take care of this first," she teased, pressing into his aching cock.

Luke shook his head. He was sore and barely hanging on to his control as it was. As good as an orgasm would feel, he needed something even better right now. "Get this thing off me," he said, running his hand over the beard.

With a towel wrapped around his waist, he sat one hip on the vanity and let her lather his face and scrape the beard away. When she wiped his skin with a hand towel and stepped away, her eyes gleamed with tears.

"What?" he whispered, cupping her cheek.

She put a hand to her throat. "Looking at you right now just... It took me back, that's all."

He swiveled his head to check himself out in the mirror. Damn, he looked almost human again.

"I'd nearly forgotten how stunning you are under all that hair."

He turned back to her, the wistful note in her voice pulling at him. Beat up as he was, he still wanted to carry her into the bedroom and lock the world away for a few days. He wanted her naked body flush up against his so he could hold her and feel her heartbeat, reassure himself she was safe in his arms. To know they were finally back together.

He ran his hand down her neck to cradle her nape in his palm. "Take me to bed, Em."

With a watery laugh, she leaned up to kiss him. Her lips were warm and tender, and she sighed as she nuzzled him, rubbing her petal soft cheek against his. A million nerve endings sparkled to life in his freshly shaved face. But when he touched her cheek again, she flinched. He pulled back and immediately found the faint bruise forming under her translucent skin across her cheekbone.

"Did he hurt you?" He ran his eyes over her slim frame.

"No, just this. Because I wouldn't...stop attacking him."

The visual that gave him damn near made his heart stop. "Jesus, Em..." He wrapped her close, locking his arm around her fiercely. No, screw it. He needed to know. "Why'd you do it?"

She didn't answer for a moment. "I wanted you to be free."

He set her away from him. "What?"

"I wanted you to have a life again. I figured I don't have much longer anyway, so…"

So she'd tried to sacrifice herself for him. To save him.

What the hell did he say to that? Didn't she know losing her would have killed him anyway? All the emotion he'd shoved into the vault inside him threatened to burst free when Emily sniffed and pressed her face against his chest. Her slim shoulders shook in a silent sob.

But then she lifted her eyes to his and got control. "I'm glad it's over. But I'm so sorry you had to be the one to..."

Kill Tehrazzi. He didn't know what to say because he still didn't know how he was supposed to feel. Too much had happened too fast.

Emily's eyes glittered with unshed tears, laced with pain and confusion. "He let me go, twice. Why?"

Luke swallowed past the constriction in his throat. "He knew it was the right thing to do," he answered softly. "And he... I think he did it as a final gift to me." Because Tehrazzi had assumed they would both die on that boat. Everything he did had a pointed motive. Tehrazzi was all about poignancy. Releasing Emily had been a last gesture of kindness to acknowledge the close friendship they'd once shared. Luke was sure of that.

Her fingers were gentle against his bare cheek. "I'm so sorry, sweetheart. It must have been hell for you."

Emily had always known what was in his heart. Better than he did. And she knew how torn up he was over having to take Tehrazzi's life.

The tears he'd kept at bay suddenly flooded his eyes and he looked away. Maybe it was because he was exhausted or still suffering the after effects of the anesthetic, or the fact he kept seeing Emily jumping on that damn boat as it pulled away from the dock, but he couldn't keep up the brave front anymore. His voice cracked despite himself. "I stayed with him," he said unsteadily. "'Till it was over."

Nodding, she stared up at him with loving eyes. But they were bruised underneath. And her skin was too pale, almost transparent. Fragile, yet she was loyal and goddamn brave enough to break his heart. "So he wasn't alone at the end," Emily finished quietly.

*The end...* The words echoed in his head as he stared through tear-blurred eyes at the woman he'd never stopped loving. She believed she didn't have much time left. Sweat bloomed on his upper lip. Oh, sweet Jesus, she couldn't die.

Reeling from the spurt of panic, Luke grabbed Emily's shoulder in a desperate grip. "Don't you leave me, Em." She'd been through hell and back, but she had so much strength inside of her. Enough to fight this.

She stared at him, lips parting in surprise. He was coming unglued and he knew it, but he couldn't stop. The thought of her dying made him feel like someone was clawing out his insides with a red-hot poker. "I couldn't take that. You've gotta fight this, Em." He didn't deserve her. He'd never deserved her, but he was going to make up for that. He would *make* her live, God dammit.

She licked her lips. "I'm trying, Luke."

*Not good enough.* "No. You have to *beat* it." He shook her once, aware he was on the verge of having a meltdown, but his legendary cool was gone. "You understand me? You have to *win*. Promise me."

Emily smiled and wiped his tears away before they could fall. "I've waited over twenty years to get you back. You think I'd leave you now?" She pressed a hard kiss to his lips, as good as a vow. "Not a chance. Now come on. Let's get you tucked into bed."

The sick, hollow feeling in his gut remained as she got him back into bed and tucked the covers around him. Her hands were so gentle.

"Need anything else?"

"You," he answered roughly, pulling her down beside him, desperate to feel her warm and alive up against his body. "God dammit, Em, I need *you*."

Grabbing her as tight as he could with his bandaged arm in the way, Luke buried his face in her neck and shook. Holding onto her, he fought his darkest fear and prayed he wasn't too late. "I'm sorry," he managed finally. "For everything. For every damn time I did something that hurt you." Sorry didn't come close to cutting it, but he didn't know what else to say. Christ, if he could go back in time to the day he'd left her, he'd undo all of it. So many things in his life he wished he'd done differently.

"I know," she murmured, her voice soft and full of understanding. "And I forgive you. Now it's time to forgive yourself."

He wasn't sure he could. Not yet. Maybe never.

He couldn't go back and fix everything. Now he could only go forward. He bit down on the inside of his cheek to hold back the sob that rose up from the depths of his chest. "Need you," he repeated hoarsely.

"Luke, you've got me. You've always had me, and you know it."

He did, and he had. God, he was *such* an asshole.

She cradled him like a child and broke his heart all over again. "I'm willing to start over if you are," she said softly.

He nodded, unable to speak, and pressed his face hard against her. A shudder wracked him and then a sob burst free, shaming him.

"Shhh," she soothed, cradling him tighter. Her hands smoothed over his hair and neck, the gesture achingly familiar, so comforting. "It's okay to let go now. You know you're safe with me."

He stopped fighting the inevitable and lost it. Held

securely in her arms, Luke put his head down and cried for the first time in memory. It all poured out. The guilt over leaving her and Rayne; the lonely years without her; the regret of not fixing things sooner. Losing Davis. The pain of having to kill Tehrazzi and the fear he might still lose Emily. It all came out in an agonizing blast. Em handled it perfectly because she didn't say a word. She held him through it, caressing his hair and his shuddering back. When it was over, his eyes were so swollen he could hardly open them. He'd soaked the front of her sweater. He tried to wipe at it, but she merely sat up and pulled it over her head.

*Oh, Christ yes.* "Take it all off." His words were rough and gravelly. He needed to feel her naked against him, to reassure himself she was safe and real. He was starved for it.

She paused only a moment before taking off the rest, including her bra. Facing him naked with the morning sun filtering through the blinds, his heart swelled at the sight of her, scars and all. So beautiful and courageous he thought he might cry again. Then she eased down beside him and drew his head to her naked chest. The scent of vanilla and clean female skin drifted up, surrounding him like a cozy blanket. Luke rested his cheek on the softness of her left breast and kissed the scars on her right side, humbled by her trust. "I love you so much, Em."

In answer she kissed the top of his head and cuddled in closer. "Love you too. Now go to sleep."

The demons that had driven him for so long had finally been laid to rest. After all these years apart, they would finally have a second chance. He was damn well going to get it right this time.

Surrounded by Emily's loving arms, he heaved a weary sigh and let himself fall into a deep, healing sleep.

# Chapter Twenty-Two

*Charleston, SC*
*Three months later*

"Morning, sleepyhead."

Emily smiled at the feel of Luke's lips against her bare shoulder. "Morning," she said without opening her eyes, and fought a yawn. She was so damn tired all the time.

More delicious kisses skimmed across her skin and she sighed in pleasure. "Keep that up and you might turn radioactive."

"I'll risk it." He leaned over her and kissed her forehead, his thumb rubbing across the new wedding band on her left hand. He'd had her old one melted down and remade for the ceremony at St. Michael's a few weeks back. "Still tired?"

"Yes." *Always.*

"Want some tea?"

"Mmm, please." She didn't want to face that she had another radiation treatment in a few hours. Five days a week, for six weeks. She was only on day four.

The first treatment had made her so queasy she'd made Luke pull over on the way home so she could throw up at the side of the road. He'd tried to hold the ends of her wig back for her but she'd slapped him away, annoyed and embarrassed. Later, she'd felt badly. He'd only wanted to help. He'd been fussing over her like a mother hen ever since he'd come back to Bryn's house in Beirut.

But she didn't want to think about Beirut anymore. That was all in the past. She needed to focus on the future. Right now though, her eyelids were too heavy to pull open. She wasn't nauseated anymore, and that was a gift in itself. The mattress was soft beneath her and the warmth of the comforter was so delicious that she let herself slide back into sleep.

She stirred sometime later when a puff of cool air hit her legs, then Luke was rubbing his face against her naked stomach. The perfect smoothness of his cheeks made her smile. He must have shaved again before coming back upstairs. He was always considerate of her that way, careful not to abrade her tender skin now that she marked so easily. The absence of the beard pleased her immensely, and not just because his clean-shaven skin felt good against hers. It meant he wasn't going back overseas, and that nobody would call him in the middle of the night to respond to some terrorism crisis. Though she gave him another month, tops, before he dove back into some kind of security consulting work. Otherwise he'd wind up pacing around like a caged animal being in the house with her all the time.

Hot kisses and slow caresses trailed across her stomach and over one hip bone, starting a delicious throb between her thighs. Sighing, Emily eased a hand into his short, thick hair and stretched out, waiting for him to reach the vulnerable folds between her legs. Dying with the anticipation of it.

His fingers brushed over her swelling flesh, drawing a soft moan from her throat as he teased her. *More*, she willed him, opening for his touch. He shifted a little, and she caught the faint click of a teacup being placed in its saucer before his hands went to her thighs to hold her still. Without warning, she felt a shocking warmth between her legs. "Oh!" she cried, jerking up on her elbows.

A hot, smooth stroke followed her exclamation, right over her most sensitive flesh. His tongue, but superheated. It felt so good it loosened her muscles and made her head fall back. "Luke..." God, had he taken a sip of her tea before going down on her?

The low growl of enjoyment that vibrated against her core was his only response before he parted her with his fingers and lapped at her like melting ice cream. She moaned and lifted her hips, helpless under the lash of decadent pleasure. He stroked slow and steady against her sensitive flesh, licking tenderly over her swelling clit, flicking his tongue over it. Her hands sank into his hair again. It seemed like forever since they'd been intimate. "Luke..."

He stopped, and a second later his hand shot out from beneath the blankets to grab the fragile handle of her teacup. It disappeared beneath the comforter and a moment later his hot tongue treated her to another luscious caress. Her eyes closed in bliss as she fell back against the mattress and let him love her. The pleasure rose soft and bright inside her, sharpening when he sucked on her clit gently. He slid a finger inside and rubbed right over the sweet spot that made her twist and moan, his tongue licking slow and soft until he had her panting and pressing into his touch.

It was always like this with him. He turned her on so fast she was on the verge of coming within minutes, and knowing he relished every second of her response only made it hotter. The feel of his fingers moving inside her amplified the pleasure tenfold.

Her body moved intuitively beneath his touch while he held her in place, drawing out the pleasure. Emily was liquid with it, desperate for release when he suddenly stopped. Gasping, she raised the covers. "What—"

Luke moved over her, settling atop her as he raised her legs and gently brought her knees over his broad shoulders. "I want to feel you come around me," he whispered, leaning down to kiss her.

She tasted herself and spicy chai tea on his lips before his tongue delved inside to caress hers. Then he shifted and entered her with a smooth thrust that made her body sing. She cried out into his mouth and grabbed his upper arms, the muscles bulging beneath her fingers as he shifted forward.

Trembling, she opened her eyes and stared up at him, waiting. His bottomless brown eyes gazed back at her, full of hunger and tenderness. "I love you," he murmured, pulling back.

God, he was so thick and hard inside her. She struggled to form the words, her body throbbing, straining for release. "I l-love you t—"

Luke surged forward, the position seating him impossibly deep. It could have hurt if he hadn't been so careful with her. But he moved gently within her, using that smooth pumping motion he knew made her wild.

The intense friction was incredible. "Ohhh…"

"Mmm, I know." He kissed the tip of her nose. "God you're gorgeous."

Emily clenched her hands around his biceps and cried out, catching fire in his arms. When he finally reached one hand between them to stroke her aching clit, she thought she'd scream from the pleasure. "More," she begged, struggling to open wider, give him better access.

Expert fingers moved in sweet, unhurried circles over her slick flesh. “Yeah. Feel me, Em. Feel how good it is.” He was magnificent rising and falling above her, his whole body a fluid ripple of muscle and bone, eyes intent on her face.

“Ah God, Luke…”

“Come for me then, baby.” He crooned it, moving faster now in an endless, sensual rhythm. Short, sharp strokes that caressed her inner walls and hit just the right place over and over.

Her body tightened around him, throbbed, the pressure building impossibly high. Throwing her head back, she let out a fractured moan as her body exploded around him. Waves of pleasure coursed through her, her heart turning over when he reared back and groaned with his own release, muscles standing out in his chest and shoulders and arms. When it faded, he gently unhooked her quivering legs from his shoulders and settled them on the bed before laying his head on her, right over her incision site and the scar where the IV port had been.

Trying to catch her breath, Emily wrapped her arms around him. She stroked his damp hair and smoothed her fingers over the healed scars in his left shoulder.

Luke sighed and nestled in closer, tucking his hands beneath her back. “I love retirement.”

Laughing breathlessly, she kissed the top of his dark head. She loved this part of it too. Things hadn’t always been easy since they’d come back stateside, though. He still slept with a loaded pistol in the bedside table. His startle reflex was more noticeable now that they were home and she picked up on the tension in him whenever they were in a crowd or in heavy traffic. As though he was still on alert for threats. It would probably fade in time, but he’d always carry that trait with him to some extent. His time in the military and the field had changed him forever.

They were learning about each other all over again, but this time without her walking on eggshells. She was simply herself, and more than a few times her stubbornness or strong opinions had shocked him into silence. She didn't go out of her way to avoid conflict with him, and she'd had to learn how to give up some of her responsibilities around the house. He'd told her he needed to be needed, and she was taking him at his word. All in all, the transition was going smoothly.

Luke still had nightmares sometimes, and he was pretty closed up about them. Didn't want to talk about whatever had made him wake up in a sweat. At least he let her hold him most of the time, unless it was a really bad one. Like the other night when he'd risen from their bed without a word and not responded to her calling after him. When those kinds of nightmares came, he retreated downstairs or out of the house for a while. And she let him go.

As for her, she tried to put the dark memories behind her and focus on her life with Luke. Though these days it seemed most of her energy was consumed by her ongoing battle with the cancer.

At least she'd responded well to the chemo. Better than her doctors had anticipated. But she faced plenty more radiation treatments that left her feeling like she had a permanent flu. After that, they'd give her body some time to heal and keep monitoring her blood for cancer cells. Though no one had said "remission" to her yet, everybody had their fingers crossed. It kept her going. Well, that and Luke. Not that he gave her a choice, but so far she was winning the war, one battle at a time. She prayed it stayed that way.

Emily moaned a protest when Luke pulled away and went into the bathroom. He came back and cleaned her up with a warm damp cloth, then pulled on a shirt, boxer briefs and jeans. "Come on," he said, handing her a robe.

"But we don't have to leave for at least another hour," she grumbled, already dreading the next dose of radiation.

"The sun's out. I want to take you outside for a bit."

Sighing, she sat up and slid into the robe, then let out a squeak when he gathered her up and lifted her into his arms.

"Your shoulder," she admonished, squirming away.

He held her tighter. "My shoulder's fine. More than strong enough to carry you, lightweight." Pushing the door open, he took her downstairs and through the kitchen out to the back porch. He set her on the porch swing and tucked a quilt around her before disappearing back into the house.

Snuggled up beneath the wedding ring-pattern quilt, she looked out over the garden awakening from its long winter slumber. Spring in Charleston was a glorious thing. The bright morning light spilled over the tender, unfurling plants that raised their tentative faces toward the warm sunshine. Life. So fragile and sweet. Precious beyond measure.

The screen door on the porch creaked as Luke came out carrying a steaming mug in one hand and a cup and saucer in another. Emily smiled and lifted the quilt so he could slide under it next to her, and accepted her fresh cup of tea. "Thank you."

"Welcome." Settling back, he laid an arm across her shoulders and set the swing rocking gently with his foot. The steam from their drinks curled into the breath of cool, salt-scented breeze that ruffled the palmetto fronds. His loving smile warmed her to her toes.

It was eerie, sitting there with him. Like she'd been swept back in time to when they were first married. She hated that they'd lost so many years in between...

*No more of that.*

They were together now, and that's all that mattered.

She intended to make the most of whatever time they had left together. Whether it was a day or another few decades.

Tilting her head, she admired Luke's chiseled profile, and the leanness of his square jaw. Every day she woke up with him cradling her tight against his body, she wanted to pinch herself. However hard he pushed her in her fight, it was worth it just to have his arms around her each morning.

"What?" he asked, meeting her gaze. The swing rocked forward, and a shaft of sunlight filtering through the crepe myrtles transformed his eyes into a kaleidoscope of chocolate and coffee. A robin twilled somewhere in the yard.

"You sure you're not going to go crazy being cooped up with me? Could get boring real fast for a man who's lived on the edge his whole adult life." He was already feeling it, though he'd never admit that.

His fingers toyed with the ends of her wig, the long one she wore most often because it was his favorite. "Bored? Trust me, I'm not bored. And as soon as we get the all clear, I'm taking you somewhere tropical with white sand beaches."

Sounded good to her. She loved travelling with Luke. He never failed to impress her with his knowledge of so many languages and different cultures. And she never worried they'd get lost. He was a human GPS and loved exploring new places. It had been a long time since they'd had fun together, she mused, studying him. She'd like to have fun again. To hear him laugh the way he used to. Luke had an infectious laugh. Best of all, he made her feel completely safe, no matter where they were. "I'd like that."

But a lingering fear crept in. That dark whisper in her head that never let her forget what she was fighting.

*I'm still here. Inside you, just waiting…*

She brushed the thought away. Luke's fingers trailed over her cheek, bringing her gaze to his. His eyes held hers, magnetic and forceful. "I'm in no rush to go anywhere. We've got another fifty years together, Em, so we'll fit it in when you're ready. We've got future grandkids to spoil and places to travel to. One day at a time, remember?"

It's not like she could forget, because he said it to her every day. And when it came to her getting better, he wouldn't take no for an answer. He was going to push her, every step of the way through her treatments while she fought her battle. Bully her, if necessary. He also wasn't going to let her give up when things got hard. And they *would* get hard. When they did, he would be her anchor in the middle of the storm. The man who carried her when she was too weak to go on. He would give her his strength and his love and his unyielding support. He would hold her when she needed it, let her cry on his shoulder or give her space.

But whatever happened from here on out, he would never desert her. She would have him in her corner every step of the way. That meant everything to her.

Emily's heart was full to overflowing when she grinned at the only man she'd ever loved. So long as Luke was with her, she could face anything. And dammit, she was going to beat this shitty disease and relish every minute of those next fifty years with him. "I can't wait."

Twining their fingers together, she squeezed his strong hand in a silent promise. Enjoying the sunshine, she tipped her head back and closed her eyes. A wide smile stretched her lips. She was going to win this fight. She was going to *live*.

*Just watch me.*

**—The End—**

# Complete Booklist

**Suspense Series** (romantic suspense)
Out of Her League
Cover of Darkness
No Turning Back
Relentless
Absolution

**Titanium Security Series** (romantic suspense)
Ignited
Singed
Burned
Extinguished
Rekindled

**Bagram Special Ops Series** (romantic suspense)
Deadly Descent
Tactical Strike
Lethal Pursuit

**Empowered Series** (paranormal romance)
Darkest Caress

**Historical Romance**
The Vacant Chair

# Acknowledgements

Thank you so much to my wonderful readers for supporting this series, and to my amazing husband and kids for tolerating me while I pursue my dream.

And to Katie, for always being there for me.

# About the Author

NY Times and USA Today Bestselling author Kaylea Cross writes edge-of-your-seat military romantic suspense. Her work has won many awards and has been nominated for both the Daphne du Maurier and the National Readers' Choice Awards. A Registered Massage Therapist by trade, Kaylea is also an avid gardener, artist, Civil War buff, Special Ops aficionado, belly dance enthusiast and former nationally-carded softball pitcher. She lives in Vancouver, BC with her husband and family. You can visit Kaylea at www.kayleacross.com